I0787997

Behind Even The Shadows

Cloaked Heart

Second Edition

Molly Moles

Scriverdea Publishing

Lewisville, Indiana

Scriverdea Publishing
4886 East 1100 North, Lewisville, Indiana, 47352
Printed by IngramSpark with permission

For additional information, contact Molly Moles using the above-listed address or email behindeventheshadows@gmail.com. Be sure to follow @BEtheShadows on Facebook (with links to other social media platforms) for author updates and fan forums.

Cloaked Heart second edition, 2020
First in the *Behind Even The Shadows* Series of six novels.

Cover artwork and illustrations by Bekah Koen
Photomanipulation, logos, and accents by Jacob Moles
Concept editing by Janet Hughes
Map created using Inkarnate.com with proper licensure

ISBN: 978-1-951499-04-4 (paperback)
978-1-951499-05-1 (hardcover)
978-1-951499-03-7 (eBook)
978-1-951499-02-0 (Audiobook)

LCCN: 2020905065

Novels in the

Behind Even The

Shadows

Series:

Cloaked Heart

Unveiling Thorns

Paradox Puzzle

Mental Tempest

Verity Pursuit

Callous Closure

~ Dedication ~

To The One Who gave me the ability to produce the work I do ~ my Lord and Creator, God Almighty. May He be glorified in all I do, and may this book — and series — be a reflection of young Christian adults striving, growing, renewing, maturing, and perfecting day-by-day to follow Him and be in the world but not of it. Standing up to the sinful nature of those who do not submit to God's commands, while at the same time, showing them they do not have to continue in hopelessness and sin.

~ Acknowledgements ~

Thank you to all those who made this dream overcome insurmountable odds and become an amazing reality. You've all been a great source of encouragement and gave me help when I desperately needed it:

Sarah Moles	*Justin Dobbs*	*Evabeth Koen*
Janet Hughes	*Bekah Koen*	*Olivia McCauley*
Jay Moles	*Jacob Moles*	*Laurie Koen*

~ Table of Contents ~

Chapter 1 _______________________________________ 1

Chapter 2 _______________________________________ 8

Chapter 3 _______________________________________ 25

Chapter 4 _______________________________________ 28

Chapter 5 _______________________________________ 47

Chapter 6 _______________________________________ 50

Chapter 7 _______________________________________ 55

Chapter 8 _______________________________________ 61

Chapter 9 _______________________________________ 67

Chapter 10 ______________________________________ 71

Chapter 11 ______________________________________ 82

Chapter 12 ______________________________________ 85

Chapter 13 ______________________________________ 109

Chapter 14 ______________________________________ 128

Chapter 15 ______________________________________ 135

Chapter 16 ______________________________________ 158

Chapter 17 ______________________________________ 210

Chapter 18 ______________________________________ 241

Chapter 19 ______________________________________ 256

Chapter 20 ______________________________________ 261

Chapter 21 ______________________________________ 272

Chapter 22 ______________________________________ 291

Chapter 23 ______________________________________ 301

Chapter 24 ______________________________________ 306

~ Pronuciation Guide ~

NOTES: Underlining: "hard" vowel. Capitals: stressed syllable.

First Names:

Baleck: B<u>A</u>Y-lek

Calli: KAL-<u>e</u>

Callimay: KALI-m<u>a</u>y

Creigam: KR<u>A</u>Y-gum

Dakoe: d<u>a</u>y-K<u>O</u>

Destan: DES-tan

Fairove: F<u>AI</u>R-of

Gallia: GAL-l<u>e</u>-ya

Gerould: <u>J</u>AIR-<u>o</u>ld

Orpha: <u>O</u>R-fu

Rocher: RAH-cher

Toreon: T<u>O</u>R-<u>e</u>-yon

Last Names:

Berchoff: ber-KOF

Davenpond: D<u>A</u>V-en-pond

Nevrille: ne-VRIL

Ionba: <u>i</u>-<u>O</u>WN-buh

Swinchpuck: SWINCH-puk

Places:

Aridigobe: ARID-i-g<u>o</u>b

Berchshire: BURK-sh<u>i</u>r

Brigon: BRI-gon

Crosswall: kroz-WAL

Faberton: F<u>A</u>Y-bur-ton

Gastonia: ga-ST<u>O</u>N-<u>e</u>a

Hagzell: HAG-zel

Heirway: H<u>A</u>IR-w<u>a</u>y

Kae-Nu: K<u>A</u>Y-new

Kerogen: K<u>A</u>IR-<u>o</u>-gen

Quaverly: KW<u>A</u>Y-ver-l<u>e</u>

Quidoria: KWI-d<u>or</u>-<u>E</u>A

Quimbergo: KWIM-bur-g<u>o</u>

Trawnvane: tron-V<u>AI</u>N

Veinyet: V<u>A</u>N-yet

Miscellaneous:

(Era) Augury: AH-gar<u>e</u>

(Neckline) Bateau: bu-T<u>O</u>

(Era) Catharsis: KU-thar-sis

(Knife) Sai: S<u>I</u>

~ Map of Quidoria ~

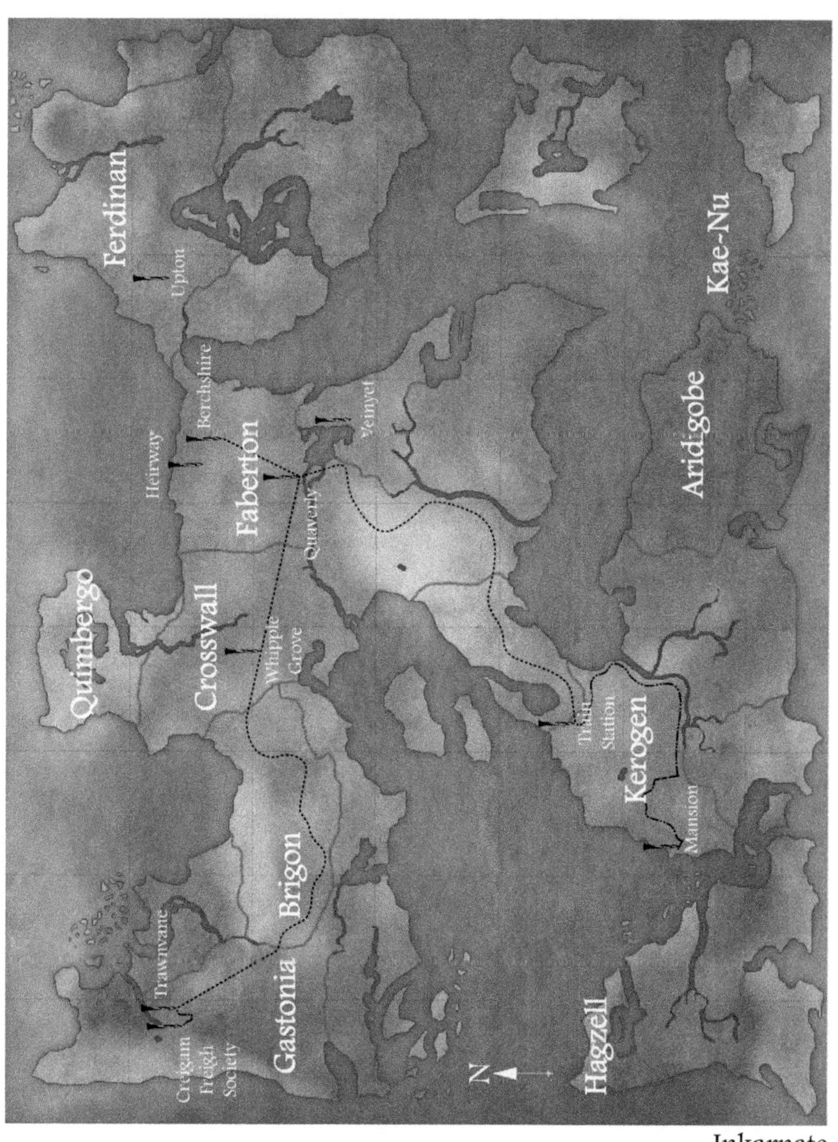

Inkarnate

~ 1 ~

"Creigam Freigh Society: ensuring future society through proficiency of self." Mr. Freigh stated in his resonating and calm voice as he looked over all of the finished artwork. His eyes shone with pride while he readjusted his glasses and handed the paper to the man standing beside him.

"This is quite the undertaking. Are you sure 'all' this is necessary?" Baleck Willgun, Mr. Freigh's lead assistant questioned; his deep voice cracking. "Shouldn't we con—"

"Baleck? Sometimes you have to be willing to make sacrifices to ensure the stability and even reality of the future. This 'is' necessary… you understand this better than most."

Looking at the scattered plans, paperwork, formulas, research, and financials which littered the desk the two of them were standing behind, he responded rather defeated, "I understand the necessity for it, but the manner in which—"

"We are ready. They are too; they just do not know it. … I know you are concerned. I believe in one way or another we all have our own reservations. But we cannot let our fears and concerns cripple what society needs. We all know our roles. And providing time is on our side we will succeed."

"You're right. We cannot afford to wait any longer. Things are to the point of no return. I only hope this approach is successful."

"It 'must' be. There is no time to find another way."

Mr. Freigh was a man who looked to be in his early to mid-sixties, average height, and a bit heavyset. His polished persona was on display through and through in his wardrobe that complemented his salt and peppering hair. But this lifestyle was not stagnate or unwilling to show emotions; and he was by no means someone who looked down upon others around him. Case in point would be Baleck Willgun who had become his most trusted colleague in this undertaking. He was a good twenty years younger but showed his worth through his knowledge and willingness to be involved.

Though professional in his attire, his thin — yet not thinning — brown hair resembled something along the lines of a scraggly mullet in its length; slicked against his neck as if it hadn't been properly cleaned. And then there was his voice. It was better suited for someone of Mr. Freigh's build, not his long and lanky frame.

But he was a man who broke stereotypes left and right, holding true to the culture of the country he was from — stereotypes were seen as nothing but challenges to conquer. And so, even though it was natural for him to wish a position of power and authority, he truly enjoyed and appreciated having such a man as Creigam Freigh to depend on for the finality of decisions and the responsibility contained in such matters.

ॐ

"Many are calling this the civil revolution of the Augury era and what will forever change education as we know it." The reporter stated in his upbeat tone — though some might call it photogenic or fake. "Creigam Freigh Society is projected to be the most sought-after institution for higher education in the world! Applications have already been pouring in from all over the globe for the opening semester this fall. With Creigam Freigh Society being a tuition-free institution, every single application is personally reviewed by founder and conductor: Creigam Irvin Freigh. From what he shared with us in our exclusive interview: being accepted will not be an easy task, yet not out-of-reach for those wishing to impact their communities."

The television screen switched to a string of clips from an interview done just after Mr. Freigh met with Baleck. He was poised and looked comfortable taking questions, "Creigam Freigh Society is pleased to present this revolutionary form of development for the young adult through their interaction with fellow classmates. Plainly stated: we are not looking to revolve education around academic test scores in the classroom… which inevitably cause stress for the individual; but rather, through the simplicity and casual nature of the social hierarchy. — By pushing young people to excel in this way, it has shown in our studies to bring about better social interaction and influence. Through this, we as a world can render more rounded individuals who are staples in their communities. — With the Void and Catharsis eras at an end, we can look toward a brighter future. Now is the time to rebuild; and this rebuilding starts by making sure we prepare the next generation for their roles in society. — By accepting those from around the globe, the Society can help impact more areas to spread our mission of: 'Ensuring future society through proficiency of self'. — Our aim—"

"I'm going to apply," Callimay said determined as she turned the television off and stood up. "This is a perfect opportunity for me."

"Applying does not mean getting to go, my dear." Mrs. Berchoff reminded in a soft yet firm tone; still focusing on what she was doing. "Plus, you are fifteen and have yet to finish your schooling."

"I understand, Mother. But I have to try! If what the reporter said is right, and this is going to be the most sought-after institution… it could take them a couple years to get to my application. If I get it in now, I would at least have a better chance than waiting until I graduate in three years. This may be my only chance to make a difference on a grand scale like this! I want to help. I want to help make good things happen. Maybe by going to this Society I can."

"What you said was beautiful, Callimay." Mrs. Berchoff smiled as she laid her knitting project on her lap; her crow's feet showing her age and yet reminding others of her love for joy and happiness. "Perhaps you should include what you said on your application if they have a place for such an essay. Explain it in depth though. I know the memories hurt, but it may make an impact on Mr. Freigh… and even help you. He seems to want students like you. Though I must say, his tactics seem 'very' unconventional. I would think it to breed dissension and hatred rather than those who work as a team and are caring by looking at how they act in social groupings. But I am old…"

"You mean you'll let me apply?"

"Of course I will, Callimay. I know how much you yearn to help everyone; what little things you do so often to try to help. And this would be safer for you than to step between two arguing young men like you did yesterday. Whatever made you think to do that?"

"They weren't listening to each other. I was just trying to get them to understand they were agreeing… because they were! Everyone else knew it." She recounted as she glanced down at her bandaged arm. "I was the only one who was willing to step up."

"Callimay? You cannot fight everyone's battles for them." Mrs. Berchoff sighed as she stood and took her in her arms; stroking her glossy, long, brown hair with the softest touch — as all mothers do. "I know you want to help. But… but sometimes people do not want help. And as hard as this might seem, they will not listen to people who try to show them the truth. And then there is the whole added concept of men. They need to work through things in their own way, which to us as women can seem backward and unproductive. … Say what needs to be said, but know they have to make the decision to respond. You cannot make them do the right thing."

"I know." She sighed, her voice sounding crushed.

"Keep yourself strong and others will see it. It will only be that some choose to ignore what they know and see. Do not let them discourage you. There are those who are watching to see how you will react. They are waiting to see if what you said matches what you do. And they will flock to you when they see the consistency. Now it might not be a flock that comes to you, but those who see it will not leave you. They would not be able to and live with their conscience if they did."

"I love you Mother."

"I love you too, Callimay." Mrs. Berchoff stepped back, smiling as she sighed. "Now. To get back to what brought this all on: you will most likely need to go to the town hall to see about where to get an application. I was not planning on starting supper for another hour yet if you would like to go now."

"Alright!" She nodded as she perked up.

"It is so good to see you in such high spirits, my dear. I hope you do not hang everything on this. You may not even qualify to go."

"Perspective. Perspective and contentment. This would be a great way to achieve what I would like to do, but it doesn't have to be the only way. — Wouldn't it be something if I… I met someone!"

"Oh my dear Callimay!" Mrs. Berchoff laughed as she clapped her hands together. "Let us wait to hear back on the application first, shall we? Then we can wade through all the details."

"I was only dreaming, Mother. I will be back soon." She bade farewell, and then turned back as the screen door closed, "Is there anything you would like me to get while I'm in town?"

"Well…" she thought as she tapped one of her needles against her lip. And then pointed at her with it when she remembered, "Ask Fairove if he has any fresh tomatoes."

ॐ

Callimay was a bundle of joy and excitement, to say the least, as she ran down the hill and into town. Life seemed to have that little spark in it again. She knew there was the chance she was getting her hopes up for nothing: *I do need to calm down. ~ Land sake, Rose Petal! This place can't be so difficult to get into that you wouldn't qualify. Why would they have announced it on the news if it were? ~ I might be too young, though. Life isn't always easy or fair. ~ Well, duh! But this has nothing to do with that.*

There was this inner chatter which continued as she walked down the edge of the road. The town hall wasn't actually in the town of Berchshire itself. It was east of the rail station in the business sector of what was still considered Berchshire.

The evening trains had just arrived and people were off to their homes for supper. Callimay always had to make sure to pay special attention when at the rail station… it was a hectic and somewhat chaotic place to be on a Friday evening. Why sugarcoat it: it's a hectic and chaotic place whenever a train is there. It's the fastest and newest form of transportation in the country of Faberton, and so it always draws a crowd. People use it since roads for cars aren't in the best of shape. And most of the higher-paying jobs are in cities closer to the capital, or farther north across the border in Ferdinan.

But as always, Callimay made it through unscathed. She stopped for a moment to see the train heading south pull out. Watching the huge machine of metal struggle to start, then have that light bulb moment and catch the rail, it always mesmerized her.

"What are you doing out on a Friday evening, Callimay Rose?" She heard an ever-familiar voice call to her.

"Hi! Running an errand of my own, then coming to find you." She waved as the middle-aged man in scrubs walked up to her.

"Oh? What for?" He raised his bushy eyebrow and panned his fingers across his mustache like he always did.

"Mother was wondering if you had any tomatoes that you would be willing to part with. We're having spaghetti tonight."

"Well now. Tomatoes come at a high price, miss." Fairove wagged his finger at her… jokingly of course, and she knew it. "I may require a full-sized loaf of zucchini bread this time."

"Since when did the price go up?"

"Since I had the bread you gave me last week."

"Oh for the love of— I'm creating a monster!"

"You keep it up and I may end up with all your zucchini and you all my tomatoes, Callimay." Fairove laughed as he patted her on the shoulder. "I was actually on my way over there, so I will stop by my house and pick a few to give to Carla."

"Thank you! And be sure to ask mother if you can stay for supper. It would be wonderful to have some company!"

ঌ

She ran the rest of the way and found that she wasn't the only one who listened to the news report. There hadn't been a crowd like this at the town hall on a "normal" day in ages!

All those her age and a bit older looked upset and put off by their tones as they walked out: *Oh no. Maybe I won't qualify. If everyone here doesn't, then there's no way I will. They're the smartest ones in school! ~ Wait. They're talking about waiting for something, Rose Petal. ~ Waiting? Waiting for what? The news report was just today. How could there be a wait list? ~ Don't ask me. I was just listening. ~ Well, let's find out. … Where is— aha! There's an open window.*

The gentleman behind the counter looked exasperated as Callimay came up, almost rolling his eyes as he asked, "How can I help you?"

"I was wondering if you could tell me where I could get an application for the… umm…"

"Creigam Freigh Society?" The man finished, fearing he knew why she had come.

"Yes. I'm not sure if I need to go somewhere else, but my mother thought it best to start here with you."

"We won't be getting those papers in until late next week, unfortunately. I only have pamphlets they sent to describe who is qualified and give some overview information about the area and complex itself."

"Oh!" *So that's what they meant by waiting.* Callimay said relieved as she took the paper from him. "That's not a problem at all. Thank you for your help! I appreciate it. I guess I will be back sometime next week for the application. Goodbye!"

The man looked stunned by her reaction and acted like he didn't know how to wave as she looked back.

ꝑ

As she wandered along, Callimay flipped through the pamphlets. She stopped by the rail station at the park and sat down to look at them, not concerned with how long it took her to get back home.

The information contained in such a small amount of words and pictures had her about jumping out of her skin in a way: *I'm excited about this! They have biking trails and the scenery looks breath-taking! And look at the size of the rooms! Wow! ~ Looks like they spent some money on uniform design, wouldn't you agree? ~ More than some. There are a couple designs to choose from. My gracious! The suede alone is worth~ With it being an institution they've got to have money coming out their ears. ~ True. ... Look! They have those fancy mazes. What does it say—labyrinth. Oh yeah. I remember that now. ... Wow. This is fantastic! I can't wait to show this to mother!*

~ 2 ~

Ten years passed for Callimay before any response was issued. She had dismissed the thought of getting to attend after two years came and went with no word. Being a teenager who had never been rejected in such a way, she struggled at first. But even so, she picked herself up and found things to keep her occupied and do what would allow her to help where she could.

What broke and devastated her heart was the passing of Mrs. Berchoff mere weeks after her graduation; on her eighteenth birthday. It was so sudden and the two were bonded so deep, Callimay was still in shock for almost a year after her death.

Mrs. Berchoff had left her everything, but she felt empty and alone each day: waking up only to find endless reminders of her throughout the house. It seemed her reason for doing everything in life was for Mrs. Berchoff. Yes, she had a job, but it was just that: a job. Callimay found moments where it did make her happy, but still, she was struggling daily to cope with the loss.

❦

The day the response from the Society came, Callimay got her courage up to do a deep-clean of the entire house. It was early on a Saturday as she opened the windows to let the fresh breeze in; along with the sweet smell of the countless flowers and melodious songs the birds would sing in thanks for their beautiful resting place.

She corralled her hip-length hair and began winding it and twisting it into a bun — unaware she was doing every movement exactly as her mother would have — her hairstyle looking every inch like Mrs.

Berchoff's. Callimay grabbed one of the cleaning cloths to tie over her hair and then grabbed what supplies she needed.

Do note: this was all before she even knew the letter was coming.

Well. Do I clean it first or last? I… it's the part that needs it the most. It's been how many years now? Callimay debated as she stared at her mother's bedroom door. *Maybe I shouldn't b~ You can do this, Rose Petal. It's okay. Just do what you can and then work off the emotions by cleaning the rest of the house. ~ Yes! That's a wonderful plan. ~ Deep breath. You can do this.*

The door stuck, exactly as she remembered it to, but then it snapped as some paint on the door frame cracked off. Callimay jumped back because of it, but then calmed and bowed her head as she walked in. Without raising it, she made a beeline for the windows to open them and then to Mrs. Berchoff's vanity.

While she was going through things, she stumbled across something hidden in the vanity. There was a box, beautifully wrapped, with a letter atop it addressed to her.

Callimay almost stumbled to the bay window to sit down, staring at the package for a while. It had been so long since she had seen her name written by her mother. Cursive was something Mrs. Berchoff was very strict about — the strokes had to be just so or it had to be written all over again. But even bearing that in mind, the embellishments on this envelope were much more lavish than she was known to make.

As Callimay opened the envelope, she caught the sweet smell of her mother's perfume. She struggled but kept opening it, eventually taking the heavy-weight ivory paper out.

Before she had a chance to unfold it, she saw Mrs. Berchoff had written a note for her on the outside of the paper.

Open the present first, Callimay.

She set the letter down and took the box in her hands. It wasn't very heavy, but then again, it wasn't feather-light. Her heart started racing as she began opening it. The paper ripping would cause her to jump, her trying so much to keep it from doing so; but it appeared that was close to impossible with this paper.

Inside was something that brought back so many memories. It was a framed picture of the two of them from her graduation day. Mrs. Berchoff was in what seemed to be perfect health up until the night before she passed. The picture confirmed this.

Callimay had forgotten what she looked like when she smiled. She hadn't in so long… she didn't even know if she could anymore. With tender care, she took it out and stared at it, the occasional tear trickling off her cheek and splashing off the glass.

Amidst the sadness, she laughed to herself as she recalled how windy it was that day. Right after the picture was taken, a gust of wind came along and blew her cap off her head, smacking the person who was standing to the left of them.

Mrs. Berchoff had made the white satin sundress she wore for the graduation ceremony. Callimay still remembered the endless hours of work her mother put into it to have it fit just right. Her eyes were sparkling, her silvered hair rolled into a braided bun… like she always remembered it to be.

"I miss you." She cried in anguish as she clutched the picture and held it close. "I miss you so much."

After a few minutes, she opened her eyes and saw a small box which was hidden by the picture. She picked it up and found it was a music box! These were an extremely rare find since the craftsmanship needed to make them was something only a handful of people had learned from their ancestors or before leaving the Homeworld themselves. They had all been gone for years though because of the Eradication: *Where did— how did you afford this!*

She wound the key, being careful to not turn it too fast or too tight, and turned it over again to admire the hand-carved vines, scrolls, leaves, and roses which covered the top of the blonde cedar box. Upon opening the lid, she heard the ever-familiar tune Mrs. Berchoff taught her to play as well as sing. She began crying again as she heard the little box clink and pluck the notes; as if they were plucking her heartstrings themselves. It only played a short piece of it… but it was enough to bring back even more memories.

There was a small, velvet-lined compartment inside, which was hiding a silver chain with a heart pendant dangling from it. Callimay took it out and admired the workmanship. The heart was ballooned and hollow, like a cage. It had a scroll design and hung off a silver, cable-chain necklace.

She immediately put it on and then picked the letter up after she checked the box once more for any other surprises she had overlooked. Callimay opened it and began reading the hand-written letter as she gripped the pendant with her left hand.

To my Callimay:

I wanted to make this birthday as special as possible because it will, and I say this with much sorrow and pain: be the last one I am blessed to have with you.

When I went to the doctor three weeks ago because I was having trouble breathing, I was told I had an extremely invasive disease with no known cure. It had already progressed to the point where my right lung was all but gone and my left one was deteriorating day-by-day at an alarming rate. The doctors were shocked I had no other symptoms and was faring so well, but they have given me only a month, or two — at most — to live.

I know this is not the best way to tell you, Callimay; but for my sake I chose it. I do not think I could bear seeing the anguish and fear in your eyes if I were to tell you face-to-face. It is most likely selfish of me, so please forgive me, but I just am at a loss of how to keep myself composed and see you devastated. I am faring well. Please do not think of yourself as not noticing I was in pain or anguish. I am not.

I wish I would have taken a picture of us when you first came to me to put beside this one. I wish you could see how much you have grown and matured and blossomed. You have made my life so full of joy and happiness, Callimay.

My heart which felt like it could know no love again was brought back to life when you showed up at my door. The loneliness in your eyes gave me a purpose I had lost. I had found someone who so desperately needed my love, and it forced me to push myself away from the past and work myself far beyond what I thought I could, to see to the needs of this tiny, fear-stricken child in front of me.

There is not a day that goes by, during which I do not thank The Lord above for sending you to me. You have been like a visiting angel to me during this time we have had together. Through what I initially saw as you giving me a purpose again, you helped remind me it is each individual who chooses whether or not they have a purpose, as well as choosing who will be their foundation for what can be called, one's "life goal": not their circumstances, not people who come and go in their lives, and not even the loss of loved ones or friends. He is to be everyone's purpose. It is each person's choice to seek the good in everything and remember there is a grand plan set in place by our Lord and Creator.

You have had a sheltered life up to this point, and I am so concerned after I am gone you will abandon living and choose to stay in an empty form of existence. I know the secrecy in which you must live — to a certain degree — will cut you off from people, but do not let that or me being gone keep you from enjoying your life. Do not let the emptiness in your heart cause you to shut down and not seek someone to fill it. You know there already is, and He will never leave you. But remember others in this world love you too. I know you will say: "it isn't the same", but Callimay; I pray and have faith: one day you will find someone capable of showing you a deeper love than I ever could. I know marriage is not a promise from God, but what He has given you with regard to the type of heart you have, I cannot see it being anything but His plan for you to marry and have a family of your own.

Please do not give up hope or think I would say you did not love me if you found and began to love and care for someone else. I expect it. It is the way things are supposed to be. This is what I have raised you for. You were never meant to stay mine forever. You were meant to fly free and find another free bird — for lack of better term — who would keep you for their allotted amount of time in this life. You know this is what God Himself said.

That is what the pendant is for. To remind you my love will always stay with you, His love is always in you, and you must keep hope that you will find someone during this life who will, over time, overfill your real heart.

God bless and keep you safe, my Callimay. Happy eighteenth birthday.

With all my love,
Mother

Callimay curled up on the bed and wept after she finished the letter. Mrs. Berchoff's passing wasn't unexpected… truly. Knowing this made her so upset with herself, not noticing she wasn't feeling well. She felt horrible, letting her spend so much time making the dress, taking care of things around the house, and traveling to and from town with all the other preparations needing to be made for Callimay's graduation. All that time she should have spent resting and conserving her energy. Maybe she would have lived longer!

After what felt like an eternity of self-blame and scolding, Callimay opened her eyes and saw the picture of the two of them on what was a joyous day for them both.

She was reminded Mrs. Berchoff was in complete control of what she did and did not do. She didn't have to make the dress or have an open house. She didn't have to explain everything to her in the letter. She didn't have to do anything — she chose to. That underlying message in the letter began to sink into Callimay's head as she muttered, "I get to choose. I am in control of my emotions. I am in control of how I react. Things will always change around me, but I get to choose to go along or not. I even get to choose if my memories will bring me happiness or… or even sorrow."

Mrs. Berchoff had taken Callimay in when the state orphanage asked for people to take some of the children displaced due to the bloody civil war their country was finally bringing to a close. Some remembered the events surrounding the loss of their parents while others' parents could not be found or reached due to the child not knowing; Callimay being one of those from the latter group. She would at times scream out in her sleep, or describe a horrible event of people dying, but there was never enough information to piece everything together and discover her true identity. Aftermath workers found this poor little five-year-old girl wandering the streets one late night while it snowed: splattered with blood, alone, shivering from the cold, and with only a single toy to cling to for protection and companionship.

It was no secret to anyone that Mrs. Berchoff had just lost her husband. Hearing the news of her taking in a child worried some, but they supported her nonetheless. She had always wanted a daughter, but four early miscarriages proved she and her husband would have to adopt to have a family. The money was never there, so they began building a home to suit the two of them. They found contentment in their situation and were very happy with the home they built.

Then the Eradication started, and not much later, civil war broke out. The longer it dragged on, the more casualties there were. After a few years, Mrs. Berchoff's husband — who was in his mid-forties at the time — felt compelled to help end the needless bloodshed.

He offered his services, picked up his uniform, and said his goodbyes to his wife with the promise he would never leave her alone and he would see her before long. He died two short weeks later. Mrs. Berchoff was grieving in her heart for the love she lost and the regrettable, hasty promise he made and was unable to keep.

But even so, at least she knew who to grieve for! This poor child who came to her had no concept of what was going on, who she was, where her home was, or what in the world happened to her life before this! She had no one to grieve for but still knew something was not right. In a way she was grieving.

Mrs. Berchoff had been busy cleaning all day; waiting for Callimay to arrive on the evening train. The doorbell rang as she scurried to finish those "final touches"; but she rushed out to see the little angel she was going to be raising.

Two of the orphanage workers accompanied the little girl who had a look of terror burned into her eyes. The child, who was now at what she would know to be home, only had a small stuffed dog given to her by someone named Lanta according to the attached tag.

To my Callimay. Happy fifth birthday, Rose Petal! October 5th, 2468

The toy was splattered with blood and caked with debris just like Callimay. Nice clothing — which had seen better days — fit her petite frame like a glove, her still beautiful hair was tousled, delicate skin grayed from debris and dirt, and her almost-black eyes were wide with wonder and fear as she looked around the fancy and frilly bedroom.

Callimay clung to the toy and didn't touch a single thing, it appearing she was terrified something would hurt her… though she seemed to be intrigued by the lace on just about everything.

Mrs. Berchoff attempted to take the toy to clean it, but Callimay refused to part with it. She could relate to this outburst and didn't reprimand her for it: she lost someone herself and only had "little" things of them left… and she protected them with everything she had because she knew deep down it was all she would ever have.

Once they both endured a few trial-and-error episodes, she was able to figure out how to appease Callimay and wash it.

While she looked at the dress, Mrs. Berchoff remembered the small dress she'd seen in a shop and bought years ago. She'd never had anyone to give it to, so she stored it; clinging to the hope that someday, she would be able to give it to her daughter.

After all the visible signs of war and terror had been washed off Callimay and her toy, Mrs. Berchoff put her robe on her and began to dig around in her expectation chest for the dress. Her heart was fluttering at the thought of having someone of her own to give it to. The momentary fear of her wondering if it would fit was there, but her joy would not be quenched.

"Do you need hewp?" Callimay tugged on her sleeve and then scurried back to the door and peeked around, still clinging to her toy and looking worried.

Mrs. Berchoff was taken aback by hearing the child's voice for the first time; but was able to say, "I would love help. Thank you."

"Otay." Callimay nodded as she crept up and peeked in the chest, eyeing her the entire time.

The two of them spent a while going through everything, Callimay finding it necessary to remove every single item and open any box to see what was inside. She asked a million and a half questions about what things were and what they were for and why she had them.

At first, Mrs. Berchoff found it sweet and was glad she felt comfortable, but after a half hour of Callimay doing it, it began to wear on her. Thankfully the next thing she grabbed was the dress and so the questions had to stop.

As she pulled it out, Callimay began reaching out to grab it; her tiny arms drowning in the long sleeves of the robe. Mrs. Berchoff helped her into it and could barely hold back the tears when she stepped back. Her still wet, straight, brown, hip-length hair framed her near-white face… but she was smiling.

She fussed with the sleeves on the dress a bit, but exclaimed in her lisp-filled way, "It's my cuwer!"

"Is it now?"

"Yes. Mommy always makes surer I have at weast won dwess wike dis. But de sweeves hurt."

"Well… I can fix the sleeves. Do you like it?"

"It's just wike my bedwoom — ownge!" Callimay threw her hands in the air. "Mistu Wuff's cowar es ownge too!"

"I see." Mrs. Berchoff nodded as she backed her face away from the wet toy which had been thrust into her face. "I'm glad you like it, Callimay. … Are you alright if I call you Callimay?"

"Surer!"

Mrs. Berchoff immediately took to making everything special and joyful for her little Callimay; doing all she could in every aspect to make sure she had a full and happy childhood. There was never much money, but she spent every dime she could spare on things for her. Apart from that though, she gave her the invaluable lessons of being loving, selfless, compassionate, patient, and honest. Things bought with money would break or lose their appeal, but those lessons would be able to carry Callimay throughout her entire life. The way in which she "spoiled" her child was much different than what others would expect.

She adjusted to her new life with ease; soon beginning to refer to Mrs. Berchoff as her mother. Callimay would ask about "daddy" if a man came to drop something off or visit. The answer was always short and pained; Mrs. Berchoff only saying he was gone while she gripped the necklace she wore — where she kept her husband's wedding band.

For the first few years, Callimay was taught at home. When she was old enough and Mrs. Berchoff felt she would be safe, she attended the local school.

When she turned twelve, Mrs. Berchoff summoned the strength to sit her down and explain how she came to live with her.

She was worried about how Callimay would respond, but was so happy when she answered, "I may have had other parents, but you are my mother."

All the while, Mrs. Berchoff never used the nickname written on the stuffed animal's tag when she spoke of or to Callimay: *It was a special name Lanta gave her. I will not infringe upon that.*

But now she was gone and Callimay was left just as she was when she was five. Yes, things were different: she was an independent young lady, had a job to pay what few bills there were each month, and she even had friends where she worked as well as in her congregation. Yet everything seemed the same. Everyone she knew reminded her of Mrs. Berchoff; she couldn't bear those reminders... she still felt the loneliness and hurt.

She realized this needed to change. It took her a while, but she finished what she knew needed to be done and took the time to sit down for a light lunch. Callimay heard the whistle of the lunchtime train and knew the service carrier would be by soon. In working toward this goal of change, she decided to go out and say hello when he came by.

This may not seem important, but she tried to make a point on Saturdays to not see him. Granted, she tolerated his attitude but found it hard to be a real friend to him. He seemed like a lady's man... which repulsed her to no end. It wasn't that she was now deciding to approve of his lifestyle; she was, more or less, making an effort to come out of her comfort zone and be more sociable.

It was a beautiful summer day, and so Callimay sat on the porch swing and waited. The butterflies congregated on the flowers which filled the numerous flowerbeds in the small yard. Birds sang their sweet melodies in the branches of the apple and peach trees down by the road. The wind rustled as it made its way through all the tree limbs and plant leaves. Then there was the groan and creak of the swing as it swayed back and forth, Callimay having her legs curled up on the seat, not caring if the swing was moving or not.

She saw the service carrier coming, so she wandered down to the collector. A few flowers called for special attention, so she startled the young man when she popped up from behind the gate.

"Hello… Miss Berchoff." The younger man paused as he glanced at the letter he had and then looked back at her, offering a friendly smile. "How are you today?"

"Hello." She answered, sounding a bit stunned, finishing in a tone of bewilderment: *He's not the usual carrier. ~ I told you it wasn't Trever. No uniform, wrong colored hair, and then he was too short. And I could see that all that w~ Hush. Trever's not worn his uniform — especially on Saturdays; and you can't always tell someone's hair color that far away or their height. ~ Well what happened to Trever? Did he finally get fired? I know he'd been warned ab—*

"Are you alright, miss?"

"I'm sorry?"

"I was just asking how your day was." The young man smiled as he put his hand in his pants pocket.

"Oh. It's going well." Callimay apologized as she bowed her head and blushed, and then looked back and finished, "And you? I… I'm afraid I don't know your name. Are you new by chance?"

"I'm doing fine, miss. Thank you." He nodded as he handed her a single letter. "My name is Dakoe. Dakoe VanGild. I'm actually not the normal service carrier. I think I passed him a little while ago. I'm with the Creigam Freigh Society."

"With who!"

"Creigam Freigh Society."

"But it's been…" Callimay said under her breath as she stared at the envelope, and then addressed him directly, "Thank you."

"You're welcome."

She stood there in a trance for a while and then looked up to find he was leaving, being quite a bit down the road now. She opened the gate and ran after him, calling out, "Wait! What does it say?" *Ah! What's his name? ~ You forgot? ~ Not helping!* "Please wait… sir. Did I get accepted? Is that why you came?"

"I'm not at liberty to say." Dakoe turned back and shook his head, him at eye-level with her now. "I'm sorry."

"Oh. Th… thank you anyway. For bringing this, I mean."

"You're welcome, Miss Berchoff."

Callimay moseyed back to the gate, still in shock from the news… and how the news was brought to her.

A minute or so later, she could hear someone calling out to her a few times, but never paid much attention until they were right behind her, practically yelling in her ear.

"Oh! Hi." She backed up and turned her head away when she realized who it was. *So he didn't get fired. ~ You sound sad, Rose Petal. ~ Do you mind backing off? ~ What? ~ I didn't mean it that way. ~ He's laughing at you. ~ It's your fault.* "Anything for me?"

"I'm afraid not." Trever slapped the bag on his hip, and then after a moment scratched his forever unruly, rusty red hair, "What's that you got from the man I just passed? Anyone special I should know about? Didn't recognize him. You even ran after him once he left. … Are you importing guys from other places, Callimay Rose?"

"No, Trever." She shook her head and sighed heavily as she made a face. "He was from the Creigam Freigh Society. He said he came to give me this letter."

"Well now! That's pretty fancy stuff right there." He perked up, his freckled face smiling. "What's it for? Why in the world did you apply there? And when did you? I never mailed anything f—"

"I… I don't know what it is. I applied years ago."

They stood there, Trever staring at Callimay and Callimay at the letter. There seemed to be no inkling of her opening it, so he prodded, "Well, are you gonna open it?"

"Not with you around." She turned to face him and put the letter behind her back.

"Don't get all keyed up now, Callimay." He backed off, seeing the irritation in her eyes. "I was only asking. — Oh! There's a dance tonight at the town hall. Would you like to go? I know tomorrow's Sunday, so I'd make sure to have you back early. … They're supposed to have some really good food."

"No thank you," she answered as she shut the gate behind her and focused on the envelope in her hand. "I'm not hungry."

"But I didn't—" *What's a guy got to do to gain the trust in you that's needed for a relationship of any kind, Callimay?* He sighed as he shook his head and turned around, shoving his hands in his uniform pockets. "I'll see you tomorrow then? … Callimay?"

"Sure." She nodded, though at this point she wasn't paying much if any attention.

ℬ

When she got inside, Callimay ran for the letter opener. But not a moment later she stopped short, having the opener inside and ready to rip it open. Her hand started to shake and her eyes darted back and forth: *Why would they wait ten years to respond? I know the services we have are not the best… but they didn't even use them to respond! ~ That's true. They did it themselves. I didn't think there was anyone slower than our services. Ten years is a bit ridiculous. ~ I thought there might be a little bit of a delay, but ten 'years'? This isn't ridiculous, it's insulting. Why even bother at this point? I haven't been waiting on pins and needles for the response. Not now. … Anyway, I know what it says: 'We appreciate your interest, but due to the volume of applications and talent seen, we cannot accept you at this time. We wish you the best in your future endeavors.'*

She worked herself up so much; she was frustrated with everything now. Callimay threw the paper down on the coffee table and flopped onto the sofa, screaming.

But even in all this emotional upheaval there was the eye of the storm: something deep inside her was curious. Something in her still hoped. Something in her refused to accept she was seen as useless or unqualified. Something in her remembered she was worth so much. Something in her fought for her even when she didn't think she could anymore. Something couldn't see the response being a refusal since it was hand-delivered. Something couldn't see those at the Society as being heartless. And this something inside of her that was awakening — her heart — knew the letter was nothing but good news that was a long time coming.

After she gathered herself, Callimay pulled the thick-weight, champagne-colored page out of its protective covering. Her heart couldn't help but start racing as the crisp-folded paper began to unfold like a blooming flower. It was watermarked with the seal of the Society and had the faint smell of pine sap on it. There was quite a bit of writing on this single page… could this be bad?

As she read the hand-written letter, her eyes got wider and wider.

Dear Miss Berchoff,

I would personally like to take a moment to thank you for your sincere and poignant application which you submitted to me now ten years ago. I understand my time in responding to you is quite delayed and I hope you will forgive me for that. Thousands of reasons could be offered for my neglect, but those do not have any bearing on the news I have for you.

After careful consideration and consulting with the lead assistant here at Creigam Freigh Society, Mr. Baleck L. Willgun, I am thrilled to invite you to the complex near Trawnvane, Comstock; Gastonia.

Classes are set to begin on Monday, September tenth. You have been assigned a room and two roommates who will be disclosed to you when you arrive on the third of September for your orientation and tour.

Please do remember that due to the limited room and large distance from surrounding towns, you will need to come alone. We trust all personal farewells will be seen to before your arrival. All efforts are made to provide a level competitive field — no formal, in-person introductions which could plant seeds

"I got accepted?" Callimay muttered, full of confusion and shock.

She read the letter a second time and then set it down on her lap, stunned and still trying to process what was happening. Her eyes darted back and forth as if she could still see it and were reading it in the air in front of her. Her facial expression ranged from this stunned look to a deep furrowed confusion.

The light dawned as she cheered, "Mother! I got accepted!"

Not but a few seconds later, her echoing voice not finding an ear to fall on, she crumbled to the floor. Callimay dropped the letter and stared at it, now admitting: *I played this scene over and over in my mind as to how I would tell you I got accepted. I was so full of excitement I wanted to do it before the letter even came — I was that sure. You were always so supportive of me. I feel as if I let you down by not getting in before I lost you. You never got t...*

The tears became too much for her to hold in, and so, with one mournful scream, a flood poured down her pain-ridden face and onto the acceptance letter.

Seeing the hand-written letters bleed into the page and become illegible made Callimay "snap out of it". This single piece of paper was a prized and coveted possession. Few qualified to apply for the Society, and even fewer were accepted. Let alone the fact you were competing against others from around the world for those highly sought-after five-hundred spots each year.

Callimay glanced around at everything she would be leaving. Was this worth that much to her anymore? Was this something she needed? For that matter, did she even want it anymore? She already had a life and was doing as well as could be expected. How could she pick up and leave so soon?

If her emotions weren't in a whirlwind already, this certainly was going to make sure they were! She ran to her room and grabbed a book off of her dresser and sat on the floor. The soft, malleable, orange leather of the book had her name imprinted on it. On first glance, one might have thought it to be a journal; but it was, in fact, her Bible.

The spine was so well trained, it fell open to a frequented passage she read which covered the emotions she was dealing with at that very moment. She closed her eyes and looked up; mumbling something for a few minutes, then opened her eyes and stood up.

When she came back into the living room, Callimay's wandering eye caught the framed picture of her and Mrs. Berchoff at her graduation: *She wanted me to go. She wanted me to make a difference. She knew this was what I'd wanted all along — to help others. She wants me to live. I need to go. No. No, I 'choose' to go.*

~ 3 ~

And so, with this drive and purpose, Callimay set out to make sure things were set in place. There wasn't much time to prepare, but she somehow squeezed everything in. Saturday night she lay on her bed and stared at the lacy canopy, realizing just how much she did.

The house was the first and biggest issue, but Fairove jumped in and agreed to keep it in order. What a relief! The paperwork was lengthy and confusing, but next she applied for and secured her border pass, had some co-workers help her find the cheapest way to travel to Trawnvane and then help her make reservations, then last but not least: she spent an entire day packing what she could fit into the luggage bag a lady from the congregation she attended at gave her.

The morning she left; the weather was picture-perfect. In fact, the whole trip there was going to be nothing but sunshine. Things seemed to be falling into place perfectly.

After Sunday morning Assembly was over, Callimay was inundated by everyone who said goodbye again and again; wishing her the best and sharing in her excitement for the trip.

"Take care, Callimay. We will all be praying for your safety. I know we all wish your experience to be encouraging."

"Thank you, Mr. Ionba. I appreciate it. I really do. I know I'll miss you all so much. I am excited about this, but I still know my heart will be lonely for home."

"I know you did, but I made sure to speak with the Evangelist there yesterday. Before I say anything, what is your view?"

"I was impressed with what he said and sent me. Granted, I know people can put up a good front, but I'm optimistic about him. When I first applied, I admit it wasn't something I considered. When I got the letter, I made sure to call Mr. Freigh himself and ask who would be available. They both seemed very grateful and pleased I saw it as so important to ask; even saying others had done the same. I'm encouraged by hearing about there being others interested and concerned about having a place to Assemble."

"I'm glad, and felt the same. If I remember right, he said he had thirty students request information. It is not a large group of the entire student body, but still a sizable number for you to draw encouragement from. … I know you are on a tight schedule as it is, so I will let you go. We will all be anxiously awaiting your return, Callimay."

"Thank you." She said choked up as she gave him one last hug.

ℬ

She picked up her bags and took a quick trip out to her last stop before leaving: Mrs. Berchoff's grave. Callimay set them down on the path and then walked up to the headstone which had wind chimes hanging from it and a cluster of flowers planted around it.

The graveyard was positioned on top of one of the tallest hills in the area; overwhelmed with newer graves over the past couple decades due to the civil war and it being the largest one in the area.

Mrs. Berchoff's grave was in a lovely spot next to her husband's, under a great willow tree. The graceful, wistful branches and leaves of the silent giant kept watch over the person Callimay dearly loved.

It's almost hard for me to believe this is it. She sat there and looked out across the scenery, the wind just gracing the tree's branches and causing the wind chimes to plink and tink every now-and-again. *I'm so unsure of what to expect and if I can do this anymore. I have changed so much since you left, mother. I feel like I somehow lost myself when I lost you. Maybe this is a good reason for me to go: to find who I am. If who I was before I lost you is my true nature or who I have become is. I'm not saying 'find who I am' in that I don't know who I am in Christ. I don't mean that at all. … I mean, the only way I can help others is if I have myself under control. Only then can I truly care for and love others the way they need to be. And for me to have myself under control, I need to find out where I fit into the mix of everything: where*

I'll function best as far as reaching out to others. Oh, I'm probably making no sense, like usual. Ugh. … It's hard without you here. Somehow I imagine things being so much easier if I knew I were coming home to you, but maybe I am grasping for rainbows. I miss you so much. … Though, it's like I can hear your voice; telling me this is how things are supposed to be. That nothing ever happens by accident, there is a purpose and design to everything — just like what was spoken of this morning. I'm struggling with seeing the bigger picture of everything right now. Maybe in time I will. … Surely! … And then on top of everything I'm so nervous I'll be found. Gastonia seems to be one of the more lenient countries if you will— but, it still terrifies me to be somewhere I have no one to trust. I hate things are so… so hard. — I would rather stay here and talk to you, but I do need to get to the rail station before I'm too late. I love you, mother. No matter what happens, I will take the good out of it and make sure I am doing what is right. I— I'm getting excited now. Now I want to get there so I can come back and tell you about what all happened and what I learned! Goodbye for now, mother. I'll see you next spring!

~ 4 ~

Traveling alone was fine for her and not the issue she was fighting at first, but when Callimay got to the rail station this entire outlook changed. She realized she had almost always gone where she knew most of the people and the area; so of course, all her experiences with traveling were good. And then if she did make a trip to where she didn't know people, it was always in the company of those she knew and trusted.

This? This was foreign to her in every way. Not one face was recognizable or even resembling someone she knew.

It seemed though as if everyone else were accustomed to having so many strangers around them and kept going, ignoring Callimay. There was the occasional eye contact made followed by a smile, nod, or friendly hello; but that was the extent of it: *It's so odd I never noticed how detached and secluded people are when they travel. Of course, going to the town hall or hospital isn't the same as actually walking 'into' the rail station itself. And when you're in a group, you don't notice. At least I never did.*

Knowing this pushed those fears away. Yet, on the heels of this victory, she knew some lurked around these places on a regular basis; looking for people like her. Most of them were easy to notice, but every once in a while they would be crafty: *Knowing me, a Falconer would see me the 'one' time I make a mistake.*

℈

It was over four times as long — traveling by train than plane — but for one thing it was financially easier. In addition, heights were one of her greatest fears… and she didn't feel like testing how she would hold up on a flight being alone. Then there was the plus of enjoying the scenery of the ever-changing countryside. Altogether, she had to travel through Faberton, Crosswall, and Brigon to get to Gastonia. These countries alone boasted vast changes in terrain. If she flew she wouldn't see anything. At least that's what others told her.

Trawnvane was the second to last stop on this line. The town itself was at the base of the snow-capped, tree-covered Brussel Mountains which formed the western edge of the country of Gastonia. Barely visible from the train station, Creigam Freigh Society was situated on the edge of the Foothills… though distinguishing it from being on one of the mountains was somewhat hazy.

She remembered the footage she saw on the television, but was blown away! No video could come close. This place was beyond breath-taking! And she would get to be here for almost a year!

The number of people at the station wasn't nearly what she was expecting. But then again, Callimay knew she was going to be one of the last ones to arrive since she left around midday on Sunday.

As she continued along, she found a welcoming committee at the entrance of the rail station. She breathed a sigh of relief, smiling as she asked chipper, "Could you tell me which way it is to Creigam Freigh Society? I'm planning on walking th—"

"I doubt you'd make it very far in those shoes, deary." An older lady laughed as she looked at what she had on. "It's all of a thirty-mile stretch from here to there. And uphill the entire way at that."

"Oh! I guess that won't work then!"

"There's a bus just about to leave and head in that direction." The older lady pointed to her left. "It's only twenty brass cleats as well as the safest and easiest way to get there."

"Thank you." Callimay took off, waving as she glanced back.

"Good morning… yeah, morning. Where are you headed to, miss?" The driver asked as he closed the door behind her — the lady was right when she said it was about to leave.

"Creigam Freigh Society," she beamed with pride as she worked to catch her breath and hand him the money, them making their usual high-pitched clinking sounds as they hit each other.

"You're my only passenger for that stop." The driver cautioned as he glanced at the money to make sure she gave him the correct amount. "We don't usually go up there… but seeing as how you're wearing those hi—"

"How long of a walk would it be if you dropped me off where you normally would?" Callimay asked without a second thought, and then apologized, "Pardon my interruption."

"Oh, you're fine. I usually stop where the private drive starts. It's another five miles or so from there. Uphill the whole way."

"I'll be fine. I'm from an area of similar terrain and walked to and from work in shoes like these, so I'm used to the kind of walk it will be. I appreciate your concern though."

"Whatever you say, it's your feet." The driver shrugged his shoulders and reached for the wheel. "Have a seat."

"Thank you." Callimay nodded as she turned to find one.

❦

When she was dropped off, she looked at the task ahead of her and didn't flinch at all. Callimay had been sitting in a train for almost an entire day, so she was glad to give her legs some exercise. And in those thoughts she laughed at what the driver was expecting: *I'm sure I surprised him. The roads here are so much better than back home. This will be a breeze of a walk. It's so beautiful here. It reminds me of home in little ways. Surely this will help me feel more at ease, right? ~ It's okay, Rose Petal. Just calm down.*

The walk was a scenic one, only the sound of her heels clacking as they hit the pavement and the wheels of her one bag being heard above the sounds of nature. She looked out at the vast valley below, hearing a low roar. Callimay figured out what was making the rumbling roar and became excited to watch a plane land: *They do look like birds. ~ I guess so. If you stand on your head and~ From this distance, silly.*

After seeing a half dozen or so, she turned back and kept walking; soon coming into view of the main gate. Seeing the stately appearance of the fence surrounding the complex, she became more and more nervous. The closer she got, the more she could see the large crowd of young adults her age. They were all standing around and chatting.

She stopped at a table near a raised platform with a podium and sound system set up, speaking with the few people who were there.

Upon checking in, Callimay then turned to who were going to be her four-hundred and ninety-nine classmates for almost a full year. Thinking of the number made a feeling of intimidation set in. Being what would be called a socialite was something she let fade from her life after Mrs. Berchoff died.

The more she looked around at what everyone else was wearing, the more Callimay felt underdressed. It seemed as if she were the only "plain" one there. She knew what she had was her best: her pair of high heel pumps which matched her skin tone perfectly; a pair of cream-colored slacks; and a warm orange, tunic-length blouse with ruched princess seams and elbow-length sleeves. Callimay wasn't much for doing her hair, so it was only pulled back into a tight bun with her side-swept bangs tucked behind her ear.

By a quick glance, everyone else looked to be of higher standing than her. She even guessed the jewelry most of the other girls and young women were wearing had real pearls and diamonds; but she wouldn't trade her heart pendant or Mrs. Berchoff's wedding band for any of them.

Refusing to accept defeat, she summoned her courage, and within an hour realized those gathered there all seemed friendly.

"Hello, I'm Callimay Berchoff." She smiled as she walked up to a couple young women who were looking around.

The one who spoke first was very short in stature and had a freckled face just like Trever. Her bright blue eyes stood out, but matched her silk sundress. Callimay could tell the dress was of high-quality fabrics and unique design… and thus was most likely tailor-made for her.

"Well hi! I'm Gallia. And this is— I'm sorry, I forgot your name already. I told you names were difficult for me." She giggled as she addressed the other young lady in the now threesome.

This young lady was tall and extremely slender… like some models Callimay had the… "unique" experience of working with. Her hair even resembled theirs: the edgy high/low cut with stark blonde and lavender highlights. — Why that combo was so popular is anyone's guess. — Her moto outfit complemented her edgy style; being made of white leather and lavender cashmere.

She tried and tried, but couldn't deny she knew this type of woman. They were snobbish to some degree or another… so Callimay wasn't sure how this would go.

"That's fine; and completely understandable." She laughed. "My name is Ingrid. It's nice to meet you, Callimay. Where are you from? I originally hail from Upton, Ferdinan."

"I'm from Whipple Grove, Crosswall." Gallia offered.

"Wow! Those are cities I have always wanted to visit." Callimay began to daydream; inside being ashamed of the little town she called home. "I'm from a small town in Faberton."

"Oh really?" Ingrid asked rather inquisitive, still sounding polite. "That's amazing there are three of us so close together! We're practically neighbors. … So, what part of Faberton are you from?"

"The Northern Hills. Berchshire."

"Oh, the Northern Hills is a beautiful place." Gallia sighed loud.

"And you know," Ingrid began to add. "I think I've been through that area—"

"Well hello," a young man's voice interrupted.

The girls turned and saw the embodiment of what was idolized at the time in a vast majority of the world: a handsome young man about six-foot with striking blue eyes and strawberry blonde hair done in what was known as "the James" style — named after a famous actor from the Homeworld who took the scene by storm in his day. And then there was his attire. It was of the quality only seen by Callimay in articles of nobles.

He flashed a pleasant smile there way as he strolled over. Callimay was more star-struck meeting someone of such a high standing than "noticing" him like it appeared Ingrid and Gallia did.

"Hi," Gallia giggled as she twirled her already tightly curled, bright red locks around her finger.

"And who might you be?" Ingrid smiled as she tossed her head to move her hair away from her eye.

"I'm Toreon Philpod." He bowed. "Let me say I am 'so' pleased to meet the three of you. Might I be privileged to know your names?"

"Gallia Vernon," she curtsied and rested her chin on her right index finger which she had bent; a sign of regal standing in the country of Crosswall for women.

"Ingrid Davenpond," she smiled as she shifted how she stood and put her hand on her hip.

"I'm Callimay Berchoff," she bowed her head in respect. "I'm pleased to make your acquaintance."

"And I, you." Toreon flashed a smile as he took her hand and rubbed it; and then cleared his throat, "Well! Allow me to introduce you to a few young men I've met so far."

Following the direction in which he gestured, the three girls saw a small group of younger men; all whom were of equal desirable physical appearance — in their own way.

Callimay stared at the one young man in particular: *I know him from somewhere.*

Meanwhile, Toreon finished introducing those he knew to the three young women, "And this is Callimay Berchoff."

"It's nice to meet you," the familiar young man offered his hand.

"Do I know you?"

"I'm glad to see you remembered me. I'm the one who delivered your acceptance letter. Dakoe. Dakoe VanGild."

"Now I remember! Do you work for the Society?"

"I was accepted early and asked to be a correspondent who would deliver letters to others." He smiled but shook his head.

"You gave me mine as well," Ingrid added as she offered her hand. "Glad to see you decided to show. I know you said you weren't sure when we talked last."

"Oh. Well then! What do you know? I feel like I know someone here now." Callimay laughed, causing everyone else in the group to erupt in laughter as well.

The group talked for a while and added in a few more young women and men along the way. Callimay was thrilled to be fitting into such a wonderful group so quick. They all chatted about what their homelife was like, as well as their likes and dislikes of different topics and things... the normal group chatter.

She was quite thankful the homelife sharing died off before the question made it to her; she wasn't quite ready to open up about some things to those she just met. Really? As far as every question went, she was content to listen to everyone else's answers.

It seemed like their small group was from all four corners of the world: the archipelago of Kae-Nu, one of the newest countries of Hagzell, the frozen tundra of Quimbergo, and the desert wasteland of Aridigobe to name a few.

As the conversation continued, she began to realize how late it was getting when she saw where the sun was in the sky. At first, she was talking to herself, but found she was now talking to the group, "Shouldn't our orientation have started already?"

"Oh. I guess you're right." Toreon agreed as he consulted his watch. "I wonder what could have happened. I don't see the Society as being an institution which takes many, if any, liberties with scheduling."

"You are quite right, young man," a rather familiar voice to them all stated in a clear and agreeable tone.

"Why, Mr. Freigh!" Toreon exclaimed as he whipped around.

"It is fine." He encouraged as he put his hand out to help calm everyone's gasps. "You are Toreon, is that correct? Toreon Philpod?"

"Yes sir."

"It is nice to meet you. The essay you submitted on the need for social equality within different financial brackets was very inspiring. I am looking forward to seeing you work and grow toward being able to fulfill that desire. I would say humanity as a whole needs help in that area. — Now as for what you— Callimay Berchoff?"

"Yes sir." She nodded in the same respectful manner as earlier.

"As to your question, there is still one student who has yet to arrive. He informed us of his possible tardiness, so this delay was something we had prepared for. Our lives demand so much of us that priorities must be made and upheld. I value the willingness of young adults who see the importance of having such an awareness of decisions and their consequences. I hope your welcoming of this student will reflect your shared admiration for such character. — All efforts have been made to assure everyone can go through this process together so you can begin to lay a foundation to be built upon during your year here."

"Oh. Well that's completely understandable. We should make an extra effort as a group to include the last person since they will not have had as much time as us to get into a group." Callimay offered as she looked to everyone else.

"Sure thing. Sounds great." Toreon replied rather nonchalantly, several others also nodding in approval.

"Splendid." Mr. Freigh agreed, and then turned back to where he was headed, "In fact; I think I see him coming now. … Yes, it is him. I will let him formally introduce himself, but let you know his name is Destan Nevrille."

"Thank you Mr. Freigh," Callimay said appreciatively.

"Yes, thank you." Toreon echoed.

"You are quite welcome. I am looking forward to being better acquainted with you all. And: welcome to the Society!" He said jovially as he left to greet his last student. "I am so glad you were able to make it, Destan. Thank you for informing us early about your possible tardiness. It was appreciated."

"Mr. Freigh," he addressed in a serious tone as he shook his hand with a firm and professional grip. "I want to thank you for your willingness to give me that leeway. 'I' am the grateful one. And I will make every effort to ensure there are no more incidents of this nature."

"The information surrounding your possible tardiness was more than enough to constitute our compliance. We are grateful you joined us. The group there agreed since you have not had time to find a home-group they would like to include you while you search for your own."

"I appreciate they are willing to," Destan replied in the same tone as he picked up his smaller sized duffle bag and glanced over to where Mr. Freigh motioned.

"The young lady, Callimay Berchoff, was the one who spoke up first for the idea." Mr. Freigh informed as he nodded toward her.

She grinned and waved when they both looked over, Destan replying, "I will make sure to convey my thanks to her."

His appearance was rather subdued compared to the vast majority of students there — like Callimay herself. He was wearing a basic black suit, but his jacket was slung over his shoulder and the white dress shirt he was wearing had the top button undone, cuffs unbuttoned, and sleeves rolled up almost halfway — not to mention no sign of a tie anywhere. This "break of protocol" seemed strange, but he surely had his reasons for not wearing his jacket and rolling up his sleeves.

Yet his appearance compared to everyone else couldn't hold a candle to the noteworthiness of his height: six-foot seven-inches — maybe a tad taller. And yet for as lean as he was, he wasn't gangly at all and he didn't "look" awkward. His thick, black hair wasn't a mullet, but it was a bit longer. Just think, if he would have his hair spiked… that would have that made him even more of a giant!

Regardless of what is said either way, Callimay still felt like a young child due to this vast difference in height. She wasn't short in stature by any means compared to the average woman; it was due to Destan's extreme height. Even though she was wearing four-inch heels she felt tiny. Usually when she wore these shoes she was at least eye level with most people. Now? Nowhere close.

What caught her attention more than anything when he got close enough — which was farther away than you might think — were his dazzling green eyes. Callimay stood there for a moment as they stared at her… she'd never seen someone with this color green before. Really? She'd never seen anyone in her entire life with green eyes. She was so drawn in by how they appeared to show his emotions.

"Hi Destan!" She smiled, offering her hand in friendship.

In that split moment of silence after she spoke and before he replied, his eyes became very soft and sincere in their gaze. It's not that he was glaring at her before, but Callimay couldn't help but notice that there was a change in them as they looked at her.

"I wish to thank you for your hospitality, Miss Callimay," he replied in a formal tone as he bowed his head; seeming oblivious to her outstretched hand.

Oh. This is awkward. ~ Well say something. "You… are quite welcome. Come and meet everyone. I know there won't be much time before Mr. Freigh starts speaking, so don't feel bad for not remembering them all. I can't either."

Destan broke somewhat of a smile and followed Callimay back to the group. For some reason having him following her felt funny; not bad though. It made her smile to herself.

Everyone was thrilled to meet him and started the rounds of introductions. Well, all except for Toreon. It wasn't that he hated him, but there felt like there was some kind of tension between them.

But Callimay put the thought out of her mind because she knew she had to be wrong: *It's fine, Rose Petal. ~ Are you sure? ~ Seriously? You don't even know them. Maybe they know each other and that's how they greet each other. Webb and Toreon know each other. ~ But what if~ Shush. They're starting.*

♮

"That was. Intense." Toreon said exhausted, though everyone could tell he was exaggerating the entire issue, as he unbuttoned his blazer and sat next to Callimay.

"It is quite a bit of information to take in, and in such a short amount of time." She answered and then continued: *It looks as if some were able to keep up with everything a bit better than others. I wonder where Destan is. I never did catch his last name. Did he even tell us? It seems like Mr. Freigh said it before he left. Oh, why can't I remember it? Ugh! … Anyway. It's strange how he disappeared after orientation started. Maybe he's found another g—*

"You alright, Callimay?" Toreon asked as he tapped her shoulder.

"I'm sorry?"

"You didn't hear me?"

"No. I tend to talk to myself and I can kinda zone out when I do. What were you saying?"

"Oh," he nodded and then looked around the room at the array of expressions. "I was just saying I'm not the only one who is exhausted. … I can even see there have been group changes."

"Well, I'm glad he was able to find a group." She smiled when she found Destan sitting on the other side of the room, his back to her. "I just wanted him to feel included. I know I was nervous when I showed up, so I didn't want him to feel any more awkward and nervous than he probably was. Being the last one to any type of event like this has got to be stressful. And it gave him some time so he would be able to calm down a bit and find the group he wanted."

"Sure," Toreon replied nonchalantly.

I wish he would have stayed. Callimay sighed as she leaned her arm on the table, resting her chin on it while she looked over at Destan and then down to her food. *Something seems different about him. He's— I don't know. More mature? No. More responsible? He's very serious and formal in his demeanor, that's for sure. I just hope there's a group here he can fit in with and do well…*

"I must say, wearing uniforms is going to be a change for me. I'm used to being allowed to have my tailor make outfits to conform to the newest fads and my tastes. I mean, at least we can wear the clothes we brought with us after school hours and on Saturdays and Sundays." Ingrid sighed as she turned her focus to Callimay. "What about you? What do you— what in the world are you doing with your fork?"

"Oh!" She jumped when she saw a few people staring at her. "I'm sorry! Was thinking about things again."

"It's 'so' much to take in, I know. Don't worry about it." Gallia smiled as she put her arm around her and gave her a quick hug. "Ingrid just asked if wearing uniforms would be a change for you."

"It will be, very much so. The little school I attended wasn't much for strict dress code or timekeeping… or anything, really. Where I'm from, school has been seen as a distraction from farm duties and work needing to be done at home. It's gotten better, but most everyone wore their working clothes which were muddy already, just to go back home and get even more mud on them. We started whenever there were enough of us to have a study partner and then left when it was time to begin afternoon chores. With it being so soon after the civil war, education wasn't on the top of many peoples' priority lists. We oftentimes shared books since they were so…" Callimay offered, fading out as she saw everyone's facial expressions.

"That 'is' a change," Ingrid answered slow and stunned.

"The name tags will help me remember everyone's names." Gallia giggled, deflecting attention and changing the subject.

"That's for sure." Callimay chimed in. "And since they are sewn into our uniforms and the access key to all the buildings, it makes things so much easier for me."

"Lose your keys?" Dakoe jabbed as he looked at her out of the corner of his eye.

"More times than I care to remember!" She rolled her eyes and laughed. "I was so relieved when I found that out."

To that response, the entire group had a hearty laugh and forgot what Callimay said earlier.

You need to watch what you say out loud more, Rose Petal. ~ I'm so used to being on my own I forget there are people there listening. ~ The last thing you need is to let it slip—

"We hope you all enjoyed your first dinner here. Please report to the main lecture hall for the evening orientation session." Everyone heard Baleck inform. "Presentations will begin in ten minutes."

"Let's get there first so we can sit in the front, letting everyone see what a great group we are," Toreon announced as he stood.

"Alright!" "That's an awesome idea!" "Let's lay a foundation for our reputation!" "Lead the way, Toreon!" "Nothing like getting a head-start, am I right?" Those in the group answered.

As she passed Destan, Callimay stopped and said, "I'm glad you were able to find a group which fits best for you. I hope you didn't feel I was forcing you into this one."

"You weren't. I thank you for your kindness, Miss Callimay." He replied, glancing at her and then back at his empty lunch tray.

"You're very welcome, Destan." She smiled, though she felt something was bothering him and started asking, "Is everything—"

"Callimay!" Toreon called out as he turned back to find her.

"Coming." She answered as she became a bit flustered. "I… I will talk to you later, Destan. Bye for now."

He never responded or looked up at her, and she couldn't wait any longer by seeing the look on Toreon's face. She rushed over and was rather shocked to hear what he said as he rolled his eyes, "Just ignore the guy, Callimay. He's not worthy of our company."

"Well…" she hesitated as she looked back to Destan who was looking straight at Toreon, the same serious expression on his face.

"Look at him. He's way too serious for us." Toreon snapped as he nodded toward him. "There's no way he could ever fit in with us. I wouldn't be surprised if he ended up at the bottom of the class. If he doesn't lose that serious tone, it will be what happens. That's not what the Society is about at all."

"He's probably nervous since he was late, that's all." Callimay defended, offering a sweet smile Destan's way.

"Come on guys. Remember? Front row, set an example, lay our foundation, take the lead." Ingrid interjected as she put a hand on each of their shoulders. "Sound familiar?"

"Right. Focus." Toreon smiled with determination as he turned around. "Let's go!"

🕉

"Quite a group," Baleck stated as he watched the screen. "They're polarizing faster than any of the other groups thus far."

"We have yet to have talent and personalities like we do this year." Mr. Freigh answered satisfied as he sat back in his chair. "Do you still think my choice in accepting Destan was in error?"

"It's still too soon to know. He's reacting exactly as you predicted, but only time will tell."

"Believe me. He is the best chance we will ever have for Challenger. He has great potential. Let us hope the composure and seriousness he shows is reflected in his true emotional nature."

"Potential is always there. Look at Toreon Philpod. Upstanding young man with a great endeavor to help—"

"Nothing but lies." Mr. Freigh interrupted as he shook his head. "He is a manipulator of situations for his own good: financially, socially, economically, and personally. His family history shows this tendency, and he is showing every earmark he plans to continue with it. … I understand, Baleck. I do. I commend you for looking for the good in him. You want to see it because of his potential for being an example of overcoming the status quo… much like yourself."

"Yes," he admitted as he hung his head; and then a moment later looked at his superior out of the corner of his eye, "Though could it be said you are doing the same for Destan. … Are you?"

"I am not saying it is impossible for either side, good or bad. But we have to see people for who they are now in reality and not who they 'could' be. We have matched them all to who we would want them to be with perfect reasoning to create a future we would like… and would be best with what we are faced with. In reality though, everything hinges on whether or not they prove to be the potential we see." Mr. Freigh answered as he went through a file of papers with all the students' names, pausing as he finished, "I am saying this as much for myself as you, Baleck."

"I just don't want to judge someone on the first day due to their excitement, or…"

"I see where you are going with this," he sighed as he took his glasses off and retrieved the handkerchief from his jacket's breast pocket. "I am just as frustrated as you are. Our efforts have not been nearly as successful as either of us had planned. We have only found two dozen qualified candidates over the past ten years, with only half of those completing their training. The cliffhangers were not— we cannot give up now. We cannot. If we do, our last sin is greater than the first."

"Emotions are a hard thing to control. People hide so much of who they are: saying things to themselves they would never dare utter to the outside world. And yet they hold a perfect façade for everyone else to see. This deception is, in and of itself, an art; and one requiring the person to lie to themselves; which is more pain than bearing the weight of people knowing the truth, I believe. … Though, it 'is' admirable that we've been able to master almost all we've encountered."

"But the one we need be able to control 'cannot' be!" Mr. Freigh lashed out in anger and threw the file down on the table, spreading all the paperwork across the desk. "It is the one we see the most of and the reason why we lost the twelve cliffhangers!"

After a minute or so of silence, Baleck looking across the room at him rather shocked, Mr. Freigh gathered himself and replaced his glasses as he sighed heavily, "I am showing by my own example how dangerous anger can be. I apologize for my outburst, Baleck. I am grateful I have you here to help keep me in check."

Hearing his comment caused Baleck to pause. He returned the book he had in his hand and hurried back to the desk. While he picked through the scattered pages, he suggested, "Could it possibly be while we are looking for independent persons, we have needed a team all along? Not a group, just a two-person team."

"Excuse me?"

"Hear me out, Mr. Freigh," Baleck leaned across the desk. "The biggest deterrent we encounter with cliffhangers when they fall into frenzy mode is the disconnect in communication, correct? What if we team one with the highest probability of this happening with one who could reach them even in that state? What if we have been looking to impact too many areas at once and not seeing the wisdom in teaming them up to strengthen their abilities? You just said it is beneficial to have a second person to keep watch."

"Do you think it could be possible?" Mr. Freigh asked in a hopeful manner as he looked over the page which was handed to him.

"I don't know why I didn't think of this before now. If Destan 'is' Challenger, he 'will' need this person's help. His cliffhanger index is the highest we've had. I don't see us needing to take the route of altering his situation. It is best to work with him as is."

"Agreed. But…"

"I made sure I left a few spots for operatives," Baleck informed as he picked up another couple papers. "I was rather surprised you didn't notice them. And as it sits right now, there are a couple who are in close contact with this person who would benefit Destan. I can get word to them to help things along so we can see how this person reacts, and if they will match up to what we anticipate."

"Forcing someone's hand — not to sound too cliché — comes with many risks. And the kinds of risks we cannot afford to meddle with. You said so yourself."

"Yes, but these operatives are seasoned and understand their purpose for being here. This person does not show any signs of being noncompliant or rebellious. … I know this was going above you, but I knew something needed to be done as a precautionary measure which would not show our hand to everyone. — Remember I get the same reports as you do. I know it's now or never. — The only problem might be: seeing if they will be able to work with Destan. He seems to have pulled away and made himself everyone's enemy just about, and it's only midway through the first day of orientation."

"So you 'do' believe Destan is Challenger?" Mr. Freigh prodded. "Baleck? Why else would you plant operatives in the student body? Do not sugarcoat it with your 'objective, scientific views'. Tell me."

"Yes." He admitted as he picked up Destan's paperwork. "He's a perfect match… more so than anyone I have seen. This first day has solidified so many of our findings as him being Challenger. Our developers have told us time and time again this is the strongest serum they have developed. Keeping him stable is the most optimal choice, but this second person could bring a huge variable into check if he does end up being a cliffhanger."

"Do not start anything too soon, but we only have limited time to get them into optimal preconditioning. But who knows? Things may change between them and they may come together on their own."

"Very well. — Now I think it's time for you to address your student body for the evening session."

"So it is." Mr. Freigh acknowledged as he checked his watch. "This is a major breakthrough, Baleck. If this works, I mourn for those twelve cliffhangers all over again. We may have murdered a dozen innocent young men without seeing the wisdom of altering our objective by just one person."

Baleck could not find any words of counsel. What Mr. Freigh said was true. The twelve they lost — nor the ones who were successes for that matter — knew of or consented to what happened. What ended up happening in every individual case was squarely left on the shoulders of all those at the Society.

"Just one person." Mr. Freigh repeated in anguish as he leaned his forehead against the doorframe.

₰

"W. O. W. That's all I've got to say," Ingrid collapsed onto a bed.

"Tell me about it." Gallia checked her makeup in the mirror. "This is 'so' much more than I thought! I cannot wait to get started."

"It's a tall order, that's for sure. And structured like nothing I've ever heard of." She continued as she stared at the ceiling. "Regular academics can be hard enough, but this whole social thing? I know they told us how it works… but how does it work again?"

"Oh, you worry too much."

"Think about it: everything we're supposed to do to succeed at this school has nothing to do with what school has always been about for us. And this is college-level classes." Ingrid continued, somewhat annoyed by her indifference about everything. "This social thing is foreign to all of us as far as grading goes."

"Being a social bug isn't foreign," Gallia answered a bit arrogant. "It's the game of finding who the top dog is and riding on his coattails… like any social hierarchy."

"Well, if nothing else, at least we have each other!" Callimay said to help defuse the situation as she closed the door. "Who knew the first two girls I met would be my roommates!"

"Our optimist: Callimay." Ingrid smiled as she sat up, and then fell back again, "If you want this bed, I'm sorry. It's comfortable so I'm staying. Go find another one."

All three of them laughed.

"Things will be really different and challenging, but there are so many conveniences we have!" Callimay continued as she looked around the spacious rooms. "Just look around us."

"Like name tags for instance?" Ingrid insinuated; not moving to look over at Gallia.

"Very funny," she responded, annoyance still in her voice.

"Well… that, the integrated keys which will unlock anything we are allowed into, no combinations to remember for our lockers — or locks that don't work, the fact we each have our own bike, we don't have to do any cooking or laundry. There's not even any need to take out the trash… though I guess it might not be something you see as a convenience." Callimay stated, and then gasped, "Oh, I'm sorry! I—"

"Don't be," Gallia looked over to her and tossed her head in a rather carefree manner. "It's true. Isn't it, Ingrid?"

"You've got that right." She agreed as she sat up again. "Don't worry about saying things from your perspective, Callimay. It's nice to hear how others see things. Makes a person all the better knowing how others see life."

"Thank you girls." She smiled as she walked over to the room Ingrid had claimed as her own. "This is going to be a great year; I already know it."

"Seems like you and Toreon hit it off extremely fast." Ingrid winked as she nudged Callimay. "Or was it Dakoe?"

"They're both nice," she answered unconcerned but polite.

"Toreon. Nice? That's all you can say?" Gallia gasped in horror. "I mean, I get Dakoe… but Toreon!"

"What else am I supposed to say?" Callimay asked as she walked over and inspected her room.

"Why… why how dreamy he is and just… amazing. I would give anything to switch places with you." Gallia twirled around.

"I don't quite follow you," Callimay replied, looking confused. "He seems like a very nice young man. I'm glad I have him as a friend. Like Dakoe and the rest."

"Playing it coy. I love it." She grinned as she shook her hands with joy as if she were about to burst at the seams because of it. "How I would love to be in your shoes."

"Really, Gallia. I don't know what you are talking about."

"You two are practically a thing… a couple." She stated blunt, a bit of jealousy in her voice now as she put her hands on her hips.

"Whoa!" Callimay panicked, waving her hands in front of her as if to flag down a bus. "I just met him! I don't know who he really is!"

"No need to freak out." Ingrid intervened, getting out of bed and shoving Gallia to the side. "I'm sure you were just teasing. Right?"

"I'm sorry. Really. I'm sorry I scared you, Callimay."

"Let's all get some rest. We've got the rest of this week to get to know each other better before things get serious." Ingrid sounded like the exhausted older sister who just wanted to go to sleep and not deal with her squabbling, younger siblings she was left to keep watch over. "We're tired."

"Sounds like a wonderful plan." Callimay began to yawn.

~ 5 ~

The next week flew by, everyone scrambling to build a strong and loyal group. Callimay saw it as almost too much of a fuss because things would change throughout the year. At least from what little she had experienced in life: people came and went, so you just needed to hang on and be who you knew you needed to be. Everything would work out in the end. Sure, it was understandable everyone wanted to start with a good foundation, but Callimay knew no one was going to build that flawless group in less than a week.

With all this going on, everyone thought they were on top and began to draw lines, causing rifts in the class body. Callimay wasn't a fan of this happening, seeing as how the ones who determined who was on top were the faculty at the Society. This social hierarchy wasn't decided by the students themselves.

Every student was required to sign waivers stating they understood they would be monitored visibly and audibly in all public areas of the complex during school hours — excluding the obvious areas which should never have spying eyes. All faculty were observers — including Mr. Freigh and Baleck.

Mr. Freigh made regular appearances throughout the week, but even though he was the conductor of the Society, these appearances were in a pure observation role. Baleck ran interference if students attempted to converse with him, reminding them when they could speak with him.

Anything approved through the scheduler was booked during leisure time. It was then that students got to talk with Mr. Freigh and Baleck about their questions or concerns.

But if issues arose, unlike what Callimay assumed would happen, students first had to seek help from other students. Faculty was only to be approached if no student could or would help, Mr. Freigh and Baleck being the last resort. This was said to help reinforce the objective of the Society.

Leisure time was just that: leisure time. All observation during those hours couldn't be used in the grading of students, nor what was overheard or seen by faculty. Even though they weren't allowed to leave, normality still seemed to find its way into these short times.

Though, with such a limited number of students — and those being so polarized due to their different social groupings and disagreements — any organized sports were irrelevant and unsustainable. The sports complex was degraded to the place for pickup games, as well as a place offering exercise areas for students who enjoyed such things.

Aside from this, there wasn't much entertainment. Students had to be inventive when organizing something, satisfied with mingling, or find contentment in time alone.

❧

Callimay already knew it, but was reminded any contact with family or friends was revoked to help them focus on themselves and what they wanted to achieve without any outside influence. It didn't have much bearing on her seeing as how she had no immediate family, but she was concerned about those who did.

This all made her think of Destan when she saw him walking the grounds on Sunday morning before Assembly: *Maybe leaving his family was hard. He seems so alone. I wish I could help.*

She was rather shocked to see who was and wasn't there, but remembered her focus wasn't supposed to be on people but on God.

There were obvious differences in how things were conducted, but Callimay knew this coming in. And then as far as how things "looked" she knew preferences were just that: so what if they had padded pews and stained-glass windows. They were just things.

Introductions were soon over, followed by announcements about different opportunities for students to participate in extra studies. Being in an environment that was geared toward social interaction, there was quite the list given, and encouragement on the part of those speaking about students signing up for more than one so that their grades would be helped by this "practice".

The answer to what was the "why" question for these studies didn't sit very well with Callimay: *You don't glaze it over by saying it helps with school. Study in and of itself is what is expected of any Christian. There's no need for any other motivation than to be closer to God. ~ Well, maybe it was a 'slip of the tongue'? ~ One way to find out for sure. ~ Very true.*

As she sang, Callimay could hear what sounded like Destan's deep and clear voice coming from behind. She almost laughed a couple times, hearing the rather strange way he pronounced some words due to his thick accent. During that time, she became more and more at ease. She had a strong foundation already but was thrilled she was going to have what she was hoping for so she could continue to grow while she was away from home.

ℬ

When Assembly was over, Callimay turned to see if Destan was there but found a small group blocking her view. They talked for a little while, mainly getting to know those they had not met yet.

By the time she excused herself from the group and got to where she could see, Destan was gone… if he was there at all: *Oh well. I'll check tonight. ~ Maybe it wasn't him. ~ Maybe. But what if it were? ~ Then he'd be lightning-fast to get out like he did. Who runs out like that? ~ I guess you've got a point.*

$$\sim 6 \sim$$

When Callimay woke up for the first day, she was gleeful as she grabbed the few items she needed to get her hair and makeup done. The rooms were quite generous in size, so it gave the three girls privacy as well as plenty of room so they weren't falling over each other. Callimay was still adjusting to sharing her space with others but knew it wouldn't take her long to get used to it.

"Are you ready?" Ingrid called out from the hall.

"Just give me another— oh, head on without me. I'll catch up with you in a minute or so." Callimay paused, changing her mind.

"You alright?" Ingrid poked her head back in.

"I'm fine. I… I'll be fine." She hesitated as she looked down at the floor. "I need a minute to— I just need a minute. Okay? I… I promise I'm alright."

"If you need anything…"

"I'll let you know. Thanks." Callimay nodded and then finished when Ingrid shut the door, looking at herself in the full-length mirror: *This is actually, really, truly happening. I— it has to be because I just realized I'm doing this.*

She tried to be positive, though she sounded more and more terrified as she spoke, closing her eyes and mumbling under her breath, "Maybe a part of me is scared I'll be found. I can't expect defeat though. I'm the one who gets to choose how I feel. And I want to be excited about this… I do! I'm going to be nervous but I don't want to be scared. I know I can do this. I know I can."

Callimay opened her eyes and finally saw herself smile. It wasn't as bright as it had been, but it was there.

"I can do this. I 'want' to do this."

One, last, deep breath and she grabbed her book bag.

❧

As Callimay walked out, she noticed almost everyone was at the main school building. Without thinking, she took off — forgetting the fact that taking her bike would have been quicker. A large roar of applause and cheers rose from the school building, diverting her attention long enough she didn't see the other person on the path and ran into them.

"Oh! Oh my goodness! I'm so sorry!" She gasped as she reached for their book bag, and then looked up rather shocked, "Destan!"

Callimay was now embarrassed, seeing she ran into a young man. Though she felt even more so since it was Destan for some strange reason; blushing as she got up and handed it to him. He took the book bag without saying anything and not looking fazed. But at least he looked at her, and she couldn't help but think his eyes changed.

"I… I hope I didn't— I'm sorry." She stammered, trying to pull her thoughts together on the fly. "I should have been—"

"It's fine," he answered flat, shrugging his shoulders.

His lack of worry caused her to look back up at him, staring at him for a moment. Callimay all of a sudden felt something she hadn't before; but wasn't sure what it was. Not only did Destan seem different from everyone else, but he also made her feel different. She felt like she was truly smiling now… not like earlier.

As she was about to ask a question when he turned and left, the first bell ringing as well, "I—"

She gasped and took off running again. Destan's strides were so long, it took her a little to catch up with him. He didn't seem disturbed by the bell and kept going at the same pace. Callimay was confused he wasn't speeding up, but something in her told her it would be alright and she shouldn't abandon him. She slowed down a bit to go his pace — though she was still walking at a quicker pace than usual.

While they continued along, she kept her head somewhat down, the only sounds filling the air being her shoes clacking on the paved path and the rushing wind through the nearby trees. The wind was so strong it didn't take her much time to regret how she did her hair, scolding herself and finding it necessary to toss her head to get her bangs out of her face: *I should've looked outside be— ugh! This is 'so' embarrassing.*

She now had to push her hair — not just her bangs — out of her face, and she could tell her earrings were now tangled in it. Being fed up, Callimay kept one of her hands over her hair so she wouldn't have to deal with it and could hopefully keep it from looking like an absolute mess. She knew it had to be laughable, what she must look like: practically her entire uniform flapping in the wind like a group of flags. What a sight!

After a bit, she glanced over at Destan to see if he might be laughing at her, but he kept his focus in front of him and didn't seem to notice she was looking at him at all… let alone it looked like she was going to be swept away by the wind at any moment. And then she noticed how the wind didn't affect him. His hair bobbed a little but didn't move much; his uniform not showing one sign it knew there was any wind.

❦

As they came up to the door, Callimay saw Toreon and a few others waiting. It was rather strange to see everyone in the same style of clothing: white or cream-colored shirts, charcoal pants, and sandy or dark-brown jackets. Even their accessories matched. — This was matchy-matchy heaven. — But then again it was an equalizing factor she saw: giving everyone the same fighting chance since this was all about social interaction, though many others — Ingrid for sure — saw it as a major inconvenience.

But the more she thought, the more she began to doubt. Maybe she was wrong: *Just because others have more money doesn't mean they can't socialize with people like me, or be nice. We've gotten along great so far. At least that's what I've seen. Maybe this whole matchy-matchy thing isn't so great after all…*

Callimay reached for the door as she waved to the group with the other, not realizing Destan already had his hand on it, "Oh! I…"

He — again — didn't appear startled at all.

Once he finished opening the door he stood there, staring at her: *Well this sure is awkward. ~ Why is he just looking at me? ~ You really are dumb. ~ What?* — "Oh! Why, I… I don't— Than—"

"Come on, Callimay!" Toreon called out rather irritated. "We'll be late for first lecture."

"I'm coming." She sighed as she turned to leave, and then stopped and turned back, "Thank you for letting me tag along, Destan. I hope you didn't think I was intruding. I'm sorry if you felt that way."

Everything inside of her was begging him to say anything, even tell her he didn't want to walk with her again. She didn't like him being so quiet. It made her feel like something was wrong… and she was the cause. If he said something, she'd at least know one way or the other!

Sadly, Destan still didn't say a word, so Callimay rushed over to the small group and headed in.

"What was that all about?" Ingrid asked a bit wide-eyed as she snickered. "Can't walk to class alone and need help opening doors?"

"Nothing of the kind!" She shook her head; talking in a hushed tone as Toreon looked at her displeased. "He— I… I was running late and it just so happened he was too. I didn't plan it that way. Really! How would I know? We haven't talked any since the first day. And as far as what happened at the door, I… I was j—"

"I'm just teasing." Ingrid laughed as she nudged her shoulder. "Relax, Callimay. I'm not going to rail you like Gallia would. Come on. Let's head on inside."

"Nothing, huh?" Toreon muttered as he glared back at Destan. *Oh really? Somehow I doubt that.*

~ 7 ~

"Callimay? Oh! There you are. Did you see!" Gallia shrieked after she looked back, having to hop a few times to see where she was, then pushed her way through the group of students.

"No. What?" She answered rather puzzled, taking a step back when Gallia ran into her to hug her.

"We did it! I mean I knew we would, but it's official!"

Toreon said triumphantly as he walked up, "We are the top dogs; the ones to be looked up to."

"We are?" Callimay asked in disbelief as she walked toward the large crowd of people around the posted reports.

"Yep. We sure are." Toreon walked up and casually put his hand on her shoulder. "We can go all the way. I know it."

"Our group is very strong," she answered in agreement as she looked down the lists.

"That is true, but I mean you and me, Callimay." He clarified as he slipped his hand in hers.

She was scared.

Sure, she thought Toreon was a nice young man, but this was way too fast for her. Some may not have seen it as anything, but to her, holding hands the way he was wasn't something you did with anyone. Yes, she had entertained the thought of finding someone special, but she never imagined it happening this way or this fast; let alone the fact the way he did it made her skin crawl. She didn't know what to say or do to get her point across without offending him in front of everyone and putting her grade in jeopardy — he seemed to be the type to be easily irritated and offended.

Callimay smiled rather nervous and hesitated as she said, "Maybe, but there are others who are even better than me. I mean look at Ingrid: she's in third right now overall."

"She is good, no doubt about that. But still not for me," Toreon explained, pulling her to him.

"Well, umm… we do need to keep the group as a whole in mind and not cause divisions."

"The group is strong like you said," he repeated as he tossed his nose in the air and began to saunter, parading Callimay around.

"It does look like some of our members are struggling in the individual ranks though." She reminded as she stopped and turned to point at the screens.

"I couldn't care less about their individual rank. In that aspect, I want everyone else below me. … Well everyone but you. I want you right beside me."

There were so many people around, but Callimay felt alone with Toreon. It seemed there were so few she felt like she could turn to for help at the time. She thought she knew so many people, but it was quite apparent she just knew them; she didn't truly trust them yet.

What do I do! Does anyone even know I'm uncomfortable with all of this? She cried in horror. *Does anyone even care!*

"Hey boss man!" One of their group members called out when he saw Toreon. "Wait up."

"Hey Webb," Toreon responded rather annoyed as he stopped, practically clenching Callimay's hand in his.

"Hey Callimay." He greeted when he noticed her.

"Hi Webb. How are you doing?"

"Oh, not too bad. The group's really got it going on! Individually? You two are soaring. Hopefully I can catch a ride so I can make a last-second move and win this all for myself." He bantered as he winked his eye. "What do you think about that plan?"

"Very funny," Toreon rolled his eyes. "But Callimay and I are going all the way. Nice try though, Webb."

"Is that so?" He asked as he raised his eyebrow.

"Oh, we are," Toreon answered in a firm tone, grabbing Callimay's hand again and pulling her over next to him.

"Whoa!" Dakoe interjected as he came over. "I was hoping you would save at least Callimay for someone else."

"Only the best for me, Dakoe," Toreon replied, sliding his hand around Callimay's waist. "You know that."

"Okay. Okay. No need to go all 'pub affec' on us." He responded as he put his hands up and turned his head.

"Excuse me," a familiar voice called out as they came through the crowd of gathered students.

Destan? Callimay asked in disbelief almost, though hoping with everything the voice she was hearing was indeed his.

Overall, the accent a person had was very unique to their country; Destan being no exception. She hadn't talked to him much, but his deep voice was so distinct. Callimay couldn't help but think she recognized this voice, but she didn't want to get her hopes up… not now.

"Sorry. Excuse— me." Destan stopped when he saw the look on her face and how Toreon was holding her.

"Hi Destan." She greeted, sounding frightened.

"Hello, Callimay." He responded in his usual flat tone.

"Move along. You don't belong here." Toreon stormed up to him, letting go of Callimay — more like shoving her to the side.

She bolted for the door, not stopping or turning back to see what happened. Who would?

"No need to worry. I was just being courteous to Miss Callimay." Destan backed off, putting his hands up.

"Leave me to do that," Toreon warned as he gritted his teeth. "And don't ever say her name aloud again. Your type of chivalry died ages ago. Drop the act. — And speaking of dying ages ago, it appears your social aptitude has as well… cliffhanger."

"Well, when you're hanging off the edge you have something to fight for… even the older traditions of life." Destan came back as he looked down at Toreon who was a good five inches shorter. "Come to think of it; when you're on solid ground, you can get too comfortable and not be ready for the ground to give way. You know what they say: when you're on top there's only one way to go… 'down'."

"Whoa!" Webb gasped, shocked to see this spunk in Destan. "I'm impressed. That was a burn there, boss man."

"Put a lid on it right now, or so help me!" Toreon snapped as he whipped his head around and glared at him; hissing through his teeth. And then turned his focus back to Destan, "Listen: punk. Don't let me 'ever' catch you talking to Callimay again. You hear me?"

"I hear ya," he tried to keep from laughing as he started to walk away. "Keep it secret. Not a problem."

"Don't walk away from me until I'm done," Toreon said infuriated as he stomped his foot. "Nevrille!"

"Okay." He stopped, turned to face Toreon, and waited for a few seconds; all the while looking dead serious. "You're done."

"You're gonna regret that, Destan Nevrille! I swear! You. Will. Regret. You 'ever' said that!"

ℬ

"He's showing promise; I'll be the first to admit." Baleck stated as he nodded in approval. "He's stable under pressure and beginning to show concern for others, even on a small scale. And if nothing else he has a keen way of making sure he has the last word."

"Very true." Mr. Freigh chuckled as he wiped a tear from his eye. "I am curious though, to see if this was an isolated incident or something he would be willing to repeat in the future to help Callimay."

"If nothing happens by week's end I will start the plan in motion. What about Destan? If things escalate— do I need to put any measures together to help him?"

"Oh believe me," Mr. Freigh laughed boisterously. "Toreon would be the one needing help, not Destan. He will be just fine."

"Very well. — Oh look. Destan seems to have followed Callimay."

"Interesting." Mr. Freigh said as he enlarged the feed from one of the surveillance videos. "Let us see what happens."

The footage showed Callimay seated on a bench, facing away from Destan. Her body language suggested she was frightened and scared, sitting curled up with her arms wrapped around her legs, head bowed. It even appeared she might be crying since she shivered. Destan stood a little way off down the path and watched her. He started walking toward her — having a hand stretched out — and then stopped short. He turned back the moment he heard people coming down the path.

Mr. Freigh sighed as he leaned back and rubbed his eyes, "Well, that was rather disappointing."

"He did follow her."

"True. But we need a solid case of him helping her for me to know for sure about this. We cannot afford to go off of assumptions and speculation. We are too deep into this to risk it all."

"Understood."

℈

Callimay found herself in somewhat of a bind: she needed to stay in this group to keep her individual ranking and she did like those in the group, but she didn't feel safe now. She didn't like Toreon's attitude toward her: too much uncalled-for attention and unwanted affection. In fact, she wasn't interested in him.

He seemed as of late to be quite full of himself; which she didn't approve of. Toreon was now constantly criticizing her attending Sunday Assembly and mid-week Study since he found out Destan was there; which made her upset he would say such a thing since he didn't go himself: *I'm not doing this to be around Destan. I didn't even know he was there for sure until Toreon said something. Every time I tried to look, no one was there. … Why is he so upset with me? Why doesn't he at least come at this all with some level of tolerance? It's not like I'm forcing anything on him. ~ You refuse to change; and he is the type who enjoys control. ~ Maybe. But that isn't an excuse. ~ I wasn't saying it was; don't start arguing with me now. ~ Ugh!*

And then on top of everything, it was baffling to her why he would treat her the way he did. He seemed to have at least three, maybe four girls clinging to him already. Why would he need another girl?

Dakoe, on the other hand, was someone Callimay had become quite close to. She began to value him on a deeper level and enjoyed the moments they would get to talk. They sat together on Sundays and during mid-week Study, and would even chat afterward.

As time went on, Toreon's authoritative roll pulled on Dakoe so he stepped away and left her altogether. She was sad he didn't value her like she did him; but at the same time, she was grateful to find out the truth sooner rather than later. She wanted to talk with him about it but it was quite apparent he'd fallen under Toreon's thumb during the past week; him not coming to Assembly even.

Him not coming saddened Callimay more than words could say. He wasn't just walking away from her; he was starting to walk away from God! She couldn't understand how one person could have such a strong pull on someone who was supposed to be a Christian!

All these thoughts ran through Callimay's mind, beginning to horrify her: *Who can I speak with? ~ You're supposed to go to classmates first before even thinking about faculty, Rose Petal. ~ But Toreon's got the few I would trust under his thumb now. What is he trying to do? I thought he was so nice? Why is he changing? Was it something I did? ~ What if this is who he truly is? ~ Oh, what do I do! I'd talk to Mr. Freigh, but what if he doesn't see it as anything important? ~ What about the scheduler? ~ Oh no. I forgot about that! If that doesn't work I have nothing left!*

But she stopped. Dakoe's comment earlier; it made her question if he "did" care. Could it last? Would he come back? Was he strong enough to stand up to Toreon?

~ 8 ~

For the rest of the school week, Callimay began to doubt why she came. The next day she arrived as late as possible in hopes she would have to find a different seat than her normal one next to Toreon. Unfortunately, he made sure it was left for her. She sighed as she walked over and sat as far to the right in the seat as possible.

"A bit behind this morning, Callimay?" Toreon leaned close.

"Just a little," she said a bit nervous as she looked down and away from him. "It's not like I was late or anything."

She made a point to go sit with some of the struggling members of their group during lunch, thrilled they asked her to sit with them for the afternoon. Some of the group wondered why she changed her seat, but thankfully they asked Callimay and were completely on board when they found out her reasoning… or at least the part of her reasoning she told them. She did want to help the others in the group, but she also wanted her distance from Toreon. So, it worked hand in hand… right?

The final lecture let out and Callimay went straight back to her room. She usually went for a bike ride in the afternoons to get away from everything and enjoy the beautiful scenery but she didn't think it best to be out and about by herself. Gallia and Ingrid both took an extra class in the afternoons on cosmetology so she was left alone.

&

The next day she sat with those same struggling members again which started making things with everyone else strained. Questions began to be asked, rumors began flying, sides were being taken, lies spread; and by day's end, Callimay was ousted. All the group members who tried to stand up for her earlier in the day were now against her.

She spent her leisure time for the rest of the day looking for a new group. The third-place team took her with great enthusiasm.

Thursday seemed to be going better, though it was hard to change rooms. And then there was learning a whole new group of names and having more than just the regular questions asked.

Callimay was grateful to the two girls who stepped up to offer her somewhere to stay, "I know this was short notice. I really appreciate—"

"Oh, don't think anything of it." The one girl smiled as she pulled her suitcases from underneath the bed which was now Callimay's. "It's nice to have someone new to talk to!"

"You mean now you'll have someone else to annoy." The other girl laughed as she shut the door behind Callimay.

"Hyra. Come on." The first girl huffed as she shoved her suitcase under her bed as best she could.

"What? I'm just telling the truth."

"New people open the door for lots of questions; I get it." Callimay inserted, trying to keep things from escalating. "I'll answer whatever questions you have."

"Now you did it." Hyra rolled her eyes and shook her head. "Don't say I didn't warn you when you're bombarded."

❦

Friday morning rolled around and she arrived for morning lecture only to find she was dropped by unanimous decision of the group members

She scrambled to find anyone willing to take her before lecture began. At this point, it was for sheer survival. The second to last group took her on rather begrudgingly, but by the end of the day even they had decided she wasn't going to work. Callimay attempted to ask the bottom group, but they were convinced their efforts were enough to improve their standing for the next report card. They were clear: they weren't about to jeopardize their chances just to help her.

That evening, Callimay got back to her room only to find her belongings in the hall: *Well, at least they gave me back everything that is mine. I wonder where I'll go now.*

"Miss Berchoff?" A lady asked, sounding curt and authoritative.

"Yes?"

"I was informed your living arrangement needed to be changed, so I came to escort you to your new room." The lady who looked to be in her late thirties stated as she walked up to her.

"Oh thank you. I was wondering what I was going to do."

"This way please."

Callimay was moved to an empty single room on the northwest corner of the third floor. It was a bit dusty, but nice nonetheless. The lady took a handset device and used it to sync her key to the lock, "If there are any issues with the lock not responding, please let us know. This one can be temperamental."

"I will. Thank you again." Callimay nodded as she followed the lady to the door and saw her off.

ઝ

As he opened the door, Baleck could hear the sound of something being smacked against the desk in a steady and repetitive manner. His face was coated with a look of confusion as to what the sound was; him taking a quick glance around since it stopped. It was not a sound of something in the background. No. This was meant to be heard and stopped for a reason.

"I thought I instructed you to wait to move until next week?" Mr. Freigh said extremely displeased. "Why did you go behind my back yet again, Baleck?"

"Mr. Freigh?"

"Your operatives. I gave explicit orders for you to hold off on starting anything concerning Callimay until next week." He restated as he folded his hands in front of him on the desk. "So I will ask again: why did you go behind my back?"

"But I haven't contacted them."

"Then what in the world is going on?"

"I'm sorry, but I'm not sure what you're talking about."

"I cannot understand how in the world— you did not know? Callimay has been ousted."

"From her group?"

"Not only that, but she's been shunned by 'every' group. She has taken a total free fall in three days, practically."

"What started it all? Or do you know?" Baleck inquired as he sat down on his seat at the side of the desk. "There has to be some logical reason for this all."

"As close as I can tell, a rumor was started as to Callimay's disdain for Toreon." Mr. Freigh recounted, still eyeing him with a look of displeasure. "So much of the beginning of this happened during leisure time behind closed doors that I do not have too much to go on."

"Do you know who started the rumor?" Baleck leaned forward.

"As best I can deduce it was Gallia. Gallia Vernon."

"Now that would make a bit more sense. I could tell she has been jealous of the attention given to Callimay by Toreon from the first day."

"That was what I was seeing as well." Mr. Freigh agreed, looking like he was beginning to soften in his tone. "I think the scene in the hall on Tuesday was the tipping point for Gallia. It seems she saw the refusal from Callimay as her perfect opportunity to remove her obstacle and solidify her standing with Toreon."

"I can see the effect of her losing standing in her original group because of her refusal of their leader, but why would everyone else choose to leave her?" Baleck inquired, taken aback by the situation.

"I was wondering that for a little while, but then I came across a conversation of group members prior to first lecture today and I had a moment of clarity…"

"Did you hear the truth about Callimay?" A girl whispered as she leaned over her desk, looking this way and that to make sure no one was listening.

"That her and Toreon had it out and so to get back at her he threw his weight around to get her kicked to the curb?" A guy answered as he turned to face her; rolling his eyes as he scoffed, "I've heard it at least a dozen times this morning alone."

"No!" The girl shook her head. "She's been hanging with Destan on leisure time behind everyone's backs! Who would have guessed it? She seems like such a sweet girl. I never would have guessed her to lie."

"And who told you that, Hyra?" The guy rolled his eyes.

"Gallia and Ingrid, her first roommates. … You need to keep your voice down, Jesko. What if she walks in and hears you?"

"Her roommates, huh?" He asked, rubbing his mustache from intrigue. "Well it seemed like there had to be more to the story than just a lovers' spat. Love triangle makes so much more sense."

"And a love triangle which includes the Loner and Toreon at that! Can you believe it, Jesko!" Hyra replied with enthusiasm.

"With the way people's pasts are starting to surface I'm not surprised really. And this all makes sense now."

"So what are we going to do?"

He thought for a bit, rubbing his nose as he made a face, then sighed as he answered, "With her hanging out with Destan, I don't think it would look good on our report card at all. — I don't even understand why he's here. He's at the bottom and doesn't seem to care about it. Complete loners don't belong at a place like this. He either pulled the wool over Mr. Freigh's eyes or they brought him so he'd be the fall guy. — Regardless, faculty has got to know about that all going on between him and Callimay. If we keep her, we're going to suffer for it."

"Agreed." She sat back in her chair, content with his answer. "Now tell her when she comes in."

"Oh thanks, Hyra." Jesko scoffed as he threw his hands in the air. "Way to pass the peacock. Very subtle."

"Well, you're our leader."

"I know, I know. I'll take care of it."

"So this is what was spread to the rest of the groups?" Baleck asked.

"Exactly." Mr. Freigh nodded as he paused the video. "I have done enough digging to find several other clips with the same story being told from the same source."

"Amazing how this student body is working to further our agenda without even knowing. — What about Destan's reaction? I know there was the confrontation on Tuesday, but has he done anything regarding Callimay since? Said anything to Toreon? Any comment because of all the rumors which are being spread?"

"No on all counts, I am afraid. He may not accept her even though she is his equal as far as things go in regard to our grading process."

"Do we push ahead or allow him some time?"

"Let us give him some time. … Two weeks. If nothing happens, we will attempt to force the issue, and then if nothing happens yet again, we will need to start shifting our focus to others in the student body. I do not want to risk another cliffhanger. We cannot." Mr. Freigh said rather defeated. "We would lose Challenger but I would rather lose it than sacrifice another innocent life."

"He's got two weeks, Mr. Freigh. If this all happened in three days, there's no telling what can happen in two weeks. My goodness, this group has barely been here a full month!"

"Very true, Baleck. I must say I am glad things are progressing quickly on their own. This will benefit our timeline in every way."

~ 9 ~

Callimay didn't sleep much at all Friday night. She felt miserable from all that happened, but it was also the anniversary of Mrs. Berchoff's passing — and her birthday. It seemed like this day could hold nothing but sorrow for her. She got up extra early on Saturday so she could at least enjoy the fall colors by herself in peace and quiet for a while… if that would help at all.

It was all but lost to her as far as what it was like to be all alone. She had adjusted to being in a group and everyone getting along and being happy… something she had always wanted for everyone. Why did it all have to change?

Trying to get her thoughts in a better line, Callimay remembered the perks to being alone — especially when it came to living space. The familiarity with how life used to be started coming back in a way that comforted her. She would smile to herself or laugh; but even those moments of happiness were drowned out by her utter confusion with the whole issue.

Why can't everyone be happy and get along — work to help others? Why can't they enjoy what they have and not hurt others? What is gained from being so cruel and selfish? I still don't know what happened and why. No one will tell me. I deserve to know for Heaven's sake! It's my life being torn apart!

As she reached the major fork in the trail, she decided to take the hill trail back so she could see the sunrise from the highest point on the complex. The brisk air against her pale skin seemed somewhat comforting; the wind felt as cold and alone as she did.

She stopped short of Lookout Point when she saw who was there.

"You're up early," Destan commented as he looked to see who was riding up the trail; the same blank, serious expression on his face. "You've never taken this path before on a Saturday morning."

She was shocked by his comment, but if he came this way every Saturday morning at this time, he wouldn't see her, "I... I couldn't sleep any and needed to see something which reminded me of home. And better times."

They both stood in silence, enjoying the fall foliage and early soft yellow sunrays; though by the expression on Destan's face, it felt like he was just existing and staring off into nothing.

Callimay had a question but felt uneasy about asking it. She wasn't the only one who had it, so maybe he'd already answered it and she just never found out. He didn't seem to be the type to repeat himself when it came to such questions.

It was well known he wasn't part of a group since she offered to have him join the one she was in on the first day of orientation. His social interactions with people were limited and most of the time ended up being confrontational.

Rumors flew constantly about why he was even there and how he got accepted. Some knew of the Nevrille name but couldn't see him as being part of that prestigious family. Most thought there had to be the one loner in the group so someone could be at the bottom of the social ladder without hurting someone who was trying. Others said he was there for some personal vendetta: there was some conspiracy at the Society he was working to uncover — all those joking of course and playing off of his cold and aloof personality. Some said his isolation was due to his being late the first day. And this thought continued with saying: something terrible happened to change his emotional state and he didn't want to or know how to move on. Of course Callimay was the only one who thought the latter.

Looking at the two of them, someone would almost laugh. Destan was well over a foot taller than Callimay. He was wearing a black, moto leather jacket with all the bells and whistles that came with such a style of jacket: *Is he from Hagzell? ~ That would match their fashion. ... Naw. His demeanor doesn't match: too formal. ~ Then what's with the drastic change in clothing? He didn't look like this when he first came.*

And then there was the cheerful, colorful, yet simple clothing gracing the petite young woman standing beside him. She could have easily been mistaken for his younger sister because of the height difference — and the fact her hair was up in a ponytail. Siblings always do their best to look as different from each other as possible and she had that down pat. But then again, there was something sweet and endearing about seeing the two of them together. But why was there so much silence!

Enough is enough; Callimay cleared her throat and said light-hearted, "I… I guess we're in the same boat now."

"Oh?" Destan questioned, no fluctuation in his voice or turning his head to even address her.

"Well what I mean is we are both without a group now."

"Welcome to the bottom of social society," he said cold.

He 'is' heartless, Callimay agonized, wringing her hands and staring at him… though too scared to tell him how she felt. *I was hoping— that's what I get for trusting others. Why am I so gullible! Why do I keep putting myself out there just to get hurt? Why can't I be satisfied with being alone? Why do I keep looking for someone — anyone — to be around?*

Besides this, it was crushing to her to see him like he was. He didn't look like he wanted to show any type of compassion or kindness. How could anyone exist like this? How could someone cut off someone else who was trying to be kind to them? What did she do so wrong! And if he were a Christian, why was he acting like this!

She stood there for a minute, tears beginning to stream down her face. It scared her when she let the first sob out, but since Destan never looked, she let all the bubbling emotions out.

Still nothing!

At this point, Callimay couldn't bear to stay any longer. She got on her bike and took off back to the complex.

Destan hung his head as he heard the sound of her bike trampling the leaves on the trail. Even the faint noise of her still sobbing was audible… and made him feel worse. He clenched his fists and leaned them on the railing, saying under his breath, "I'm sorry, Callimay."

~ 10 ~

Monday rolled around, Callimay having to summon every ounce of strength she still had so she could go to morning lectures. When she arrived, she had the eerie feeling she was being watched — and not in a good way. The thought ran through her mind to try and defend herself, but seeing the looks on people's faces discouraged her.

No one said good morning to her, and soon she began to feel like she did the last couple years at work after Mrs. Berchoff passed: empty, alone, and rejected. And so, she dragged herself to her locker that was covered with sticky notes of insults and belittling name-calling. She removed them without saying a word, uncovering what had been posted on her computer screen. Callimay wanted to cry, but she didn't want to add insult to injury.

Someone hacked her computer and uploaded a picture of her and Destan walking hand-in-hand with roses and hearts everywhere. After a few moments it disappeared, but it did its damage: the sound of snickers and jeers behind, beside, and all around her audible to anyone within earshot of the building itself: *Please stop. I know you all hate me.*

She took a deep breath and opened her locker, placing the papers on a clear shelf and then took out her books she needed. With each moment, she looked more and more defeated. By the time she turned and walked to the main lecture hall, Callimay was practically dragging herself there.

❧

No one was there since the bell hadn't rung for first call. It wouldn't ring for another fifteen minutes. Everyone was using every moment to work on improving their true report cards… and this now apparently included tormenting her.

It was hard, but she resigned to the fact she wasn't going to succeed in this type of school, but she wasn't going to give up and run away. So, she decided she would gain what knowledge she could from the academic side of the classes. Even though she had gone to school; with it being a rural one, it wasn't very advanced or in depth.

So this was enjoyable for her: learning new things… for the most part. Some subjects drained her, but overall, the experience was helping her understand more.

As the door closed behind her and she saw all the empty seats, another thing dawned on her: *Where am I going to sit! I don't even want to, but there's no way I can sit in the front anymore.*

She looked around and began rattling off where everyone sat; giving her a map of where she "could" sit. It was easy for her to imagine what the room looked like with everyone there and soon nodded.

While she ascended the steps to the back, she noticed she wasn't the first one there. On the back row in the far corner was Destan. He was leaning over the desk so much, she wasn't sure if he was asleep or reading what looked like his history book.

So this is where he sits. Callimay commented a bit shocked, then finished as she sat down, "Good morning."

"What's so good about it?" Destan retorted in a muffled voice, not moving to look at her.

"Well… we're alive and have another day full of opportunities like what was talked about yesterday morning. That's something to be thankful for. At least I'm thankful for it." She trailed off, then took a deep breath and said much more chipper, "And if nothing else, this time is a chance to gain academic knowledge."

Destan sat there and said nothing.

Callimay was about frantic, trying to think of something to say so she could gain some type of civil communication with him. She wasn't about to let another day be miserable. There was a new determination in her to make things better… or at least exhaust every avenue available: *There has to be a heart in this young man somewhere. I can't believe there isn't. I know I said that yesterday, but maybe it's hurt and doesn't want to try anymore. Who knows! Maybe he lost someone very close to him and he's struggling to cope with it. Maybe he's never known someone who is nice for the sake of being nice. I know there are so many who do it to gain something for themselves and throw you out when you're of no use to them anymore… or if someone interferes they aren't dedicated enough to stand up and fight back. But there are those of us who want to do the right thing and be nice.*

Looking at her books — physics in particular — she thought of one thing to say, but felt like she was playing with a grenade by asking. Her throat was dry and she found herself fiddling with her cardigan hem again, but she didn't want to wait too long, "Umm… you wouldn't by chance be good in physics, would you Destan? I never had advanced math where I went to school and it's difficult for me. I mean, if you don't then I guess we'll struggle through it together, right?"

He sat up but said nothing in reply.

Callimay could tell something was bothering him. His eyes were flashing back and forth, he seemed to be talking to himself since he was mouthing words, and then his knuckles were white from him clenching his fists so tight.

"Is something wrong, Destan? If I can help I want to, but I can't read your mind…" she trailed off as she started rambling unsure and scolding thoughts to herself.

"How do you keep doing it day after day?" He almost whispered in a tone of aggravation.

She was more than concerned at this point, *Something is wrong — very wrong.* "I'm sorry? How do I do what?"

"How do you stay who you are when everything around you has all but exploded in your face?"

"I… I'm not quite sure. I feel like I have changed. Quite a bit. But maybe to everyone else it doesn't seem so because they can't see what is going on inside me. I guess I just want everyone else to be happy so much I don't see myself as that important or needing to be noticed or helped. My emotional wreckage won't ever change so I learn to survive it and keep everyone else happy. God never said being a Christian would be easy. Well, I know in some ways it is. Like t— I… I'm probably making no sense. I'm sorry."

"See. Like that." Destan turned and looked at her square in the eye. "Why do you apologize for doing your best?"

"Because sometimes I don't feel like it's enough. That I could have done better." She answered, wanting to cower from his piercing gaze but feeling things would be worse if she did.

"Well I know I could have yesterday." He sighed as he hung his head and looked away, still sounding rather cut off and cold. "You were just being you — optimist and peace-keeper. I was taking the aggression of my circumstances out on you."

"You were right in what you said though." She let out a small laugh. "I am at the bottom of social soc—"

The door opened as first bell rang. Destan shut down and became the cold person everyone knew. Callimay then began to realize — he talked with her! And he'd even noticed something about her: she always tried to be the peace-keeper and positive person. But it didn't seem in character for him to say what he did. How did he know that? No one could say such a thing unless they paid attention.

He's 'not' heartless! I was right! I was right all along! Destan must be fighting some horrible battle inside of himself. But how do I help? I don't even know what is wrong! Callimay pitied him as she glanced over and saw he resumed his normal, hunched over position; cut off from the world. *If I could only reach out to you without talking. It's eating me up inside not knowing what is wrong while still knowing something 'is' wrong! Maybe you'd open up to me if no one else could hear. It's not that I want to pry; I just want to be the person God wants me to be and help if I can. And the only way I'll know is if you talk to me. I... I'm sorry, Destan. Please~ He can't hear you, silly. ~ I know...*

⚭

Mr. Freigh and Baleck couldn't find words. They watched the footage over and over again; almost expecting it to change.

"She is doing it." Mr. Freigh muttered.

"How though?" Baleck asked in bewilderment.

"I doubt we will ever truly know. Some things are never explained but need to be appreciated. ... Now comes the question: do we move now or wait a little while?"

"In my opinion, we should hold off; let them bond a bit more. Talking is just one part of the puzzle. They need to have trust in each other before we proceed. The only thing is, I don't see them setting up an appointment with us during leisure time like everyone else has. Let alone the probability of them asking for the same day or dare I even suggest together."

"What you say is very true." Mr. Freigh sighed as he pushed his chair back. "Not only do we need them on the same day, but to be most accurate, we need them at the same time. Do you have any suggestions as to getting them here without arousing suspicion on any level?"

"Well," Baleck began as he leaned back in his chair, appearing to be in deep thought. "It's not the most covert way, but… what if on the next report card we were to put Callimay and Destan in a tie for last place in the individual standings?"

"We have never had a tie before."

"Exactly. It would open the door for a meeting with them to discuss what happened." Baleck explained further as he stood and began to pace the floor, putting a great plan together from the look in his eyes.

"Answer me this," Mr. Freigh challenged as he pointed at him. "It would be on a school day. How could we coordinate it so we have them come in?"

"We could call them in just after the last lecture of the day."

"I have made it very clear their leisure time is to be their time; not ours. 'We' would be calling them in for this meeting."

"I apologize Mr. Freigh. … Well, we could do it at the beginning of final lecture."

"The time it takes to complete processing would take the entire lecture period," he disagreed, shooting down every idea Baleck had. "And I do not want them to miss the entire lecture."

"We can slow down time if you will. Slow the clocks' progression while they are with us, and then when they get back, speed them up to help make proper adjustments. Only our watches are allowed, so we would have complete control."

"Better." Mr. Freigh nodded slow, sounding more supportive. "Run through it from beginning to end. I need to hear it all together for clarity and to make sure it could work."

"Very well," he began pacing the floor again; slower and more methodical this time. "We would position Callimay and Destan in a tie for last place this grading period. There will be no lack of chatter once report cards are posted. I'm sure it will be loud and ever-present all day. We will instruct faculty for physics to give Destan and Callimay directions to the office at the beginning of lecture; ensuring them any work they miss would not count against them. Then, while they are gone, the clocks will be slowed to make proper adjustments for the time they will be gone, so it will appear they are able to make it back for the last few minutes of lecture. Once they are processed, reorganized, and sent back; the clocks would be sped up to help compensate for the time adjustment. I doubt it would be an exact match off the top of my head, but it should be within a fairly small margin of error, and one easily compensated for over the course of the first hour."

"You have done it again, Baleck." Mr. Freigh nodded with full approval as he stood. "I am at a loss for words about how everything is coming together so perfect… and fast. It is like this is all staged!"

"I agree. No plan could have ever brought about these kinds of results. I hope we can utilize what has been given to us."

"It sounds like a very solid plan. So, the first day of next month… which would be… a Wednesday? — No. Wait. I forgot. We will not be having classes on the thirty-sixth through the first. Midterms are not until the second. Which also means report cards will not be posted until the third, a Friday."

"I completely forgot about Conclave, Mr. Freigh."

"Oh, think nothing of it, Baleck." He brushed off as he looked at the calendar. "I forgot as well. So it would be the third. Yes. Third of November. End of day during physics. Get our team working and all the necessary items in place. I have some reorganizing to tend to."

"Understood."

"We cannot afford to lose these two. If anything starts, do not bother taking time to ask me: use our operatives."

"I will keep a constant watch from here on out," Baleck promised as he shut the door behind him.

❧

As with all classes, labs, and lectures; it was the established routine for students to be dismissed according to their group social status from the last report card, and within that, their individual standings.

This realization came to Callimay as the faculty began assigning homework: she was no longer part of any group, but the last report card showed her as being with the first place one and seventh individually: *Surely this has happened in the past, but I have no idea what they're going to do.*

Needless to say, the tension in the room made it apparent: Callimay wasn't the only one wondering what was going to happen. So many stared and glared at her that she wanted to disappear into the wall.

"I know you all must be wondering about the conduct of dismissal in light of Callimay's new status." The faculty said politely. "This is something which does not happen very often here at the Society, but rest assured it has, so we are aware of how to handle such things. — Callimay? To best suit everyone, you will be dismissed after all other groups since you have none. When the next report card is posted, you will then be dismissed in relation to your individual standing and how it best fits in between groups."

Callimay nodded in acknowledgement while everyone else began to whisper amongst themselves. It humiliated her to be singled out like that in front of everyone and made her worried what the rest of the day would bring: *Maybe he didn't mean it like that. I'm piling faculty in with everyone else… and I shouldn't.*

☙

Thankfully though, the rest of the morning and lunch flowed silky smooth. But… Callimay had this feeling she was being watched and it was very unsettling. In fact, it was quite similar to how she felt when Toreon was "claiming her as his own".

This got worse when she began hearing others whispering after pointing at her. But in all honesty, everyone was looking down at her, so to feel that way wasn't too concerning. Everyone was talking about her; this feeling had to be coming from that.

Callimay instead began to learn how to block everyone out to help save her sanity: *It makes no difference they're talking about you. You know you won't be listened to if you try to defend yourself, so you~ I might as well start learning to ignore everyone, is that what you're suggesting? ~ There's some who would probably say you're good at that right now, Rose Petal. ~ Ha! You are right. Everything is lies anyway. Listening will only aggravate me. Some peace and quiet would be nice come to think of it.*

Afternoon lectures went well, ending the day with physics. Callimay dedicated herself to listening to everything the faculty member said and what they were teaching, but found it so difficult to keep up with the advanced math.

At one point, her mechanical pencil broke. She sighed and began to click the end so she could continue writing… but the piece was too small to use. Callimay jiggled the pencil a little to seat a refill, but there weren't any extras in it. After taking a deep breath, she reached down into her book bag. A thorough search proved she'd forgotten to put any sleeves in her bag — or an extra pencil for that matter. All she had left was her ink pen.

Now at her wits-end, Callimay put down the pencil and laid her head on the desk. Since she sat in the back with five-hundred students in the room, she knew she'd be able to vent her frustrations without anyone noticing… which was all well and good until she looked to her left and saw the one person who also sat at the back.

Destan was looking right at her, his usual austere look on his face. His eyes seemed to be softer in how they looked at her, like a sincere gaze; not the piercing look everyone saw most — if not all — the time.

She flinched at first, then sighed heavily and sat up again.

ℬ

After dinner, Callimay hurried to leave and went to get her bike so she could go for a ride and clear her mind. It was a beautiful second summer day and so she decided it would be nice to enjoy the last few warm days of the year before the snow moved in. With them being at a higher elevation they'd have snow until at least March, which would be a vast majority of the remaining school year.

Callimay decided to head up to Lookout Point again and enjoy looking at all the different colored trees and hearing the birds sing.

With the leaves now falling and leaving certain types of trees bare already, she noticed there was a path following a small river at the foot of the hill on the same side as Lookout Point — which was more of a cliff but naturally-occurring since the size of trees right at the base were rather large and thus old.

As long as Callimay looked straight out into the distance she was fine. She never ventured too close to the edge since the railing wasn't high enough as far as she was concerned; which was most likely the reason she hadn't noticed the path until now: *I need to find where that path joins the main one sometime. It looks… well, it looks so peaceful. It would be a great place to go during the winter while the river is frozen over. Maybe I could even go ice skating if it is thick enough! Well, if I had skates with me. Ha!*

When she reached Lookout Point, the sun was beginning to set. The sky was splattered with what looked like tufts of pink and purple spun sugar stuck to the burning yellow to red ombre sky. She sat on the bench at the edge of the path and closed her eyes.

Callimay wanted to cry, but then again, why should she? She did nothing wrong. Everything was due to the selfishness and dishonesty of others. But bearing all the emotional turmoil because of this was in and of itself enough to make any person cry. It wasn't that she was crying because she wanted people to feel sorry for her and join in what they would see as a pity party… she just needed an outlet.

I know things are hard, but I've been through hard times before. Maybe losing you was preparing me for this. Maybe I'm meant to be here and fight for the truth. Not giving up isn't enough. I know I cannot control others, but I will not change who I am and give them that victory. I am hurting~ Burning up inside sounds a bit more accurate, Rose Petal. ~ I know. It's hard to stay strong but I know others need me. Not everyone is like Toreon and Gallia. There are good people here. Maybe not strong, but still good. I have to show them by my example. While certain types of people may excel in this school, they, in the reality of life, will never be able to stand against me. They don't have true strength. They parade around in their façade to intimidate others into thinking they are strong. People with true strength know those people have nothing in reality. The strong who value others will ignore fake people. They will not indulge the façade of others who are bullies. Like— Callimay stopped as she opened her eyes in shock and whispered, "Like Destan!"

She jumped up and whipped around, running into him.

"Whoa there," he said startled as he stepped back. "Where are you headed in such a hurry?"

"Destan!" Callimay exclaimed, shocked and caught off guard.

"Yes. … Let me take a wild guess: you were looking for me?"

"I was looking for you!" She exclaimed at the same time.

"What is it?" Destan sighed as he almost laughed.

"I… uh… I don't know exactly how to say this."

"Well neither do I."

"True. — I remembered what you did for me last week when Toreon was… shall we say: being a jerk?"

"That's putting it mildly," he mumbled under his breath.

"Well anyway. I could be wrong, but I've come to the conclusion you did what you did to help me and not to take a stab at Toreon's ego. Am I right? … Destan?"

"Well. … I—"

"I just wanted to say thank you for what you did, regardless of your motivation, really. I've never been in a situation like that before and I had no idea what to do. All I knew was I wanted out." *And I 'never' want it to happen again.* Callimay recalled, not waiting for him to answer. "I know I said it, but thank you for being willing to step up like you did. I appreciated it in every way possible."

"I could tell—"

And yet again he was cut off. It was the curfew bell this time. So the stereotypical "saved by the bell" phrase was turned on its head. And of course it was at the most inconvenient time.

"I forgot it is a school night." Callimay sighed. Hoping he would finish what he was saying, she finished on a more positive note, "That's only first bell and I still have a minute before I need to leave so I can get back. What were you saying?"

"I was going to say I could tell by the look on your face you weren't comfortable." Destan finished rather rushed.

"You were right. Thank you. I really do appreciate it."

She waited for a few more seconds, Destan appearing to look like he had something on his mind he wanted to talk about. But at the same time he didn't look like he wanted to say anything, so she walked over to her bike and got on. She felt awkward just standing around and nothing being said.

Just as she started off, he blurted out, "I'll help you."

"Excuse me?" She asked after she hit the brakes, a half puzzled, half worried look splashing over her as she whipped her head around to look at his uncomfortable expression.

"With physics that is." He clarified, fading off as he finished, "I could tell you were about ready to walk out today."

"You have no idea. I want to understand it. I really do. I just don't know the math behind it to be able to get any kind of foothold."

"I can help first thing in the mornings. I don't know everything, but I'd be willing to help you with what I do have a good grasp on. I'm in the hall by five-thirty."

"But that's two hours before class even starts!"

"Allows me to have less time dealing with the likes of Toreon," Destan explained rather gruff. "When should I expect you?"

"I can get there at six-thirty, maybe a couple minutes earlier. Would it be enough time?" Callimay began to cower.

"I'll make it work."

"See you tomorrow then!"

❦

Callimay felt carefree and happy as she rode back. She ran to her room, somehow thinking the sooner she got back the sooner tomorrow would come. Though, when she finally got ready for bed she struggled to calm down and sleep; time crawling by. Tossing and turning did no good, and she became more and more frustrated with how slow time was moving by when she checked her watch every few minutes.

I can't sleep when I feel miserable, and yet I can't sleep when I'm happy. She threw her hand back against the pillow. *What is wrong with me? ~ Just calm down. You'll go to sleep, Rose Petal. Quit, checking, your, watch. Stop it! ~ Alright! I'm done. Happy? ~ Goodnight, Rose Petal.*

<h1 align="center">~ 11 ~</h1>

After a long-fought battle, she fell asleep. She woke up early and started doing her hair and makeup in a flurry of excitement. Callimay always did those things, but her motivation for doing it shifted. Before, it was something she did out of routine and as an expectation, not because she wanted to.

This sudden change prompted her to ask: *Why am I doing this? Why all of a sudden am I happy like this? Why is having the attention of Destan making me feel better? Is it because I like him? Is this what Gallia was talking about when she was referring to me and Toreon at the beginning of the year? … I guess in my mind I did 'choose' Destan over Toreon when we first met; but why was he better? In what way did I 'choose' him? I mean, in reality, I 'chose' Dakoe. Really. Maybe I'm not the best judge of people. … Destan's not even paid attention to me. W— am I getting myself all psyched up just to have everything crumble around me like with Dakoe? Should I back off? ~ Come on Rose Petal, get it together. You could push yourself off of Lookout Point talking like this. You're just excited someone is willing to talk with you and help you where you need it. Enjoy it for what it is. ~ Perspective and contentment. I know.*

ɓ

It was still pitch-black outside which made her feel a bit uneasy not being able to see everything in her surroundings, but the walkways were well lit. Even so, she rode her bike at a brisk pace to avoid any possible dangers that lurked in the shadows… like there were any.

She arrived at six-thirty on the nose: *Great timing, Rose Petal.*

Some students were there eating an early breakfast while cramming to finish homework, but with Callimay nowhere on the radar no one noticed her.

Her view of being unnoticed changed when she went to her locker and there was a cryptic love note on it. She took it down and laid it on the bottom shelf of her locker with the others; assuming that was the cause. But as she got her books, she felt the same strange feeling again. She tried to ignore it, but it made her feel so uneasy she ran to the main lecture hall.

Callimay all but slammed the door shut and breathed a large sigh of relief as she leaned against it. A quick surveillance of the hall showed there wasn't anyone there, so she shook her head, thinking it would help the feeling go away.

"Good morning Destan." She greeted cheerfully.

"Morning," he answered rather flat as he sat up.

"I'd say there's something specific I need help with but I'm really not sure," Callimay admitted as she pulled out her physics book.

"You did say the math was difficult for you."

"Yes. Yes I did."

"We can start there." Destan suggested as he took her book and opened it, continuing without hesitation even though their fingers touched each other as he took it from her, "We aren't far along, so we won't have to go too fast to catch up..."

"I quite literally cannot believe my eyes and ears, Baleck." Mr. Freigh said in disbelief. "This girl is a Godsend. How did we find out about her in the first place?"

"Ingrid Davenpond. She was sent through that area... three years ago was it? Yes. Three years ago. ... It says here she originally sent in her application when we first opened our doors — when she was fifteen. She must have been a later entry that we shuffled because of Primary. ... It wasn't reviewed until midway through the school year, so— yes, here is the note."

"This is a miracle. I am so tempted to move up our timeline, but we need to keep it as is."

"Agreed. They still aren't a 'team' yet. They are close but still have some work to do."

"Even after they are processed and reorganized, they will have to work on their relationship. We have not tried this approach yet. Things need to be watched carefully."

"I couldn't agree more, Mr. Freigh." Baleck nodded as he stood. "If you wouldn't mind my absence for the rest of the day, I need to speak with my uncle."

"Oh yes. He is the one with the…" he gestured in such a way that appeared he was grasping for the answer that was floating in the air. "Crypt Syndrome, was it?"

"Yes."

"By all means. Take the rest of the day. I hope today is one of his better days."

"I appreciate your constant concern for him." Baleck smiled as he checked his watch. "Ginger said she wanted to speak with him as well to give me a deeper understanding of his condition… if that was alright with you, of course."

"I doubt she will be needed." Mr. Freigh gestured toward the door. "I hope for a good report on his condition."

~ 12 ~

Things continued with the new status quo for both Callimay and Destan as they continued to spend mornings together, bonding over the mathematics of physics. At first it was nothing more than two people doing homework, but, over time, things began to change.

She arrived at six most mornings which in turn gave her two benefits: she got to spend more time with him and she didn't have the uneasy feeling when she got to the main school building. The ride wasn't much different — pitch-black is pitch-black — so she didn't have a problem with coming earlier.

Destan's reaction didn't appear to change from her coming sooner. In fact, if it did anything, it only helped him work with her in more depth so she could understand things better and quicker.

He had a way of explaining things so she could understand them… something faculty lacked. Even though there wasn't much emotional reaction from him, everything between the two of them was civil.

There were moments Callimay and Destan would look at each other and his eyes would change like they did the first couple times they saw each other. These often occurred when she would struggle to learn something completely new and was ready to give up.

It baffled her at times how patient he was. She tried and tried to find words to tell him thank you in a way that conveyed her true feelings, but nothing ever seemed to show it the way she wanted it to… or his reaction just wasn't what she was expecting.

During this whole time, they had no idea of the looming deadline. Mr. Freigh and Baleck kept constant surveillance of them; including the extended team in on the observations whenever possible.

❧

And then… Thursday came. Students were knee-deep in their last-second efforts to improve their report cards or maintain them. Callimay found it ridiculous to see people all of a sudden act kind toward each other when only the day before they had spent the entire day stabbing this same person in the back — emotionally and socially that is.

Such hypocrites! She fumed while she watched them scramble as if an air raid was going to be issued at any moment.

Mr. Freigh had not made any appearances around the complex in the last week. He was not completely satisfied with where Callimay and Destan were, but with recent reports, they were out of time and had to move forward.

His absence from the public eye put a large majority of the student body on edge and allowed Rumors to begin flying as was the new norm with every little thing not in the ordinary. The faculty even seemed on edge, which fueled the rumors even more.

And with these rumors being started and spread, this morning was like the occasional late one for Callimay. Just as she opened her door to leave, she saw Toreon in the hall talking with Gallia. She never left while he was there, so she didn't know for sure if it would, but she couldn't imagine it going unnoticed. Dealing with him was something she was hoping she could steer clear of, so as usual, she stepped back into her room and tried her best to be quiet as well as patient in waiting for him to leave.

The door was cracked only enough so she knew when he left, but closed enough so he couldn't tell it was open. She overheard them whispering — though their ability to seemed very lacking — about the absence of Mr. Freigh and what it might mean: *Oh please you two. There's not enough gossip for you with the five-hundred students here that you have to start something against the conductor of the Society? You keep this up at school and I'm sure that'll backfire on your report card. Goodness.*

Callimay watched the clock with an impatient eye as precious moments slipped away. She wanted to be with Destan; not sitting and hearing these two giggle and laugh like they were.

86

Time felt like it were flying past; but he left right at six-fifteen without Gallia: *At least he's punctual when he leaves. I wish he would be the same with the days he comes by.*

❧

When she got outside, she found her bike was missing which puzzled her since it would only unlock with her thumbprint. But she didn't have a second to lose, so she didn't take the time to figure out what happened and walked there— well, ran. She knew she was going to be late no matter how fast she ran, but she didn't want to lose any more time than she had.

It was no surprise she found her locker like every other day when she got there late. On top of this, she had the unsettling feeling of being watched; as if her skin were crawling with the feeling: *It's fine, Rose Petal. Get your books and go. You're just nervous because you're late.*

She shut her locker door and shrieked when she saw who was responsible for her unsettled feeling. He was leaning against the locker next to hers, "Toreon!"

"Hey Callimay," he said in his suave voice as Webb and Dakoe walked up beside him. "I've been missing my girl."

"I… I heard you and Gallia got together," she stuttered as she gripped her books. "That's great."

"Yeah, but I can make her disappear. Don't worry about that minor detail." Toreon answered as he took a step closer. "There are some girls out there who are a dime a dozen."

"I'm sure there are. Gallia may end up being that girl for you. — It was good to see you guys but I don't want to take up your time—"

"Oh, you are worth my time. That and more."

"I appreciate that, but I don't want you to lose any points with this being the last day of the grading period. I know how crazy the last day can get." Callimay began to cower, panic setting in. "I really would feel bad if I cost you your position."

"With my reputation, I could get away with anything and no one would say a word. Nothing can affect my position."

I wouldn't be so sure. She took another step back and found herself against the wall. *There are limits to everything… right?*

"Looks like you've run out of real estate there, Callimay." He smiled fiendishly, ripping her books out of her white-knuckled hands.

"Look Toreon," she begged as she looked at everyone else who had their backs turned. "I don't want to cause any trouble. I just want to get to the main lecture hall."

"For what… exactly, Callimay? You get here so early. What are you doing?" He questioned, a sharp point of irritation in his voice as he continued to step closer. "It's like you're sneaking around. Only those who are hiding something do that. So what are you hiding from me? … Tell me, Callimay!"

"She's getting tutoring from me for physics, you moron." Destan interrupted as he grabbed Toreon's shoulder, pulling him out of the way and motioning to Callimay so she would come to him.

"Moron… ouch." Webb groaned as he made a face and turned away. "That's a burn t—"

"Shut it, Webb," Toreon hissed.

Callimay flew to Destan's side and gripped the front edge of his blazer, turning her head to bury it against his chest.

"Punk, you'll stay out of this if you know what's good for you. Or have you forgotten what I told you last time you tried? You seriously think you can take me on?"

"Really? That's a laugh." Destan snickered as he looked down at him. "I know I could, and you do too… but I'm not going to."

"Why not?" Toreon challenged as he backed up and looked around with confidence. "If you know you can then why not show it?"

"Because I wouldn't be proving anything by beating you," Destan reached out and ripped the books out of his hand, making sure to keep Callimay as far away from him as possible. "Just because fighting is how you prove yourself doesn't mean I have to stoop to that level to do the same. Go bully someone who doesn't see any worth in themselves or anyone else. — Oh wait… you've run out of people like that here."

"Pfft!" Webb let out though he tried to contain his audible reaction — the second comeback more noteworthy than the first.

"Who are you; calling me a bully, punk?"

"Give it up Toreon." Destan rolled his eyes as he pushed past and put his arm around Callimay. "Everyone knows this is over."

"You better watch your back, Nevrille! I swear: you better watch. Your. Back!" Toreon fumed, rattled by Destan's comment and making it necessary for Dakoe to intervene and hold him back.

಄

This whole time, Callimay was trying to catch her breath and stay upright. As soon as they got to the main lecture hall and Destan shut the door, she couldn't stop the sudden sobs that would come. It was almost impossible for her to catch her breath. She was so scared that her entire body began shivering.

Callimay grabbed his arm to try to steady herself but was so exhausted from everything she collapsed.

He dropped to his knees beside her as she put her hand out, "I— just give me a moment."

It took her some time, but she was soon able to get up with Destan's help. Having him right next to her, holding her practically, didn't register at all. The fear Toreon put in her was holding her hostage now. He was the one who "owned" her; similar to how he owned Dakoe. She couldn't do anything without being in fear of his wrath.

After she sat down and looked like she had calmed herself enough, Destan asked in a quiet tone, "Did he do anything?"

"He got me to walk back into the corner and then took my books," Callimay whimpered between sobs as she shook her head.

"Anything else?" He leaned forward, his brow beginning to wrinkle from what looked like worry.

"No."

"You're sure?"

"Yes."

"I should've come out sooner. You've never been any later than six-thirty. It's my fault for waiting. I am s—" he began to apologize as the bell rang and people began filing in.

Oh, Destan. Callimay cried in desperation as she reached out to him while he turned away and leaned over the desk like he always did. *Please don't leave me... not now.*

಄

89

"We cannot afford another close call like this, Baleck. What happened is unforgivable." Mr. Freigh lectured as he grasped his clenched fist with his other hand. "And do not act like you have no clue about what I am talking about. I know for a fact you arrived an hour ago."

"Yes I was here early. And while I understand your concern; this scenario solidified several details surrounding Destan's emotional state. — And actually, this works in our favor."

"In what way?"

"Why not use this incident as our fuel for bringing Callimay and Destan into the office together?"

"To correctly address the events we would need to do it today."

"Yes. It's just one day. Everyone is here and everything has been prepped. It wouldn't take but a moment to get the serums mixed."

"I am not sure." Mr. Freigh hesitated, tapping the desk.

"We've noticed that what happens without us interfering causes the best results between these two. We need to seize this opportunity like you mentioned earlier." Baleck reminded, sounding firm.

"Maybe so, but it does not excuse the fact things got out of hand this morning. — And I say that in the most lenient way possible. — The whole reason we have her is to keep Destan stable. We lose her, we lose him." Mr. Freigh paced the floor. "I will not have anything upsetting our plans. After so much death and disappointment we finally have the chance to do what we purposed this entire time. We are already taking the largest risk by doing this during the school day. If we lose one of them, the damage control is going to be astronomical and some—"

"Please do not concern yourself with the hypotheticals."

"I know they can usher in more stress than necessary, but we must understand these risks are real. And even after processing, things will still be difficult because they will have to navigate through the stressful discovery period. That is the most critical time."

"Yes Mr. Freigh." Baleck nodded, trying to alleviate the situation. "Please rest. We are all uptight today; but we need to be able to present ourselves as controlled and 'status quo' individuals to help ease the rumors being spread about the shift in priorities behind the scenes."

He sighed as he sat down, now relaxed so he could think clearer, "Thank you for the reminder, old friend. Now with regard to your request… I must be honest and straightforward: I am more than just hesitant. Last-second changes make situations vulnerable to mistakes which we cannot afford.”

“I understand.”

“But, I also do agree this is an opportunity we cannot pass up. Inform every one of the changes and prepare for this afternoon.”

“Very well,” Baleck bowed his head as he took his phone out.

ℬ

Callimay seemed to be better at lunch, but just seeing Toreon made her frightened. She made her new home right next to Destan, and without saying a word, it appeared he was making sure to shelter her. Though, for as much as he tried, the reality of Toreon being there could not shake the deep-seated fear in her.

“Not hungry?” Destan asked, noticing she hadn’t touched her food in a half hour. “Callimay?”

She never said anything, not even nodding or shaking her head. It was as if she didn’t hear him.

A side effect of this emotional damage was that she didn’t have an appetite anymore. She didn’t even want to walk to the main lecture hall or back to her room. The harsh reality of everything that happened was building to a breaking point.

“I… I’ll be back.” Destan calmed when she jumped in her seat because he got up. “I’m just taking my tray back. Do you want me to take yours? … Callimay?”

Her face didn’t approve, but there wasn’t anything she could do to make him stay. All she could do was sit and watch him walk away.

For as much as she could feel at the time, she felt as if he were walking away with part of her. — Maybe it was lingering emotional turmoil from earlier that didn’t have a thing to do with this? — Whatever it was, it hurt and got worse when Destan left. And then when he disappeared from her line of sight, a small yelp of a gasp escaped from her mouth; but no one paid a bit of attention.

She gripped the edge of her cardigan and rubbed it between her fingers as if trying to keep her mind off this pain. Callimay wanted to cry, but her eyes were too tired to… her whole body was.

The afternoon was going to be long, and she didn't eat breakfast this morning. Callimay knew she needed to eat something. As much as she hated to, she looked away from where she knew Destan was.

After taking a painful sigh, she ate a few bites of the mashed potatoes and pot roast he put on her tray. He actually got everything that was on her tray; putting a little bit of everything since she wouldn't say anything about what she wanted and wasn't doing anything but following behind him.

All of a sudden, someone reached around Callimay and grabbed her tray. She whipped her head around to see who it was and almost fainted when she saw Toreon grinning at her.

"Come on," she heard Dakoe say as he jogged over, causing Toreon to stop reaching out to her. "First bell is about to ring. Let's go."

"You again? What is wrong with you? You and Webb both. You spoil just about everything. I was only having some fun."

Out of nowhere, Destan appeared. Dakoe backed off when he saw him while Toreon stood there grinning even more.

"Wanna finish it now, punk?" He prodded as he hid his readied fist under Callimay's tray.

"Put. That. Down." Destan growled as his green eyes flashed.

"Make me."

"It's fine." Callimay managed to say as she slipped past Toreon and over to Destan; almost tugging on his blazer as she came up to him. "I was pretty much done anyway."

He moved aside to let her pass, while not taking his eyes off Toreon; commenting, "Since you were 'so' eager to take the tray, looks like you can keep it and take it back when 'you're' done. Enjoy your lunch."

"How does he do it!" Webb remarked in awe of Destan's ability to pit Toreon against himself — looking like he was going to applaud. "I don't think I've 'ever' seen someone—"

With that comment, the gloves came off: Toreon began arguing with Webb, shoving the tray at him. Everyone was in shock and began to worry what was going to happen between these two.

Why won't he leave me alone? Callimay shivered as she clung to Destan. *How can he think this is funny? How can anyone else? I don't... I don't understand!*

༄

The afternoon was long, but midterms for the classes and lectures were — for the most part — easier. Callimay didn't leave between classes like she oftentimes did… she had enough as far as run-ins with Toreon to last her a lifetime.

Destan's demeanor hadn't changed much; though he did switch times for some of his classes so he could be with Callimay.

Right before physics started, Callimay hoisted her book to the desk. It was a large book anyway, but it felt so much heavier today. She groaned as she opened to where they would be for the day, realizing she hadn't been able to talk to Destan about her list of questions on the sheet of paper now in front of her.

As she stared at it, Callimay heard something strange: ripping paper. She looked over and was stunned to see Destan's hand on top of a ripped piece of paper he was sliding toward her. He wasn't looking at her — quite the opposite, actually.

When he felt her book against his hand, he lifted it. Destan looked nervous; his hand was shaking as he drew it back.

Just as she was going to pick it up, she heard the faculty say her name. She jumped in her seat, whipped her head around, and jerked her hand away from the paper.

It couldn't be to reprimand her. Why would they? The class hadn't started yet and they never cared if notes were passed during class! … Let alone she was in the back. How did they see her?

No. No, this was an announcement, "You two are to report to the conductor's office immediately. If you do not return in time, missing your midterm will not count against you. P…"

She looked at Destan with pure fear all but tattooed on her face… he was the other one instructed to leave. He had an intrigued look as he listened; leaning his chair so the back feet were the only ones on the floor and shoving his hands in his pockets.

When faculty finished, the two students addressed came to the front of the class; Destan letting Callimay go first. The faculty offered both blank envelopes at the same time, "Open them once in the hall. … Knock on the door before coming in if you return after the meeting."

93

Callimay was in a daze at this point, so she wasn't paying attention to all the comments being made out loud about her. Destan overheard Toreon's specific comment and turned back, stomping his foot on the floor and glaring at him with his piercing green gaze — never saying a word but speaking volumes from the expression on his face and his overall body language.

Silence fell over the entire class when they heard what Toreon said and saw how Destan reacted, the sound of his stomp reverberating with power and disgust toward the crude comment flippantly voiced. They thought there was going to be a brawl earlier? That was playful banter compared to this.

After it appeared Destan was satisfied Toreon got his message, he left to join Callimay who was already in the hall.

ᚻ

"What did I do wrong!" She asked in horror as she looked at him, tears streaming down her face. "I… I haven't done anything all day! Why would Mr. Freigh want—"

"We don't know this is a bad thing."

Both envelopes contained directions to Mr. Freigh's office and specific instructions to not disclose the location to anyone.

They never had access to the doors they were directed to, so Callimay wondered how they were going to get there — there wasn't anyone out in the hall to escort them.

As they came to the first door, the light flipped from red to green and they could hear the lock releasing. It was a maze to get to Mr. Freigh's office, but as they came down the last hall she hesitated for a moment: *This can't be a bad thing. I mean if it's about this morning~ And lunch hour for that matter. ~ Then it must be to get Destan's and my accounts of what happened. Right?*

"I think this is it," he looked up from the paper to the door on their right, and then over to Callimay.

Not hearing the rest of what he was saying, she reached for the door only to find he had as well, "Oh! Why I— I'm sorry. I— thank you."

ᚻ

As the two of them entered, they saw Baleck seated beside the desk where Mr. Freigh was. Once the door made a hushed wafting sound as it closed, the two men stood and greeted their expected guests.

"It is good to see you." Baleck smiled.

"Thank you for coming to speak with us." Mr. Freigh concurred.

"These are for you, Mr. Willgun." Destan turned over his paper — him taking Callimay's since she was still in a daze.

"Thank you Destan, Callimay," he took them and then sat down.

"Please be seated." Mr. Freigh ushered as he resumed his place.

"Thank you," Callimay said in a rather nervous and quiet tone.

"I'm sure you are quite curious as to why we brought you here." Mr. Freigh started, sounding calm and conversational as he clasped his hands in front of him on the desk. "Well, let me offer to you it is not for punishment in any way. In fact, it is to congratulate you."

"What?" Callimay asked louder, now puzzled.

"We here at the Society have been working over the past ten years to find individuals like you who aren't afraid to stand out in the crowd when the right thing needs to be done. Those who are willing to go against the grain as it were and be the voice of reason." Baleck informed in a semi-rehearsed fashion, gesturing with his hands every so often. "So many times we find students falling for the luxurious and addictive thought of emotional superiority. Though, this outcome is beneficial to us so we can find students like you much quicker."

"I knew it," Destan said under his breath as he became tense.

"I… I'm afraid I don't understand. What do you mean students fall for emotional superiority and you're looking for those who go against the grain?"

"What my colleague is saying, Callimay, is the true mission of Creigam Freigh Society is very different from what the world knows it to be. Over the past twenty-so years, there have been sightings of humans with extraordinary abilities. Most of them are on the side of law and order, but the small remnant of them which twisted the power entrusted to them into their mode of gaining power has now outgrown those who are law-abiding persons. We call these people Rogues. In recent years, the number of these Rogues has spiked exponentially. Governments around the world have been able to contain knowledge about them up until now in view of the panic it would ensue amongst those in the general public. They have even made attempts to find the origin of these Rogues but have yet to discover it. — Mr. Willgun and I met through these efforts from our respective countries and came together to see if we could pool our personal resources to fight an elusive enemy. Mr. Willgun has the scientific background and technical team while I have the facilities and status to fund research and development. After extensive collaboration, Mr. Willgun and I formulated a team which could develop serums to give candidates the same abilities as these Rogues to help curb the global crisis we are now faced with. — We found early on your age range was the best suited for adaptation to the serums. Our team formulated specific ways to test subjects without them knowing to aid in determining the best suited ability for each individual. — The process is quite lengthy as well as involved, so I will not bore you with the details. — Not all who come to the Society prove to be qualified for this honorable task. In fact, the vast majority prove to be nothing but selfish children who desire nothing but attention." Mr. Freigh explained as he handed Destan and Callimay each a folder with their name on it. "Callimay? We have discovered you have a way with people through the words you convey. You seek to bring the good out in people. Through initial determination and then observation once you arrived, we have confirmed your ability will be telekinesis. You will be able to hear what others are saying to themselves and should, by our determinations, have the extension of mind-speak with Destan. — Destan? You have been on my radar from the very beginning. I met you long ago and knew you were going to be very special and help this world in an immense way, even then. While developing this program, I kept you as my motivation and hoped you would apply. I was overjoyed when I saw your application come across my desk last year. You stated you sometimes missed the mark, regretted missed opportunities, and were frustrated you were not where you were needed at an earlier time. This fits the ability of super speed with what I would refer to as detailed precision. There is not a better match. While in focal point, as we refer to the state where you are using your ability at its optimal rate, you may find your strength is heightened as well. … I will warn you both there can be side effects from gaining these abilities, but I have faith they will be of no importance since you will be working as a team. We wanted to begin the process earlier, but needed to see that you wanted to work with each other. … I know this is quite a bit of information to take in, but please know this is for the good of everyone and is being done to ensure the future of life here on Quidoria. Your emotional states going into processing will determine the amount of control you will have over your abilities. Please keep this in mind because once the process starts it cannot be stopped. Of course I say all this, but you will not remember any when we are done."

"Wait. What?" Callimay challenged as she stood up, afraid what she thought she heard and even thought she was reading was correct. "I never signed up for this. I don't want superpowers or abilities or whatever you want to call them. I don't want to fight these Rogues you keep talking about. I won't— you can't 'make' me do this."

"Sometimes what we want and what is necessary are two 'very' different things." Mr. Freigh said in a calming voice, motioning for her to sit back down. "It's not what—"

"That's God's choice to decide what is necessary versus what is wanted; not man's." She argued as she threw the folder on the desk. "What do you think you're doing!"

"The discovery period you will go through will hopefully not be very long. We wipe your memories to enable you to tap into them at your own pace so your body will accept the abilities you will have been given." Mr. Freigh continued, seeming to ignore the uncharacteristic outburst made by Callimay. "Please understand we have only come to this point of what some might refer to as 'drafting' due to necessity. We need you. Especially you, Destan. The ability being given to you has been tested to have more than just an effect on speed and strength, thus dubbed the most powerful ability: Challenger. Though what that powerful extension exactly is will be determined by you yourself. … You have also tested high to be a cliffhanger — one who could spiral out of control while in focal point — which is why we have Callimay to help guide you through any stress you may encounter."

"I just…" she pleaded; her hands and voice now shaking as she flopped onto the chair. "I want to help others. That's why I came."

"And you will," Baleck reassured as he motioned to someone.

Callimay was about at her wits-end with everything that had happened up to this point in the day. She was scared and bewildered as to why they were being told this and expected to go along quietly.

Destan, on the other hand, sat there this whole time with his head slightly bowed; no emotion or change in his body language as Mr. Freigh and Baleck spoke… nothing. This lack of emotional response was encouraging to Mr. Freigh, seeing as how those who undergo processing with the strong negative emotions of hate and anger have always become cliffhangers. Though to Callimay, this complete lack of emotion frightened her almost more than the news Mr. Freigh and Baleck gave her: *Destan? Destan don't just sit there. Do something! Please! You can't agree with what they're doing!*

The side doors to the office opened and two men walked up behind Callimay, two behind Destan; one holding a cloth drenched with ether and the initial serum for each of their abilities while the other was there to help restrain each of them.

They took Callimay first, catching her completely off guard. She screamed out in a muffled voice since the cloth was over her mouth and nose, reaching out with the hand she was able to get free, "Destan? What's happening? — Let me go! —Destan I'm scared! Destan!"

Unforeseen to everyone, he lunged at the men holding Callimay, bellowing as he grabbed one of them, "Let her go!"

There was a brief struggle, the other two men rushing over and grabbing hold of him, barely keeping him constrained long enough so the anesthetic and serum could begin to take effect.

"No!" Mr. Freigh called out mortified as he jumped from his seat, seeing the man throwing the cloth over Destan's mouth. "We cannot allow him to go through processing with his emotions like this!"

"It's too late." Baleck reminded as he grabbed his arm. "He's already been exposed. To stop now would be worse than to finish and make sure Callimay is as strong as she can become."

As Destan began to slip out of consciousness, he kept looking for her while fighting those who were restraining him. He called out, no longer hearing her voice or being able to see her; him becoming more and more lethargic, "Calli? Calli where are you? — Let me go you hijackers! Don't hurt her! Stop! Don't do this to her! — Calli…"

"It was not supposed to happen this way." Mr. Freigh sighed in anguish as he sat down and put his head in his hands.

"We did all we could." Baleck consoled. "We cannot control every variable, but we at least have Callimay this time around."

"And that is our pitfall: one loose variable is a recipe for disaster." Mr. Freigh took his glasses off. "Callimay is his— 'our', only hope."

❦

Callimay was injected with the remainder of the serum which would then be distributed to the various areas of her cranial cortex and inner brain to heighten her perception and communication abilities. To throw these into super drive, electrodes were placed at certain points around the skull and stimulated at certain intervals to fully amplify her ability and solidify the serum's location.

"What is that monitor showing?" Mr. Freigh asked over the intercom as one of the machine screens began flashing red.

"It's monitoring her pain levels; and it appears the stimulation is causing her more than anticipated." One of the technicians responded. "It is within tolerable levels, but may cause her to have migraines while using her ability. Her history does show she already suffers from them, so it is an unfortunate as well as inevitable reality."

"Can you slow the process to cement the serum so these are not so… severe? She is our key to keeping Destan under control."

"Yes Mr. Freigh. We can try. I cannot guarantee anything, but there is no harm in slowing the process."

Destan was injected with the remainder of the serum which spread to the various portions of the nervous system interacting with his legs as well as the muscles and bones in his legs and lower torso. Electrodes were placed in key areas and stimulated at certain intervals just as was done with Callimay.

"How are things going?" Mr. Freigh asked over the intercom.

"Very smooth sir." The technician replied optimistically.

"No variances at all?"

"None so far. This has been the smoothest one to date."

"Keep a close eye on him. Do not fall into a false sense of security."

"Absolutely, Mr. Freigh."

Within the next half hour, the entire process was completed. Their short-term memories were wiped clean — only including what took place after they sat down. Everything was timed so there would be no overlap or gaps when they were given new memories.

"Are you ready for your part, Baleck?" Mr. Freigh asked as he handed him some papers. "I know there is not much time, but I did not want there to be any confusion about what should be said."

He nodded as he glanced over them, "I agree. In light of what happened this morning, things needed to change."

"They're coming to." The technician said over the intercom.

"Let us get ready." Mr. Freigh encouraged. "Bring them in."

While they were still groggy, Callimay and Destan were moved from their recovery units to the office. Once they were fully awake, it was as if they just sat down.

"I am sure you both are quite curious as to why we brought you here." Mr. Freigh began to replay; saying everything exactly as before just in case the memory wipe was a few seconds off — making this nothing but a déjà vu moment. "Well let me offer to you it is not for punishment in any way. We just wanted to speak with you about events from this morning."

"Oh." Callimay hung her head and wrung her hands.

Destan sat there, his head bowed a bit, hands gripping the armrests and eyes fixed on the floor just in front of him.

"Neither of you are going to be punished. Especially you, Callimay. I regret the compromising position you were placed in this morning. We are changing the time faculty arrives to prevent this in the future. — Destan? Both Baleck and myself wanted to thank you personally for your willingness to step up today." Mr. Freigh commended as he stood and offered his hand. "I know you have been struggling with regards to your social report card, but let me assure you: this is a very solid case for raising your standing — as well as lowering Toreon's. I am saddened to see he has opted to take this path toward fulfilling his desired goal; but hopefully through this he will see the error in his way and amend the broken trust with some of his fellow classmates."

He responded slow and uncertain as he stood and shook his hand, a bewildered look on his face, "Thank you, sir."

"Thank you very much Mr. Freigh, Mr. Willgun." Callimay smiled as she stood; sounding more and more relieved with each word. "I appreciate the concern you have shown and the openness to fixing this issue. I don't want to tear people down, but I don't want someone else to go through what I did."

"You are very welcome, Callimay. — Again, thank you for meeting with us." Baleck reiterated as he looked to Mr. Freigh and then them. "Please remember that the location of this office is not to be disclosed to anyone once you leave here."

"Yes sir," Callimay and Destan said in unison.

The initial stillness that was equally calming and strained was interrupted by Callimay blurting out after she saw the clock, "May I ask a question?"

"Anything," Baleck answered cheerfully.

"The faculty for our lecture said before we left: if we didn't make it back in time our midterm would be excused."

"Yes. That is correct."

"With what time it is, there's no possible way — at least for me — to get it done. Would it be possible to get a copy so I could work on it during leisure time? I am struggling to understand physics in general and would like to get as much practice as possible."

"I will see you are given a copy," Baleck answered as he nodded.

"Thank you Mr. Willgun." Callimay smiled as she began to walk to the door with Destan.

"Goodbye." Mr. Freigh waved as Destan opened the door.

"Goodbye." Callimay returned the gesture.

The moment after the door clapped shut, Mr. Freigh asked, "So. What is your estimation as to the length of their discovery periods?"

"I would give them upwards of a month. But in all honesty? That's an overestimation. I see Callimay discovering hers rather easily — and quickly — due to her constant inner chatter and probable extension of wondering other's thoughts. I would say Destan will take a bit, but—"

"True, Baleck. We need to keep an eye on him."

"But for now, we wait."

❧

The clocks in the main lecture hall were slowed to make it appear as if Callimay and Destan were only gone for a half hour, when in fact they were gone almost an hour and a half.

He walked slowly behind her the whole way, seeming disconnected and distracted. She wanted to stop and ask him what was wrong, but she knew they needed to get back… and then she wasn't sure if he would tell her.

Callimay sighed as they came in view of the main lecture hall, "I really don't want to go back in. I wish today were Friday."

Destan didn't respond.

His face was still full of confusion, him ignoring her and walking to the door to get the faculty's attention.

The lady looked over — as did a few students who sat close to the door — and came outside, saying hushed, "Oh good, you two made it."

"Is everyone still working on their midterm?"

"I appreciate the respect you have for your classmates, Destan. Almost all of them are finished and working on a class assignment. If you would like, I wrote down the assignment on the board. Do not feel obligated to complete it though. — Mr. Willgun notified me you wanted a copy of your midterm, Callimay. I will have it ready for you before you leave. — I can also have the midterm ready for you if you would like, Destan."

"I would appreciate it, thank you."

"Very well then, please take your seats."

No one raised their heads in acknowledgement when they walked in, which was fine with Callimay. She scurried to her seat, Destan lagging behind, and sat down to open her book; ready to begin solving the problems assigned.

The second he sat down, she remembered the note: *Where did it go, Rose Petal? ~ Oh, I hope someone else didn't take it. Destan won't ever forgive me if someone did because I didn't pick it up!*

As she worked, she could tell it was getting more and more difficult to hold in the emotional hurricane inside of her. Yes, the meeting was encouraging; but the extreme high was conflicting with the extreme low from earlier — and then there was the question and worry in her mind of where Destan's note went. And then what about the measures Mr. Freigh said would be put in place? Faculty being there earlier might have helped, but what happened over lunch hour was while they were there!

And what about Toreon? Was he going to be spoken with at all? Surely! Right? Why wasn't he pulled out when they were? Were they trying to keep things from boiling over again like they almost did during lunch? It made sense. She knew she didn't want to be around him anymore than she had to; and she didn't want to make Destan feel he "had" to protect her all the time.

She couldn't focus: her palms were sweating, hands shaking, and Callimay could tell she was getting a migraine by the little white specks that danced and darted across the page and table as well as her eyelids when she would blink.

A quick glance at the clock made her sigh in relief when she saw there was only another fifteen minutes left.

Destan was in his usual cut off, isolated position; working at a steady pace until he noticed a repetitive noise which was somewhat irritating. He looked over at Callimay and saw she could barely hold her pencil because her hand was shaking so much, it tapping the paper instead of flowing over it as she wrote. She flinched when she noticed him looking and immediately dropped it, clenching her hands together so he couldn't see her trembling.

He turned back to his work without saying anything or looking directly at her.

The bell rang not a moment too soon and the announcement was made concerning report cards being posted in the morning; the suggestion given to arrive early so they would have plenty of time to see their updated scores. Everyone filed out as usual, though the chatter among them was more than normal.

"Here is the midterm." The faculty stated as she handed Callimay a small stack of papers.

"Thank you."

"Destan, here is yours." She offered as she switched her focus. "The answers are on the last page."

❦

After she put her books in her locker she headed out for the evening; stopping where her bike was: *There you are! … It would be nice if I could go to Lookout Point — or even down to the small river to eat dinner. It would be a little bit more time I could have away from everyone. But I don't know if I could go by myself. I don't feel safe now with Toreon acting so brash and bold. Oh I wish there were a way I could ask without actually asking Destan! ~ What would make it even better is if he would think to ask you, Rose Petal. ~ If only. … I can tell he's slipped back into his old self somewhat. Something must have happened during our visit with Mr. Freigh—*

Typical of her zoning out, she didn't know the person she was talking about was in front of her. Destan repeated for the fifth time in a loud voice, waving his hand in front of her face, "Hey!"

"I'm sorry," she apologized as she shook her head and looked to him. "I can zone out when I talk to myself. What is it?"

"I was asking you about tomorrow."

"Oh. Right. Tomorrow is Friday."

"I was wondering since everyone will be arriving early to check report cards— would you be willing to come in earlier?"

It took her a few moments to understand why Destan would ask that question, but then it dawned on her, "I guess I could. … Yeah. Yeah, it would be fine. Five-thirty is when you get there, right?"

"Yes."

"Okay. It shouldn't be a problem."

"I will see you in the morning then."

Callimay was crushed. She was hoping he would at least ask her if she was feeling better after everything that happened. Now knowing who he could be, she so desperately wanted back the Destan she saw earlier. At least she wanted to end the day better.

With each passing moment he was walking farther and farther away, but she still hadn't gotten her thoughts together. She shook her head and ran after him, reaching out and grabbing his wrist, "Would you— if you don't I completely understand. I don't feel like staying around everyone during dinner. And if it was okay—"

105

Destan turned and looked at her with nothing more than his blank, serious expression.

"Never mind." She stepped back and bowed her head. "I… I will see you tomorrow. I'm sorry I… never mind."

"Alright."

What happened to you? She clasped her hands together as she watched him walk away. *Why have you slipped back? Is this who you really are and the Destan I saw this morning was the façade? What is wrong! This isn't going to all of a sudden disappear. As long as Toreon is here — as much as I hate to say it — I'm going to have to deal with him to some degree. … Why did you change? I thought we were starting to form a friendship. It seemed like you were opening up to me the one morning. It seemed so raw and real; like it was the real you coming out. What happened today? What happened during our visit with Mr. Freigh? What did he say that would make you cut yourself off again? What happened to make you leave me?*

℘

"I'm picking up several concerning readings from Callimay's emotional responses," Baleck sounded nervous as he entered the room.

"Already? What are they?" Mr. Freigh asked as he looked up from the paperwork he was going over.

"Doubt, fear, anger, frustration… I know due to the circumstances from today they are understandable, but she's extremely suspicion."

"What would make her suspicious? I do not recall there being anything that changed. Was the memory wipe successful?"

"From what I can see, everything was within the parameters set. There should be no gap from erased to new memories." Baleck stated as he rechecked the report.

"This is very concerning." Mr. Freigh said as he shook his head.

"I know—"

"Not just that, Baleck. This."

He had the video feed from morning lecture next to the feed from after they got back from processing. Destan was withdrawn in every way possible. No emotion or attachment of any kind to Callimay, "How did this happen?"

"Let me look at his paperwork again." Baleck said rather calm, knowing there had to be an easy explanation; but after a few moments gasped, "Oh no."

"What?"

"We were uninformed though it was a needed variation, for them both to wake up at the same time, his memory wipe had to take place later since Callimay's processing was slowed. It says here an adjustment was made in the STM dosages for them both; but they were nowhere near the same amount. By my best calculations — off the top of my head — Destan was given a dosage which would put him where he was last night... not just after coming into the office today."

"Idiots!" Mr. Freigh lashed out as he shoved his chair back. "Who made the calculation?"

"Well. ... That's strange. There's no name."

"Let me see that. ... How could this be the only thing not signed? Any and all variances have to be signed by both the person making the variance and a witness! Where is the footage for Destan's processing?"

"It should be in your private folder. It hasn't— oh. Remember that we set it to delete automatically at the end of the day so no one could access it?" Baleck recalled defeated as he looked at the clock.

"So we have nothing!" Mr. Freigh slammed his fist on the desk.

"I'll gather the team. They're still here." Baleck reassured as he took his phone out. "We will get to the bottom of this."

"Oh!" Mr. Freigh said abruptly as Baleck closed the door.

"Just a moment— yes?"

"Since everything happened today, the report card can be changed. And since I made a point of telling Destan he would be rewarded and Toreon reprimanded, make sure it is reflected as such. I will leave it up to you about how much and where Callimay fits into all this."

"Okay," Baleck responded rather preoccupied and then continued talking on the phone.

⅌

Callimay skipped dinner that evening altogether. She was so torn up about everything and her emotions were so out of control she was ready to fall into an emotional breakdown.

All this stress was causing the migraine she had earlier to progress to the point where the smallest movement, light, strong smell, or sound would cause her excruciating pain. She pulled the curtains, turned off the lights… even put a towel at the base of the door and dampers in her ears; yet the stabbing pain radiating from her right eye wouldn't lessen.

Callimay could barely move, and because of the debilitating pain she stayed in bed. Crying only made things worse — she knew this all too well — but the pain was horrible enough being bottled up like it was. She lay there in the dark and let go of everything she was holding in, all but wailing in agony and frustration.

Once she was done, she laid her hand on her forehead and sniffled: *No one is around. It's not like anyone will hear or see me. And even if they did they wouldn't care. The only person who cared about me died seven years ago. Everyone else cares as long as it's in their best interest to. Once they gain no benefit from me they leave. Everyone wants what is seen as the easy way out. They only want to take care of themselves.*

After a while, she was finally able to stop crying. But she now couldn't breathe very well. It was as if she couldn't catch a break: *Why is it: if it's not one thing it's another? Why can't I just go to sleep so I don't know I'm in pain? Please! Please God. Let me sleep.*

The pain kept her awake for most of the night; her getting to the point she was sick to her stomach. She had migraines similar to this in the past, but never one based on emotional stress only. Callimay was baffled why it was the sole trigger for this severe type of migraine. At least she couldn't think of anything else that would contribute to it.

For some unknown reason, every time the pain settled in or behind her eye it would swell shut. Not only was it present this time, but she could tell her jaw and neck on her right side were also doing the same: *This is by far the worst one I have 'ever' had.*

As she lay there, making sure she stayed motionless, she began thinking about home and what it was like when Mrs. Berchoff was alive. She was trying to keep her mind on happier times and maybe help her not notice the pain long enough so her body could at least rest; hopefully letting her drift off to sleep.

~ 13 ~

When her alarm did go off, Callimay could barely move. Not only was the pain still in her eye and her jaw and neck swollen, but since she didn't move any, she slept in the exact position she was in: awkward. Her muscles, on top of everything else, were complaining.

If I can get up and take some medicine it will have enough time to kick in before I need to leave. And since everyone will be there early— "Oh no! I forgot!" She screeched; realizing what she promised. "He'll never forgive me for— oh what have I done!"

She struggled to get out of bed and stand upright but eventually did.

After staggering to her desk, she took her pain medicine and got ready as fast as she could. Callimay was trying to make every effort to look presentable, but she couldn't bear the light being on so she could see to put her makeup on. Her face was visibly swollen, so no amount of makeup was going to be able to fix or hide it anyway: *I'll just have to make sure I only show my 'good side' today. My hair can cover it.*

Last thing on the to-do list before leaving: she walked over to her dresser and took down her perfume bottle. When she tried to put it on she about passed out.

Simple Kathy it is, Callimay turned her head away and threw the stopper back in the glass bottle, the sound of the glass clanking causing her pain as well.

$$\mathcal{B}$$

When she stepped outside, the crisp autumn air felt good, but it quickly began to intensify all the pain she had. She didn't want to ride her bike, but knew if she didn't she wouldn't make it in time for first lecture.

Just as she was about to get on, everything around her started spinning. She fell to the ground, though thankfully to the side her book bag was so it took the brunt of the impact. Callimay came to after a few moments but stayed there for a while; trying to calm herself so she could open her eyes, let alone move. Her hands were plastered against the path to help her mind remember it wasn't spinning.

Right as she started getting up, she heard what almost sounded like someone talking. She wasn't sure if it was someone talking or the birds chirping in the trees, though. Every noise was so overly amplified in her brain she couldn't distinguish what was what.

She was shocked and almost scared, seeing who was jogging over, "Mr. Freigh? Mr. Willgun?"

"What is wrong, Callimay?" Baleck reached out to help her. "Your right eye— did you hit it when you fell?"

"Thank you," she said gratefully as she took his hand and got up rather ginger. "I just have a migraine. It started yesterday afternoon and hasn't gotten any better." *Really, if anything it's gotten worse.* "I'm extremely sensitive to light, sounds, and smells when I have these; and there is an ample supply of them all right now. A side effect I can have sometimes is: where the pain settles I also get inflammation… hence my swollen eye and jaw."

"Are you well enough to attend lectures and classes today?" Mr. Freigh asked, a deep furrow of concern etched in his brow and voice.

"As long as…" she paused as she grabbed Baleck's arm again for support. "As long as the medication I took kicks in I should be fine. I thank you for your concern."

"Do you remember where my office is, Callimay?" Mr. Freigh asked as he nodded to Baleck. "The door before it is where one of the medical rooms are. Go there first. I will explain to faculty for first lecture about the situation. You look like you need actual medical attention. I am not sure if there is anything that can be done to help, but it is better to try than give up."

"I… I guess so. … Alright. Thank you."

"Are you sure you will be able to ride there?" Baleck asked.

"As strange as this may sound, it's less painful than walking. Plus it will get me there faster. I should be fine. Thank you."

Mr. Freigh questioned in a hushed tone, "You don't think—"

Baleck replied after she was out of earshot, "I don't think this is 'all' due to her processing. Not by her response. But I do think it was the seed which started it."

"This was supposed to go so smooth this time." Mr. Freigh sighed as he watched her ride away. "Destan had too much taken away and Callimay had too much given. Both are our fault."

"They will balance. Give them time. This discovery period is the most critical time for us to not poke or prod. They must find their abilities on their own. Then we can help them with reaching and exiting focal point."

"Time is something we are running out of. I just read over two dozen reports which had been posted within the last week. Whoever is responsible for unleashing the Rogues has apparently found an unlimited supply to draw from. And they are flaunting and flexing their muscles in this area by not holding anything back. I know they need this time, but then again: we need them. Right. Now."

☥

As Callimay walked in, everyone was crowded around where the report cards were posted. She remembered what happened yesterday at this time and shuddered at the thought of it happening again. Those memories prompted her to look for Toreon, but she didn't see him. So, she let her shoulders drop as she breathed a sigh of relief. No one else made note of her, so she kept walking down the hall.

Something felt strange, though, as she got closer to the end of the hall where the first door which led toward Mr. Freigh's office was. It felt as if someone were watching her. — Not again!

When they weren't but ten feet off, she heard their harsh question, "What happened?"

"I'm sorry," she moaned as she did her best to hide the right side of her face. "I had a migraine last night and forgot to take something for it and reset— oh why try to explain. I'm sorry, Destan. I know I promised you I'd come earlier."

Seeing her weakened state, he softened a bit and asked, "I didn't know you weren't— where are you going?"

"Mr. Freigh found me this morning. I passed out by my bike. He told me to go to the medical room which is the door before his office to see if there is anything they can do to help."

"Oh. What about morning lecture?"

"He said he would inform faculty," Callimay answered as she grabbed the side of her face, beginning to get dizzy again.

"Are you alright?" Destan asked concerned as he reached his hand out, seeing her beginning to sway back and forth.

"I'll be okay." She assured as she stumbled back, him catching her so she wouldn't fall.

Destan saw her face, his eyes gasping as he asked extremely serious and concerned, "What happened, Callimay?"

"I'm sorry." She answered scared as she reached for the door handle and turned away so he couldn't see her. "I… I'll be fine."

"Callimay," Destan spoke softly as he walked beside her and put his hand on her shoulder. "What 'really' happened? You can tell me."

"This is all from my migraine," she hesitated and then looked to him; sounding flustered. "I know it may look like I got hit in the face, but believe me when I say this is all due to my migraine. If someone did this to me I'd be bruised too."

"Okay," he responded slow and unsatisfied as he stepped back. "Can you get back there by yourself?"

"I think so." Callimay tried to smile as she sighed.

"If you're sure."

"I am."

"Alright," he sighed as he walked away. "I hope they can help and you start feeling better soon. No offense, but you scared me just now."

"I'm sorry, Destan. I didn't mean t—"

"Excuse me?" He asked as he stopped and turned around.

"Oh, I'm sorry. I thought I heard you say something." She said rather weak, looking worried and confused.

"No. I didn't say anything." He responded a bit shocked.

"Oh. Okay. I thought I— I'm probably…" Callimay rambled on, her voice sounding muffled as she opened the door.

❦

As she walked down the hall, she tried to understand: *I could have sworn I heard his voice as clear as I'm hearing my own. ~ Really Rose Petal? Of course you can hear yourself; you're talking to yourself in your mind. ~ Please stop. My head hurts too much right now. I'm not thinking clearly, you know that. I'm probably imagining things I would want. Like Destan caring about me.*

She made it to the door and knocked a couple times. It was getting more difficult for her to stand upright, so she leaned against the wall while she waited. The cool brick felt so good against her skin… why did it have to be so hard? Her body trembled and quivered as she stood there slumped over. She was breathing rather hard and the expression on her face looked as if she were about to cry.

It seemed like an eternity, but the door finally opened and a younger woman came out, "You are Callimay, aren't you?"

"Yes ma'am."

"Mr. Freigh made sure to let me know you would be coming. I'm so sorry you're not feeling well." The young woman consoled in a soft tone, a sweet smile on her face. "Please come in. Let's see if we can figure out if I can help so you can get back before your second lecture starts… hopefully before breakfast."

"Thank you." Callimay moaned as she dragged herself to the medical bed the younger woman ushered her to.

"I thought this would be more comfortable than an exam table or a chair. Please lie down and try to rest. I know it's hard, but try. This shouldn't take very long."

"Alright," she replied as she got into the bed.

The bed was so comfortable and relaxing, the room dimly lit and the only sound being the pitter-patter of water on a window. This whole time, the young woman moved the least amount possible and at a snail's pace to not disturb Callimay. She took some blood and then did a couple tests before sitting at a computer.

After everything was completed, she walked over with what looked like a metal ring, "I have inputted all the information into this device. I am going to have you put it on so you can situate it where it will be as comfortable as possible. I know with migraines any pressure on the skull isn't pleasant, but with you doing it as opposed to me, your body doesn't see the pain as 'that' severe. This little device will show me what parts of your brain are irritated and to what degree so I can program it to give those points therapy to calm them and help you."

Callimay took the device, following the young woman's instructions and adjusting it several times before she let go of it and lay back.

"What medicine did you take? Mr. Freigh said you told him you had taken some."

"It was 600 milligrams of ibuprofen."

A few minutes later she returned and explained, "I'll give you an injection which should help with the immediate pain. The device you have on has determined where the points of irritation are and will treat them for long-term relief. The only thing you'll feel is the prick from the injection. The rest of the treatment will be undetectable to your senses. Are you alright if I do this?"

"Please," Callimay begged without any hesitation.

"Pain is no fun. I used to have migraines myself, so I understand."

"You did?"

"Yes. Yes I did. Now you rest until everything is done. Take a nap if you want. I'll wake you when everything is done."

"Thank you."

Now having immediate relief, her body could rest and begin to heal: she fell right to sleep. The halo-like device was done treating her brain in forty-five minutes, but the younger woman ran a test again to make sure it had treated everything. She then nodded to what looked like the wall, and then went back to her paperwork.

"Callimay?" The younger woman whispered as she stroked her hand softly. "Callimay you're all done."

She opened her eyes in complete shock with how well she felt.

"You can take the Halo off."

"Oh! You mean this little thing fixed my migraine all by itself?"

"Yes, it did. Pretty amazing, huh? — Now I wouldn't run out and act like everything is crisp cucumbers, but you are free to go whenever. The medicine I gave you may make you feel a bit dizzy, so keep that in mind. I'm going to adjust the lighting so you are not shell-shocked when you leave, okay? There's no need to add insult to injury right now. Just take your time. I'll be here."

"Okay." Callimay acknowledged as she closed her eyes and felt the right side of her face. "If I had my way, I'd stay here and sleep for the rest of the day. I haven't gotten rest like this in so long."

"I know exactly what you mean." The younger woman laughed as she continued to turn the lights up. "And I mean this in a good way: your face looks much better."

"So, I can go… now?" Callimay asked again, unsure if what she heard was what was said.

"Whenever you feel you are ready. Yep!"

ʤ

Callimay left after her eyes were adjusted to the full brightness of the lights and made her way as fast as she could to the main hall, quickly realizing the young woman was serious when she warned her about the medicine making her dizzy. She caught herself and sat down in the corner of the hall, closing her eyes to help her mind reorient itself.

It just so happened to be right between the first and second lectures when she got back. As she shut the last door, she glanced to see if anyone noticed her. For a split second, it felt very strange that the hall was empty. She checked her watch and saw it was ten after nine: *Everyone must be at breakfast still.*

Just then she saw the faculty from first lecture exit the main lecture hall. She walked as fast as she dared, waving down the middle-aged man, "I was told Mr. Freigh explained my absence?"

"Yes he did, Callimay. I'm so sorry you have to live with those slices of torture. I'm glad to see you're doing well."

"Thank you. I was wondering if there would be any chance I could have a list of the in-class assignments and homework? If you can't I understand. It could be seen as—"

"Destan already took care of that for you. He spoke to me after lecture on your behalf. I left all the work with him. He said he would give it to you before next lecture starts."

"Oh! Oh, thank you."

She immediately turned to head to the main lecture hall and ran right into him… again, "Oh, I'm so sorry Destan."

"We need to stop meeting like this." He cracked a tiny smile.

115

"And wouldn't you guess you are the person I wanted to see this time as well," Callimay replied, almost laughing herself.

"Guess I need to make sure from now on I don't walk or stand too close to you, huh?"

"Maybe. I wanted to say thank you for getting my assignment from last lecture. You didn't have to but I am grateful you did."

"You're welcome. I remember you asked about it yesterday, so I assumed it still applied. I take it by how you are acting they were able to help? Your face looks a lot better."

"Oh yes. I feel so much better now." She grinned as she nodded, then paused when she realized who it was asking her this, "Thank you for asking, Destan."

"You're welcome." He replied as he turned and walked away.

ℬ

When Callimay entered the front area for breakfast, she noticed several people glanced her way and then started talking to others: *I'm sure they're just gossiping like they always do.*

She glanced around the room again to see where Toreon was. No sign of him anywhere: *Well that's strange…*

A while later she heard him call out, "Where were you?"

Oh no. She shivered as she turned toward the sound of his voice and finished; her void sounding timid, "I wasn't feeling well."

Toreon was standing a little way off and didn't say a word in response. He had this disgusted look on his face and left when Gallia walked over.

Some people are never pleased no matter what happens. ~ Maybe his report card wasn't what he was expecting. Callimay sighed as she turned around. *Well, at least he didn't keep things going. It worked out better this way. … Right? ~ Yes, Rose Petal. Now let's get something to eat. 'I' at least am starving.*

ℬ

The rest of the morning went smoother than she expected. Not being at first lecture was a blessing: she didn't have to be around Toreon and deal with the migraine at the same time. That would've been torture.

116

Lunch was uneventful and carried into an equally uneventful afternoon; putting Callimay at ease and allowing her to rest from what happened yesterday — including both what she knew about as well as what she did not.

When physics let out, everyone made a mad dash since it was Friday and thus leisure time until Monday morning. Callimay didn't really care to look at the report cards, but she was curious as to what had been done for Destan and to Toreon.

But, she got sidetracked when the first screen she looked at was for the girls.

As expected, she wasn't anywhere near the top. She let her hand slide off the screen when she found her name, "Last place."

"Kinda," a voice interrupted.

"What do you mean by that?" Callimay asked as she turned to Destan who was leaning against the far wall.

"Look again." He gestured to the board.

"At what? It says I am in— a tie for 499th?"

"Look at the other one," Destan pushed off the wall.

"You're 499th too? How did that happen? I thought ties weren't allowed? Let alone Mr. Freigh said yesterday what you did would show on your report card. That was supposed to be a good thing."

"It's not that they aren't allowed, it's just they've never happened before. And it appears that was just talk."

"That's… troubling. — How would you know this all about the ties? Who did you ask?" Callimay looked over her shoulder at him.

"Mr. Willgun."

"Oh. I wonder why they did that."

"Maybe they think we make a good team?" Destan suggested, no emotion in his voice. "Or they didn't want you to feel alone at the bottom so they left me there."

"You never know." She sighed, though she was taken aback by what he said. "Anything can happen for any reason."

"I guess," Destan responded slowly as he stared at her.

"Well, what I mean is: since everything is based on the social hierarchy. Things can change so much and what people say doesn't always reflect in their actions like they should. Maybe I'm not making any sense, but you have to admit this whole structure is difficult to make much s—"

"Are you eating at your room tonight again?"

You noticed I wasn't here last night? Callimay asked stunned, taking a few moments to process everything before saying, "Well, I hadn't given it much thought. Last night was— well yesterday was a day I am glad is over for just about every reason. I don't ever want to have to go through that again."

"Go through 'what' again?"

"What do you mean by that? You were there… both times!"

"Excuse me?" Destan defended in a raised tone.

"You mean to tell me you don't remember yesterday morning at all? That you forgot what happened in the morning 'and' at lunch?" She clenched her fists at her sides and stomped her foot. "Are you so detached from any emotion that you can shut off memories?"

"I…" he paused, a look of bewilderment plastered over his usual stern one. "I really don't know what happened yesterday."

"I mean it's like— you don't?"

"No, I don't. I remember going to bed the night before and then it's blank until we were in Mr. Freigh's office. I don't even remember getting up that morning, let alone going there."

"You mean you don't remember anything? Nothing at all?"

"Isn't that what I just said!" Destan said in a raised tone, his green eyes flashing at her. "Didn't you hear me?"

"I'm sorry." She cowered, trying to keep from crying.

"I just don't— I don't know what these big incidents are that everyone's talking about. All I heard was: 'supposedly' something happened yesterday morning between Toreon and myself. I know people lie, but I can't help but think something 'did' happen and I just can't remember it for the life of me. That and what they talked about sounded like something he would do. You know what happened, don't you?" He calmed down as he leaned his back against the wall next to where she was standing. "How does a memory which should be so big go missing like 'that'? I just don't understand."

"I… I feel horrible now."

"Why?"

"I thought ever since last night you didn't care," Callimay explained as she hung her head and began to cry. "I assumed you had decided to kick me to the curb like everyone else. I'm sorry I thought that of you. I shouldn't have but I did. Please forgive me."

"I…" he hesitated; but finally confessed, "I do care about you. Really, I do. It's just… I'm scared to."

"Why are you scared, Destan?" She looked up.

"What?" He flinched.

"I was asking why you're scared to show you care. If I'm pry—"

"I didn't say that out loud," Destan sounded suspicious as he shook his head, standing up again. "I was talking to myself… in my mind. How did you hear me?"

"But I…" she paused as a look of fear came over her face. "But I heard you say it. I swear I did!"

"Well I didn't." He leaned back against the wall, and then finished in a critical tone: *Only someone with telekinesis could hear me while I'm not talking. Someone who can 'hear' thoughts. That type of ability doesn't exist in real life.*

"Your lips didn't move!" Callimay shrieked as she jumped back. "How am I hearing you if your lips aren't moving? What, are you some coyote or something?"

You can hear me? Like now: you can hear everything I'm saying?

"Stop it!" She screamed as she covered her ears and crumbled to the floor. "Stop talking! Stop… stop thinking! Destan, please! Just stop! Please! Make it stop!"

"Callimay." He tried to comfort as he kneeled in front of her, hesitating before putting his hand on her shoulder.

"Please go away." She cried as she pushed his hand away. "I can tell you're scared of me."

"I won't and I'm not."

"Don't lie to me! You don't want to even touch me. Just go!"

"I'm not scared of you. I'm just confused and shocked by all this, I'm not scared. Okay? I'm trying to figure out what's going on."

"What's happening to me? When did this happen? Does this have anything to do with you not being able to remember yesterday?" She asked, tears streaming down her face.

"Remind me what happened. If you say it happened I trust you."

She sat there and didn't say anything.

"Please Callimay," Destan repeated desperately.

"I was late in getting here yesterday like some days because of Toreon's random visits to Gallia at her room before the start of the school day. They were gossiping as usual so I sat there and waited for him to leave. He finally did, and so I left as fast as I could. When I got down to the bike racks, mine was missing. — Come to think of it, I never figured out why it was still here. — But anyway. After running all the way, I got to my locker and was hurrying to get my books when Toreon showed up. He had Webb and Dakoe with him… and they cornered me. You showed up and got me away from him. You walked me to the main lecture hall and helped me when I collapsed. You askcd…" she recounted and then paused.

"I what? What did I ask?"

"Nothing. I guess I just now realized what you meant." Callimay brushed off. "But I guess I don't know if you a—"

"Please tell me," Destan begged as he looked at her and put his hands on her arms. "Please. I need to know. I need to remember. And the only way that will happen is if you help me."

There was a short pause, Callimay not speaking until her eyes began to well with tears, "You were concerned about me. You asked if Toreon did anything. I didn't understand what you meant by that until now. Y… you blamed yourself even though it wasn't your fault. You never finished since the bell rang, but I think you started to say, 'I am sorry'."

"Why can't I remember any of it?" He asked, a defeated look on his face as he hung his head and tapped his fist on the floor.

"T… the other time was at lunch."

"What happened then?"

"You left to take your tray back to the front while I was sitting there staring at my food I hadn't eaten. I… I really didn't want you to leave me, but you promised me you'd be right back. I ate a few bites, and then Toreon came over and grabbed my tray to get you to fight him." Callimay folded her arms across each other and looked at the floor; finishing in a worried tone, "H… has any of this helped you remember anything? Anything at all?"

"Unfortunately no. But maybe it will help jog something later on. You were suspicious of how I was acting, weren't you? That's why you acted so scared yesterday evening when you were trying to ask me something. I wasn't acting the way I had earlier."

"I didn't understand how you could switch so fast. I didn't want to believe you were like so many others here who would kick someone to the curb if they weren't being 'helpful'. Though I must say: your actions were adding up to just that."

"I'm so sorry," he agonized; seeming to finish what he started to say the morning prior. "All afternoon I couldn't focus or think about much anything other than why there was such a large gap in what I could remember. I was trying to piece things together myself, but never gave any thought to how that might affect you… and even what danger I was putting you in. … Well, I take that back, I did think about you. But I admit it was because I was suspicious of you. Geez, I'm suspicious of everyone. With me not knowing what in the world happened for over a half a day— I didn't know who to trust. You, Mr. Freigh, and Mr. Willgun seemed to be so in sync with each other and what you were talking about. I assumed you were all in on why I lost my memory. When I saw where I was on the report card I became even more suspicious. Then you were late this morning and I saw you heading back toward Mr. Freigh's office, I— but when I saw you and heard your voice, I realized then you couldn't be capable of what I was accusing you of. 'I' should be the one asking for forgiveness."

"Oh, Destan. I don't know what to do to help."

"You've helped so much." He ensured as he helped her up. "Really Callimay. You have."

"But you said you still couldn't remember."

"You've given me the truth; I know you have. I'll eventually put all the pieces back together."

Callimay could barely comprehend what was being said. No one had said that to her. She was so accustomed to being used by others and not appreciated. The only one she ever remembered valuing her like this was Mrs. Berchoff, "I… don't know how to—"

"Don't worry. There's nothing you need to say. — I do have one question if you don't mind."

"What is it?"

"When you were evaluated today, what did they do?"

"She drew some blood, did a nerve-response test, took my vitals, gave me some pain medicine of some kind, and then used this ring-looking device — I think she called it a halo — which analyzed and treated my migraine somehow," Callimay recalled, using her hands to describe things. "You don't think I gained this ability like a superpower do you? I mean… that's just fairy tales and ancient folklore from the Homeworld. Legends, right? … Destan?"

"I'm curious because you asked 'when' this happened. Not that my two-cents matters but I'm gonna give it to you anyway: I don't believe in the devil's art of magic or what some call 'gifts', so the only logical conclusion can be that you were given this ability through some type of treatment. Did you lose consciousness at all this morning?"

"I slept for almost an hour."

"Hum. You could have been given it then. This was the first time you 'heard' anyone… right?"

There was a moment of silence, Callimay looking up to the sky as if looking for the answer, then replied, "No."

"When?"

"This morning. You."

"When you said you thought you heard me talking to you… you heard my voice like you did earlier?"

"Yes. Exactly the same way."

"Incredible," Destan mumbled under his breath.

⅌

"Usually it is the older individual in a partnership who starts forgetting things first." Mr. Freigh walked up to Baleck in the hall that morning while Callimay was being treated. "Is everything going alright?"

"I'm sorry, what?" He asked rather confused.

"I guess it is my own fault for interjecting like I did, interrupting you while you were trying to get the team before they left yesterday. The report card. We—"

"Oh my— I totally let it slip my mind. I should have taken care of it the second you mentioned it. I apologize for that. I know this is—"

123

"We were both thrown into a frenzy with the ordeal surrounding the miscalculation in Destan's counteractant." Mr. Freigh sighed as he patted him on the shoulder, more upset with himself than anything. "I should have taken care of it myself."

"I was wondering why Destan stopped me first thing this morning to ask me about ties. I should have put two and two together. I take full responsibility for that error. "

The two of them then began to walk back to the office, Mr. Freigh commenting, "I am putting too many responsibilities on—I am, Baleck. It is time I take some of them back so you are not stretched so thin. You are never this nervous or unorganized. … Is there something going on in your personal life, your uncle perhaps? You know I am not one to pry, but I cannot ignore when a colleague and friend is distracted."

"I appreciate your concern. I am willing to concede the thought of finally having Challenger is still shocking. Other than that I am fine. Really. And as far as responsibilities here, you brought me on for this very reason."

"I know. But the fact remains I am an equal partner in this, so I bear the same amount of responsibility for errors as well as victories. Do not be afraid to speak up if I am giving you too much, or to remind me I am fully capable of doing things myself."

"Very well. But I assure you, everything is fine."

༷

As Destan and Callimay were about to leave after finishing dinner, Toreon and his entourage walked by. He looked at Callimay with a Cheshire-cat smile and then switched his focus and glared at Destan. There was a moment where there seemed to be some type of battle between the two of them though neither moved an inch or said a word, but Toreon finally turned away and scoffed in disgust, leaving without ever saying a word.

He really thinks he can intimidate me? Destan laughed.

"He does it because he has to keep his façade up for even himself to believe. It seems everyone's starting to doubt he can take you on."

"Geez, Callimay!" Destan jumped.

"I'm sorry."

"Did you 'hear' that from him or was it you observing?"

"Just observation," she shivered; appalled at the thought of listening to Toreon on purpose. "As far as I'm concerned, one extra person in my head is more than enough."

"Well thanks."

"I didn't mean it that way." Callimay rolled her eyes as she walked outside. "I'm going for a bike ride before it gets dark. You're welcome to tag along if you'd like."

"I appreciate the offer."

"My bike is over on the side. I'll be back as fast as I can. If you don't want to go I understand." She offered as she turned and ran as fast as she could; not waiting for a response.

ℬ

Callimay kept running until she turned the corner and saw Toreon standing there. His gaze fixed on her as she stopped dead in her tracks. Those in the group he was talking with paused and looked in the direction he was. He said something to them to which they nodded and then left.

"Well, well, well." He started as he strutted over, slipping his hands out of his pockets. "Where is your tutor at, Callimay?"

Destan? Destan I need you right now! She stood there, frozen with fear while Toreon walked toward her.

"You seem… worried." He suggested, seeming to be holding back laughter. "And why would that be? Hum?"

She didn't say anything.

Toreon walked right up to her and then leaned over and whispered in her ear, "I'm enjoying this game we're playing."

ℬ

Destan was waiting out front this whole time when he noticed movement out of his peripheral. He looked over expecting to see Callimay but took off running when he saw Toreon. Seeing him was bad enough, but the look on his face? This wasn't good.

Toreon blocked him, snickering as he spoke, "Why are you so concerned about her? I'm taking good care of her."

125

Not bothering to say a word, Destan responded by shoving Toreon aside and running to find Callimay, "Are you alright?"

"I… I'm fine," she answered shaky as he kneeled in front of her.

"Callimay," he said firmer as he took her by the shoulders and looked her in the eye. "What. Happened?"

"He asked where you were and then walked up and whispered he was 'enjoying the game we were playing'. … What did he mean?"

He's not gonna give up. He's going after the one thing he knows he can't have — you — but wants to flaunt as if you're his for the taking while 'he's' the one playing hard to get. Such a jer—

"I don't like being around him, Destan. He scares me!" Callimay confessed as she threw her arms around him and refused to let go.

He was not expecting an embrace from her, so he wasn't quite sure what to do or how to handle it. Destan didn't want to shove her away, but he didn't feel comfortable either.

Trying his best to keep his cool, he took a deep breath and cleared his throat as he stood; helping her at the same time. It wasn't hard to tell he was frustrated — him keeping Callimay at arm's length — but she knew he wasn't directing it at her. If anything, she felt embarrassed for what she did.

"I don't like it either. I may not remember what happened yesterday, but I know what happened now, and it won't be something I'll forget. He's got another thing coming if he thinks he can torment you."

She couldn't believe what she was hearing him say! There were all these little glimmers she saw of the true Destan, but they were few and far between, unfortunately.

Exhausted and still scared, she said rather rushed, "I'm just going back to my room. I don't feel like going for a bike ride anymore. I… I'm sorry Destan."

He nodded and started escorting her back, neither saying a word.

Right before the path split toward each dorm, Destan said rather quiet and caring, "If you ever need anything, let me know."

Nothing.

"Hey." He stopped and tilted his head so he could see her, that sliver of a smile starting to form. "It'll be alright, Callimay. … I know he shook you pretty bad, but he's just one guy."

"I'm sorry." She flinched.

"Easy. I'm not saying you should man up and deal with it like nothing happened. I… just try to—"

"I can't." Callimay covered her face and ran up to the door.

This would have gone unnoticed if it hadn't been for the fact that a small group of young women were coming out of just as Callimay got to the door. They rolled their eyes and snickered as they whispered to each other, then stopped dead in their tracks when they saw Destan… who was less than thrilled with how they were treating Callimay behind her back.

What he did in response to Toreon's comment just a day earlier was fresh — to say the least — in their minds. But their knee-jerk reaction wasn't one to stay, "What? Are you looking for someone to scold? — Aw. Who hurt your baby doll this time? I— hey! Come back here."

Destan wanted so much to put an end to their cruel thoughts and intentions, but knew this wasn't Toreon he was dealing with. It wasn't even another guy.

Just hang in there, Calli. Don't give up. He repeated as he stomped off; inside feeling miserable.

~ 14 ~

Over the next couple weeks, Callimay and Destan steadily became closer to each other. Part of this was her accepting him for who he was. She wasn't thrilled he wasn't very conversational, but she was glad for the talks they had and the ever so subtle hints at his true self coming out — or what she wanted to believe was his true self.

On occasion he would seem harsh, but she knew it was what he had become used to showing for whatever reason. She never let the thought cross her mind that he was doing it intentionally to be cruel to her.

Callimay, by Destan's suggestion, began learning how to control her newfound ability. It didn't take too long for her to discover she could only hear people she was directly looking at or intentionally focusing on within a seventy-five-foot radius. She also found she could only hear what the person was saying to themselves; not random thoughts that ran through their minds. — This line may seem somewhat fuzzy, but it was the best way Callimay could come to explaining it.

When she had to focus hard due to the person being farther away from her, if they were moving rather than standing still, or if she had been utilizing her ability for a long period of time: she would develop a migraine. It was never anything she wasn't used to or unable to control easy; it was more of a nuisance than anything.

Of course, Destan was her assistant — he preferred the term guinea pig — in these experiments. But even though he poked fun about it, he truly wanted to help her and wasn't about to leave her alone. Not with Toreon around.

♄

One side effect she had not encountered was in true focal point she would lose her peripheral vision and hearing. It wasn't something she even noticed until one day while they were out riding their bikes. Since Destan was quite a bit ahead of her and they were moving, Callimay had to try extremely hard to stay focused on him. In doing so, she wasn't paying attention and ran into a tree. A student who was walking by tried to warn her, calling out to her and waving their hands in the air, but it was as if she couldn't hear or see them at all.

"Are you alright!" Destan exclaimed as he rushed over, finding her lying on the ground face down. "Calli?"

"Ouch." She groaned as she rolled over.

"What happened?" He took her hand to help her up.

"I don't know. It's like I couldn't see anything while I was trying to focus on you. It was hard enough to hear you with us both moving and you being so far away." She explained as she tried to balance herself, grabbing his arms to help her. "I guess that's one bad thing about really exerting myself — other than the migraines of course — not being able to see things around me."

"Well I know you can't hear anyone."

"Dakoe!" Callimay greeted in a chipper tone as he came up.

She still wanted to consider him a good friend, but a one-sided friendship wouldn't have much if any chance of lasting. Toreon made it clear he wouldn't permit any socializing outside the group… especially with her. Well, that was unless it was himself.

"Are you alright? Took a hard hit there." He asked as he looked over at the bike. "Brakes not working?"

"I just zoned out for a moment." She shrugged off.

"Well, at least it was a tree and not the edge of Lookout Point."

"Isn't that the truth? Thanks for stopping, Dakoe. How are you d…" Callimay faded out when he turned and walked away.

She sighed a bit, seeing he still feared the so-called authority Toreon had over him more than his fear for someone who was "off limits" but might have been injured.

"Well it's nice to know how concerned he is," Destan growled.

"Oh, leave him be. He didn't do anything wrong. … Anyway! This means I need to add I can only see or hear anything the person I'm focusing on when I'm really using my ability. Strange how that's not what we were intending to try today; but it worked out!"

"Are you keeping a journal?" He asked concerned as he picked up her bike. "Seriously, Callimay. This isn't physics class."

"More or less I'm writing down keywords or phrases so if someone does find it they won't understand what it's for. And so you can stop asking me why I would keep it written down at the risk of someone finding it or taking it away from me."

"Hey, leave my thoughts to myself."

"You said you'd help me learn to control my ability." Callimay reminded as she closed the book and looked up to him. "And by you talking to yourself, you're leaving yourself open to me hearing it."

"Yeah, I know."

Callimay shivered as the wind began to pick up, "It's almost getting to the point it's too cold to go for bike rides."

"Just about."

"At least the howlers held off as long as they did so the change in the leaves could be enjoyed," she looked off in the distance at the flood of falling leaves, using her hands as she talked. "It reminds me of home. The hills are always covered with different shades of crimson, orange, gold, and so on. It's nice to have those little reminders of home. I do miss it, but it's good to get out and do new things."

He didn't say a word.

"Is there anything here that reminds you of home? ... Destan?"

"It looks like there might be a storm rolling in. We might want to call it a day." He averted as he pointed to the west. "Looks like we may get some snow."

"Oh. Okay then."

She so wanted to listen to him, but she'd promised herself when she asked questions like that she wouldn't. Callimay wanted to hear Destan say it out loud. She wanted him to be committed to opening up to her. It was still hard for her to control, but she could do it well enough to give Destan privacy when she knew he needed it most. She was sad he wasn't able to trust her enough to tell her, but understood how events wrapped up in strong emotions were difficult to tell others: *Maybe soon. Just not right now.*

It was time for another report card to come out, so everyone was busy gaining last-minute points. The hierarchy was well-established, but there were still spaces being vied for. Callimay often wondered if these last-second sprints even did any good.

The structure for how the grading was done was kept secret. All of the information they were given — though quite lengthy during orientation — was nothing more than a bunch of five-point words describing the basic and broad concept of social life. Callimay herself was caught up in it at first and then began to realize how much was left untold.

Toreon was still an annoyance at times, but Destan was much more present which kept him at bay. He never went out of his way to keep Toreon away; it was more or less him being close to Callimay which detoured Toreon from even trying. There were still times they would be separated for a while — which were the times Toreon would try his best to manipulate — but each time she braved it and knew Destan wasn't far away if things got out of hand.

The last day of the month, Callimay opened the door and smiled as she waved. With it being bitterly cold in the mornings, Destan suggested she come later so it would be warmer; even going as far to state he would walk with her. She assured him she was fine with the early walk even with it being cold — plus she didn't want to cut off their study time in the mornings — but he told her they could do it between school and dinner.

How he approached the situation seemed like a polite gesture — some might even say a demand — but she saw it as so much more and treasured his offering that small slice of time for just them… and not over physics.

Today was as any other as they walked along. In a slightly comical way, it was endearing to watch the two of them. They were so polar opposite and yet got along the best of anyone there; each of them having their own way of contributing to the friendship that was clearly there. — For those opposed to this type of education, Destan and Callimay would be their strongest evidence. They didn't bother much with what others said or did, and if anything else, just let those moments strengthen their bond.

"The stars always shine so much brighter when it's cold," Callimay stared up at the sky. "I heard on the Homeworld they connect them into shapes. They're called… constellations if I remember correctly."

Destan didn't respond.

"I also heard that on the Homeworld you can't see where we are." She tried to ever so slightly nudge him to talk with her. "Isn't that crazy to think about?"

Still nothing.

Callimay couldn't stand the silence. She took a deep breath and let the first thing she thought of fly out, "Well, it's been almost a month and you haven't laid a hand on Toreon."

"He ought to be grateful," Destan said under his breath as he shook his head and clenched his fist. "He deserves—"

"I'm sorry. I was just trying t— I so epically failed."

It took a few moments, but he calmed, "Don't worry. I wouldn't invite it to happen, but I wouldn't stand aside and let him have another chance to… well…"

"And I appreciate it in every way, Destan," Callimay said as she stopped and put her gloved hand over his fist.

His fist softened the moment she touched it, him putting his hand in his pocket and starting to walk again; sighing as he glanced down to her worried eyes.

⌗

When they arrived, they stopped at Callimay's locker first — now their new routine — and found it "decorated" with notes. Just as she did every time this happened, she took them off and placed them with the rest in the bottom of her locker.

Why don't you throw them in the trash? Destan asked as he beheld the ever-growing stack of notes and papers. *They're doing no good, sitting there, reminding you. They torture you enough, Callimay. Don't add to it.*

Well if you must know, it's because if I did throw them out they would put them back. — Believe me, I know. — And by doing this, I make them put forth the effort to keep it up. Gotta give them credit: they're hard workers when it comes to belittling others. … But I guess the biggest reason I do this is because I'm the only one who has access to it and I'm the one who holds it and hides it. I control what others see. These notes are like all the pain I have in my life and this locker is my heart: I keep everything locked away in there so no one sees it and I don't have to deal with it. Maybe it isn't the best, but it's worked for me so far. I'm trying to be better about moving on and not let those who don't wish to know about God cause me to cut myself off like this. I want to; it's just not always easy. She sounded depressed as she fingered the pile of papers. *Do you thi— never mind. You can't hear me.*

"What did you just do?"

"Huh? What?"

"Let's get to the main lecture hall and I'll explain."

"Oh… okay. — Where are you going?"

He stopped and whipped around, all but plowing into the same group of young women he met the other day, "Sorry."

One of them eyed him as she stepped back, "You're fine."

ℬ

When they got to their seats, Destan said in a whisper, "I heard everything you said back at your locker."

"You're kidding me!"

"I thought you were talking out loud at first, but something seemed different. So I moved to be beside you and your lips weren't moving. Now I know how you felt when you heard me."

"That is crazy! So what you're saying is not only can I hear you but you can hear me? … Are you sure you don't have what I do?"

"Umm, I'm fairly certain that's a no," Destan responded without hesitation, a bit of sarcasm seeming to be in his voice.

"Well, have you ever actually tried?"

"Well, no," he began to wonder.

The bell rang so Callimay knew personal conversation time was over. She'd grown comfortable with the routine they had developed over the past few weeks. There were things she wished were different, but she was content with things for now.

❦

With winter break looming, it was going to be interesting to see how things unfolded. They were told academics would be as any of the regular school systems throughout the world, but added the social report cards would continue to be updated during that time. And yet, even though they would have this long break, they weren't allowed to leave… not even for a couple days to see family or friends for Jubilee.

Destan helped Callimay continue to develop her ability and began attempts at seeing if he had the same ability. Each time he tried every avenue she knew, nothing ever came of it. There were no similar episodes since, so he was even more confused.

She was quick to learn new skills and how to control things while in focal point — though she didn't know that was the name of it. When she was under stress, she was learning how to handle it so she wouldn't have a horrible migraine after; though there were those days when it would rear its ugly head.

Callimay was ever grateful for Destan's help and understanding, but couldn't quite understand how calm he was about the whole thing. She knew he wasn't much for showing emotions, much like any typical man… but still! Knowing someone who had this type of ability — or any for that matter — you think would cause a person to be wary around her and reluctant to help.

~ 15 ~

The week before academic finals for the semester, Mr. Freigh called a special session just after the last lecture to discuss winter break, "I know there have been many rumors flying around concerning what is the expected conduct during winter break, so let me clarify a few things. This break is your leisure time. This may be confusing as to how report cards can be posted if it is leisure time, but bear with me. … First, this month's report cards will be posted as usual, so do not neglect that. Similar to most higher education facilities, assignments will be due during break. With it being one and a half months, these assignments will be due halfway through: four weeks from the last day of this semester. — They will be handed to you as you leave today. — Please take note; these special assignments will be all we use to grade you for the entire month. Do not take it lightly or procrastinate completing it."

Mr. Freigh continued for a bit, discussing the overview of how things were going as a generality and the schedule for next semester; saying signup sheets for extra classes would be posted next week.

He spoke briefly of a week next semester when students, who were not foreseeing themselves improving, having an opportunity to meet with himself and Baleck to discuss leaving early. There was a warning to students who failed to show any improvement by the appointed time; saying they would be summoned to discuss possible expulsion.

To this comment, everyone's eyes turned to the back of the room where Callimay and Destan were sitting. Comments were made in hushed tones all around and then focus returned to the front.

Why can't people be nice? Callimay sounded grieved while at the same time perturbed by the attitudes everyone was showing even with

Mr. Freigh present. *It's as if everyone here has gone insane! Is there something in the air? Things used to be like night and day in how people acted because they wanted to show their 'good' side for their grades. Now they don't care at all. People who were so nice when we arrived are so back-stabbing! Everyone is so enthralled with themselves and how they can do things for themselves. They're missing the point of everything! We are supposed to be working so we can go back home and help others! This isn't about ourselves! I don't understand. Just because a report card shows one thing doesn't mean that's who the person really is. — And quite frankly, the ones who remember this fact aren't doing well. The ones putting others first and standing up for what is right are being shoved aside, ostracized, and treated like they are the problem. In light of the rejection they have received, they don't see the help and honesty from the other few who are trying to do just that. … Have faculty even fallen into this delusional belief and lost sight of what this Society was founded for? My goodness! It's as if they 'want' this to happen! … They're basing things off what they observe during school hours. But are they even paying attention to that? — Mother was right; this can't bring about nurturing caring people. It's a breeding ground for the selfish.*

How are you doing that? Destan asked, thinking she was listening to him. *Callimay?*

No response.

Callimay? Aren't you listening to me? He sighed. *Callimay.*

❦

The meeting was soon over and so everyone filed out and picked up their break assignments. As they left, Destan could tell Callimay wasn't acting like herself. He wanted to see if he could get her to talk, but it was apparent something was messing with her so much she couldn't function very well anymore.

Nothing was said during dinner and she only nodded when he asked if she wanted to go for a walk.

So, the two of them strolled at an uncharacteristic pace to the rec complex in complete silence and somewhat detached from each other. Anyone who looked at them would have either said they were sworn enemies forced to walk next to each other or they just fought. Though anyone truly paying attention could see there was something of a different nature altogether wrong. The two of them seemed to switch places… emotionally speaking. Callimay was cut off while Destan was in a frantic panic trying to figure out how to fix things.

Callimay?

Nothing.

"Callimay?" He repeated.

Again, it seemed she wasn't going to respond, but then she looked up and replied in almost a whisper, "Yes Destan?"

Hearing the grief in her voice, similar to what he heard during the conference Mr. Freigh called, he shifted what he was going to ask, "Are you alright?"

"I'm okay."

"I…" Destan tried to say, and then closed off: *I want to help, Calli. I know something is wrong. Well, 'really' wrong. You always talk about what is on your mind even if something is bothering you. Why are you so cut off? This isn't you, Calli. … I know I should ask, but I'm scared to get too involved because of what happened— losing those you care about is extremely hard. I cut people off for this very reason. It kills me to do it, especially to you, but if anything were to happen to you I'd kill myself— well, I mean at least I'd die inside.*

When they made it to the door, she forgot he was with her and reached to open it herself. She pulled back when she felt his warm hand touch her ice-cold one; looking at him with a blank face.

He had come to easily understand how she was feeling by the expression on her face, but this was a completely new side he'd never seen. It had been a learning curve as it was to get to this point and he was pretty proud of himself for figuring that out; and now she changes. Why? What was going on?

Callimay didn't say anything; she didn't react emotionally to what happened — she stood there and stared through him. Destan wanted to ask her what was wrong but wasn't even sure if she would answer him. He opened the door and let her in without saying anything.

❦

Callimay looked like an owl in a spotlight as she took her coat off. Her eyes never focused on anything, yet she was completely aware of what Destan was doing and where he was.

They walked on the indoor paths for what seemed like forever. There was never a word spoken between them and he only glanced at her a couple times. Callimay stared off just in front of her and looked like an empty shell: her hands clutched around her necklace and her eyes glazed over. The poor thing looked devastated! Destan walked at the same speed as her to be next to her but she didn't seem to notice.

Is this what you think of me? Are you repaying me for being cold to you for so long? He asked as he walked along, unaware she stopped. *I guess I deserve it. — Oh, Calli. Why won't you talk? Say something… anything! Tell me you hate me. I don't care!*

A minute later, Destan realized he was alone. He looked back and saw Callimay standing there. Her eyes followed him as he came back; them not blinking once. As he got closer, he saw she was crying.

What he had mistaken as her being detached was, in reality, her being utterly exhausted on the emotional side of life. She had nothing left to give, and it was quite apparent nothing had been given back.

"Calli?" Destan asked concerned as he wiped the tears from her ice-cold cheeks. "What's wrong? You're never quiet like this."

She said nothing.

A few seconds later, she hung her head and started to sob; not letting go of her necklace this entire time.

Destan wasn't sure what to do. She was so different from him as far as how she worked on the inside. Callimay was emotionally driven in everything. He didn't understand or know how to handle emotions — let alone such strong ones. And he apparently didn't know how to understand someone else's. Yet, it didn't stop him from trying to think of what he could do to help her though. She needed to have what was taken given back in a big way right now. And unfortunately, he was the biggest taker in recent times. He had to figure something out.

Anything Destan thought of didn't seem to be anything which would help. She needed something else… but what? What did he have that he could give? How could someone who didn't know how to control or fully express emotions be the kind of support she needed?

"Callimay, please talk to me," he almost whispered as he lifted her chin so he could see her face again.

She closed her eyes and turned her face away.

"Oh, Calli," he said under his breath as he sighed, wrapping her in his arms. "It's going to be alright. I promise."

What she did next threw Destan for a loop: she pushed him away and ran. She never looked at him, never said a word — she just ran. He stood there in complete disbelief as she pushed others out of her way and threw the main door open, looking like someone was chasing her.

Those she pushed past looked back to see what in the world was going on, and didn't do anything but stare at Destan with contempt and scrutiny. But it wasn't his fault! Was it?

Callimay had looked to him for protection this whole time, and when he had finally fit that one piece of the puzzle together, she rejected it. He wanted to try to give the benefit of the doubt; but with her utter refusal how could he even think of going after her? What else could he say or do to make her see he was trying to help?

Unseen this whole time, Toreon lurked on the deck above and watched this all take place. He was thrilled to see the confrontation between the two of them and the fact Callimay was alone; Destan not appearing to care and go after her. He went in search of and found his entourage, immediately leaving to find her.

ℬ

Destan's frustration and anger were hard for him to contain at this point. This made no sense to him at all. He stormed out and took off toward the northern portion of the complex.

A vicious circle of thoughts began swirling through his mind as he walked down the dimly lit paths which crisscrossed this wooded area of the complex. By his body language alone, you could tell he was angry and unwilling to listen to anyone: his stiff arms shoved deep in his coat pockets, steps firm and quick, and head bowed to hide his fiery gaze from anyone who might walk past. Though, if he did meet anyone, he might run them over due to him not watching where he was going.

He looked up when the lighting and noises around him changed. In front of him was a small lake. The dim moonlight flickered off the rippling water, and at its brightest points, burst like the gleam of a diamond in the sun. A slight fog set along the far bank, giving an extra glow to the area from the moon's rays. The soft and repetitive mutter of the water hushed the other sounds around.

Something about seeing this body of water made him stop and stare. His expression looked like he was seeing something impossible: his eyes so wide and full of fear. Or was it shock?

As he stood there, a slight breeze kicked up an ever-familiar smell. It was carried from across the lake and gently surrounded him; him now changing his expression and body language. His arms were less rigid as he pulled his clenched fists out of his pockets.

Destan fell to his hands and knees and kept muttering while he gritted his teeth, "Why her?"

ℬ

When Callimay left, she took off for the largest labyrinth garden. She had been through there so many times she had the shortest path to the center memorized. The crunching sound of the gravel beneath her feet mimicked the feeling of being devastated and crushed inside. The tall and well-manicured shrubs resembled the strictness and formality of authority others had over her; showing the predetermined path she was allowed to take. Yet, the farther you got into the labyrinth, vines began creeping out and soon enveloped the shrubs to show the treacherous nature and true lack of care this authority had. The darkness present from the height of the shrubs instantly reminded her of her ever-present loneliness. Occasional fallen blossoms which were wilting reminded her of how fragile everything was: how even the smallest change in wind or weather — circumstance — could devastate someone... if they allowed it. This last little bit seemed to fade from Callimay's memory.

When she got to the center, she glanced around and looked at the fence of shrubs which surrounded her. They all seemed to have their backs turned to her. It was as if they would invite ones in, but once they were in, there was no concern or guidance given.

She walked to a bench by the small water fountain which had been drained for the winter. Callimay's knees gave out, her falling beside it and convulsing from sobbing and wailing; getting out in broken repetition, "Why Destan?"

Her head began to pound from her crying so much, but the pain inside was greater and needed to be let out. She wanted so much to be comforted, but who was there willing to do it or be honest about it? Callimay clutched the necklace she was wearing to the point her hands were stark white and red.

After she was there a while, she was able to calm herself to a gentle cry. She looked at her hand since she could feel the pendant "peel away" from her skin. Seeing the indent it left reminded Callimay: no matter what she did, people were going to leave an impression on her heart. She had to control how much it affected her… and if it was going to be a good or bad thing.

It was silent in this innocent-looking prison; only the soft sound of a breeze through the shrubs being heard. This made it quite easy for her to hear footsteps on the gravel path in the inner portion of the labyrinth. She then heard whispers but couldn't distinguish who it was.

Callimay got up and crept toward the opening, her stuttering voice showing her fear, "Who's there?"

More gravel shuffled from footsteps, but no answer.

"I know you're there."

"Well it took you long enough to figure that out," the cringe worthy voice laughed. "I've known you were here the whole time."

"Toreon!" Callimay shrieked as she froze with fear.

He stepped out, accompanied by his usual entourage of Webb and Dakoe. The look in his eye made Callimay desperate and helpless. Who was going to save her from this wild person standing in front of her?

She had to work harder than she ever had before to get her legs to move. When she did, she took off in the opposite direction.

Unfortunately, the way the labyrinth gardens were constructed, you couldn't skip through them. — Well, that is unless you wanted to shred your clothes and skin. — You had to know exactly where you were and or you would for sure be walking around in circles. In Callimay's case, she could not afford to get lost. Toreon was no fool. He knew his way around the labyrinth as well as she did. He wouldn't have followed her in if he wasn't able to get through it fast enough.

The sound of the gravel beneath her feet rung out so loud: *Even if he does forget where to go, he can follow the commotion I'm making. If I could only outrun the noise I'm making!*

As she got toward the outer rim, she forgot which way to turn! Callimay looked around her, her face looking frantic and panic setting in, "Oh no!"

"Lost my little plaything? Why did you stop?"

She looked up and saw which side the moon was on and finally remembered which way to go. The only thing was: when she started off again, she felt someone grab her shoulder. She screamed as she tried to pull away.

Toreon had a strong hold on her as he turned her around. She slapped him in the face and screamed again. He was stunned by what she did, but instead of loosening his grip he tightened it.

While she kept trying to pull away, she heard something ripping. Somehow she got free and instantly took off.

By now, she was in the large, open area surrounding the labyrinth. Callimay wanted to relax, but knew she was even more vulnerable at this point. The cold night breeze began to pick up, her now aware that where Toreon had grabbed her shirt was ripped. She frantically began looking around for somewhere she could go to for immediate cover and protection. Her dorm would be the best, but Toreon was between her and it. And to add to the cruel turn of events, he had her name tag. Now he would be able to get in without any questions while she would be locked out.

The only promising lead was the foot of the path leading up to Lookout Point. It was somewhat wooded. She ran as fast as she could across the open area, calling out for help every few seconds.

This whole time, Toreon kept answering her calls to toy with her.

Callimay was getting to the point she could barely keep going, but hearing his voice gave her reason enough to forge ahead. She leaned against a tree every so often to catch her breath and then continued up the hill for as long as she could.

There was the railing! This mad dash was over; she was at Lookout Point. She took a deep breath and turned, but shrieked: Toreon and the others were right there! Callimay felt like a rabbit cornered by wolves.

Destan! She cried as she screamed.

"What is the big fuss?" Toreon asked, trying to hide the fiendish smile he knew had to be on his face. "I just wanted to say hi and talk with you. And what do you do without any cause or giving me a chance to explain? You slap me."

She begged as she inched back toward the railing, "Please."

"Please, what?"

"Please leave me alone, Toreon. I don't want to cause any trouble." She continued as she looked back at the huge drop-off, finishing: *Destan, I know this hasn't worked since the first time, but if you are close enough to hear me: I need you! I'm sorry about earlier. Please don't leave. Please, Destan!*

"Why would I want to leave my girl alone? And why would I think she is trouble? That would be rude… like what Destan did earlier: trying to do what he wanted when you didn't want to do it. I agree, what he did was totally uncalled for and you did the right thing by leaving and waiting for me to find you."

Callimay screamed, tears starting to streak down her face, *Destan I'm begging you: please listen to me! Destan!*

But the problem was: he was a good three miles or so away from Lookout Point. Callimay obviously had no clue of this and kept trying even though there was no way her ability could reach him even if he wanted to hear her. At this point, she was against the rail; heart pounding from the danger in front of her as well as lurking at the base of what was behind her.

"Oh come on. Let's cut to the chase." Webb rolled his eyes.

"Shut it! How many times do I have to say—"

"What are you really here for, Toreon?" Callimay shuddered as she grabbed her arm.

"Like I said: I just wanted to say hi."

"Why chase me? Why grab me? Why toy w— why!" She screeched as she threw her fists to her sides and shook them.

Dakoe said as his eyes began to dart, "If we hang out here much longer with her carrying on like this, someone is bound to notice."

"Oh, I know how to make her quiet down," Toreon answered as he grabbed her wrists. "This is easy."

"Never!" Callimay jerked away from his grasp.

She lost her balance and fell over the railing, grasping to hold onto it but missing. Dakoe rushed up to grab her, but Toreon held him back.

Callimay screamed as she focused harder than ever before: *Destan! Help me!*

ℬ

He heard what sounded like faint screams, but the owls and such were out so it could have been them. So, he ignored it. The smell which had come on the breeze was now gone and Destan noticed it was getting very late, so he turned and began to head back. He looked calmer: he wasn't so rigid and his pace was more of a stroll.

Those faint shrieking noises came back, but he wasn't sure what he was hearing… until he heard Callimay's voice in his head.

"Calli!" He called out as he started running.

The leaves were all but down from the trees, so he was able to look around to see where she was. He questioned what was going on as he roughly judged the distance between them: *How in the world am I able to hear you?*

Destan was still about a half-mile away when he saw Callimay fall over the edge. Hearing her scream in his head like she did sent chills to his bones, almost to the point it paralyzed him. He wanted to save her, but how in the world was he going to get there in time! His mind knew it was useless but his heart couldn't give up.

There wasn't any time to lose. He broke free of these paralyzing emotions and ran.

Her fall was broken by a large branch, causing her to become limp and stop screaming, "No! I can't lose you too!"

Not but a moment later, things slowed down… or he was speeding up. Destan was covering more ground with each stride and it seemed as if Callimay were falling slower. He was worried, but was able to clear the small river without any trouble when he got to it.

For some reason it dawned on him: he had no idea how in the world he was able to do what he was doing. And then with his emotions the way they were, he couldn't think straight enough to figure out how to stop. What was he supposed to do?

144

In desperation, he threw his arms out and lunged forward; digging into the ground as he launched. He wanted to yell out, but it was hard enough for him to breathe. … And what would that do anyway?

Destan caught Callimay — just before she hit the ground — but this wasn't going to be a pretty landing. He did his best to shelter her and take the brunt of the fall; wrapping her in his arms as tight and fast as he could as he turned himself so he'd hit the ground first.

When they stopped tumbling, there was a brief moment where time felt like it stop. Destan was out of breath and about scared to death with what almost happened and what did. Callimay was in his sure grasp but she felt like a ragdoll: limp and lifeless. Her skin was ice-cold to the touch and her complexion was practically white. He could feel her warm breath on his neck, but something wasn't right; he knew that.

For the first few seconds, he lay there trying to catch his breath and let his mind catch up with the rest of his body.

After taking a deep and shaky breath, he rolled to his side and laid her on the ground as soft as he knew how.

"Calli? Please. You've got to be alright." Destan begged as he rubbed the side of her face with his quivering hand. "I can't have come so close and messed up again. I can't bear to lose— Calli, please! Wake up!"

He looked up and saw movement: the three perpetrators peering over the railing. It was no surprise to see who was responsible. Destan couldn't understand what they were saying, but by their reactions he knew they were in self- preservation mode and not about to see if she'd survived. Filled with rage, he turned his attention to Toreon. His anger was clouding his thoughts, preventing him from hearing Callimay.

After a few moments of no response or acknowledgement, Callimay gasped, *He's not listening to me!* "Destan, please. I just had the wind knocked out of me. Destan! Come back! Don't do this!"

Unsure how he harnessed this ability, he relied solely on his natural running capability to catch up with Toreon.

Callimay's head was still pounding, but the only thing she could think to do was to try to "talk" to him. It was successful once before — that she knew of. Maybe it would be different this time? It had to! Since she was already in so much pain and he was running so fast, she knew there was a short window of opportunity for her to reach him.

Even amid his anger and rage, he heard her pleading voice: *Please don't leave me Destan. Doing to them what they almost let happen to me won't fix anything. This is all my fault. I should have never done what I did. I'm sorry! I wasn't trying to pay you back; you've been so wonderful to me. Please forgive me and come back. I need you. Please don't do this! Destan I'm sorry!*

Hearing those words and her sorrowful tone completely disarmed him. He somehow stopped, dropping to his knees and heaving from being out of breath. His whole body began to tremble; him terrified with how out of control his rage was and what thoughts he was letting take root in his mind.

Once he got up, he jogged back to Callimay who still looked like she was unconscious. Her uniform was snagged, ripped, and torn; a few blood stains from when she hit the tree … he hoped. She had gashes in her right arm and leg and a deep cut in her right cheek.

As Destan kneeled next to her, she opened her eyes and answered his silent questions so sweetly, "I'm okay. In light of what could have happened I'm doing really well. — I… I'm sorry about earlier. I was cutting you off when you saw I needed your help. This is all my fault, so don't blame yourself. You didn't do anything wrong."

He cradled her in his arms, his body letting out one large shiver as he sighed heavy, "Oh Callimay."

"I just…" she tried her best to explain as she began to cry. "After what Mr. Freigh said about those not doing well getting kicked out, I couldn't help but think it would happen to myself or you… or both of us; and I'd never get to see you again. I've already lost someone I love—in fact the only person in this world I loved. I don't want to feel the pain again by losing you, Destan. With what he said, I began to shut down and cut everything off; preparing myself for the inevitable reality I thought was coming. I let thoughts keep circling in my mind and clouding what reality was. I was forgetting to enjoy what I had now. … In that state it seemed like the logical thing to do to help keep my sanity; when in fact it was driving me insane. I'm starting to remember what you did earlier and I regret everything I did and didn't do or say. I ended up rejecting the one person who was willing to protect me and left myself out in the open, practically begging for what happened. I've made a mess of everything. I shouldn't jump to conclusions like I did tonight. … In my selfish pity party I neglected to think of you and what you needed. I know you're hurting, Destan. I know something deep inside you is causing you horrible pain. And by me doing what I did, I know I've damaged the trust you have in me. I know there were and are areas our trust hasn't shown, but what we had I treasured. What little ways you showed your trust in me meant the world to me. I know I've lost some if not all of it. I'm so sorry."

Destan held her closer and closer as she begged for forgiveness; and realized at the end, despite his lack of emotional "involvement" in their friendship, she still cared for him. And it was on a deeper level than he could have ever imagined. It wasn't what she could gain that she desired, but what she could do for and give to him.

Hearing her say why she acted the way she did reminded him so much of himself. He felt miserable for reacting the way he always had in some situations, whereas Callimay has for so long pushed through and kept going. She was working to keep others above herself, and in doing so made herself feel better. The only thing was, she was running on empty and starting to panic; trying in desperation to figure out how to fix everything when it didn't need to be fixed… and the fact there wouldn't be anything she could do if it did need fixing. How could he continue to treat a heart like this with such coldness?

He was trying to understand how the little moments they spent together meant the world to her. How nothing flamboyant or romantic had to be done to show affection to her. And furthermore, those little things showed his trust in her.

It wasn't news to him that things could and should be so much better; but it was getting to this point he struggled with. Now knowing how she felt made him feel a bit more open to admitting to himself how even he felt about her… as well as more willing to do what he knew he needed to so he could keep her safe and make her feel he trusted her.

"I wish I could have done more," he said defeated as he continued to hold her, tears beginning to well in his eyes. "I'm sorry I took from you for so long without giving anything back."

"Destan." Callimay corrected as she looked him in the eye. "You saved my life. What more could I ask for? What have you taken?"

"I haven't been there for— I should've gone after you. I should've tried harder to remind you that I was here for you and never leaving. I should've stopped everything from coming to this. I—"

"Calm down. I told you none of this was your fault. I was the one who flipped out. You were trying everything you could. You had no idea what I was thinking about."

"I knew enough," he admitted in a mumble as he looked away.

"What do you mean?"

"You're ice-cold," Destan drastically changed the subject as he felt her hand and saw her shivering. "First I need to get you inside where I can tend to those wounds and get you warmed up. Umm… here. Put this on for now. — I promise Callimay. I'll answer your question when we get there. Alright?"

"Okay. But I don't want you to freeze to death."

"I won't. I promise. … What in the world ha— what did he do?" Destan asked in a dead-serious tone when he saw her shirt.

"I promise I'm alright. I was actually the one who did it." Callimay replied rather weak as she put his coat on and began to get up. "Would you mind it very much if we take it easy? I don't k—"

"Hold on. You took a nasty fall even with me catching you. I don't want to risk you getting hurt any more than you are. Are you alright if I carry you?"

She was stunned by his offer and sat there staring at him for a good minute; then replied, "It's such a long way. I could walk until I get tired so I'm not burdening you. You've got some scratches on your face."

Oh Calli. Destan sighed and then finished in a tone which sounded so tender, "It's not very far and you are in no way a burden to me, Callimay. We'll stop at the rec complex for some first-aid supplies and I'll grab your coat. These scratches are nothing. I'm fine."

"Alright then."

He picked her up, making sure he wasn't near any of her injuries, and began walking back. It didn't take Callimay long to slip her arms around his neck and curl her head in toward his chest. The initial feel of her ice-cold hands against his neck startled him.

"I'm sorry!" She exclaimed, jerking her hands away. "I w—"

"You're fine. Your hands are cold and I just wasn't expecting it."

For the first little while there was no sound; not even the call of a night owl. Nothing but the calmed air that only comes after a violent storm. Callimay was able to rest and not worry about anything, and so she was starting to notice her wounds from the stings of pain she would feel from the cold late fall wind hitting them. Strangely enough though, the pain she was expecting to feel was gone. Her migraine vanished. It was horrible, especially after she "talked" with Destan to keep him from doing something they would both regret, but now it was gone and she couldn't remember when or understand why it stopped.

Destan was in a bit of shock from how he was able to open up to Callimay so easily about such "sensitive" things. It might not appear to the average person what he did was much… if anything. But, for him, it was a major step. And the fact he offered to and was carrying her brought back painful memories he had to fight through. The last time he carried someone… he didn't make it to them in time.

It was hard for him to process all those emotions, but then something happened. The wind kicked up and blew some of Callimay's hair in his face. It was only for a moment, but it helped snap him back to reality and away from the painful past. The smell of her perfume was something Destan instantly recognized and enjoyed the light scent of because it meant she was close enough he could smell it. It reminded him of her personality: light and cheerful; never overpowering or forceful — what he so deeply cherished about her.

A moment later, she realized her hair was flying around, so she did her best to corral it and stuff it inside the coat. She glanced up and saw the small smile on Destan's face she remembered from when they met. Seeing it helped her even more.

"Do you mind if I ask you a question?" Callimay asked rather timid as she fiddled with her cardigan.

"Not at all," he responded, his small smile vanishing.

"Were you ever in track and field?"

"No. Why?"

"You were, well… sprinting when you were going after Toreon and the others. I was only wondering if maybe you were—"

"Oh. About that." He laughed a little; taking this question and answer very light-hearted. "I guess I 'do' have an ability."

"What! You mean that wasn't 'you' running?"

"Nope. — Now don't get me wrong, I run quite a bit, but the pace I was moving at was unbelievable. It wasn't anything I could ever do by myself. … When I heard you scream for me and saw you fall, it's like something clicked in my brain. The next second everything around me was going in slow motion. I'll admit though, when I went after those three something was different. Something wasn't, well… right. You remember when you ran your bike into that tree a while back?"

"Yes."

"I now understand what you meant by you 'zoned out': narrow and focused vision on what I was running toward. I was so angry at Toreon. Making him pay for what he did was all I could think of, nothing else seemed to matter but to get revenge." Destan admitted as he stared off into the distance.

"I was wondering what was going on. I tried to call out to you but it's like you didn't even know I was saying anything."

"Only because you got through to me did I think of stopping," he looked down to her, that small smile creeping back on his face. "You're getting good at it. I've heard you once this afternoon and three times tonight now."

"It's so strange it's working now. I'm not exact— this afternoon? What do you mean by that?"

"That's what I was going to talk about when we made it back."

"I'm sorry."

"You're fine. Don't worry. … How about you relax for a bit? We'll talk more about this once we get back."

There were a few moments of silence before Callimay asked, "Just one more question… please?"

Destan looked deep in thought, but answered, "Alright."

"Why, how, and when did we get these abilities?" She asked rather scared as she clung tighter to him. "What in the name of— what's happening to us?"

"I don't know if I have those answers, Callimay. I'm sorry." He answered somewhat rushed as he shifted his grip and kept going.

"If you need me—"

"Just rest. Okay? I'm fine."

Callimay felt safe around Destan — there was no doubt about that — but something was different. It felt like he was in a different type of protective mode than before; as if he wasn't going to let one single person or thing hurt her ever again. The reason this switch happened was left to her imagination: him finding out he had an ability, her close brush with death, that she reminded him of someone from his past, or his complete disdain for Toreon. Maybe a combo of all the above?

Whatever the reasoning, she was glad to have someone willing to fight for her; to know she wasn't alone. She tightened her grip and curled closer as these thoughts ran through her mind.

"Are you alright Callimay?"

"Yes. Yes I'm fine Destan."

ℬ

By the time they made it back, everyone had left for the night; which was of no surprise since it was after midnight. Destan took her in and found supplies to clean and dress her wounds.

Feeling the warm, rough skin of his hands against hers gave Callimay chills. It was so strange she felt the way she did, but she wasn't going to say a word about it. He stopped and asked if she was still cold, but she assured him she was fine.

"I'm no doctor, so you need to see someone to make sure you don't have internal injuries you don't notice right now," he commented as he continued to wrap her arm. "Plus, these dressings won't be what you'll need long-term. I'll see about contacting the scheduler for Mr. Freigh and Mr. Willgun in the morning to see what can be done."

Callimay was sad this all had to happen, yet she was overjoyed to see the tender side of Destan for so long. His eyes were so soft, his touch so gentle — yet strong — and his tone… it made her sigh: *How are you so good at hiding this side of you? And why?* "I appreciate this all so much, Destan. I don't want you to think you owe me some debt. I am the one indebted to you."

"Remember: you aren't a burden to me. I'm doing this because I want to." He reminded as he paused and looked to her, then changed the subject as he diverted his attention to her cheek, "I… I don't know, Callimay. This one may need stitches."

"You really think so?" She asked as she attempted to touch it; and then winced, "Ah!"

"I'll do what I can to keep it clean for tonight, but if any of your wounds need special attention it would be the one," Destan remarked, sounding uneasy as he began to clean the area. "I really don't want to hurt you. Here. Why don't you do it."

"Alright," Callimay took the cloth, trying not to smile too much.

ℬ

While she finished taking care of the cut on her cheek, he went and got her coat. As he turned to walk back, something in his peripheral caught his attention. He looked over and saw Toreon and Baleck outside the main school building. As if a knee-jerk reaction, Destan jumped back into the shadows and away from their direct vision: *How did he get in touch with him? It's not like Mr. Willgun walks around the complex this late at night for anyone to talk to. At least I've never seen him do it. Faculty is always in their residences by ten so there's no way Toreon could have contacted the scheduler.*

Destan stood there, out of sight, until the two parted ways. Toreon appeared to hand some kind of cloth to Baleck and pointed out toward the direction of Lookout Point. Nothing suspicious seemed to be in how Baleck was acting, though Toreon looked frightened… which was out of character for him. They eventually stopped talking, him heading to the dorm while Baleck went in the direction he pointed. Destan knew something was up, so he followed — waiting though for him to have a sizable lead.

He kept hidden, but where he could see. Baleck didn't go to Lookout Point but rather took the base path. Destan was able to stay closer now since they were in the wooded area but was careful to hang back.

Baleck stopped on the path just below Lookout Point and began to survey the area where Callimay would have fallen. He took out a flashlight and started looking for something… but what? He didn't spend much time before he took his phone out. Destan couldn't catch everything, but what he did was enough to convince him.

"There's no sign of Callimay," Baleck remarked, bending down to have a closer look at the ground. "I can see footprints in the softer areas, but they will need to be analyzed to know if it was indeed Destan. … If he has, then we need to get the two of them in soon. We can't have them using these abilities as toys or conveniences. They need to be taught there is a purpose and mission for their new gifts."

So I was right. How could you? Destan fumed as he dragged his fingers across the tree bark.

Destan heard enough at this point. He didn't appear a bit nervous as he left; and yet he watched his back while he ran.

֍

Seeing her coat that he'd tossed on the floor reminded him what he'd come out to the front for in the first place. It'd be a dead giveaway if he went back empty-handed. As he rounded the corner, he tried not to sound winded or upset, "Well it was easy to find. Warmed up some?"

"I'd hope it would be, and I am, thank you," Callimay said, trying to smile but stopping because of the cut on her cheek. "Ouch! Well this isn't gonna be fun at all. Let alone easy. Not smiling for a while will be difficult for me to remember."

"You said 'you' were the one who ripped your shirt. So I assume you know what happened; and when?" Destan gestured as he double-checked the dressings.

"Well… it's complicated."

"Try me."

"I was running through the large labyrinth to get away from Toreon when he reached out and grabbed me. I slapped his face and pulled away… I still don't know how I got free." She tried to explain as she did her best to cover her shoulder; shying away from his gaze that was piercing now. "When I got ou—"

"That jerk!" He gritted his teeth as he jumped up. "I swear I—"

"Destan." She calmed as she reached out toward him.

"He didn't do anything else, did he?"

"Other than this, no. I could tell by the way he— n… never mind. Nothing happened, Destan. I'm fine." Callimay shook her head, trying to forget everything.

"Does he have your key?" He mumbled, sounding a bit calmer.

"Yes."

"Do you have your pass card?"

"Umm, well… I've always had a knack for losing keys so I was nervous about carrying it and decided to leave it in my room. Come to think of it, I guess it isn't a smart place to keep it, huh?"

"If he has your key then you won't be safe going back to your room tonight anyway — I don't know why I asked in the first place. I'll sleep in the lounge area of my dorm so you can stay in my room." Destan paused when he saw the stunned look on her face. "I mean… that is if you are alright with it. I just don't know where else to take you so you'll be safe for the night."

"You're right. I can't go back even if I did have my pass card. … This is such a mess. Ugh! — I don't want to kick you out of your room just beca—"

"You're not, Callimay." Destan reminded as he picked up the supplies and headed to put them away. "I'm the one offering, so that means I'm alright with it."

"Okay then," she nodded as she put her coat on.

"I'll let the scheduler know about him having your key so they can deactivate it and make a new one." He tossed his coat over his back in a somewhat strange fashion, slipping his arms in the sleeves in one fluid motion. "I don't want you going back until it's fixed."

"A… alright," Callimay said shocked as he picked her up.

"Are you feeling better?"

"Much. Thank you." She leaned her head on his shoulder. "So… about what I asked earlier?"

"Oh yes. — When Mr. Freigh was speaking this afternoon, I heard you talking about how you were frustrated with people who weren't doing the right things were the ones rewarded."

"You did! That's so strange."

"Maybe so, but what's really strange to me is how you were able to reach me tonight while I was over a half-mile away from Lookout Point. That type of distance never worked before."

"You were how far!"

"Over a half-mile as close as I can figure. Maybe three-quarters."

"That's never worked before!"

"I know. … Do you maybe think it only works when you are under quite a bit of emotional distress? That's the only thing I can think of being related to each incident."

"It's possible. … This is all so much to take in."

"I'm sorry about d—"

"It's alright. It's just crazy how so much has happened today."

And you don't know the half of it. Destan sighed; flinching when he realized she could hear what he said if she wanted.

ക

As Destan got to the door and it unlocked, he put his face near the window and glanced around in the front common area. The marble floor made walking quiet about impossible, but he somehow managed to be whisper-silent. In a strange turn of events, he was the one holding on tight as he crept along.

Most of the room lights in the immediate vicinity were off and no one was out of their rooms. Destan whipped his head around, focusing on the ones with lights on — looking like he was trying to listen for voices. A few seconds later, he heard a couple so he dashed over and shoved the door to the stairs open.

Oddly enough, Destan calmed and walked into the hall on the third floor without checking to see if anyone was near. His grip on Callimay softened and he strolled to the far corner where his room was. Granted there wasn't one light on in any room, but still.

She tried to tell him she was well enough to walk around the room, but he refused and set her on the bed. While she took her coat off, he pulled the curtain back and looked out, seeing Baleck walking back, "What's wrong, Destan?"

"Nothing you need to worry about."

"Thank you for all this. I don't know how I can ever repay you."

"Don't worry about it. I'm glad to help. … I'm just down the hall. If you need me for anything, please don't wait or hesitate. Even if you're not sure, call for me anyway."

"I promise."

"Are you sure you're comfortable?"

"I'm sure. Get some rest, Destan. Thank you again."

"You need rest more." He commented as he opened the door; and then finished quiet and slow as he glanced back over his shoulder, "G… goodnight, Callimay."

"Goodnight Destan."

❦

He lay there for a while and stared at the ceiling, everything still running through his mind at the speed his ability now allowed his entire body to. It was hard for him to put all the pieces together. Destan had so many of them, but there were major holes left which needed to be filled to understand everything.

Tomorrow was going to be interesting — to say the least — in light of what Baleck told Mr. Freigh on the phone and what Destan had already made plans for: *I'm not telling her we're not going. She needs to be checked. But how am I going to watch her and…*

Knowing he would need to be focused and as observant as possible, he did his best to stop thinking about everything after a few minutes and get some sleep. He rolled his coat up to use as a pillow and settled down. Since Callimay wore it, her perfume was on, in, and all around it. He sighed as he closed his eyes: *I will protect you, Calli. I promise.*

~ 16 ~

As the first glowing rays of sunlight poured into the lounge, Destan jumped up and headed back to his room. He knocked and waited for a minute, but didn't hear anything. After knocking a second time and still nothing, he threw the door open and saw his bed made… Callimay nowhere to be seen.

The first thing that ran through his mind was that faculty had taken her, "Calli? Calli, where are you!"

"I'm right here. It's alright." She came up behind him and laid her hand on his arm.

"What are you doing up?" Destan asked in a raised tone, his eyes still darting around in fear.

"I wasn't sure when you were coming back so I got up early to try to clean up a bit."

"Don't scare me like that again." He sighed as he put his arms around her.

"I'm sorry. I didn't mean to scare— what did you call me?"

"I. Uh…" he stammered as he stepped back, scratching his already messy hair.

"It's alright. Sometimes things jump out of my mouth too." Callimay smiled as she patted his arm.

Destan walked over to the sofa and sat down. After a few moments, he looked up as she hobbled over, "Callimay?"

"What's wrong?" She asked worried, noting the sudden shift in his voice — concern to serious.

"I need you to listen to me for a little bit, okay? Just remember: I'm not leaving. I 'will' protect you."

158

"O… kay," she sounded shaky as she followed his nonverbal cue to sit beside him.

"Something happened last night which has me concerned about what I'd planned to do today. … When you asked me if something was wrong last night? I saw Mr. Willgun walking back from Lookout Point. Yeah, that might seem trivial, but I saw him earlier when I went to get your coat. Toreon spoke with him outside the main school building. He handed something that looked like a piece of cloth to Mr. Willgun. I have my suspicions it was your key, but I can't say for sure. Then before he left, Toreon pointed toward Lookout Point. — The jerk wasn't even concerned as he went back to the dorm. — Mr. Willgun then headed out. I gave him a good start before I followed to find out what was going on. He went to the base of Lookout Point and poked around before he called Mr. Freigh. From what I gathered, they're the ones who gave us our abilities… and they're looking to control us. The way he worded things, it sounds like they already know you've discovered yours; but weren't sure if I had discovered mine. He mentioned that they needed to get us in soon — whatever that may mean. I probably should have, but didn't hang around after hearing that. I didn't want to leave you alone any longer." Destan explained in a serious but calm tone, his eyes set on her the entire time, never wavering. "Maybe I didn't word it all in a clear way, and I can understand you being confused; but none of this changes what I told you last night. I need to take you in to make sure you're alright. But I also wanted you to know what is going on. I would've said something last night, but with— I didn't want to put you through any more stress than you had. … They have no idea I know any of this; at least I don't think so. And there aren't any security cameras for the dorms and there's no one in the rooms around me, so we're fine talking about it. … I've had my own suspicions for a while, and even though I don't understand 'every'thing I do know that what this society is— it's a cover. Believe it or not, what you said is right: they don't care. They want those who are selfish to consume everyone who won't stand up to them. They're doing this on purpose to find people like us, Callimay. For whatever reason, they need people who care and aren't afraid to sacrifice their own standing with others to make sure the right thing is done. I can't continue with my theories because I don't have tangible proof yet. … I know this is a bombshell. I get it. But I need you to be strong for me, Callimay. I need you to be who you truly are. I need you to push ahead and not look back. I know I haven't shown it much to you, but please believe me when I say I am working every moment to make things better. I need you to trust me and know I trust you. I don't know what is going to happen today but I need you to understand what's going on."

As Destan spoke, the worried look on her face turned to fear. She couldn't understand why they would be doing this. Callimay wanted to lock herself away and not deal with it. Tears began to stream down her exhausted face, her eyes gazing so full of awe at his words. She was scared, but she also had full assurance he meant what he said when he promised he would never leave her.

Destan was always very purposeful with his choice in words, but there was something extra about his tone and voice when he spoke about protecting her. She wanted to think she knew what it was, but why think of something and build yourself up just to be let down if it isn't the case?

He sat there and gave Callimay time to process it all. Destan could tell she was fearful by the way her hands shook, but he could see the courage in her eyes that was fighting to say she wasn't going to give into the fear. And it was plain to see the joyful shock which also rested in her eyes. Even he was stunned. Things would not be silky smooth on so many fronts, he knew this; but this was not going to scare him away from what he said. He was committing to trying harder each day and asking for her help.

Callimay took a deep breath, wiped the tears away, and answered, "When do we go?"

"Right now. Since it's Saturday and so early, everyone will still be in their rooms. — Now I am just making this suggestion. I will leave it up to you. I would much rather you let me carry you. I don't want you risking getting hurt, and it will give us an upper hand by having an element of surprise."

"An upper hand? How? Element of surprise?"

"They won't be expecting you to focus and use your ability if they think you're hurt. They would be more likely to focus on making sure you are alright and not on our abilities so I can see if there is anything in Mr. Freigh's office to help explain what's going on."

"That would be a huge risk!"

"It would, but we need to know why they did this and what their intentions are… and not while they are paying attention. Don't worry though. If I find something or things just don't feel safe, I'll get you out of there."

"I… I see what you're saying," she nodded as she wrung her hands. "But at the same time— we're not spies, Destan. What if they find you snooping around?"

"If I don't find anything within a minute or so I'll come back. You can be my lookout of sorts to let me know if something's going on where you are. — I promise you'll be alright. … So, are you walking or am I carrying you?"

"Oh, Destan." She wrapped her arms across her chest and began to quiver. "I don't know now. I…"

"Callimay." He kneeled in front of her, his voice sounding soft again. "I'm not going to be by myself in the room or blind to what is going on where you are. You can get to me if you need to. You know that now. I'm always listening. I promise."

"I know. I just don't want to risk losing you."

"I don't want to risk losing you either. With our abilities though, things are going to be risky, one way or another." Destan took her hands. "But we're a team, you and I. We're in this together. I'm not leaving you. Nothing would ever make me do that Callimay. Ready?"

She paused for a few seconds, and then answered, "Yes."

"How do you want to do this?"

"We'll do it your way."

❧

Callimay's heart was pounding as Destan carried her. She was terrified knowing all she did and wasn't quite sure she was going to be able to help him the way he needed her to. Even he was on edge, regardless of him trying his best to stay calm.

When they got to the main school building, they saw Mr. Freigh walking up the far side hall. He didn't see them at first, but jogged up and threw the front door open the moment he did. His voice was just as sporadic as his words, "For the— how can I h— what happened!"

"Callimay took a tumble over Lookout Point last night."

"How far did she fall?"

"I was thankfully able to make it to her in time before she hit the ground," Destan explained as Mr. Freigh all but ran down the hall ahead of them. "I'm glad I caught you. I wasn't sure if any faculty would be here or not."

"I am glad I decided to come in today. Is she doing alright?"

"Yes sir," Callimay responded in a quiet and calm manner.

"It is so good to hear you say that." Mr. Freigh said relieved as he opened the door which led down the winding halls to the offices.

When Destan's key got within range, an alarm sounded. He tensed up as he looked around, expecting people to come out and grab them; going so far as throwing his back against the wall to guard against what might happen. Callimay clung to him, afraid of what was going happen. Mr. Freigh motioned for him to move back, after which the alarm shut off.

"I forgot," he almost yelled, still disoriented from the blaring alarm. "You are not allowed in unless I unlock your key access. Just give me a moment... there. I hope it did not startle you too much. I apologize."

"We're fine." Destan nodded, seeming to be perfectly calm on the outside but Callimay knowing he was even more on edge internally.

"If you do not mind my asking: how did this happen, Callimay? Did you trip?" Mr. Freigh asked, continuing as if nothing happened. "I only ask to see if we need to change the railing height."

"Toreon chased me up to Lookout Point. As he was trying to grab my wrists, I pulled away and lost my balance." She summed up as she felt Destan's grip on her getting tighter and tighter.

Mr. Freigh sighed and shook his head as he continued on.

When he stopped and turned, Destan said, "I did what I could, but I know she needs to be looked at. She hit a branch at one point."

"I will have you two go in here while I make a quick phone call."

"Thank you," Callimay answered.

Mr. Freigh ushered as he opened the door, "Both of your keys have access to all the doors in this area, so if either of you need anything you can come into my office through the door there. I will be in a bit later to see how she is doing."

𝕭

Destan was still tense and nervous as he walked in. It looked like any standard medical exam room, but something didn't feel right to him. It was as if he'd been here before. He laid Callimay on the bed and made sure she was comfortable, then looked around for a moment.

She was just about to ask what he was looking for, and then realized what was going on. As if trying to get back to her as fast as he could, he flew over to where there was a chair. Destan snatched it up as he raced back and set it as close as he could get it to her. After sitting, he looked around once more and then settled down.

Then there was an awkward silence, similar to when a conversation runs out of gas. Callimay wanted to say something, but she wasn't sure if he would talk with her. She rubbed her cardigan sweater between her fingers and rolled her head over to look away from him, still trying to keep herself together and not wanting him to see her cry.

Not but a second after she did that though, she felt him put his hand on her shoulder and heard the caring tone in his now soft voice: *What's wrong, Callimay?*

"I'm fine."

I'm not taking any chances talking out loud. He scolded as his eyes began to flash.

Oh. Okay. I understand.

So, you've figured it out?

I can't say for sure; but it's like something clicked last night and I just can. But I don't know how I'm doing it or if it's something I 'can' turn on and off. — Destan! I can hear Mr. Freigh.

Easy. It's okay. What is he saying?

H… how can he see us?

He casually looked around, *There's a one-way window behind us.*

The alarm about scared me to death. She sounded nervous.

You wouldn't be the only one.

I'm starting to think we're in over our heads, Destan. She started sounding frantic. *We really have no idea what we're doing!*

Don't worry, Callimay. Everything is going to be fine.

If you say. But why would the alarm sound? Whenever someone has tried before it didn't do anything… it just wouldn't open at all.

Maybe because he had the door opened. Destan theorized as he leaned back in the chair, seeming calm physically on the outside as well as emotionally on the inside. *He did motion for me to step back and it quit the second I did.*

As she usually did, Callimay started wondering: *You know? We probably should say something aloud so they don't get suspicious. You said they are aware of me knowing about my ability.*

You've got a good point. Destan realized, taking a few moments to think before he asked, "Are you feeling alright?"

"I would like some water," she replied, her voice sounding timid.

A quick search of the room proved unfruitful, so Destan said, "I'll go ask Mr. Freigh."

"De—"

"I'll be right back, Callimay," he assured as his eyes softened, seeing the terrified look on her face. "Just rest, alright? I won't be far away and this won't take me but a minute. … Okay?"

She sighed, closing her eyes and looking away again, *I'm scared. I don't think this is going to end well for either of us. Something isn't… something doesn't feel right.*

He opened his mouth to say something — only in regards to her physical reaction since he didn't hear what she said — but stopped short and turned; opening the door to Mr. Freigh's office.

Destan saw Mr. Freigh on the phone. As much as he wanted to know what he was talking about, and who to, he knew he needed to lie low. So, he stepped back and started to close the door. Mr. Freigh though, nodded as he smiled and motioned for him to come in.

"As soon as she is available. … None that I was told. … Thank you. Goodbye." Mr. Freigh finished as he hung up. "What is it, Destan?"

"Callimay was wondering if she could get some water. I didn't see anywhere to get some in there so I thought I would come ask you." He requested as he took surveillance of the room.

Mr. Freigh stood up, pushing some paperwork to the side of the desk, "Oh! Of course. Have a seat. I will get her a glass right now."

He walked over to one of the bookcases and opened it to reveal a drink station. It was so well made to look like the others in the room it made Destan suspicious there might be more hidden things in there than he realized.

"I do want to apologize for your placement on the report card." Mr. Freigh commented as he took a glass off the shelf. "I had spoken with Baleck about updating yours and Toreon's scores after we spoke, but due to other projects I had given to him, he forgot. I am not excusing it, but once they are posted they unfortunately cannot be changed."

"I appreciate your clarifying that." Destan nodded as he glanced down at the desk; noting the two folders Mr. Freigh pushed aside had his and Callimay's names on them.

"I know things have not been the easiest for you. But I want you to know I have been supporting you. I unfortunately have to compile and account for what others see and what they put in for your grades. I have tried time and time again, but they do not see the potential I see. And it seems as if the student body this year does not either."

Callimay? Destan asked abruptly.

What! She responded startled.

Don't drink the water. He's taking too long to get it. I wouldn't trust him to not have put something in it.

Okay, she answered a bit scared.

I— it's alright, Callimay. Destan tried to calm, then said to Mr. Freigh as he followed him, "I wanted to use this opportunity to grow in areas I struggle, but it is becoming apparent this may not be working."

"Why not stay here while I give this to Callimay?" Mr. Freigh suggested as he turned back. "I will be just a second and then we can talk for a moment."

"Very well." He consented, seeing he was going to have a short window to get what he found. *Callimay?*

Yes? She replied startled as Mr. Freigh came in.

Try to keep him in there for a minute. I found something. He instructed as he ran to the desk.

Her voice sounded like it was quivering as she gulped: *O… kay.*

Destan opened their folders and removed all the papers. He wanted to look at them but it didn't sound like poor Callimay was going to be able to buy him much time. There were quite a few papers in each, so leaving them empty wasn't an option. His eyes darted around the room, him grabbing what papers looked insignificant from various places and putting them in the folders so they would appear to be untouched.

As Destan stood there, he realized he forgot what to do as far as concealing what he found. His coat was still in the other room and the amount of papers was too much to inconspicuously hide on his person… let alone the noise they would make. He whipped his head around while looking to find something, and then went to one of the bookcases that held larger books. Destan grabbed the first one he could and shoved the papers toward the back.

It wasn't a moment too soon because Mr. Freigh walked in the second he closed it, "Admiring the books?"

"Do you play chess much?" He brought the book with him, trying his best to act normal as he read what was on the spine.

"I have always seen myself as a mental gamer and not a physical one." Mr. Freigh nodded as he sat down. "What about you, Destan?"

"I was never very good at it. My aggressive style seemed to falter to the enduring tactics of my opponent." He admitted, keeping a firm grip on the book the man sitting across from him was focused on.

"Sometimes brute force is not the most profitable or necessary mode of achieving one's goal. A diplomatic approach is sometimes best suited for the task. … I know you most likely want to be with Callimay, so I will not keep you long. I am sure you remember what I said during the announcement yesterday concerning possible meetings with students like yourself."

"Yes sir."

"I do want to apologize if it felt like I was singling you out. It was not my intention at all. It is the normal speech given to the student body at this time… and it just so happened that portion was going to be more obvious this year than in years past. I apologize."

"I understand." Destan nodded, becoming nervous as Mr. Freigh began moving papers and files on the desk. *He left them out on purpose? ~ You've gotta be— I'm such an id—*

"I wanted to— where are those papers?" *I could have sworn—* "In my older age, I sometimes think I have done things when I have not."

He chuckled as he got into the filing cabinet behind him; looking around for a little while before he found what he was looking for, "Destan? I feel at a bit of a loss as far as how to say this. … Please understand this wasn't a unanimous, quick, or easy decision. … As much as I hate doing this; the meeting we had a month and a half ago when classes were canceled— these are about your options for next semester. You do not have to wait until the date listed to get with me. In fact, whenever you decide and see faculty, let them know you would like to speak with me. I will be sure they know I gave you permission to contact me through them. Though, if you see Baleck or even myself, stop us if you would prefer. The next few weeks are open, so there would be no issues with getting you scheduled in a timely fashion."

He nodded as he accepted the folder, "I appreciate your waiting for a private meeting to tell me and not make matters worse than they already are with everyone else."

Destan, someone's here. Callimay interrupted.

I'm on my way.

Tact was of the utmost importance… that and speed. He opened the file while he slipped the papers out of the book; making it appear he was glancing at the papers. Quite cleaver: camouflaging the sound of him opening the book. He then closed it as he put the papers under it.

Feeling guilty, Mr. Freigh said, "Destan? I— do not worry about the book, I will take it. I would like to do some reading today and it would be a good one for me. … I am sorry about this all. I truly am. I most likely did it at the worst possible moment but— I am sorry."

Ֆ

The younger lady who helped her last time was the one who arrived first. Already knowing her made Callimay relax: *She's very nice and good at what she does, Destan. I think her name's Ginger.*

The young woman, who was indeed Ginger, was confused as to who did the dressings — they were some of the best she'd ever seen — and praised Destan for his skills when she found out it was him.

Callimay flinched a few times as she unwrapped her arm, causing Destan to flinch — even reaching out a couple times when she gasped: *I thought you said she was good at what she did?*

It doesn't hurt much. Really, Dest— ah! … I'm babying myself more than anything. She's not doing it on purpose.

Still.

After she checked the cut on Callimay's face, Ginger worked to find a solution that would avoid a disfiguring scar. She cautioned though, as she explained what she was doing, there was a risk: it could reopen if injured before having a chance to heal, "Just don't do anything crazy for a couple weeks and you should be fine."

Another gentleman wearing scrubs showed up in the next couple minutes, Ginger deferring to him; hinting he must be the doctor.

Destan wasn't happy he had to leave the room when the scan was going to be done, but was reminded by Callimay it was for his protection and he wouldn't be so far away she couldn't reach him.

Unable to have his argument heard and considered, he swallowed his pride and left… though begrudgingly. He stayed right next to the door and talked to her; his tone being critical the whole time. To him, it seemed way too long for what little they ended up doing, but in reality, it wasn't more than fifteen minutes.

Upon being allowed back in the room, Destan sat right next to Callimay, moving the chair back to where he originally had it. She found it sweet how he was reacting: so protective when he wasn't sure or saw she was in pain, while relieved when he understood what he was being told or saw she was smiling.

Mr. Freigh came in for a moment to check on everything just before they left, "How are you doing, Callimay?"

"Just fine. The scan came back alright. — I… wanted to tell you something before I left; if I may."

"What is it?" Mr. Freigh asked as he sat down.

"I lost my key last night… and so I can't get back into my dorm." Callimay stated in a timid voice as she rubbed her arm and stared at her leg. "Toreon has it. I… I don't know if there is any way for you to deactivate my key so he can't use it. It makes me feel really unsafe knowing he has it."

He must have been waiting outside and listening for his name, because how else would his timing be so perfect? These things don't just "happen" in real life. — Baleck walked in, prompting Mr. Freigh to turn his attention and ask, "Oh good. Just in time. Did you happen to bring the key with you?"

"Yes."

"Do you mean this key, Callimay?"

"Why yes!" She exclaimed as she took the missing piece of her uniform in her hand. "Where did you find it?"

"Toreon gave it to me," Baleck informed as he stood at the foot of the bed. "He said it ripped off when he tried to grab you as you fell."

Liar. Callimay fumed as she heard Destan say the same thing; then finished, "I appreciate that I got it back. Thank you."

"You are very welcome." Baleck nodded as he glanced at her and then Destan. "Do you two have plans for the rest of the day?"

I have what we need so we should leave, Destan advised, his eyes now looking concerned.

She was wondering if he would say anything more, but Destan seemed at a loss for words. Running a few different ideas through her mind finally found the answer which would keep them safe while appeasing Mr. Freigh and Baleck, "We usually go for a bike ride on Saturdays. I know I don't feel the greatest, but I do enjoy it so much. — Would you still want to go Destan?"

"As long as you feel up to it." He nodded as he helped her up.

"I can understand." Mr. Freigh agreed as he stepped back to let them walk past. "After a stressful day, some normality as well as peace and quiet can be beneficial. Enjoy the rest of your day. And Callimay, if you start feeling any pain whatsoever, please let us know and we will do whatever we can."

"Thank you." She sighed as she bowed her head.

Unsure about what in the world was going on — starting to feel like Callimay and himself were being cornered — Destan moved so he was between her and the other four in the room. She could sense his concern, and so she quickly followed him to the door.

As he started closing it, Mr. Freigh pointed out, "Oh, Destan. You forgot your paperwork."

He froze and then whipped around, "Thank you Mr. Freigh. I appreciate you reminding me."

"You are very welcome. Enjoy the rest of your day."

"Goodbye." Callimay waved as he came back to her; and then finished rather shaky: *What's wrong?*

I didn't like how Mr. Willgun was acting: asking us what we were planning on doing for the rest of the day. Destan replied rather suspicious as he looked down at the file in his hand.

That was a close call.

You're telling me. I almost kept the pages under the file and didn't put them in at all.

I'm just glad that's all done and I'm alright, Callimay took his hand and leaned her head against his arm.

Me too. Destan put his arm around her and started walking.

ঙ

"Why didn't you have them stay!" Baleck asked, sounding more than a bit irritated as Mr. Freigh walked into the office. "They were right, here! It was our golden opportunity!"

"With Callimay in her fragile state, I do not want to overwhelm her. The poor thing has been through enough as it is. And I have no doubt going into that conversation would cause her to lose it similar to the first time. I gave Destan the paperwork and I am expecting to hear from him before the end of next week. And with what happened and how he acted just now, I cannot see him 'not' bringing her. We will just have to wait and see."

"You even left their files out!"

"I did not have time to put them away without raising suspicion. I am trying to keep their trust, Baleck. They have to be willing to work with us or everything we have done is in vain. There is no time to find and train anyone else." He calmed as he unlocked a drawer in the desk to put them in. "Usually I am the one on the verge of madness when things go wrong, not you, Baleck. What is going on? Are things with your uncle going alright?"

"I apologize Mr. Freigh." He sighed and closed his eyes as he worked to regain his composure. "My uncle is fine. It is only the events over the past couple days catching up with me. I know how crucial deadlines are right now— you are right: we need their cooperation. Doing things under these circumstances would in no way help."

$$\mathfrak{B}$$

Destan and Callimay stopped on their way out and ate breakfast. It was late enough that most everyone else was gone, which was all for the better as far as she was concerned.

After he asked if it was possible, they took something for lunch so they wouldn't have to cut their bike ride short to come back.

She was rather surprised he asked; all butterflies on the inside: *So we're going to have lunch somewhere else? Just the two of us? I wonder where would be a good place. Maybe he wants to be able to get to his room and not worry about coming back. I wouldn't mind not having to see Toreon, that's for sure…*

Those who were there stared as Callimay's appearance, so as they left she stopped Destan, "Would it be alright with you if we stopped at my room first so I can freshen up first? I look a bit worse for wear and I'd prefer to—"

"Oh. I wasn't thinking. I'm sorry I wasn't paying attention." He shook his head a couple times and shielded her as he ushered her on. "I gotta say, the fact you got your key back is a shock to me."

"I don't know why Toreon did it other than to save his skin by his lie about how he got it. I doubt even 'he' could have talked his way out of that mess… though I guess he kinda did."

"I've given up trying to understand him. Pure evil can't be—"

"I at least have it back."

They walked side-by-side, looking like the complete opposite couple from a little over a day prior. There still wasn't anything said, but they were walking as close as two people could without touching each other, and their faces helped paint a brighter view of things.

As they came up to the dorm, he stopped at the front door, "You go ahead. I'll wait here."

"I wouldn't think of leaving you out here in the cold. You can wait in the lounge if you'd like."

"It's fine. I need to go get my bike. I'll meet you here."

Callimay opened her mouth a couple times to say something, but couldn't quite get the words out. She finally sighed and said, "Okay. I won't be long, I promise."

"Take your time. No need to rush." Destan assured as he turned and walked away, stopping and turning back — that small smile on his face: *Really. I'll wait, Callimay.*

𝕭

She got done as fast as she dared and then they headed out. Destan usually rode point, but in light of everything, he rode right beside her. It was so cold that no one was out and about, but he wouldn't have put it past Toreon to be the one to brave the weather just for the sake of his "game" of tormenting Callimay.

They were such a strange couple: she was bundled up like a trapper in the forests of Brigon during the winter hunting season while Destan looked like he was out for a casual stroll down the central strip in Veinyet during masquerade week. They really couldn't be any more different in this aspect, "The cold doesn't bother you much, does it?"

"Not much. I'm used to it." He replied in a rather flat tone.

"You would think I would be since I grew up in a similar climate as this… but the cold still gets to me." She continued as she spread her gloved hands so they were lying on top of the handlebars.

He didn't respond.

Callimay sighed to herself. She knew it couldn't last forever. And so, now the time had come for Destan to sink back into himself and away from her.

The time she had with him she was ever grateful for; it was just that now since she knew what it was to have him around, she didn't want it to stop. She didn't want to, again and again, go through this push and pull with him as far as things were emotionally.

For quite a while, they rode along in silence; the sound of leaves crackling and gravel grinding under their bike tires filled the hush. Destan took the lead now and headed down a narrow gravel path Callimay had never been on. She wasn't sure where they were going, but began to recognize it when it twisted around and crossed the small river quite a few times. It was as pretty on the path itself as the view of it from Lookout Point.

What? Destan asked sarcastically, knowing she stopped.

No answer.

Worried Toreon was nearby, Destan slammed on his breaks and whipped his head around. He took a deep breath and leaned his head back when he saw her; but then looked where she was staring.

Callimay? He asked as he rode back; repeating himself a couple times since she didn't respond.

She was beginning to look frightened again, unable to look away or move from where she was: the horrific memories of what happened playing over and over in her mind.

As quick as he could get back and stop his bike next to hers, Destan reached over and put his hand on her arm, "Callimay?"

With her frightened reaction of jumping back and gasping as she jerked her arm away from him, he steadied her bike as he tried his best to calm her "It's me, Callimay. Destan. You're alright. I won't let you go up there by yourself ever again. … Let's keep going. Okay?"

"O… kay."

℥

He kept next to her again, which in turn helped her calm down and put the memories of last night away as much as humanly possible. They continued for a few more minutes, Destan pulling over and stopping when they came to the small lake. Callimay was ecstatic, "It's beautiful! This has been hidden back here this whole time?"

"Yeah," he responded, a blank look on his face.

"You picked a perfect place for lunch."

Being so happy about the new scenery made her forget she was injured. And unfortunately that wasn't a good thing. As she turned around, she smacked her arm on her bike's basket.

"Calli!" Destan gasped as he kneeled beside her.

"I… I just smacked my arm. It's not too bad. — Ouch! — Don't worry. I'll be alright. Just give me a minute."

Destan helped her up and then picked up what he dropped, helping her spread out the blanket she brought.

Once they were both satisfied, he sat beside her.

The sun was glistening as it mingled with the crystal clear water, splashing little spotlights and rainbows all over her face. He couldn't help but comment to himself how beautiful she looked. Even though her fur hat was covering and hiding much of her silky, straight, rich-brown hair as well as her cheerful and glowing face; he could still see it was shining. Her wool winter coat somewhat obscured her figure, while her delicate hands were hiding in her tan gloves; but Destan still saw her beauty which couldn't be hidden. No matter how hard she tried, he still saw the beauty Toreon ignored. Her attitude was one of being selfless and caring no matter how hard things were for herself. And no matter what happened, she was honest and true. And that "part" of her was more attractive and beautiful than her entire physical appearance… though it was nothing to be ashamed of.

Destan recognized this valuable beauty and also knew Toreon couldn't care less about it. All he cared about was what others saw on the surface. If they liked what they saw, they wouldn't poke and prod to find out who he truly was. He saw Callimay as a pretty face he could manipulate. There was no love or care for treating her as a human being who deserved at least the basic level of respect — especially when she decided enough was enough and didn't want to play the part of his plaything. But for one to show respect, they had to be at least civil if not honest; which Toreon had shown in several ways on many occasions that he wasn't.

Callimay could tell something was occupying Destan's thoughts, but she didn't want to force anything. They both had been through so much over the past twenty-four hours. She couldn't blame him for shutting down. He wasn't used to putting forth so much effort with his emotions. It had to be that he was just regrouping: *He might be embarrassed about how open he's been with you. ~ Oh I hope not. I don't want him to feel that way.*

No matter what was causing this disconnect, she knew whenever she needed him that he would be there. … This was something she hadn't been able to say in a rather long time.

Coming to this conclusion, Callimay closed her eyes and sighed, remembering the sage advice Mrs. Berchoff gave her time and time again while growing up. It's not that she taught her to give up on wanting something better, but she wanted to keep her grounded: those hopes and dreams weren't guaranteed. Now was the only thing that was guaranteed.

Destan glanced over and was concerned when he saw she closed her eyes, but realized she was smiling. She looked relaxed and happy. After breathing a sigh of relief, he reached into his lunch bag. He saw the folder Mr. Freigh gave him and was reminded they needed to look at what he was able to find… but he didn't know if he could bear to tell her about the other papers. He'd seen her unhappy and miserable, and he didn't want to cause her to feel that way again.

The sun looked so lazy as it made its daily climb to zenith, Callimay and Destan sitting there the entire time. It tried its best to keep them warm while providing them with a lavish display of glistening water ripples, but it knew it could only — in the end — do so much.

Surprisingly, she didn't say much. Callimay found it nice to relax and not worry about anything or feel the need to say anything to fill the void. Destan was there. Plus, what was there to talk about? They'd talked more up to that point in the day than they would in almost an entire week! And aside from this all, Callimay still found it hard to believe how close she was to dying. She couldn't find the words to tell Destan how grateful she was for everything he did and was still doing.

A quick glance in his direction hinted to her he was somewhat relaxed. He never was much of the type to live and let live — at least not by what he showed everyone else. It begged the question if him being relaxed like this would last.

After they were done with their lunches, she could sense he was on edge yet again. But this wasn't the on edge feeling she had sensed from him earlier, "Is everything alright?"

"Everything's fine." He deflected as he shoved the file away; but after a few moments finished, "I… I do have a question to ask you."

"Okay."

"Last night you were holding onto something around your neck. Would you be willing to tell me what it is?"

"It's the only two things I have left from the person I lost… well, as far as what I have with me that is." She said a little sad as she put her hood back and pulled the chain out. "I didn't know we weren't allowed to wear rings, so I didn't have anywhere else to keep it safe. It's my mother's wedding band. Of course I say that, but— she's the only woman I've known as my mother. She took me in when I was really young. … The other thing is a heart pendant she intended to give me for my eighteenth birthday."

"I didn't mean to dig up unhappy memories. I'm sorry Callimay."

"They're not unhappy like you might think. I cherish every memory I have of her. It's just hard at times to remember she's gone." She corrected as she put her hand on his shoulder; and then let go, rolling the ring between her fingers. "I wouldn't say it's not painful; but the pain just means I loved her."

"Would you mind if I looked at it? The ring I mean."

"No. Not at all. Give me a second… here. It's not very fancy. She told me her husband couldn't even afford a betrothal ring, but it didn't matter to her. I remember that she wore it all the time. I never saw her without it. After she passed, I understood why she kept it so close. It's memories which make things valuable, not their monetary v— I'm sorry. I started rambling."

Destan sat there for a little while and looked at the band, then replied sounding nervous, "You're fine, Callimay. It doesn't bother me; you talking like that. … This may seem rather spontaneous and out of the blue, but I have another question."

She scooted so she was facing him, sounding chipper as she closed her eyes and grinned, "Alright. What ya got?"

"Like I said, this is going to more than likely be out of the blue for you. It's been on my mind for a while, and I see it as the best way to keep you safe." He started rambling as his eyes shifted back and forth.

"Destan?" Callimay soothed as she put her hand atop his fidgety one. "Are you alright? I've never seen you nervous like this. Can I help? Is something wrong? … You can tell me."

"I just don't want to sound heartless or cold when I say it. You always use your emotions so well to convey what you want to say to others. Me? It's more like I slap the person in the face with a spike-studded board." He quieted to a mutter, avoiding her gaze. "And I don't want to do that to you."

"Oh, Destan. You don't have to be fancy and flamboyant when you talk to me. Just tell me what you're thinking. It may be a bit more abrupt or blunt than what I would say, but that's just it: you aren't me. I wouldn't want it any other way. Just hearing you talk to me makes my heart smile. It doesn't need to be all flowery. And if it would help you any: I'm not 'listening' to you. I made a promise to myself to refrain from doing so if you felt unsure or didn't want to talk. So, if you need a moment to get it all straight inside before you let it out, don't worry."

"You have done that this entire time?"

"I admit I really wanted to at times, but more than that I wanted you to tell me because you wanted to. I wanted to gain trust with you and not take whatever I wanted whenever I wanted. It's not fair to you."

Destan sighed in relief, "I never would accuse you of doing it on purpose, but I know things can happen if we forget. And I know you're still trying to control— thank you, Callimay."

She wanted to say more, but she knew she needed to give him a moment to gather his thoughts. Callimay sat there and smiled so soft as his eyes bounced around, "I don't want you to think I came to this decision purely based on me wanting to keep you safe. I 'do' care for you. I do. I just see both as working together."

Doing her best to not talk to herself so she could hear, she just smiled as he helped her to her feet… though, at this point Callimay was completely baffled. He was being cryptic, which wasn't that strange, but he was never nervous like this. What was wrong!

"I know this isn't the best way of doing it, but sometimes you have to use what you have. God never said it had to be done a certain way, so…" Destan took a ginormous breath as he got down on one knee and looked up to her. "C… Calli? Do you remember how I said we are a team now? Well, I got to thinking about it afterward and it isn't true. We aren't a team. But I want it… I want it so very much. I want to protect you more than I can right now. I want to be the support you have always been for me. I want to show you how deeply I do care for you. I want you to know you're not alone in this world. I… I know we don't know each other very well, but I believe I know enough. God is Who is important to me, and I know how important He is to you. And I know we've never talked about this directly, but— would you wear this ring as your own until I can get you one of your own? Would you wear it for me? Would you be my wife? Would you marry me… Calli?"

What was she supposed to say to that! She was too shocked; unable to take her gaze off of Destan's green eyes. They were so soft and gentle, looking like she remembered them to so many times; the signs of tears welling in them quite evident.

Callimay finally realized what it was she felt when she saw him the first day of class — his love and care for her. All this time she had been so focused on everyone else; she neglected to see someone was showing her the same. She felt a bit selfish, being given this wonderful gift. But as she looked into Destan's eyes, she knew it was just as much a gift for him as it would be for her.

Her thoughts wandered back to when she first said she wanted to apply and had the thought cross her mind about finding someone. And then it all shot back like a boomerang when she saw the look of worry begin to grow on his face.

"I don't— oh I don't mean no! Please don't think that! I meant… I— that was beautiful, Destan." Callimay finally got out as she smiled; pushing aside the pain from her cut cheek. "I know things have been challenging for you when it comes to emotions, and I know you've been around me long enough to know there's no short supply of them with me. … But what you said was so— you are right: God is important to me. More than anything. And I've seen that same love and zeal in you. I would consider it a joy to wear this ring as my own: for you. I would be thrilled to be your wife."

For the first time, Callimay saw Destan actually smile. And when he did, a flood of tears started racing down his joy-filled face.

With his now clumsy hands, he struggled to take off her glove and put the ring on her finger.

Without a second's hesitation, he stood up and wrapped her in his arms as he cried. He wasn't sure why he was, and it scared him to an extent: not knowing why he was showing such a great amount of emotion. How could just one question cause this? Why was this decision so emotionally involved?

Whatever the case, Callimay's ever-abounding encouragement and patience gave him courage to let his guard down. He knew there was much they still didn't know about each other, but he couldn't see why they couldn't work through things as they came up.

The wind picked up and his lunch bag fell over, the file of papers sliding out. He knew the decision concerning his future at this institution would now be made by the two of them. It was already a hard decision to make, but it was one he now dreaded; not because he feared they would agree… no, it was the fact she was now tangled in this web he'd let himself fall into.

And the more Destan thought, the more he worried about her. He didn't want anything more to happen to her. She'd already been hurt enough. Both by him as well as others.

At this point the file had him hypnotized, not allowing him to take his eyes off it. It was sucking him deeper and deeper into these dreadful thoughts, picking away and stealing what happiness he was feeling. There was no mercy, no shame, no reservation. It wasn't going to be satisfied until it ruined this moment for both of them.

Callimay's side of the blanket seemed to see this happening and did what it could to help snatch him from the file's grasp. It let itself get caught by the wind and spread over the hideous papers.

It did the trick! Destan closed his eyes and took a big deep breath. He pushed those thoughts aside since he couldn't see the reminder.

Knowing there was a shift in his emotions; Callimay brushed her hands back and forth across his back to remind him she was there. He leaned his cheek on top of her head and pulled her closer.

After what was something along the lines of an amazing lifetime of beautiful silence, Destan let Callimay go. There were still tears running down his face, so she wiped them away and said so soft and sweet, "It feels good to be able to let things go, doesn't it?"

He nodded as he took a shaky, deep breath.

"You know, Destan? I think you're more emotional than you believe yourself to be. Don't mistake emotion for weakness."

"I've never had the luxury of being able to show emotion and feel I'm being a strong man and leader. I always been taught I had to push emotions aside because they were something women showed."

"Anything can become a weakness if it isn't controlled; not 'just' emotions. Sometimes it takes more strength to show them and vocalize you need help or encouragement than to 'suck it up' and be brave. I'd never think you to be weak by asking for help. And pushing them aside doesn't get rid of them. They only fester and build to a breaking point." *Like what I did.* "I understand though: sometimes there doesn't seem to be a person in the world who can help you through or you don't want to sound like you're complaining. That's why you need an outlet: like me and bike riding. It gave me something to do that was constructive and yet allowed me to be by myself so I could figure things out. Plus, being out in more remote areas where the scenery is always changing and beautiful; it reminds me of— I'm rambling now. I'm sorry."

"Don't be," he reached out and touched the side of her face.

They both froze for a few seconds. Callimay was shocked to feel his warm and rough, yet somehow gentle hand caressing the side of her face. Her heart started racing and she felt similar to how she did the night before when he was tending to her injuries.

Destan was so taken in by her beauty. Her soft skin seemed to beg him to never let go, her eyes showing him his future: her.

By the way the two of them looked at each other, the woodland creatures who were spying on them would have been gasping and covering their eyes; waiting for the two of them to kiss.

A few seconds passed and then he barely moved his thumb, causing Callimay to close her eyes and sigh.

"You know the perfect time to say the right thing, Calli. I— you just know exactly what needs to be said." Destan stuttered; taking his hand back rather awkward and looking down at his feet as he shuffled them. "So… would you like to stay longer or head back?"

"Why don't we start packing up. We can go down the path a bit before we head back… if you want." She replied as she sighed, looking like she felt awkward as well.

𝕯

Amidst the calm, Destan's mind wandered back to where it had been. Callimay was talking, but he wasn't paying attention; being consumed with these reoccurring, unsettling thoughts. Now he wasn't sure how things were going to play out. He wasn't sure if she would be willing to leave the Society when he planned to. The fact she was fed up with everything going on hinted to her not objecting, but he didn't want her to feel she had to "give up" because he was leaving.

He knew they needed to talk things through, he just hated to ruin the wonderful time they were having; especially when he saw the smile

on Callimay's face. They both deserved a break from all the stress and frustration they were going through. But would waiting end up adding to everything instead of dealing with it head-on now and being done with it? Or would doing it right now cause more issues to arise? And then apart from that, there were going to be countless other things needing to be dealt with and decided upon between the two of them.

Destan's thoughts left those heavy things and focused on the present when the same scent he caught the last time he was there came back. It was a warming note to the bitterly cold air and worked wonders with his emotional state, "Callimay? Hold up."

"Okay. Where are you going?"

"I'll be right back. Just stay here. Don't worry."

Seeing her smiling face, he couldn't help but feel like he'd known her his whole life. She felt so familiar to him. But in reality, he hadn't known her very long at all: just around two and a half months! And then most of their time together was focused on physics and advanced math, or merely being in the same room during Sunday Assembly and mid-week Studies. Backstories were never openly shared, so they were — in so many ways — just acquaintances. Knowing this, it was now crazy to Destan to think that he committed to her as fast as he did; but it seemed like the logical thing to do. It felt right.

While she waited, Callimay sat there and stared at her hand. This was a whirlwind for her, too. It didn't seem real... just like what happened the night before didn't. All these thoughts made her unable to sit still. She kept taking her glove off to looking at the ring and then putting it back on when her fingers couldn't take the cold any longer. This little band had been on her hand before... but it being on the left one felt odd while at the same time reminding her how special it was.

She heard a rustling sound and whipped around, fearful of whom it might be; only to find a snow owl: *Why... that's odd.*

Callimay got off her bike and crept over to the dead tree where the fluffy bird was perched. It only moved its eyes as it watched her, "What are you doing here? It's day and it's not snowing yet. ... You're so beautiful! And quite the rare bird to find. I've only seen pictures of you! But I've never seen you with purple eyes before. You must be a 'very' rare bird! Your eye color reminds me of—"

Footsteps caught her attention, so she looked back in the direction Destan went, "What are you doing?"

"I was looking at— it's gone!"

"What's gone, Callimay?"

"It was a— why do you have your hands behind your back?" She paused when she noticed. "What did you leave to get?"

"The last time I was here I smelled these. I did again just before I stopped." He explained as he revealed a bouquet of red roses. "They reminded me of your perfume and you. I thought you might like to have some. At least this would be something I gave you which wasn't already yours."

"Oh, Destan! They're beautiful. … They 'do' smell like my perfume. But I had no idea you paid any attention to it."

"It was one of the first things I noticed when you came up to me and introduced yourself," he admitted, his face becoming flushed. "Then our little run-in the first day of classes cemented it."

"You did? And I am so sorry about that. I really should've watched where I was going. … I got the perfume as my graduation present. I never used it until I came here. It was the first day I'd ever worn it. My mother passed away so soon after I got it… I c— I'm sorry."

"It's alright, Callimay." Destan comforted as he rubbed her arm.

ℬ

They ended up staying out for the entire afternoon, riding around. It wasn't anything romantic, but it was something they could do together and be alone… and that was more precious to Callimay than having a candle-lit dinner or going to a fancy show.

Nothing was said much by Destan — she did all the "rambling" as she referred to it. She felt bad being the only one talking, but he assured her he was content to listen. … Though, after a while, he did suggest they head back to the complex so they wouldn't have to rush back since it was getting close to dinner.

As it turned out, they made it back sooner than expected. So, they walked through a couple of the labyrinth gardens. The two of them stood side-by-side and never held hands, but for whatever reason, Callimay didn't feel it was necessary to. She knew he was there and going to take care of her. Did she want that special connection with Destan right then? Who wouldn't? But Mrs. Berchoff's voice would remind her to keep her focus where it would be helpful. It sometimes wasn't easy, but she knew to live in the now was what she needed… trying to envision a future like she did the one time caused them both enough grief.

Callimay was continuing to walk along and then felt Destan put his arm around her, "What is it?"

"You got really quiet. Just wanted to check and make sure you were alright and knew I was here." He said rather light-hearted; and then paused before he finished, "And they should be serving dinner by now, so we should start heading over."

"Oh," Callimay answered as she glanced at her watch and then over to his. "Why do you wear your watch on your right wrist?"

"Why do you wear 'yours' on your right wrist?"

"Well, it's because I'm left-handed." She answered, and then gasped in fear as she looked up at him: *Oh no!*

She took off running through the labyrinth, horrified with what she did. She'd always been so careful. How in the world did she get so comfortable she let this life-threatening secret slip!

An all-new kind of fear set in. Being scared of Toreon was one thing. This? She'd never felt her heart racing faster than it was at that moment; her almost wheezing from trying to catch her breath.

It felt as if she were crawling along, hearing the sound of Destan behind her and knowing he was gaining ground on her. Her right leg was beginning to ache and eventually gave out; her smacking that side on the gravel path before skidding a couple times.

After the initial shock and pain wore off, she looked back and saw him about five feet away from her. She yelped, knowing there was no chance for her to run.

"Please don't say anything. Please." She cried as she curled up, writhing in pain. "I'll do whatever you want so I—"

Destan dropped to his knees and shielded her; his tone so soft and apologetic, "I'm not going to hurt you. I'm not a Falconer. I swear I'm not. I'm sorry you thought—" *The reason I wear my watch on my right wrist is the exact same reason as you.*

You! You're left-handed too!

Believe it or not. He nodded as he jerked up — his face flushed — and then offered her his hand as he finished, "Are… are you alright?"

"I'll be alright." Callimay winced once she got to her feet; leaning on him for support and scared half to death. *So wait. Your family actually taught you proper etiquette stating watches are to be worn on the non-dominant hand? It's so old-fashioned to follow etiquette now… let alone illegal to be left-handed. — How have you made it? Is this why you're so reserved and cut off? Can you write with your right hand as well? It was a bit of a learning curve for me, but I can do it good enough to get by.*

I've never worked out how to write legibly with my right hand. It'd be a dead giveaway right now, let me tell you. Destan shook his head as he turned. *And as far as my watch goes: just because things are old doesn't mean traditions are worthless. That, and I forgot.*

But how do you hide when you write!

Well, I either lean over my work if absolutely necessary — lay on it like you've described — or what I try to always do is use the computer.

I never noticed it when you were helping me with physics.

I never wrote anything while we were together. He corrected. *I always had you write it. If I did have something, I had it done before you got there or used the computer.*

That's right, I remember now. — It was so hard for me while growing up to understand why it was wrong for me to be able to use my left hand the way I could. Callimay admitted as she followed him, favoring her right leg still. *I know it was part of the reason my mother kept me home for a while. She is the one who taught me to use both hands. I admit I have to watch myself sometimes when I'm out in public… I was so scared the first morning you and I were working together. You were watching me work the problem, and then when I needed to look back at the book I stopped and used my right hand—*

I noticed. But there wasn't any reason for me to say anything. Destan cracked a smile.

She stood there for a moment, astounded with how much he noticed little details: *It's just amazing. I thought I was the only one in the world who was left-handed and actually used their left hand.*

We're rare, that's for sure.

Living in this secrecy and shrouding isn't easy. I knew a few who were found. Things obviously didn't go well. … It's been a bit easier to get away with it, if you will, where I live since it's secluded; but I still have to watch myself. I mean: it's illegal! If I got c—

There are sympathizers out there who do what they can to help us blend in without losing who we truly are. He tried to encourage as they walked along. *It's not completely hopeless.*

Those groups were the main reason for civil war breaking out in my country. Callimay sighed as she rubbed her right arm, looking down and away from him. *Maybe you think they help, but they did nothing but cause death and hurt where I'm from.*

Several countries went through disputes over it to some extent, Destan said in the same tone as he reached for the door.

I was always confused as to why they were all referred to as civil wars, when they were all being fought due to the same international reason, Callimay asked as she looked up.

It was because it was a conflict contained internally. No country went across their borders. It might have been a worldwide issue, but it was something dealt with on a country-by-country basis. He opened the door, ending their conversation. "Hungry?"

᛭

He took her things and left so he could hang them up in his locker. Everyone got their dinner to go so they could watch the pickup games at the rec complex or head back to their dorms to hang out with their "friends". This left a nice, quiet environment for Callimay and Destan to enjoy. — And with all the special things that happened today, having that alone time was even more appreciated.

As she came up to the faculty at the first counter, she asked, "Would you happen to have a flower vase by chance?"

The middle-aged lady looked at her with a puzzled expression and didn't answer.

"I know it seems like a strange request," Callimay laughed as she showed her the roses. "But I got some earlier today and I have nothing to put them in. I didn't know if you would—"

"Oh! Flower as in the plant. I was so confused there for a moment." The younger lady exclaimed, cutting her off. "Of course. Let me go get one. I'll only be a moment."

She left for a couple minutes and then returned with a water-filled vase, "Here you go. Do you need any help? Oh wow, the thorns are already gone. That's nice. … Those are so beautiful and fragrant."

"I know." She smiled as she brushed the velvet-like petals.

"Where did they come from?"

"Out by the lake," Destan answered as he came over.

They filled their trays and then went over to their normal spot. In keeping with tradition, they sat next to each other: Callimay on the right and Destan on the left; silent as they ate. She was somewhat glad for the fact she didn't have to fix her own food all the time — especially when she wasn't feeling well — but what she liked to call "mass-produced food" wasn't the same quality as home-cooked.

There were times, like today, she would laugh to herself when she would compare his tray to hers. Destan's was very generous in portion size and would be all but licked clean by the time he was done. Callimay's was very minimal. She wasn't ever in fear of starving, but she wasn't used to having a five-course meal all the time like was available there at the Society for each meal.

Then it dawned on her: *I'm going to have to fix food for both of us! Oh dear. Quantity isn't the issue… though it will be more than I'm accustomed to. But what if he doesn't like what I make? I don't want there to be the whole trial and—*

"Food is food, Callimay." Destan interrupted before he took another bite. "As long as it's cooked, I'll eat it."

"Anything?" She asked as she began to grin, looking at him out of the corner of her eye.

He opened his mouth and then paused when he heard what she said to herself, finishing as he nodded, "Okay. I'll admit you've got a point."

It hurt, but she couldn't help but laugh.

"Alright, that's enough. Are you done?"

"Yes."

As they put their coats on, Destan asked, "I didn't know if you would like to come over for a bit to go over what I found. I know it's a huge sidestep from what happened earlier, but then again, we do need to know what's going on."

"I'd forgotten all about it," Callimay replied somber as she picked up the vase. "It would be a good idea to look at it now instead of later so we have an idea about what to expect."

❦

Snow began to stick to the grassy areas as they rode back. Each flake was so carefree and lazy as it fell to the ground. It had nowhere it needed to be and all the time in the world to get there. Callimay felt a bit jealous of them in that sense, but seeing the ones headed for the pavement — melting when they hit it — reminded her being carefree and lazy had dangers to it as well. You could be doing fine and then out of nowhere have your world crash down around you.

It made her think of what had happened to her. Had she become lazy and carefree to the point that she didn't see the signs of what eventually happened? Did she not pay attention to things around her enough to see this all coming?

But in the end, was she sad about it all? She had Destan and it was the most amazing thing that had ever happened to her. Things could have still worked out for them getting together without all the baggage of Toreon and such, but the past was just that.

The hall Destan's room was at the end of actually "felt" quiet… too quiet. It was strange to her all the surrounding rooms were vacant, but now everything at the Society seemed eerie and suspicious since she knew what they were doing. He opened the door and let Callimay in, flipped the lights on since the curtains were pulled, and then dragged another chair over to his desk.

"I must say: you've proven everything I was told to be true, wrong."

"Excuse me?"

"Your room: it's well-kept."

"Oh." Destan raised his eyebrow while he took his coat off. "You didn't say anything last time. Nothing's changed."

"I wasn't paying much attention since I wasn't feeling well."

"Well let me assure you," he stated as he was putting her coat on a hanger. "This is the way it usually is."

188

"Oh please don't assume I'm complaining. I just— I was pleasantly surprised what everyone told me was wrong."

"Well I'm glad I don't fit the status quo."

"Your room is set up better for a lefty. Mine's been a bit awkward to figure things out without making it obvious."

He sat down at his desk and took the folder out of the lunch bag he had been carrying around all day; never saying a word in response.

"Destan?"

"What is it, Callimay?" He asked in his monotone voice, not looking up from what he was doing.

"Why did the Eradication happen?" She set the flowers down and fluffed them a bit

To say he flinched could be exaggerating, really. He more or less let out a large sigh as she sat beside him. She was interested in this topic more than anything else during their current history class. And it stood to reason since this single event affected how she lived her life, "It's something that was often mentioned during my schooling even before coming here… but never explained as to 'why' it came about. It seemed strange those details would be left out. I would think they would be important so future generations would know and could learn from and not repeat them. I was curious if— do you even know?"

"I know some." Destan nodded as he took a deep breath, staring at the wall. "In 2455, it was suggested the minority population of left-handed people in the world was responsible for us being cut off from the Homeworld five years prior in 2450 — what brought on the Void era. Left-handed people held key positions in industries, companies, and political offices all over the globe. These entities were the same ones the Homeworld placed responsibility for their cut off of support. The vast majority of people were still in an uproar about that, so they jumped on the skewed information. … At first, the plan was to remove them from their positions, but it quickly turned into a full-blown genocide as people fell into extremist propaganda saying 'any' left-handed person could cause even more trouble for the world; and so they needed to be eradicated. Hence the title: the Eradication. — It lasted for three, long, miserable years; millions of people losing their lives because they used their left hand as their dominant hand. Bounties were placed on those of high social, economic, and political standing; which fueled the bloodthirsty vengeance so many had. Attempts were made by groups to get help from the Homeworld, but they were all refused. — By 2460, it appeared every left-handed person had been murdered. The International Law was proposed during this time and run through every government for ratification; a unanimous decision made within months to make being left-handed illegal. Anyone caught was given a sentence of death for treason… no matter how old the person was, and no chance for an appeal. Some countries — like Faberton, Hagzell, and Kae-Nu — went so far as to say the parents of children under twelve found to be left-handed would be sentenced as well, and anyone who turned in someone 'suspected' of being left-handed would be given a standard one-thousand solera reward. It got to the point where anyone — especially children — who would pick something up with their left hand at the store, wave with their left hand, or reach out with their left hand to shake someone's hand were being carried off by greed-driven Falconers left and right. — Falconers prefer using the handshake method for catching Derelicts: the term 'they' coined to label us. — Resistance groups began popping up in those countries and neighboring ones to help aid families who were discovering their children were left-handed and didn't want to force them into a government-standardized lifestyle… or lose them. They saw being left-handed as any other genetic difference: eye color, skin tone, or even gender. It's just the way God made them; not something that made a person inherently evil. Ratio-wise, there was a super majority of right-handed people who were acting in these heinous ways compared to left-handed people. It's just since left-handed people were not as common, they were singled out for being different and seen as the problem. It was easier. But, those manipulating the power-vacuum left by the Homeworld were the source of the problem. Not to say there weren't some lefties involved with these dealings, but anyway. Those governments soon realized 'some' of their errors. But since it was signed into law, they had to abide by it. It could only be overturned by a unanimous vote: every country. — The likelihood of it happening right now isn't the greatest. — They were finding themselves bankrupt from the inundation of turn-ins and dealing with facilities overcrowding. There was no provision stating if the person was found to be right-handed that the one who brought them in couldn't receive the reward; they hadn't even devised how to test if the person was or wasn't left-handed. Beyond that, they didn't know how to test a child, so countless right-handed people and children with their parents lost their lives. I personally know some groups used this to dispose of those in their way for political or financial reasons. ... The Eradication laid the foundation for several civil wars between 2460 and 2461. Most of them died down within the first year, but Faberton's was not surface-level. Yes, it found its roots in the squabble over the implementation of the International Law, but also had the addition of radical resistance groups who were — in some ways — acting just like the governments: assassinating political and social figures who were in opposition to their agenda. Another reason for their civil war in particular was the government's financial woes. That's truly why it lasted ten years. With it being a newer country, all the upheaval, deception, and corruption made finding any common ground to build on near impossible. Their resistance groups unfortunately gave an extremist view to the general public toward 'any' resistance group; most with left-handed children going into hiding, surrendering their child, or forcing them to be right-handed. So much of it isn't true. These parents are doing what brought this all on: following blindly and giving up without bothering to check the facts for themselves. There are 'good' resistance groups out there."

It was as if Destan were hitting Callimay with wave after wave of horrendous news. She couldn't fathom what kind of evil person would think to do such a thing... to a child even! It was hard for her to find something to say. All she could get out was, "That's. Horrible."

"It's more dangerous than you think," he warned as he reached out and took hold of her right hand with his strong yet gentle one. "Neither of us should be wearing our watches on our right wrists... no matter what we were taught or what traditions we see as worth following. There's no mercy as far as this goes; and no leniency if you're caught in a slip up. Yes, traditions are old-fashioned and most people probably wouldn't notice, but don't underestimate 'any' Falconer. They know as much if not more about a lefty's idiosyncrasies as any lefty because they're natural to us — we don't notice we're doing them. Falconers are trained to notice and can be anywhere. Even here. If you're caught— I know this is being extremely blunt, but I'm going to say it: you're already dead at that point. If I would have been one when you slipped earlier; no amount of begging, pleading... nothing would have saved you, Calli. And depending— just. Be careful. Please. Don't ever — and I mean 'ever' — barter with your life. There's not a male Falconer alive who won't manipulate your situation for their enjoyment. And I think you know what I mean."

She cowered from his fiery gaze, folding her hands on her lap and looking as if she wanted to shrivel into nothing.

"I... I just want you safe." Destan pulled his chair closer to hers.

There seemed to be the type of silence in the air only achieved by being in a void. The tower clock on the complex chimed to announce the new hour, after which Callimay asked, "So... this was all because of money and power?"

"It's what it pretty much boils down to."

"Greed and power... why are people drawn to it!"

Destan didn't answer.

There wasn't much need for one, anyway. Evil couldn't be fully explained; let alone someone's willingness to participate in it.

He laid the folder down and sat there while Callimay processed everything. She eventually glanced over to see what he was doing, remembering why they were sitting there in the first place, "These are different from the rest. What are they?"

"I—"

"What is so wrong with me seeing them?" She questioned as she shooed his hands away. "They can't— wait a second. These are about— why do you have these?"

"May I have a moment to explain?" Destan asked a bit irritated as he put his hand out so she would give them back.

"I'm sorry."

"While I was with Mr. Freigh the second time this morning, he sat me down and gave me these to go over. He said he's been trying to get faculty to see the potential he sees in me, but it's gotten to the point something has to be done... basically. He said whenever I make my decision he will make time to speak with me."

"Wait. Are you saying he's letting you choose 'how' you leave: voluntary versus expulsion? That there's no hope for you to stay? You 'have' to leave?"

"Pretty much."

"But then that means—"

"I'm not leaving you behind; trust me. And it's going to work out best this way: I can get you away from here — away from Toreon — and somewhere safe."

Callimay sat there in a daze for a moment, her heart racing as she thought: *What if they won't let me leave!*

"Since we're engaged, they'll have to let you go." Destan continued without knowledge of what she was saying. "Remember the entrance application specifically stated you had to be single? To keep the façade of the Society in-tact, they have to let 'both' of us go."

"Was this why you asked me so soon?" She asked depressed as she looked down at her hand, fading out as she finished: *Or at all?*

"Oh, Calli. There're so many reasons why I did this. Don't think I did this to benefit myself alone or to use you. I 'am' serious about this commitment. I understand what it means and what my job is toward you. Maybe some of my reasoning seems a bit detached and uncaring, but they all stem from me wanting to protect you. ... I didn't want to talk about this quite yet. I was going to wait until break when the report cards were posted. And I wasn't going to make any kind of decision until I talked it over with you. — Mr. Freigh was the one who brought it all up in the first place, I never asked for any of this. Though I guess I did ask for it by how I've acted this whole time."

"I… I'm just trying to grasp this is real. That you're here to stay and what happened earlier today wasn't a dream. That I'm not alone."

"At face value, some of my motives do seem worrisome, but I won't ever leave you. Please believe me. ... It's my fault for not tossing th—"

"No! No, it's alright. I need these moments to remind me. I need to become more confident in us. I need to stop being so afraid and just live. I need to trust you. But… would it be alright if we finished talking about this a bit later?"

"Agreed." Destan nodded; observing how she was dodging his gaze, "Callimay? Are you going to be alright?"

"Yeah," she sniffled as she turned her attention to the stack of papers they originally intended to go through.

He tried once more to get her to talk to him, but surrendered and divided the papers so they could read through their own file.

One would assume the first pages would be "introductory" and not too shock-n-awe in nature, but what they read first was mind-blowing. "Progress Reports" on their behavior and actions since processing were taken by Faculty during leisure time. Granted, they were from areas under constant surveillance anyway; and sometimes it would only include descriptions; but even so, their lying and devious ways of working begged the question: what kind of people worked here?

There were medical records in Callimay's file of brain activity; all which she didn't understand. Her file in this area was more in depth due to her knowing about her ability. Destan's didn't contain much at all — only a note from yesterday about the phone call Baleck had with Mr. Freigh, and that an analysis of the area would be done today to confirm whether or not he had discovered his ability or not.

The next section contained information about their "Processing". Destan's had the extra paperwork concerning the special team meeting called due to the fiasco from the overdose in the STM (Short-Term Memory) counteractant he was administered. It noted the amount he was given would've wiped his memories from the time of processing to the night prior. It was also included that his memories of the day's altercations with Toreon would be lost to him completely. The findings of the meeting were inconclusive; no one recalling such an amount being administered. So, all they could do was watch him closely for suspicious behavior as to his lack of memories. For both of them, detailed accounts of what they each underwent were documented. A formal medical record was attached which included the concerns of Destan's emotional state during the beginning of processing and Callimay's adverse reaction to what was called "cementation" of the serum in her brain in relation to her migraine history.

"So that's what those scars on my legs and back are from," he said under his breath as he continued to look through the papers.

At this point, Callimay couldn't take any more. She dropped the papers and put her head in her hands; almost wailing. The noise of them smacking the desk caught his attention. With his focus now diverted, he noticed he was gripping the papers so hard his knuckles were white.

Destan laid them down and rolled his chair over so he was as close as he could get to her. She was about doubled over in the chair. Destan gently pushed her static-filled hair behind her ear so it would be out of her face, and noticed something. He pushed her hair back further and ran his hand over what looked like a faint scar on the side of her neck. It was exactly like his. And a closer look revealed several of them right next to each other.

What did they do to you Calli? He asked in horror. *I'm sorry you got tangled up in—*

"W… why did they do this Destan?" She stammered, sounding like she was becoming hysterical. "Is this some sick game like what the Eradication was?"

He sighed and turned his attention to her stack of papers and found the next section which was titled "Selection Phase". The first page contained the name of the ability and a list of capabilities which came with it. He scanned through their observations of her… dating back to when she was at home! The conclusion of which ability would be given to her was due to her deep care for others: her level of desire to have everyone working together instead of misunderstanding each other from internal communication was extremely high. It was also observed she would miss parts of conversations — admitting she talked to herself — which further supported the conclusion made. An addendum was added to say since Destan's likelihood of being a cliffhanger was the highest of any candidate they had, her ability to mind-speak to an individual would aid him in learning to control his unstable emotions while in focal point. It kept on, saying she would have to be accepted by Destan and that they would need to have a strong bond prior to processing for her to fully sync to and be able to mind-speak with him. This type of communication would — from their research — not be possible with anyone else. And then it ended with the statement that how she would tap this ability wasn't definitely known.

At the very back was her application. Callimay's clean and fluid cursive writing showed her caring side from all the letters being tightly joined together, and her confidence from the lack of spots in any of the words as they followed the same exact placement on the lines. The deep slant to her lettering and embellishments for the capital letters showed how she was taught and still held to the older way of cursive. Then the pen she used was so fine it made her flourishing loops look so fragile that even looking at them in a harsh way could cause them to break. Destan asked once she was calm and read her poured-out emotions.

…This may be the only chance I have to accomplish such a grand-scale goal and I want to make the most of it. I want to bring positive change to those around me. The trust between people is so lacking due to the Civil War. There is still so much hurt and anger among many due to their choosing to not be open with each other about the hurt they have. Everything stays bottled up in each person, reaching its boiling point. — In some ways, I am thankful I lost my parents when I was so young because I had no cemented memories of them, the event, or who did it. All I can remember is being alone and scared. — I know so many people feel this way, but they have the added emotion of anger and resentment because they "do" remember. This is why I want to help; to bring people together and help heal what has been hurt. To, in some small way, help them find closure and be able to move on…

Not only was her penmanship beautiful, but her words even more so. Destan related so much to what she said and could, without a doubt, confirm she was already accomplishing her goal. He still had a long way to go, but she gave him hope there would be closure accompanied by a better future.

Destan laid down the papers and softly rested his hand on her shoulder. He was going to start talking, but she cut him off, "What is so special about me, about you? Why are they doing this? I don't understand."

He didn't know how to respond. That part of the puzzle as a whole was still missing: why give young adults special abilities in the first place? "I wish I had all the answers, Calli. I really do."

"You," she started as she wiped her face. "You wouldn't happen to have some tissues would you?"

"Umm," he hesitated as he looked around. "No. But I know where some are. Would you like me to go get some?"

"If you wouldn't mind."

"I'll be right back."

Callimay glanced down and saw her application. Curiosity got the best of her and she looked to see if Destan's was in his papers. It was almost at the bottom of the stack. His writing was bold, the strokes being extremely thick; suggesting he was writing with determination — maybe even anger. The letters stood at attention and looked like they were marching in a straight line across the page. They were very plain in their appearance, showing the person who wrote this was a man most likely. Careful thought seemed to be given to the wording of the essays by the variances in spacing between the words.

Destan's style of writing was unlike anything she was used to. It was much more of a third-person narrative than a personal experience essay. She became tied up in this emotion-laden narrative as she read his passionate words.

...Many who live like this see situations in life as chances for them to gain something for themselves — even though the possible chance of collateral damage to others is present.

And yet this danger finds no root in them.

This group tends to seek power; which in reality, they have no concept of wielding correctly or truly understanding its fundamental purpose. They feed their delusion of strength and power they supposed themselves to have from the weakness of others, and make the grave mistake of basing their power off the people they have under their control. In the vast majority of cases — if not all — the only reason there are people under them is because these subservient individuals have no will-power to seek anything more in life than that of a slave.

These "leaders" are shown for their true selves when faced with ones of true strength and power which came through the foundation of trust and cooperation with others. They quickly crumble when their people (slaves) show no ability to stand beside them. This is not brought about by the one of true strength attacking them, but by the strong individual simply living and breathing the strength they have worked to earn.

Prevalent and dangerous, this imbalance in society must shift if the future is to thrive — not merely survive. So many give up and surrender to a hopeless life of servitude and become complacent, which — more times than not — leads to the next generation being the same, if not worse.

The opposite approach can be just as disastrous, though. Showing no regard for authority and resisting any form of structure can lead to much the same consequence. There must be a balance of regarding authority while refusing to tolerate those who manipulate and use people for their own gain…

She then skipped to another essay which lent itself to a completely different writing approach.

…These opportunities have slipped through my fingers to be the strong person who is able to be relied upon at all times. So many times, things have happened where I could only wait for the inevitable to occur. No chance of salvaging the situation — let alone the individual. Just the knowledge of the cruelty of reality unfolding. Seeing those I have cared for my entire life succumb to the "collateral damage" of other's lack of care or concern due to their personal and ambitious purposes, it has opened my eyes to this ever-growing disease in the world. Hearing the final words of regret and sorrow from those I trusted as they confess their betrayal to others because of this domino-effect collateral damage burned the deepest kind of hole in my soul. I have personally seen the perverted and vile nature of those seeking nothing but selfish glory…

Oh, Destan. Callimay gasped as she dropped the papers, unable to keep reading. *I… I should have waited and asked you. You probably don't want me to know all this!*

As if given the cue to enter stage right, Destan walked in. He was caught off guard by her initial reaction of gasping, and then equally so when she ran over and threw her arms around him; gripping his blazer as she cried, "I am 'so' sorry. So sorry about everything."

"It's alright," he assured as he stepped back and offered her the box of tissues he found. "I know this isn't easy for you. Don't worry about me. I'll be fine."

"I meant I'm sorry for looking at your papers. I should have waited until you came back." Callimay stuttered as she confessed, looking back to the desk where his application was. "If it means anything, I didn't read everything. … I'm sorry."

"Oh," Destan said rather stern as he picked the pages up, the look on his face changing. "I— what's this?"

He looked at the last couple pages under his application and was shocked — "Rogue". As he went through them, his expression became more focused and determined. It didn't have all the information, but it was still more than enough to understand the looming "why" question.

Callimay saw this change and began to become worried. She walked over and glanced down at the pages, though she couldn't see much more than peoples' pictures.

"I found the why part you asked about earlier."

Destan handed them to her and waited for her to look at page after page of young adults' headshots. Their names, personal information, something referred to as an incident location, listing of their abilities, timestamp, and some containing a terminated stamp were included. Callimay quickly went back to the first page and read the overview. It explained about the time frame of the appearance of Rogues and their destructive intentions. Details about the efforts of governments around the globe working together to hide public knowledge of these persons gifted with abilities were discussed. It theorized an origin for these Rogues, but the ones who were contained and questioned proved to bring about no success — all going as far as suicide to protect their source. It then went into the information of the team Mr. Freigh and Baleck put together to research these abilities in an effort to duplicate or enhance them. Observations on the prime age range for acceptance were noted… and only known through experimentation. A grim description of the first attempts of gifting persons with abilities was included — all with deadly consequences.

The most recent addition to the document was just over a month ago, detailing the number of Rogues spiking exponentially — and now reaching a number of almost two-thousand worldwide. It was getting to where governments were maxing out their resources to keep this knowledge from the public as well as keep them protected.

Previous students were listed as operatives who were sent to combat them. Their outcomes being the same — lethal. It appeared they could not match the strength of the serums used by the Rogues. Those sent out from the Society never came back.

It mentioned Destan, referring to him as Challenger throughout the rest of the document. Much of it seemed to be wordy, but what it ended with was rather astounding: the conclusion and affirmation being he now contained the power to subdue all Rogues.

The Society's last hope to save humanity.

"They're pinning humanity's survival on Quidoria as a planet... all on you?" Callimay asked as she finished reading.

"It would appear so," he grumbled as he dragged himself across the room and sat down, putting a hand over his face.

"Why this just— I don't— why in the world— what person with an ounce of dignity could think this was moral? They have no right to— neither of us asked for this. Neither of us even knew about this!" She said full of spite as she stormed to the window and pointed in the direction of the main school building; the papers in her hand smacking the windowpane. "They're expecting you to give up your life just because they—"

"Callimay stop!" Destan yelled as he flashed his green eyes at her and slammed his fist on the sofa armrest. "Just... just stop. Please."

She stood there, speechless. Yes, he was mad; but she saw fear more than anything in him right then.

Now she felt that saying she was sorry was useless. She'd said it so many times up to this point she felt she was failing fixing what she was sorry for; nullifying what she was saying.

Callimay wanted to hold and comfort Destan, but she knew it wasn't how he "worked". But it was the only thing she knew to do. She tried to think of something to help, but he offered the solution first, "I'm going out for a while. I'll take you to your dorm or you can wait here."

Not wanting Destan to get more upset by having to wait for her to answer, she weighed her options as fast as possible and replied, "I don't want you to think you need to rush back, so I'll go now. Give me a second to grab my coat."

"Alright," he stared at the wall, not showing any reaction when she laid his coat beside him.

❦

Darts of fog came from Destan's nose as they walked back. Callimay wanted to help, but it was very apparent he didn't know how to ask, wasn't used to it, or handled it himself. He was cut off and detached, never making eye contact with her or telling her what was wrong.

Destan waited at the foot of the steps outside the dorm while she started up. As she opened the door, she turned to see him walking away. Her heart began to pull and tug her; as if it were trying to stay while he walked away with it. Callimay wanted to say something, feeling she was willing to beg Destan to at least tell her goodnight, but she'd had enough disappointment for one day. She closed the door and dragged herself up to her room.

It was cold and dark as she walked in. She could hear laughter down the hall, recognizing the voices of Toreon and Gallia. This tore at her even more: the thought of them being happy while she and Destan were in so much turmoil. It didn't seem fair at all! Everyone was only concerned with themselves. Callimay and Destan were working so hard to do what was right and think of others. Why was evil being glorified? Why wouldn't anyone do the right thing?

But then it hit her: Toreon and Gallia weren't truly happy. They were never satisfied; nothing was enough for them. Actually, they were scrambling to keep themselves happy and at peace; looking to worldly pleasure for that security. They didn't have what Callimay and Destan did. Though it was becoming quite apparent that they were both at times were struggling to remember this.

Callimay took her coat and boots off, along with her gloves, and then went to her window to see if she could find Destan. She had to use her sleeve to wipe away the condensation which was starting to freeze from the cold windowpane to see anything. The lights down the paths were kept on all night, so even though the snowstorm had started to kick up, she could see his tall, slender figure as he inched down the path toward Lookout Point. He looked overwhelmed and lost: crossing his arms in front of him and then shoving his hands in his pockets every so often. There was no doubt he was far enough away that she couldn't do anything, but she stayed and watched over him regardless.

How do I help you, Destan? She begged as she clung to the curtain, watching him walk farther and farther away. *How do I fix all of this? H… what do you want me to do?*

Movement close by caught her eye. As she switched her focus, she saw someone sneaking around… or perhaps stalking Destan! Either way, Callimay knew something wasn't right. She couldn't see them very well since they hung in the shadows and the snow was falling so much, so she used her ability. Hearing that suave, yet belittling voice she could barely tolerate now made her jump back from the window.

From what she heard him say, something bad was going to happen. He was making cruel comments about Destan and how: *It won't be much longer before this is all done and I can get on with what I want.*

Toreon was getting too far for her to hear him. It worried her to the point that she didn't stop to think before making the insane decision to follow him. She shoved her boots on as fast as she could, snatching her coat off the chair as she flew out the door.

Hyra and Ingrid were in the hall, startled by her door slamming, but only stared at her as she flew around the corner to the stairs.

With snow now standing about four inches deep and there being enough trees, Callimay at least had the ability to stay hidden while following pretty close.

And as it turned out, she didn't have any trouble keeping up with him… but something was strange. The longer she followed him the more— was he sneaking around? He was strolling down the main path now: *W… why in the world is he going to the main school building? What's going on in there at this time of night?*

Callimay put her back against the last tree before the open common and thought hard as she closed her eyes and leaned her head back: *Do I follow him? Do I risk it? Does he even know I'm alive? Maybe I have the upper hand there? … I don't know what to do! ~ Destan would. ~ He always does.*

She looked back and noticed she was about to lose sight of Toreon. In a moment of panic, she glanced around to see if anyone was watching or following her. Callimay let a cloud of fog out as she took a deep breath; him leaving her line of sight as said determined: *I have to know. I just have to.*

Like so many things which can be — and often are — overlooked because they never seem important, she never realized how loud the doors to the main school building were when they opened and closed… that was until she wanted to be as quiet as possible.

Once it did close, she ducked behind the closest table in case Toreon came back. Callimay's heart was pounding in her ears from being so nervous about him finding her; she felt anyone else close by would hear it. She heard a door close, but waited to see if he closed it to make her think he went on; while in reality, he was coming back to see who was following him.

After a couple minutes and no sign of him, she cautiously followed. There were several doors down the hall: the main lecture hall, the side doors for half of the smaller classrooms, and then the one at the end of the hall which led to Mr. Freigh's office. The main lecture hall was empty as were all the other rooms.

Callimay came back out into the hall and looked at the last door he could have gone through. For some reason she got a horrible feeling: *Why is Torcon snooping around this late… here of all places? How did he get through? Our keys don't have access without permission from faculty or Mr. Freigh himself.*

Before moving, she attempted to listen for him so she could find where he was; finally being able to and realizing he was looking for Mr. Freigh's office. By what he was saying, she gathered he was almost there. — He did get through! — Callimay stopped listening at this point and took off. Even though she had only been there three times, it was more than enough for her to know the way.

Now she started overthinking, and stood there for another minute, letting these thoughts run through her mind again… and again: *What if this is a trap? What if Toreon's snooping about is just a way to lure me into this situation?*

She inched closer and closer to the door and then jumped when she heard the lock snap and saw the little red light turn green. Her heart started pounding again so much so she could feel it pulsing in her ears. Callimay glanced around and then reached for the door handle, closing her eyes and pushing it open.

Nothing happened!

Taking a small sigh of relief, she took off running: *Typical spy movie scenario: when you want to be quiet the floor is always a tile one.*

Right before she turned to be in the hall where the offices were, she tried to listen for Toreon again. She couldn't hear him, but she heard actual voices in the hall. Callimay peeked around the corner and saw Baleck and someone in scrubs — the man who had tended to her and did the scan when she was there earlier. She couldn't understand what they were saying… it didn't make any sense. Mr. Freigh came out of his office and spoke with the two of them briefly before heading down the hall in the opposite direction of her. — Thank goodness for that! — Baleck and the other man then entered the medical exam room.

Callimay doubted she would have access to get into Mr. Freigh's office, but she thought it was at least worth a try: *I got this far without setting any alarms off. Maybe I'll be able to get in his office? Maybe he didn't put the lock back on my key.*

Still hesitant as she reached for the door handle, Callimay began to wait for the alarm to go off. She was amazed it unlocked, pausing yet again: *What if Mr. Willgun is in the office! Maybe this is a trap.*

Listening only proved that Baleck with Toreon. Unsure of where they were exactly, Callimay put her ear against the door to listen for their real voices.

Nothing.

Taking another deep breath to summon her courage, she reluctantly opened the door; finding the office empty. She dashed in and shut the door, then crept over toward the side door which led to the medical exam room.

The wall was indeed a one-way window. Baleck and the man in scrubs were talking with Toreon. They spoke for a little bit and then the man in scrubs put a cloth over his face; him out cold within moments.

It struck her that the look of the medical exam room was so much different from what she remembered… it looked four times as big! There were all these monitors and machines around. She wondered what they were doing, but saw Baleck headed for the door.

In a panic, she ran behind the desk and curled up in the open space where the seat was. He came around and she heard the rustling of pages being moved above her.

She focused to listen to him and heard: *Now where are those papers? I know I left his out here somewhere. … Oh come now. Mr. Freigh didn't even notice them earlier. I know he didn't touch them. … Ugh! He's already locked the safe. … I can't be losing it just be— aha! There they are.*

He then walked over to the window and read aloud, "Make sure the solvent and serum stabilize at forty-three point eight."

It took her every ounce of courage she had to stay calm when Baleck came back and sat down at the desk. He pushed himself just close enough to the desk that he couldn't see her but far enough away he wouldn't knock his legs against her.

Callimay put her quivering hand over her mouth and closed her eyes, trying to calm her breathing. She realized what would happen if Baleck found her — and Destan was nowhere nearby to help.

Knowing she was on her own, Callimay forced herself to push the fear aside and be open to hearing anything he had to say to himself… but heard something so disturbing she almost lost it: *I didn't foresee things going this far, but I must face reality: Destan is now extremely powerful. My advantage is he doesn't know that yet. Toreon on the other hand knows the abilities being bestowed to him. It is in no way equal, but since Destan doesn't know what other abilities he possesses, Toreon will be able to master him without any problem. And it may not even need to come to this, much to Toreon's displeasure. Callimay is always with Destan and we know his weak point is her. Toreon did his job well: prodding enough to prove it. But aside from that, they are both emotionally driven — in polar opposite directions of course —

and thus an exceptional weakness to be exploited. If he can successfully infiltrate it — driving Destan into frenzy mode — there won't be any way Callimay can save him 'or' herself for that matter. … Just a little bit longer and then this will all be over. The Purge will be a success.*

Baleck got up after a bit and went back into the other room. As soon as the door closed, Callimay crawled out from underneath the desk and scrambled to her feet so she could run to the door. She opened it and glanced in both directions; and then running as fast and as quiet as she could, she fled out of the building.

Destan! Callimay would call out as she dashed out toward Lookout Point. *Destan where are you? Please tell me you're still close by. Please! Where are you! Destan!*

She would stop and wait a minute for a reply and then repeat herself over and over.

It seemed like she had been out there forever… in a way. She wasn't sure if Toreon was done or if someone was watching the surveillance footage and could see her. Callimay was so winded she didn't think she could keep going. And yet, just when she was about to give up, she saw him in the distance.

"Oh, Destan." She sighed in relief as she stooped over to catch her breath. "I'm so glad you're back."

He didn't respond.

Unfazed at this lack of response, she ran up and started gasping, "You'll never bel—"

"Why are you out so late?" He cut off, his green eyes glaring at her. "You shouldn't be here"

"Well… I'm going to explain. See I—"

"You need to go back." Destan cut off again, reaching for her.

"I— fine! Be that way!" She retorted as she pulled away.

❦

Callimay slammed her room door when she got back. She was wracked with the emotional stress of learning to cope with Destan's push and pull while trying to comprehend what she heard from Baleck.

Most of her didn't want to even look at him, but she went to the window and watched Destan walk back.

His arms were stiff and rigid — his fists most likely clenched in his pockets — his head bowed and unmoving. He looked like he didn't care about the world around him… let alone the person he swore he did.

She couldn't stand to watch him exist in such a state and believe she was there for him to treat as he pleased, when he pleased. That this was going to be the way things were: she had to learn to deal with his moments of complete and utter shutdown, and then be willing to be the "fall guy" when he needed to vent. Callimay threw the curtains over the window and flopped onto her bed, crying from frustration.

❧

Destan got back to his room; the light on his desk welcoming him back. A grumbling sigh of frustration resonated in the room as he slammed the door behind him and stomped in as if he were mad at it.

After looking at all the papers on the desk, he began gathering them; starting with Callimay's. This exercise looked like it was intended to help, but he sure didn't show it.

And yet maybe it was helping. As if pausing to reminisce, he picked up his application and read through it. He began to be enraged with Mr. Freigh and the entire hierarchy of the Society and all they had done. Not only were the ones he described losing real people; the ones responsible for them dying was the hierarchy of the Society.

When he finished, Callimay's application had somehow found its way to the top of the stack. The sincerity of her words and desire for good contrasted his pointed anger and revenge. He read why they chose her, but couldn't understand why she had to be singled out like this. Why did she have to be the one to lose everything? Destan had already lost everything… in a way. But Callimay; she had a place to go back to where people cared for her. Him losing his life in this way meant nothing. At least it meant nothing to him at the time. But why do this to her?

Destan's thoughts brought him to the conclusion: the Society was the cause of all this hurt and pain Callimay was having. In a rage, he slammed the table and threw the papers to the side.

There was a thud quickly followed by a crash. This startling noise caused him to jump back in a defensive stance. He looked over and saw the roses he had picked for her now on the floor covered with shards of glass and splashed with water.

While kneeling to pick them up, the soft petals withering in his hands, he realized the real problem: *I've done all of this, Calli. This is my fault. All of it. They may have burdened you with this ability, but it was me who put you on their radar so fast. If I would've had my emotions under more control there would have been no need to have you help me. I knew they were going to choose me. I resigned to it from the start. But if it weren't for me, you would be innocent of everything going on and doing everything you could to fulfill what you came here to do. I caused you all of this heartache. I caused you all of this pain. It's my fault. I admit it! I pulled you in and have now locked you out. I said I cared but I've proven I'm not even capable of it when push comes to shove. You were just defending me earlier when I lashed out at you. … And whatever you had to tell me this evening was important enough for you to venture out alone to find me. You looked so terrified but glad to see me at the same time. And what did I do? I told you to leave. Oh, Calli! I know you need me. I know I need to abide by what I promised: we're a team. A very special kind of team; to remember I made the commitment of marriage to you. I'm failing miserably. I'm sorry.*

Destan saw it as clear as day: Callimay had become his collateral damage. In the cruelest form of the shadow calling the night black, he was being who he loathed: a leader who bullied and saw those around him — who trusted and worked toward the same goal — as inferior and insignificant.

Was it exactly what he wrote? No. But it was fundamentally the same. He'd vowed to be her leader. He'd promised to take care of her and be the person she could always run to in times of trouble.

These roses were showing him what he had done to Callimay: scattered as if frightened, some ripped and impaled by the glass shards or soaking wet from the spilt water. Some of them didn't even look like roses anymore. And whenever he touched one, it would crumble in front of him… as if cowering from him like she had so many times.

The roses would never be the same. There was no way to fix them. They were gone forever. Could he hope to fix what he destroyed between himself and Callimay? Was there any hope left?

Destan lay in bed that night and stared at the ceiling for the longest time. He thought back to what happened in the last two days, hoping he could fix everything… but he wasn't sure. There was no doubt he wanted to fix it, but he had hurt Callimay so much he wouldn't blame her if she gave up.

Here it was the very day they were betrothed and he was making everything hard for her.

It was too easy for him to sink back into his old self and ignore her altogether. It's what he had grown accustomed to, and he was able to function well in it.

But now? Things had to change. He had someone else to consider. Someone else to put before himself. Someone who needed more care than he'd ever given.

A single tear hesitated and then raced down the side of his face, appearing to make an attempt to avoid being seen. Destan closed his eyes and begged: *Calli? If you can hear me, or if you're even wanting to listen: I… I love you.*

~ 17 ~

She couldn't find any escape from her internal pain, even while sleeping, so Callimay got dressed and went for a walk. When she looked out, it was snowing pretty hard, but by the time she got outside, it calmed to the pace of dust as it wanders through the air.

Seeing her boots almost disappear when she got to the final step made her sigh in frustration; she wasn't expecting this much snow to "stay". And then faculty wouldn't arrive for at least another two hours to get it cleared, so she was left with nothing but her brute strength.

A beautiful blanket of what was known to Gastonians as winter's purity — the first snow — stretched over everything so gracefully. The only way she knew she was on a path was because of the lamp posts. She almost hated to ruin the picturesque view of this untouched snow, but it was snow… there would be plenty this winter.

The dense layer of clouds was breaking apart and allowing the stars to peek through. They were shining so bright since it was so cold, and twinkled and sparkled as if they were jealous of the beauty of the snow; trying everything they could to gain back the attention of Callimay.

As she got closer to the wooded area, the sky began to show actual color. She stopped at the fork at the base of Lookout Point and weighed her options as far as which way to go.

After a few moments, she turned and kept heading into the wooded area. She followed the river and would look toward the sky every once in a while when a bird would call out to let everything around know she was there or to see the slow change in the sky's color.

With it now being lighter out, she started seeing shallow tracks in the snow. The occasional seed or small berry suggested birds and other little fuzzy creatures were out and about. Seeing this caused Callimay's eye to focus on where the tracks led. — She was desperate to find something happy in the world around her.

Some distance in front of her, she noticed a few rabbits hopping through the snow. They were gray, but with the snow clinging to their fur so much they looked stark white. It appeared they were playing in the fluffy water instead of accomplish something by going somewhere.

Callimay stood there and watched them playing around; laughing to herself at this equally jovial and comical sight. One would jump extra high to cause more snow to fly into the air and fall on the others. In turn, these others would dash and dart about before coming back repeat the action to the original perpetrator. Their noses would twitch in irritation when they were bombed with the heavy and wet dust cloud of snow, while their ever-perked ears would constantly survey for any unusual sounds.

This whole time they were oblivious to her presence… until one of them darted straight at her and almost ran into her leg. The rabbit let out a grunting noise and turned back. Within seconds of him gathering his friends, they scurried in all directions, vanishing from sight.

"I can't seem to get anyone — and now it seems any 'thing' — to stay close to me." Callimay sighed as she started walking again.

At one of the bridges, she stopped and brushed the snow off the railing lean on it. She sighed and started to smile, seeing that te sun was just peeking over the horizon, spraying its golden fan of warmth over everything in sight. The clouds had vanished from the northern sky, so its glow was everywhere. Before her lay an endless sea of a landscape covered in snow, glistening with such a soft nature in some areas while in others it burned hot with flares to warn of the danger of warmth.

❦

As the sun peeked into Destan's room, reminding him it was time to get up, he slowly opened his eyes. His facial expression was nothing out of the ordinary at first glance; this change only visible by him alone: something inside of him wreaking havoc. And yet, the closer and longer you looked, you could see his eyes didn't stay focused like they always did. They darted around as if searching for something. —

Someone. — They were opened so wide you could have been able to see into his mind if you wanted to.

He usually popped up and got straight into his morning routine, but today was different: the guilt inside him weighing so heavy. He pulled himself out of bed and wandered across the room, fixing his eyes where the stack of papers was along with the collection of rose stems and petals. The fragrance of these blooms was still very much in the air; a constant reminder of the one person in this world he wanted to be with, but through his own stupidity and stubbornness feared he lost forever. A heavy sigh escaped before he looked away and walked past.

ↈ

Once he was ready, Destan grabbed his Bible and ventured outside. He was the first one out of his dorm — like usual — so he wasn't surprised to find no imprints in the snow. With it being Sunday, he cut across the green area to get to Callimay's dorm. They usually got to Assembly early — like they did for everything else — so he was hoping there wouldn't be any changes. How could this be possible, though? Was she going to pretend things were alright? Why? That'd be lying.

As he walked up, he saw a set of footprints. Not fresh ones, but still there. He looked to see where they went, knowing in his heart it had to be her. Without a second thought, he started following the trail which continued as far as he could see. Faculty was late in arriving, and so the paths weren't cleared yet, giving him an exact path to follow.

Destan continued jogging along, not sure what to expect at this point. Callimay had every right to be mad at him and tell him to leave. He broke his promise. Really, the best he could hope for was civility between the two of them as talked through their emotions. He knew he needed to keep his negative ones in better check; he'd known that for quite a long time. Anything she would say would be her perspective… and most likely the truth. He couldn't argue with that.

It was easy to spot where she stopped by the river; seeing all the rabbit tracks around the area. Not much longer, Destan came across the place she stopped at on the bridge. He glanced around, looking for other tracks — Toreon. There was only the one set but he wasn't willing to risk it.

As he became more and more concerned the farther he went, now coming up on him jogging beside this trail of footprints for an hour with no sign of her whatsoever, Destan saw that the footprints looked like they had just been made. For a brief moment, he stopped to listen; closing his eyes to help him focus.

Nothing but morning callers and the breeze in the trees.

Cringing as he took a deep breath, Destan continued on.

Where did she go? When did she leave? Why did she go alone?

A little while later he caught the scent of roses. He looked around almost frantic and finally saw Callimay. She was curled up, sitting near the shore of the lake where they'd been yesterday. Just one day earlier such sweet and wonderful memories were made at this very spot. Now? Now it was most likely going to be a war zone.

Around and near her were small red spots, so he ran up, concerned as to what happened; and then slowed when he saw they were rose petals. There was a trail of her footprints down to where he knew the bushes were, a trail of the petals paralleling her tracks back to where she was now sitting.

He tried to find words, but he didn't know how to fix what he had broken. Destan wasn't ready for this.

Callimay could hear what he was saying to himself, but chose to refrain from replying. She wanted to fly into his arms by what she was hearing, but she needed him — not just a desire or want or request — to tell her how he felt and what was going on. She needed to see he was willing to be open with her and trust her.

And so she sat and waited.

And waited.

"Calli?"

"I thought since there wasn't any wind they would make it, but the cold got too much for them to handle." She deflected as she looked at the bare stems in front of her. "They are an extremely hardy plant, but even they can only take so much before they've had enough."

Destan knew what she was alluding to as he cringed, "Calli?"

Her face looked so much paler since her cheeks and nose were rosy-colored; her normal, cheerful face drawn and in survival mode. These looks didn't deceive what she was feeling inside: she didn't want to risk showing emotion of any kind, really; worried even unpleasant ones would be "wasted". And on top of everything, her eyes showed their disinterest and frustration with the situation — him.

Destan was still trying to get his thoughts together but knew by how she looked that he needed to speak his mind no matter how awkward it sounded, "I messed everything up so bad. I… I can't keep things stable in my mind for some reason. — I know excuses don't change things. — I should've never lashed out at you like I did. You weren't mad at me; you were defending me. … I wasn't listening. Later, I will admit I didn't care to. I was so wrapped up in my own problems that I didn't see I was shoving you aside. I wanted you to be safe but I know I epically failed at communicating it. In fact, it wasn't even a fail: I just didn't. — I know it's hard to see, but I 'am' trying. It was late in me realizing, but I 'did' realize. I… I just hope I realized in time. … Calli? Calli I'm sorry."

She listened and looked at him the whole time, it looking like she wasn't affected by it at all. Deep down, she knew it was hard for him to say what he just did; but at the same time: things had been very hard for her. She didn't want to sound heartless or selfish, but then again, he had to understand she needed some consideration.

The reality of everything was wearing on her and making her tired of being the one to constantly say she was sorry. Callimay wanted a man who would lead her, while at the same time listen to her. She wanted to know there would be healthy stability in their relationship.

After a little bit, she let out a heavy breath; it looking like the billowing steam from a train as it worked to gain traction on the track, "I appreciate your apology, Destan. It means so much to me. I just… it's so hard for me to relax or think I have anything figured out when it comes to you. Something always seems to come up; locking you down like there's an air raid. And all you do is leave me outside where it's dark without any protection. … I know things aren't easy but I need to know I'm wanted: actions that match promises. Don't just say, 'do'. I would say please, but this isn't a request; and I think you know that."

"I know." He sighed, frustrated with himself as he hid his eyes and ran his hand through his hair. "Words mean nothing without being accompanied with appropriate action. It isn't something you should 'have' to ask for. It's an expectation. And it's one I know I need to take more seriously. You're supposed to hold me accountable and I'm supposed to allow you to. … I'm sorry."

"I need to know 'we are a team' as you liked to call it. And the only way this is going to happen is if we talk. I know sometimes you need space, but tell me — don't snap at me. Don't leave me hanging and wondering if I did or said something to cause the stress. … Talk. To. Me." Callimay demanded as her now fiery gaze rested on him. "I know things won't be fluffy bunnies and glittering rainbows all the time. And to be blunt and realistic, I know there'll probably be very little of these 'good' things at first because of everything else going on. I'm not one-hundred percent ready and I'm in no way wanting it, but I know it's going to come. But just because something is hard doesn't mean I'm run away from it. As long as I'm not alone I will be able to get through it. — I… I know I've had my moments of doing the exact same thing to you, and I'm sorry for that. … I wish we could have some time to heal and relax. A little time— some 'us' time. Time we could have to work on our relationship instead of fighting all this chaos and frustration. Maybe I'm asking for something impossible. I—"

"You're not," Destan replied as he reached out and put his hand on her shoulder. "Anything you've ever asked for is what 'every' person deserves. It's foundational relationship conduct… let alone what's needed in marriage. You're not crazy or asking for the impossible. — I know with us being so different when it comes to emotions that it's making things difficult and challenging for me. Not impossible, please don't think that. It's just going to be a process. And there may, at times, need to be allowances made for each other. I'm not saying to brush it off or let one to mistreat the other; I just— there are some differences that can't change. For one thing: I'm a man and you're a woman."

She started to smile, but let it vanish.

"I guess what I'm trying to say is: we both need patience. An overwhelming amount of it. You're doing so much better in that area than I am… but Callimay? I know we can get through this. I have faith that we can." Destan said determined as he took her hands in his. "We just need to have the emotional and mental strength to keep at it. You are a great encourager. I'm hoping some of that will rub off on me sooner rather than later because I know you are in desperate need of it.

… Callimay? I 'am' committed to this: to us. And I know for a fact being away from this forsaken place will help. But I also know that until then, things need to keep moving forward. So I'm sorry for what's happened. I'm sorry for what I did to you. I have no excuses and I want to fix this; I messed up. Will you give me another chance?"

"There's no going back."

"I know there's not. I don't want to go back to my life and the way it was before you came. I can't lo— I don't want to think of it. Believe me: I want to keep moving forward… with you."

For a few seconds, she stared him down; somehow thinking doing so would prove something… and then replied, "I forgive you."

Destan sighed as he slumped his shoulders and let his hands drop, "I'm so sorry for what I said and did, Calli."

She sniffled a little and then wrapped her arms around his left one, leaning her head against his shoulder. He put his free arm around her and leaned his head over hers as she cried.

After what turned out to be almost an hour, he asked, "So, what were you trying to tell me last night?"

"Oh! Oh my gosh Destan. It's horrible! Just horrible. I… I don't know what t—"

"Just calm down," he soothed as he rubbed her shoulders.

"Last night I was watching you leave…" she said in a sadder tone which trailed off as she looked toward the ground; and then sounded shaky as she looked back to him and bit her lip: *I saw Toreon sneaking around last night. At first I didn't know who it was, but when I found out I thought he was following you. I couldn't bear not knowing what was going on so I followed him.*

Callimay! Destan reprimanded as his eyes started to flash at her. *What did I tell you about Falcon—*

I know it was crazy of me, but I couldn't sit back and not know what in the world was going on. She defended as she continued to explain, cowering from his gaze. *He ended up going in the opposite direction. I still don't know how he got there, but he ended up in Mr. Freigh's office. Well, the medical exam room next to it. — Come to think of it, I don't know how 'I' got back there. … Anyway. Mr. Freigh, Mr. Willgun, and another man in scrubs — the one who helped me —

they met in the hall and spoke for a bit. Mr. Freigh then left; and thankfully he went in the opposite direction of where I was. — It's as if they were expecting Toreon. They had the medical exam room all set up with these huge machines and monitors. — That one wall was a one-way window, you were right. — The room looked like it was four times bigger than when we were there. And then I had to hide under the desk when Mr. Willgun came in. He never 'said' anything so I had to 'listen' to him. … Destan? I can't— what he said has me so terrified of what's going on here!*

I'm right here Calli. It's alright.

He gave Toreon abilities so he could kill us. She stuttered as she clutched her arms across her chest; trying to stop wheezing. *He wants us dead, Destan. Especially you!*

"He what!"

He never said 'why' he wanted us gone, just with the history both you and I have with Toreon — and the emotions involved — he could easily rip us apart and kill us, Callimay repeated as the lump in her throat continued to well. *I'm scared— no, I'm terrified Destan! What are we going to do! I mean… what 'can' we do?*

"So it was them all along." He uttered in a furious tone under his breath; and then made up his mind: *We can't stay any longer. We have to leave. And the sooner the better. But we can't arouse suspicion. I just hope we get a chance before they find our files are fakes.*

But how! No one is allowed to leave.

Callimay? Did you find out what ability Toreon was given?

No. Maybe I should have stayed to—

No! No. I'm glad you got out of there. Destan initially said in a raised tone, then calmed as he reached his hand out and brushed the side of her face, *I'm so glad they didn't find you. Let's get back to my room. I want to check something from our files.*

🕭

Destan started jogging back and then realized Callimay wouldn't be able to keep up. He turned and went back for her, seeing her struggling through the near two feet of snow which still coated the path, "I'm sorry I can't keep up. My leg isn't feeling too great."

"Don't," he took her hand in his; lifting her chin with his other hand. "'I' was the one going too fast. I highly doubt a couple minutes will make any difference."

❦

Once they got out of the wooded area, the paths were cleared and thus a much easier walk for Callimay. They walked at the fastest pace she could, but nothing that would arouse suspicion from anyone: they were just a couple who had been out in the freezing weather, sitting in the snow for a few hours. On that front alone they were moving quicker; making it back right after breakfast finished.

She gasped and flinched when she saw everyone leaving the main school building, "I lost track of time! And that means— we missed morning Assembly! At least there's evening, but— what was I thinking! … Well, I guess I wasn't."

Destan groaned as he looked down and away from her at what he had in his hand; frustrated with his own lapse in priorities. "I wasn't thinking either. I should've kept track of time. I knew better."

"Well so did I. I can't let my emotions cloud my judgment like this. I've done it twice now."

"I know remembering will always be your own responsibility, but it's my job to lead you. … Do you need to eat something?"

"No. I'm fine. And yes, I'm sure. But if you—"

"Don't worry about me."

As they continued along, Destan noticed Toreon standing outside the main door to their dorm. He slowed to pretty much a standstill because he couldn't tell if Toreon was relaxing or waiting for someone.

In light of everything — mainly Toreon having abilities, but also since Callimay was with him — he didn't want to provoke anything right then. He thought as fast as he could, squeezing her hand when he decided: *I know this wasn't our plan, but I think we need to avoid my place seeing as how 'Toreon the moron' is hanging out at the front door. After what you told me; we need to stay away from him at all costs right now.*

Destan! She scolded as she veered to the left to take the path to her dorm. *Why would you say—*

What? He is.

⚜

Every single inch of Callimay's room was drenched with the pleasing and almost intoxicating aroma of roses. It made him forget about everything for a moment and just focus on her. An ever-growing part of him wanted these calm moments to last longer.

She looked back and saw how he seemed to be lost in thought, so she asked, "Is everything alright?"

"Oh. … Yeah. I'm fine. Everything's fine."

"O… kay. So what did you want to look at in our files?"

"I wanted to double-check something," he commented in a vague way as he sat on the other end of the sofa.

Callimay sighed and hung her head: *I'm over here, Destan.*

No response of any kind.

After a few moments, she scooted closer and asked, "Double-check what in our files?"

"To see from their on-site observations of us so I've got a better idea where their network of cameras is located. The number one reason is because we need to find a way out. They won't let us leave; definitely not after what you heard Mr. Willgun say. … If we can find an area where the cameras aren't concentrated, then we may be able to find a weak spot in the perimeter and be able to slip through it. We've got to be careful, though. I'm sure they would be able to notice us 'hunting' for weak spots, so we've got to be very discrete. — Secondly, if there's a large enough area, I need to work after school this week to get a feel for what I can do. I need the basics of turning it on and off at least. And I would prefer to do it out of their eyesight; if it's even possible. … Could I ask you a favor?"

"What is it?"

"Could you be a lookout? You would be able to — for lack of better term — 'hear' someone coming and let me know to stop. Helping you train wasn't anything which drew suspicion. Mine will. … But I'm not going to make you do it if you do—"

"Of course I can! I wouldn't mind it at all." Callimay answered in a cheerful voice, glad he asked her for help. "When you were reading through your papers, did you happen to see anything about what you have and how it works?"

"Some," Destan leaned forward as he rubbed his chin. "Most of it was so technical that I couldn't make hands or feet of it. But! From what I could gather, not only do I have enhanced speed capabilities but I also have heightened strength. Though, the way it was worded, it would only be in a certain 'mode' where I would be able to use the heightened strength… if I am remembering it correctly that is."

"Frenzy? Was the mode called frenzy?"

"Maybe," he said rather unsure as he sat up and looked at her. "What made you think of that? Did you read it too?"

"No! No. I was remembering what Mr. Willgun mentioned when he was talking about you."

"Oh. I can't say for sure. It sounds familiar. — And then there was that strange part at the end. It said there was something else about the serum's capabilities, but they didn't know exactly what it was since it apparently had never been tested. At least that's what it sounded—"

"So they gave you something they don't fully understand? — Pfft. — Brilliant on their part."

He sat there and stared off into the distance, his overpowering silence bringing their conversation to an abrupt end. It took her a little bit, but Callimay found the courage to speak up; her trying her best to be as quiet as possible when she got up and walked to the window, "Well. I— surely Toreon has left."

"Has he?"

"I… I think so. Unless he's hiding inside the little archway." She pressed her face against the ice-cold glass.

"He didn't," Destan answered, causing her to jump. "Easy!"

"I just didn't hear you walk up behind me is all. Where is he?"

"He's right outside 'this' door," he growled as he motioned for her to look down.

"Well isn't that great. That's the only way in or out of here… well, quietly anyway. The back door automatically triggers the alarm. Ugh! We're stuck."

"Hold on. Maybe not. … Look who showed up. He must've been waiting for her to come down and let him in."

"Gallia had a thing for Toreon from the moment she saw him. She even told me she was jealous of me after the first day of orientation. The first day! My goodness, I was being nice to everyone; not just him. And I was 'never' being nice to him in the way she was suggesting. That wasn't why I came here."

"People will see what they want to. … We should be able to go—"

"Her room is just down the hall here. If they do what they normally do, they'll stand out in the hall for a while. Why? They giggle too much when they talk for me to understand most of what they say. — By the way, how did you get to be so secluded?"

"It's always been like that. I never thought much about it after the second night. Maybe there are more girls than guys here?"

"Maybe. … I'll go check real quick to see if they are going to hang out in the hall for a while."

Destan went to pick up his coat and follow Callimay to the door, but heard her warn in a yelp: *Toreon's at my door. Hide!*

He didn't want to leave her alone, but knew she was thinking about both of their safeties by not giving Toreon any more ammo than he already thought he had. Looking around the room, the only place Destan knew he could hide was under her bed; so he grabbed his coat and dove underneath just in the nick of time.

It took only a few seconds for Destan to regret his decision… he wanted to confront him right then and there. Toreon belittled Callimay with every comment he made. This "was" a game to him… and one it appeared he was enjoying too much for Destan's liking.

"I appreciate you coming to check and see how I was doing, Toreon." Callimay stammered as he pushed his way in. "It's just—"

"I'm so amazed you survived the fall. And with only the cuts you had. No concussion, I heard?"

"It was a miracle I survived. Thankfully the only contact my head made with anything was this cut I have. — But really, I—"

"It's as if you… never. Touched. The ground." Toreon reached out to touch her face, the most unbecoming gleam in his eye. "By the way, where is Destan? You two are in—"

"There you are." Gallia interrupted as she barged in. "I've been looking everywhere for you, my Prince."

"I was only telling Callimay I wanted to check on her and then was glad she wasn't injured any more than she was." Toreon explained rather irritated as Gallia took his outstretched hand.

"That was kind of you, now can we go?" She ignored what he said as she tossed her head up and away from Callimay; her curly hair bobbing as if nodding in agreement with her request. "The stench of this air does nothing but clash with my perfume."

"Of course, my Duchess," Toreon turned and escorted her out; turning back for a moment to eye Callimay.

That was the last straw; she slammed the door shut and melted to the floor. She couldn't catch her breath, her hands couldn't stop shaking, and her heart was pounding so fast it was hurting.

Destan rolled out from his hiding place, getting to her as fast as he could and holding her.

I'm not even safe in my own room, she whimpered as she gripped his forearm. *He knows I didn't have a concussion; that something happened to keep me from hitting the ground. You don't think he—*

"He's gone, Calli. I'm here. Don't think about it or worry. He's gone. … I'm right here." He tried to soothe as he stroked her hair.

She continued to shiver and breathe heavily, making him wonder if what he was doing was helping any. Though, when he did try to let go, she seemed to get worse.

I know that was the hardest thing for you to do, but you did an amazing job, he said determined, though somehow still being able to sound gentle so he didn't frighten her. *You kept yourself together when you needed to and took care of the situation the best way you knew. — You're so much stronger than you think you are. Mr. Willgun calls emotions weaknesses, but you've shown they're your strength. — I will get us out of here. I will keep you safe. No matter what the Society tries, I won't let them take you away from me and 'I' won't leave you. I promise, Calli.*

She wrapped her arms around him and slowly calmed down. The poor thing was too distraught to even cry. She buried her head against his chest and clung to him. Callimay had one thought running through her mind over and over again this entire time: she wanted to leave this place and this "chapter" of her life.

Eventually, she was able to loosen her grip and looked up at Destan who had been so calming this whole time; being able to whisper, "I'm ready to go if you are."

"Alright," his small smile reached out to her as he helped her up.

ℬ

After checking the hall, he sheltered Callimay in case Toreon was still around; and then made the two-minute walk with her to his room. There wasn't a soul in sight as they walked there and around the dorm, giving them both an added level of comfort and security.

Destan made sure the extra lock was pulled on the door when they got in. In fact, all his actions since he found out about Toreon were very pointed and quick. It caught her off guard, but she understood things were getting more dangerous the longer they stayed. They needed to work as hard and fast as they could; and they were going to have to be quiet about it all.

Some of it was frustrating to learn as far as what the Society was spying on. Leisure time was only free from their physical presence, not their technological extensions. Nothing was gathered from the wooded area of the complex. It was like this due to the inconsistency in video feed they would have due to the change in visibility from the canopy of leaves and thick undergrowth.

"The lake area looks to be our best bet to stay near and still be protected," Destan concluded as he put the papers down.

"Alright. … But what about the 'weak spot' in the perimeter you talked about? Wouldn't you think they have the fence-wall thing guarded all the way around this complex? I mean, the fence that's out front must go all the way around, right?"

"In some way or another I'm sure they do. But there's got to be something. Some small place we could dash through and get out."

In the brief moment of silence, while the two of them thought, they heard a knock on the door. Destan motioned for Callimay to stay quiet and went to the door, asking who it was.

Another knock.

Something wasn't right. He jogged back and rushed to hand her the papers as quiet as possible.

She wasn't sure why he was so concerned, but did as he directed and made sure to stay quiet.

He motioned to the closet as he led her; and then after she got in, closed the door. Destan made sure the extra lock was secure and then opened the door to the hall, "What?"

"Don't play dumb with me, Nevrille." Toreon lashed out as he slammed his fist on the door.

"Don't have to when you've got it covered 'so' well."

"Alright, Nevrille. Alright. If that's how you want it." Toreon backed away and put his hands in the air, looking innocent. "We'll play this game your way."

If you call playing with people's lives a game then you are sick and demented. He replied in disgust as Callimay listened; finishing, "And what 'game' is that?"

"You can't win. You will lose her. You know you can't save her. Anything you do is going to be in vain. If anything, it will only delay the inevitable. … But you know? The more I think about it: when it comes down to it — you're scared. I'd like to take the credit, but I know there's someone else you're more scared of. Actually, you're terrified of them… yourself. You're scared to death you will prove to be who you've turned into, 'cliffhanger'."

"What are you talking about?" Destan rolled his eyes. "We're both adults, Toreon. Quit hacking."

"Callimay will die and you know you can't save her from it. No matter what you try, this is how it will end. — You too, obviously; but you couldn't care less about yourself. — I will relish this victory and make sure you feel every bit of pain possible."

"You called this a game, right?"

"Yeah. But that's—"

"Well correct me if I'm wrong, but aren't games undetermined until the end? — Well, fair games anyway? — And you wouldn't be the kind of guy who stoops to lies and deceit to win… would you? What kind of victory would that be? People would see right through it and never recognize you for it. … And I doubt 'you' want to be the one to sully the good name of Swinchpuck."

"Shut up."

"You're the one who came here. I didn't ask you over."

"Just watch your back." Toreon threatened as he got in his face as much as he dared. "There's not a place on Quidoria either of you can run to where I won't be able to find you. Not 'one' place. Just remember that, Nevrille."

"What in the world do you have against me and Callimay?" He asked flippantly as he shuffled his feet. "It's like we're on your hit-list or something."

Callimay switched to listen to Toreon and soon realized things were escalating quicker than she could've imagined. Destan did have a better handle on his emotions than she thought, but he was showing major disturbances internally. And aside from that, Toreon said something to himself to reveal why he came: *Destan! You've got to stop. Toreon is playing you. He's trying to get you to lose control.*

"You stole her from me, Nevrille. What more of a reason do I need to want you gone?"

"I didn't steal her. You threw her away."

Destan, stop! Please! Callimay cried out as she put her hand against the closet door. *Don't feed into his rants. He's trying to get you angry. He's doing this on purpose. He knows your weakness and he's manipulating it. Destan please!*

"Pfft. Why would I throw her away?"

"Because she wouldn't be your plaything and obey your every command," Destan gripped the door handle tighter. "I don't know what else that's called."

You have got to stop! Callimay continued to try to rein in his internal rant. *Don't let him control your emotions.*

"Oh? And she doesn't for you?" Toreon scoffed as he pressed harder on the door, causing the lock to bend. "Looks like she follows you around like a little puppy dog who would do anything to make her master happy. Ruff, ruff. Ruff, ruff. Do you pet her like a dog?"

Please don't! Callimay begged, knowing it was starting to get harder for her to keep contact with him.

"Even if I did, I'd be treating her better than the Eskimos your family butchers. — There's a major difference between her 'wanting' to and you 'demanding' it." Destan pointed out as he felt the door start to give.

At this point Callimay couldn't reach him anymore; she knew it. He was so enraged she couldn't get through: *This must be what Mr. Willgun was talking about last night! I've got to get to him. But how! He's pushed me out.*

There were only a couple second she had to think of something to do: physically intervene. It wasn't something she wanted to do, but what else could she do?

Callimay hid the papers under what she could find in the closet and summoned every ounce of courage she had, walking up beside Destan and facing Toreon. Something inside of her screamed to not do it, but she placed her hand on his shoulder and asked, "Destan?"

"Where did you come from?" Toreon jumped back.

It was easy for Callimay to tell his plan was falling apart since she was there; though Destan wasn't responding well to anything going on. If anything he was getting worse.

"I've been here this whole time," she answered confused as she bobbed her focus back and forth between them. "What's going on? Why are you here?"

"Oh… nothing." Toreon stammered as he stepped back, looking nervous. "I… I was just letting him know you were doing well. I guess I didn't know you had talked. So, I— I'll be going. Bye."

She was shocked. After all he said, Toreon was utterly terrified to see her. Was he all bark and no bite? In his own twisted way did he care for her? She quickly put it out of her mind and focused on Destan who was standing there: his hand gripping the door handle was white, his posture so rigid he was like a statue, his eyes piercing in their fixed gaze, and his emotions all dialed to rage — every known earmark of frenzy mode.

"Destan?" She asked in a loud and worried tone as she tried to shake his shoulder. "Destan say something."

No response.

The next thing she tried was grabbing his left hand to pry it off the door handle.

Nothing but death itself could lessen the grip he had on it.

Now she began panicking. Callimay wasn't sure what to do so he would "come back".

Without thinking, she raised her hand to slap him… but seeing the look on his face made her stop. But doing nothing wasn't going to help this situation either.

"Destan!" She screamed, seeing if it would get his attention.

Again, no response.

Callimay could see he was breathing heavy and fast by the fuming sound he was making and the violent recoiling of his chest: *What is wrong? Why won't you listen to me! He's gone, Destan. Toreon's gone. I'm right here. I'm safe. Let him go. Come back to me. Destan!*

She repeated herself, again and again, trying to focus more each time. Destan "spiked" — or what someone might think of the term for him emotionally "snapping" — causing her to have an extreme migraine instantly flare. He let go of the door handle, released the lock, and started down the hall after Toreon; ignoring Callimay who was now passed out on the floor right next to him.

Somehow she came to within a few seconds and managed to get to the door; stumbling as she came into the hall.

One last time she cried out with everything she had left before collapsing and falling unconscious: *Destan, please! Don't do this! I can't lose you! Please!*

ᚼ

It appeared she was trying to talk, but as Callimay rocked her head back and forth, all that came out were moans. She eventually opened her eyes and jumped up; her eyes darting around to see where she was and what had happened to Destan.

"It's alright, Callimay." He calmed as he stood up and put his hands out to help relax her. "I'm here. Everything's alright now. Calm down."

"W… what happened?"

"I'm not… 'exactly' sure. All I remember was wanting to make Toreon pay for what he said. — I could hear you, but I kept ignoring what you were saying. — Now I know how stupid that was: I forgot about Toreon having abilities. … I heard you the last time; and when I looked back, you were lying there unconscious. It wasn't until I saw you that I came back to myself. So, I got you back in here and it's been about a half hour since. Why did you pass out? Are you alright?"

"I am now."

"I… I'm concerned about getting stuck in that zoned-out area where I'm so angry and full of rage," Destan admitted as he looked down at his clenched fists, seeming to struggle to get them to open. "I know according to all those papers you are supposed to be able to help me, but I'm not sure if they're right. I do hear you; most of the time. But I'm still choosing to ignore you. I'm not… I'm not trusting you like I know I need to. It's more dangerous than I thought it w—"

"Well," Callimay started as she rubbed his shoulder. "I guess we'll have to work on it won't we?"

"Always the optimist."

"Well it seems like someone needs to be right now. Accepting defeat before you've even started will more times than not doom you to that end. Don't assume things will go wrong. … Of course I say that but I know I've done the same thing before while we're working on physics."

Destan asked half shocked, half desperate. "Will you help me even after I did this? … I don't— why would you?"

"I'd say it's called forgiveness, but there's nothing to forgive."

"But I hurt you… again. I know I did. And I didn't listen to you."

"I'm your— wow, it's strange to say this: I'm your fiancé, bride, or whatever you want to call me. Regardless, I am yours. You said we are a team, and in this type of team you're my leader. You're just as new to this as I am. Well, that is unless you're hiding something from me." She tried to be light-hearted as she looked into his frightened eyes. "What I'm trying to say is: we're both Christians trying to learn how to work with each other in a new way. This is just more challenging because of what's happening with— am I even making sense anymore?"

"Yes," he assured; looking content and more relaxed now. "Yes you are, Calli. Thank you for being my helper and reminding me what's important: God. And that if we follow His commands, everything else will fall into place perfectly."

She sighed before she finished, sounding more at ease herself, "I love you Destan. — We'll figure this out. Right? We've just got to work hard at it. … When do you want to start?"

"Right now."

"Then let's go."

"Are you sure you're alright?" He almost gasped, catching her so she wouldn't fall. "What's wrong?"

"I'm a little light-headed is all," she gripped his arm. "My head still hurts some."

It's my fault. He said in a defeated tone and then asked, "Are you sure you can go? I don't want y—"

"I'm fine." Callimay brushed off as she went to the closet and grabbed her coat. "Really Destan. I'm fine."

ℬ

As they walked outside, they heard a constant hum of conversation coming from the direction of the circular drive. Callimay was a bit more curious than Destan was, but he followed her over to the large group of students. She didn't like "listening" to them, so she asked a few of them what was going on.

No one wanted to answer.

Most ignored her; a select few did reply… but were very belittling in how they addressed her. — That was no help.

Destan kept his composure and motioned to her as he strolled to the far edge. He stood almost a head taller than the next tallest student there, so his view was never blocked no matter where he stood. On the other hand, Callimay was on the shorter side in the student body and struggled in smaller classes to see since she sat in the back… or when there was a crowd like now.

When she poked her head around the end of this wall of people, she saw a row of vehicles, "What in the— whose are those?"

"They are the faculties', Callimay." Mr. Freigh answered in a pleasant tone as he walked up beside her.

"Why are they here?" Destan put his arm around her and pulled her closer. "If I'm allowed to ask, that is."

"Of course. There is nothing secretive about it. — With this week being study hall and finals prep, the faculty which has been here this semester is leaving to be with their families. Baleck and I, along with a handful of others, will remain until the end of next week. A new group of faculty will arrive throughout that week to offer new eyes and ears for next semester."

"Oh, I see," Callimay tried nodding, but started to feel dizzy again from moving so much.

"Oh, Destan." Mr. Freigh turned his attention. "I wanted to let you know I w— are you alright, Callimay?"

"I have a migraine. I'll be alright." She assured as Destan shifted his hold on her, his eyes looking concerned as he watched over her.

"Very… very well." Mr. Freigh nodded; still looking concerned and hesitant; but continued, "I will be leaving during the middle of the week for a brief time. Something urgent has come up I need to see to elsewhere. So, if you were planning to meet during the beginning of break I will be unavailable. I apologize if that interrupts your plans."

What came up so pressing that you have to see to it like 'that'? And where is 'elsewhere'? Destan asked suspicious, and then responded, "Thank you for letting me know. I will keep it in mind."

"Very good. Well, I will see the two of you tomorrow."

"Goodbye." Callimay waved, still holding tight onto Destan's arm.

What did he mean by: 'I will see the two of you tomorrow'? He almost growled, nit-picking every word he said.

What he said seemed a bit off; but maybe something really did come up. It might be something with his family. — And maybe he was meaning he would see us around at some point tomorrow since it is a school day. We could be reading too much into this since we know so much more.

True. He bowed his head and then began scanning the area again, *I do have a healthy level of concern; and doubt everything they say.* "Are you ready? I mean… can you?"

"Let's stay and see what happens. I haven't seen the gate opened since we got here… and it would give me the time I need to rest."

You're right.

It took nothing for Callimay to notice his change in tone and expression: *What is it?*

With Mr. Freigh leaving and Mr. Willgun being left in control of everything, I want to get out of here when he does.

That's not much time at all!

I know. Destan sighed as he gently rubbed her arm. *But I've got to get you out of here. After what you overheard from Mr. Willgun and the way Toreon is now acting— things are 'way' out of hand. I've got to get you where it's safe.*

But where is that? You heard Toreon.

I'm inclined to believe it was nothing but bark. He backed off the second he saw you — right after everything he said. He might 'know' he has abilities, and he might 'know' what his mission is… but I can tell he is just now figuring out what that means. I feel pretty confident in saying the vast majority of people don't feel comfortable taking someone else's life; as in they pull the trigger. He's having a hard time implementing it because of you. Destan observed as they looked on. *I just hope he doesn't get to the point where he can follow through. — But you do have a point. We don't know what Toreon's abilities are.*

I wish we did.

I know. He put his chin on top of her head. *But this means we have to be ready for anything. And in doing so we will be able to keep ourselves safer. — Who knows. If he doesn't get his act together and do his job, they just might find someone else here to give abilities to so they take us out.*

Don't say things like that, Destan. Please. She begged as she looked up to him; tears in her eyes.

It's a hard truth, Callimay… but it is the truth.

But it makes Mr. Freigh and Mr. Willgun sound like heartless people who want others to do their bidding. To keep themselves protected at the expense of someone else.

Umm… well correct me if I'm wrong, but isn't that 'exactly' what they did to us? It's the very reason we're able to communicate without talking like this?

I… Callimay tried to figure out how to say what she meant. *I guess what I meant was: if they want us to fight the Rogues then why have Toreon out to get us? Why destroy what they see as their only salvation from the current situation?*

Destan's eyes shifted a bit and he pursed his lips, seeming to be deep in thought.

I mean, who would fight against themselves while there's an enemy out there? It just doesn't make sense. Something else is going on. Something other than giving people abilities.

There 'is' something more sinister going on and I've got a— I'm not willing to have you stay so I can find out what it is.

I wonder if he knows about our abilities? Callimay asked as she tried to be nonchalant as she looked for Toreon.

I would assume they told him. It would make sense to. But what do they do that makes sense? … Hey, look. They're getting ready to leave. Well, I think they are anyway.

We should probably talk out loud some. We don't want people — especially Toreon — getting suspicious.

Alright. He almost laughed out loud. *Though you do realize it would be even more suspicious if I said much… right?*

Very funny. She sounded somewhat sarcastic as she rolled her eyes. "I never realized how many faculty we had. Or that getting out was such a process."

Only one vehicle was allowed out at a time. The vehicle was scanned, faculty checked off of a list, and their badge scanned and handed over once they made it to the closed gate. After this, there was a small discussion between the person at the gate and the person in the vehicle prior to it opening.

They left like they were shot out of a cannon!

A variety of gasps and exclamations rose from the group of students present; which had grown to just about the entire student body at this point. The gate opened and closed at a rather reasonable rate. Why did they peal out like that?

This same process was completed for each of the following faculty, not one of them looking startled: *This is our way out, Callimay. Time how long the gate stays open next time.*

Okay… she answered slowly as she glanced at her wrist, realizing she never put her watch back on. *Umm… well. … I'd say it looks like it's about thirty-four seconds.*

It's about what, five-hundred feet from here to the gate?

Maybe. I don't know. — Wait. Did you see that?

What?

Watch the tree branch by the gate. Callimay nodded in the direction of the willow tree to their right, being careful not to point so she wouldn't draw attention. *See it? Right… then!*

The tree is moving in the wind.

Look at how it moves though. It's like the branch is pushed out of the way. It doesn't sway like it would be with the wind moving it. And it's even hanging over something not there. See?

What in the… Destan said shocked when the branch fell free and then the same thing happened again. *What is causing that?*

Is this why they have to peal out when they leave? There's some kind of invisible force field which can only be lowered for so long before it comes back on? It doesn't stay down for more than… eight seconds it looks like. That's not much time at all, Destan.

We don't have much time in any area. He commented; still amazed with the bizarre sight he was seeing. *Come on, let's go. We'll use our bikes so we can get out and back faster.*

Alright. But how does it explain the gate being wide open for so long when we got here? I didn't run through, and neither did you.

Well, maybe this is a way they 'help' keep us here. There wasn't any need when we first got here. But now 'I' sure want to leave. — Anyway! Let's go. Destan suggested; and then turned back when she stopped, "What's wrong?"

"It's… nothing."

He looked around and saw a certain someone walking in their direction, "It was Toreon, wasn't it?"

"Let's go," she began to walk away; and then felt him grab her arm, "What it is?"

"Just follow my lead."

"Quite the spectacle, huh?" Toreon asked in a completely civil and conversational tone as he focused his stare on Callimay.

"Yeah," Destan pulled her closer to him.

"You should hang out with Gallia and myself tonight. It'd be fun to have two powerhouse couples spending quality time together."

"I think our definitions of 'fun' aren't anywhere near the same." He gritted his teeth as he felt Callimay beginning to shiver. "And I know you don't see us as your caliber when you talk about power. Let alone the fact we have somewhere else to be this evening."

"You both do have that bizarre meeting you go to every Sunday morning and evening, I forgot. Oh well. It was a suggestion." Toreon shrugged his shoulders and began to walk by, then stopped and took a lock of Callimay's hair; running his fingers through it, "You used to do your hair all the time for me, dear Callimay? What's changed, my plaything? Does h—"

"Leave her. Alone." Destan said disgusted, gripping his wrist and shoving him back.

Toreon had his Cheshire-cat grin on as he stepped back and looked at Callimay. She cowered from his gaze and was now clinging to Destan whose eyes flashed like they did the day they left during physics. It appeared Toreon wasn't fazed in the slightest and stood there, his hands up as if surrendering and calling the issue resolved.

Destan immediately turned and escorted Callimay to the school building to grab something to eat before everyone else came in; making sure they weren't followed.

ℬ

She was in a daze when they got inside. It was like she was walking from muscle memory to where their usual spot was and didn't move once she sat down. Destan walked over and sat beside her, furious with Toreon and horrified with how debilitated she became.

Him touching her hand made her flinch and gasp.

"Calli… it's me." He calmed as he reached out again, her letting him touch her this time; then lifted her chin so she was looking at him as he sounded so tender, "Do you want me to get something for both of us while you wait here?"

Something — someone — stole her voice… or so it felt like. Callimay couldn't answer while at the same time keeping her emotions together. She forgot how Toreon would treat her since he stopped as of late. But today cemented how twisted and cruel he was. Not even in any distorted way could he care for her. Why did she ever entertain the thought he did? And this also brought up the fact of how Destan could only do so much at any given time… unfortunately.

It also reminded her of the danger he now was since he had abilities. She knew by what Baleck said about Toreon's abilities: they weren't superior to Destan's. She knew he would protect her, but was he able to yet? He didn't know how to control his. And where did her ability fit into all this? Was she more powerful than Toreon? She knew she couldn't be more than Destan.

"Calli?"

"I… I'll go with you."

"Alright." He sighed, letting her stick to his side like lint on a wool sweater. "Are you going to be alright? I should ha—"

"I'll be alright. I promise."

ℬ

They'd been sitting near each other for the past couple weeks, but no closer than they would sit during school. It felt strange for Destan to have Callimay sit so close to him during Assembly later on. But with her being so distracted and scared — and Toreon on the warpath — he wanted her as close to him as possible. This was his "job" now, anyway.

After a few moments of thought, he picked up the songbook and slipped his arm around her to help comfort her. She looked up to him, trying to smile; it not quite making it.

He flashed his small smile: *I'm here, Calli,*

She shivered as she looked down to help him turn the pages; she didn't want him knowing her hands were practically convulsing.

Seeing her hand and the ring on it reminded him what she said earlier. Now he felt scared. But why? Destan blinked, taking a deep breath, and then looked at the song they were going to sing, "Look, we're singing your favorite song tonight!"

"How did you—"

"You always close your eyes and sway back and forth if we sing this one. Well… more than usual for you." He observed, seeing her begin to smile. "I took an educated guess."

Callimay sighed and rested her head on his shoulder, now able to "feel" better. Him saying he noticed those small details helped her forget about what happened.

While they sang together, she could tell Destan changed. He wasn't singing because it was something they did; he was singing because it was what he wanted to do. He was relaxed, enjoying himself, and focused on what was important to the "true" Destan — the Destan she fell in love with.

It had been ages since she sat next to someone who sang bass. When they first sat next to each other, and even now, she had to work to sing her part and ignore his accent as best she could.

Since she was sitting so close to Destan, Callimay didn't think she could move any. She tried, but would either bump into his side or push against his arm. It wasn't a bad thing, just something she wasn't used to and something which made singing a bit of a challenge since she was used to doing it.

As they started singing the last verse, she felt Destan lean into her a little and then pull away the same amount. She thought it was him shifting how he sat, but he kept doing it. He did it the same amount each direction and even to the rhythm of the song.

Before long she realized he was rocking her! She felt like breaking down and crying right then… but somehow kept it together.

She rarely looked at the book since these were songs she'd been singing since she could remember. For some reason, she noticed how Destan never looked down but to flip the pages. It somewhat shocked her. Not that having songs written by men had anything to do with salvation — they'd already discussed those details — but it, in a way, helped show his dedication. This was even further cemented when he got his Bible out and opened it. She couldn't help but laugh to herself: *His is just about as marked up and full of notes as mine is. Though his is only in black ink.*

There was a pause when the two of them raised their hands when it was asked if anyone needed to be served The Lord's Supper. She'd never been gone in the morning and so Callimay felt humiliated. Completely out of character, she let her emotions cloud her judgment to the point she forgot what she'd always seen as most important. It made her stop and think if she were letting her priorities change… and obviously in a bad way if so.

When they prayed, Destan saw Callimay clasp her hands as she bowed her head. Even though they were against each other, they still quivered. He reached over and put his hand on top of hers, causing her to — what some might call — melt from his touch.

Destan took hold of hers and bowed his head… nestling his head right next to hers. He made sure to hold her hand firm but not squeeze

the living daylights out of it. It was starting to make sense to him why he was feeling so strange earlier. Things were beginning to surface as far as how some things would be different.

As Callimay looked over at him after the prayer, she noticed he still had his head bowed and eyes closed. He hadn't loosened his grip at all, so she waited. The moment he looked up, he looked refreshed and confident, that small smile shining toward her.

ℬ

Afterward, they spent the rest of the daylight hours in a secluded section of the wooded area by the lake. Destan was careful to keep an eye out for Toreon as they left. Callimay seemed to get a bit better the farther they got from the complex, but she was still very quiet.

This area was dense with evergreen trees. Even if the Society did have cameras out there, it would be impossible for anyone to see them and know what was happening.

He soon understood the frustrations she would have while she was learning to control her ability. Destan didn't know how he tapped into his, and spent a good half hour aimlessly jogging and running around.

Anyone watching would have started laughing after a few minutes, but she was so understanding and supportive. Even after everything that happened that day alone, she was still making sure he was alright. Callimay knew exactly what he was feeling and she could sense he was getting frustrated — borderline angry. She was just about to say something when he tapped his ability.

At first, Destan wasn't moving as fast as she remembered when she saw him by Lookout Point. She didn't bother to say anything because she figured the excess speed would come with time… and she didn't want him to get more upset than he already was, seeing as how it was a struggle for her to keep in contact with him.

She could tell, however, the faster he got the more volatile his emotions became: *Destan, slow down. … Destan?*

I don't know how to! He snapped back.

Can you see me? She asked as she jumped up; concerned with how he was talking "at" her.

No, he said in the same tone. *I really can't see anything.*

Look for me.

I can't!

Then make yourself look for me! She pleaded, trying to keep calm. *You control your ability. Tell it to do what 'you' want it to.*

I can't. I— wait. There you are.

When he got to her, Destan was jogging at a normal pace. After he stopped, he bent over from being out of breath.

"Are you alright?" Callimay ran up to him; reaching out.

"I'm fine," he gasped for air as he put his hand out. "I just… feel like I have the wind knocked out of me. … I don't notice it while I'm running. This must be my version of a migraine."

"I guess your abilities are driven by emotions. It's difficult for me to keep in touch with you when you start spinning out of control. — But, at least you listened to me this time before it got too far."

"They were right when they said I needed you," he sat down and looked up, taking her hand. "If you're with me from the start, it's easier for me to keep you with me and not push you out."

"Well… we've only tried once. We have to keep doing it to see if it really is a way for you to get through this or if it was a one-time thing. … The only thing is: it's dangerous for you to keep doing this for long periods of time. I don't—"

"Callimay." Destan stood her up and looked her square in the eye. "I know you want to keep me safe, but I need you to understand: I 'have' to learn to control this. If I don't do this where things are semi-controlled, then I risk doing harm to myself or you — or someone else — out there. And for me to control this I need your guidance and trust in both of us. Trust that you will be able to reach me and trust I will listen to you. Granted, maybe I am a little slow at responding. … Okay, 'really' slow sometimes. But remember: I 'do' respond. Alright?"

"Alright."

"It's going to be fine. Don't worry."

"Oh Destan." Callimay sighed as she put her arms around him and held on tight.

"It's going to be alright."

"Promise?"

"I promise. You aren't going to lose me because of this."

They searched for a while and found a flat stretch which looked to be close to the distance they were from the gate while watching faculty leave. It was agreed that they would come out there after school finished each day to get as much practice done before they left.

I really, truly, can't believe we're doing this.

Doing what, Callimay?

We're like spies or prisoners! Do you realize this? We've both basically done, albeit mine wasn't intentional, recon and surveillance… and now we're planning an escape. How in the world are we doing this without getting caught! It's not like we're some type of trained government operatives. We're just plain Kathy and Clyde.

They aren't expecting any of this. I'd say that's why we have gotten as far as we have without arousing any suspicion. I don't know how much longer we'll be able to get away with this though. I'm surprised they haven't found out our files are missing.

~ 18 ~

The next day, everyone was abuzz about the procedure for faulty leaving. And then mixed among all this was a flurry of questions concerning classes. Since all faculty who taught were gone, how would lectures or classes look for the rest of the week? None of this appeared to be out of the ordinary from what Mr. Freigh said.

And sure enough, a notice was posted on the main screens and each locker, stating the rest of the week would be study hall for a half-day, finals would be on Friday, and observations would be indirect for the remaining of the grading period. Knowing this ahead of time would've helped with the gossiping. Regardless of this lack in communication, everyone was of the impression academic finals meant nothing, so study hall was degraded to gossip central.

Right before lunch, Mr. Freigh stepped in, "I do not mean to alarm you, but I wanted to address you all before I left."

Left? Callimay asked a bit confused as she looked up from her notebook. *Is he just saying something now to everyone else?*

I don't think so. … It looks like there isn't going to be much time for me to practice. Destan sighed as he focused on Mr. Freigh whose face appeared to be drawn.

A wave of whispers rolled through the room and then everyone had their eyes glued to Mr. Freigh whose voice was extremely shaky as he spoke, "I will be leaving at the end of today for a short time. … I— I was just informed my wife has fallen violently ill and so my presence is necessary. — In the meantime, Mr. Willgun will oversee everything until I return. I wish you all the best for your finals and hope you enjoy your well-deserved break."

Everyone was shocked into silence. And even after he left, there was a few moments where everyone was quiet. But soon, little fissures began to show; the whole room back to the way it was before very long.

They can't even fake being concerned for that long, Callimay said in a disgusted tone, as she almost ripped the page out of her book as she turned it.

They are fake through and through.

That's horrible about Mr. Freigh's wife.

It's hard to believe he even has a wife.

Destan! How could you even—

Would you let me lie to young adults about giving them a higher education while I instead spied on them to find—

Stop!

I'm sorry, Calli. I guess I'm just on edge.

We both are. She closed her eyes and laid her head on the table; and then opened them and sighed as she looked at him: *Mr. Freigh is leaving today, Destan. We haven't had any time to 'do' much of anything. What are we going to do?*

I know, he put his hands in his pockets and pushed his chair back, leaning it so only the back legs were on the floor. *He said he will be leaving at the end of the day; and we only have a half-day of study hall — which is almost over. … I've got to get things figured out, and fast.*

❦

They skipped lunch and darted out to the wooded area and began working as fast as they could. Destan's emotions were in no shortage with the news, but the longer Callimay had to utilize her ability, coupled with his emotions getting stronger and stronger each time; she was falling prey to another massive migraine.

He was covering the approximated distance needed in around ten seconds, but he couldn't break that threshold which made him more and more aggravated.

She tried to calm him by saying he was really close, and reminded him that since she didn't have her watch her timing could have been off. He wasn't the least bit satisfied, though.

"Destan?" Callimay reached out right before he tried again.

"Yes?" He asked as he looked over to her and then noticed how pale she was and felt her hands shaking. "What's wrong!"

"I… I can't keep this up much longer. Maybe one more time and then I've got to stop for a while."

"Calli!" Destan exclaimed as he grabbed her before she hit the ground. "Calli, when did this start?"

"About a half hour ago."

He sighed as he picked her up and started back, "Why didn't you say anything sooner?"

"Because this is more important. … Where are you going?"

"We're done."

"But you still aren't—"

"We've run out of time. I need your help when we leave so I don't spiral out of control. If I keep doing this any longer, you won't be able to keep in touch with me when I need you."

Callimay reached for her forehead, wincing.

"I'm sorry I snapped at you." He sighed as he stopped and closed his eyes. "I'm still in an anger high, I know."

"If you can't make it through the barrier in time, then we'll get caught… and who knows what will happen then!" She pointed out in a painful tone. "And you still have to build up to that speed. You don't start with it from the get-go. This is too risky, Destan. We're just going to have to find a different way. I know it seems impossible, but we've got to have faith. We can make it a little longer."

"I just…" he struggled; seeing the wisdom in her words but knowing the direness of their situation. "I know I can do it; I just need to do it. I know I only have so long to do anything before you burn out. And once you burn out, I can't keep going because I might not be able to get myself out; but I've got to try. We need to get out of here."

"Let's get back and we'll decide what to do then. Alright?" Callimay suggested, noting the desperation in his voice.

"Alright," he sighed as he continued to walk.

❦

As they came into view of the complex, Callimay decided she felt well enough to walk. The closer they got, the more they noticed the large group gathered out front; causing him to spike again, "What in the name of— surely he hasn't left yet?"

"They could be waiting for him to come out, Destan." She tried to encourage as she winced; grabbing his arm to steady herself. *It's alright. Relax. Please.*

As they passed one of the buildings, someone called out to Callimay. They both stopped and turned to see who it was, stunned and worried at the same time. She exclaimed in surprise as she saw who it was running toward them, "Dakoe!"

"Let's get out of the open." He said in a hushed voice as he motioned and took off for one of the smaller labyrinth gardens. "Hurry!"

"Wait, Callimay." *I don't like the look of this. I don't like it at all.*

If this was Toreon's doing he would be doing it himself. He doesn't trust anyone to do anything right. You know that. He wouldn't let Dakoe be a distraction. Besides, you're here… right?

A… alright.

As they walked in, Dakoe was trying to catch his breath. He looked up and blurted out, "You… you two need to leave — now!"

"Excuse me?" Destan questioned in a leery tone as he kept Callimay close. "What do you mean?"

Dakoe explained as his eyes continually darted back and forth, "They found out your files are missing and know you took them."

"How do you know?" Callimay asked stunned.

"I was planted to keep an eye on you two from the beginning. Mr. Willgun brought a few of us in to keep an eye on things for him sin—"

"Just because our files are missing doesn't mean we're at fault for that." Destan defended, not trusting what he was hearing.

"I snitched; I admit it. I… I'm sorry. I saw you two out at the lake on Saturday and— they've searched both your rooms and found them this afternoon. They're waiting. … But I didn't think they would— you have got to get out of here!"

"Why are you helping us?" Destan asked, suspicious of his intent. "If you're working for them why would you turn on them?"

"Believe me or not, but I do care about you, Callimay. I always have. I just couldn't blow my cover. I had to blend in. Unfortunately that also meant leaving you vulnerable." Dakoe tried his best to explain his predicament. "After hearing about plans to erase you two, I couldn't stand aside any longer. I know you didn't ask for this — none of us did — but you have to understand: you can't run from them forever. … Then again, they've never had to track down a team who knows what's going on."

Callimay asked; unable to comprehend what she was hearing him say, "What? 'Erase'? None of 'us'? Track down?"

"I have abilities like you two. I was part of the Society year before last. When I discovered mine, I ran. Only thing was: I made the mistake of going home. It wasn't but a couple weeks before they showed up and brought me back." He explained as fast as his lips could move after he looked at his watch. "Up until September, all I was doing was what they called fieldwork. I got pulled with a couple others — including Ingrid — to come back and observe you two. … At least that was what I was told and why I agreed. But then things started happening and— Callimay? Everything in regards to you falling off the social ladder wasn't by accident. It was planned. Every since detail surrounding how you two even got together was planned to the second."

"Who?" Destan asked in a deep and serious tone.

"The Society."

"But 'who' is it?" Callimay asked.

"I don't know; not really. I kept thinking for the longest time that it was Mr. Freigh and Mr. Willgun because they're the leaders here and Willgun gives us our assignments; but lately I've heard the term 'the Unity' and 'the Purge' thrown around by Willgun."

Destan began to prod, "Who's in 'the Unity'?"

"I heard him talk about some code names it sounded like, but I'm not sure since he was on his phone at the time and I really couldn't hear him that well: 'Origin', 'Nightmare' and something about a 'Doyle' or something like that."

"Other people with abilities?" Callimay whispered as she whipped her head around to look at Destan.

"I don't know what's going on, but those names don't sound 'friendly'. — I swear I'm telling the truth. I wish I could explain more but there's no time. You two have to go. Mr. Freigh's car is leaving in five minutes. It's your only shot."

"Destan, I… what do we do?" Callimay asked frightened as she tried to control her breathing.

Dakoe said hushed as he stopped beside him, "You knew something was wrong all along. That's why you came; isn't it?"

He closed his eyes and took a deep breath, not quite showing his true reaction to what was said.

"Godspeed, you two." Dakoe finished as he left.

They stood there, staring at each other for a few moments. So many thoughts were running through their minds, they couldn't talk. If their lives weren't a nightmare already, this was going to seal the deal.

Was everything they just heard true! Was Dakoe trying to help? Was he setting them up? One thing was sure, regardless of whether or not this information was true: they couldn't afford to stay and find out.

"We have to go," Destan whispered.

"How are we both going to get through? I can't run that fast."

"I'll carry you."

"But—"

"We can't indulge hypothetical scenarios and all the what-ifs. We could spend a lifetime doing that." He grabbed her shoulders; looking determined. "Do you believe me when I say I'll keep you safe?"

"Yes," Callimay responded rather timid.

"Then I wouldn't put you in a situation where I couldn't protect you… right?" Destan calmed a bit as his shoulders dropped.

"Yes."

"Trust me, Calli."

A minute later, they walked out of the labyrinth and noticed the remaining faculty stationed at certain intervals around the front area: *Dakoe wasn't lying.*

There's Mr. Freigh! Callimay exclaimed as she saw him exit the main school building.

In a quiet and calm manner, they strolled to where they had been standing the day before; Destan watching the movements of the faculty. Right before Mr. Freigh got in his car, he glanced locked eyes with Destan. He said something to Baleck and nodded as he got in the car.

Callimay tried to look natural as she glanced around, noticing that faculty was closing in, "Destan?"

I see them. Are you ready for this?

Are you? She gulped, noticing his hand quivered as he took hers.

It's a luxury I can't afford, he watched Mr. Freigh's vehicle pull up to the gate and the process begin.

She continued to look around and found Dakoe. He looked half terrified, half encouraging… a strange combination of emotions to be seen on anyone's face: *I know you can hear me, Callimay. Destan's going to need you. The Society has done things to cause him most, if not all, the anger he harbors. Be patient with him. — You may think from what you read that Destan is the most powerful… but it isn't true. You're the source of his strength. And seriously, you're more powerful than he is… at least in some ways, that is. You're capable of more than even the Society realizes. You have more abilities than just telekinesis between Destan and yourself. I think you've already tapped into those abilities but don't realize it. — Maybe not, but I'm sure you will figure it out. — But aside from all that, you have the strength no ability can grant: the love you have for him and his for you. Like I said: I saw you two at the lake on Saturday. Congratulations. … I know he can seem like he doesn't care, but believe me when I say he cares for you. I met Destan a while back— don't bother asking him about me because he won't know me, okay? — He may seem cut off and cold at times, but for him, the way he treats you is more than he's ever shown to anyone else. I'd say he's a lucky guy, but we both know luck isn't real. … I hope this helps you some, Callimay. I know it raises quite a few questions, but please be content right now with being aware of these things. If I get the chance I 'promise' I'll explain everything. … I wish things could have been different between the two of us, but I know Destan is more capable of taking care of you than I ever could have. Goodbye for now. I pray we get to see each other again.*

This whole time, Destan was calculating when he needed to start so they could get through in time. His heart began pounding so much, he felt it was going to leap out of his chest. He gripped Callimay's hand tighter and tighter with each second.

It's time, he took a deep breath as he picked her up.

I'm here, she encouraged; locking her arms around his neck. *We'll be alright… no matter what happens. I love you.*

But even so, she was concerned. His emotional levels were nowhere near where they needed to be so he could gain the extra speed necessary to for the distance and time frame they had. Without anger, he wasn't able to fully engage his ability — and all he was showing at the time was fear.

As she looked over his shoulder, she saw a few faculty behind them with weapons drawn but still down.

"Destan Nevrille and Callimay Berchoff? We need you to come with us." One said as they put their hand on Destan's shoulder. "The quieter the better things will be for each of you."

We're so close. He grimaced as his eye started to dart. *Too close for me to give up. Come on, Freigh. Come on!*

Just then, he saw Mr. Freigh adjust the rearview mirror in his car and look back at him. He shook his head, warning him not to try. Destan became enraged: *You can't control me. I'm not going to sit behind the shadows and let you take her from me or hurt her.*

Meanwhile, the faculty behind them repeated what they said; sounding much more serious this time and catching the attention of nearby students. Destan ignored them and Callimay was too scared to do anything, so a faculty member grabbed her arm where it was injured from her fall. She screamed out in pain and clamored to keep hold of him; having this feeling of terror set in: if she let go she'd never see him again.

"No! No you don't." Destan bellowed as he punched the person grabbing her; taking her back in his arms and bolting.

The commotion they made caused everyone to look over at them and not Mr. Freigh who just started leaving. Stunned faces were plastered on everyone's faces as they saw Destan running faster than they'd ever seen anyone. He almost looked like a blur!

Faculty came out and drew their weapons, each firing one shot. Callimay felt a spike in his emotions but couldn't pinpoint what it was. She was doing her best to keep herself going, but the spike was making things nearly impossible for her.

We're not gonna make it! He blurted out from panic.

Callimay encouraged him, pulling herself closer so she could put her cheek against his: *Yes we can. We're almost there. Don't give up. I trust you. I'm still here Destan. Please don't give up. You 'can' keep me safe. I know you can. Don't give up. I love you.*

With this encouragement, he pushed harder.

There went the water fountain in the circular drive.

There went the last row of trees by the gate.

As they passed Mr. Freigh, Callimay was able to catch a glimpse of the defeated look on his face. Destan's emotions kept climbing, but now since they were out she started to rein him in: *I know we need to get a safe distance away, but I can only last so much longer. Couldn't you—*

Just a little bit more.

I know, but you can at least start to slow down? She tried to hide the amount of pain she was in and how tired she was. *Please Destan? Just a little bit… anything. I don't think I can keep going at this pace.*

Once we get to town. His tone started to become snippy as trees whizzed by.

But it's over twenty-five miles away!

We can't stop until then. We can't. I won't stop until I've got you a safe distance away from that place.

Okay. She sighed in anguish; her becoming more and more exhausted. *But once we get there you have 'got' to stop. … Please.*

I know. Stay with me Calli.

When they made it to the outskirts of town, Destan decided it was safe to stop. But unlike every other time he stopped, there was no warning, no down-shift… just a complete and sudden halt. Her grip wasn't enough to prepare for this sudden lack of momentum, so she went flying out of his arms and tumbling through the snow.

"Goodness," she said as she grabbed her head and rolled over. "You've never done that before. And you've never— Destan!"

"I'm fine." He said out of breath as he put his arm out, rolling over so he was lying on his back. "I'm. Just. Worn out."

Callimay was now dizzy and light-headed to the point she couldn't get upright. She couldn't stand being away from him, still terrified about everything, so she pulled herself to him. It didn't take her long to realize what the strange emotion she felt was, "Y… you're bleeding!"

"What? Oh. It looks like— ah! Geez, Calli! Don't touch it." He hissed as he shoved her hand away.

She began to cry, "What hap— were you shot?"

He threw his head back against the ground, groaning, wincing, and still out of breath, "It… it's only a flesh wound. I'll be alright. I won't bleed out."

"Oh Destan. I'm— I don't know what to do." Callimay rambled as she started panicking; but winced, "Destan I know you're frustrated that you can't catch your breath, but you have to relax. Your body hasn't fully accepted your abilities. It's tired. Relax. Please! If nothing else… do it for me. I'm tired, Destan. Please stop."

"We can't stay here very long," he said impatiently as he looked around the area. "We've got to keep moving."

"I know. … But we need to stay as long as we can. You shouldn't move much." She breathed heavy and blinked her eyes really slow. "Maybe I can find something t—"

"First thing is to get new clothes and have my wound looked at." He began planning in a quiet voice; not paying attention to her plea.

"New clothes?"

"Yes," he grimaced as he tried to sit up.

"Lie back down."

"People will recognize these uniforms and start asking questions. And then there's the whole problem of our name tags. I'm sure they're more than keys. I wouldn't be a bit surprised if they have homing devices in them."

"Huh? How could you tell if they did?"

"Look," Destan labored to move her coat over a bit to expose the red dot flashing on her name tag. "They've already turned them on. Maybe the second we got out they were tripped. In any case, we need to go. I'll just have to suffer through this a bit longer."

Callimay sighed painfully as she helped him to his feet. He sounded like he knew so much more than she did about this. How could she tell him no? She was terrified!

When they turned around, an older man greeted them. She gasped as she stumbled back, Destan now having no support.

"I beg your pardon," the older gentleman apologized as he came over. "I did not mean to frighten you. I saw you as I was walking along the ridge and decided to see if you needed my help. … I can tell the young man is injured. Would you allow me to help him to my house? It's just over the ridge a bit."

"Thank you," Destan said weakly as he worked to sit up; Callimay still struggling with pain as she tried to help him.

"Here," the older gentleman offered as he took Destan's arm. "Let me help. I do not think the young lady will be able to support you very far by herself; and you're in no condition to keep yourself upright. A— are you alright, miss?"

"I just have a migraine." Callimay defended as she got to her feet; Destan reaching out with his other hand to help steady her. "I'm fine."

ℬ

When they got to the small house, Callimay felt strange being in an actual home. She had been away for only a few months but had already "lost" that sense of the sounds and smells of one; no matter the cultural differences which were found from place to place.

The older gentleman never asked "questions" and was so kind and generous. In a way it felt like he understood what happened: they were victims in need of help. He quickly prepared a bed for Destan by the fire and then skillfully tended to his wound. And then once he found out what was ailing Callimay, he gave her an herbal remedy to help with the pain.

Destan wasn't sure about her taking it, but she calmed him and said she'd had this exact one before and knew what it smelled and tasted like… and didn't notice anything wrong.

Once he felt their immediate needs were met, he prepared them a meal and provided them with a change of clothes since theirs were soaked, "I apologize if they don't fit well."

"They're more than we could have asked for," Callimay said in gratitude as she took them. "Thank you for your kindness."

While she was away, Destan asked a bit labored, "Do you know who the justice is here, sir?"

"Of course," he chuckled as he stood and spread his arms out. "I am he. Justice Goodall Wan of Trawnvane. What can I do you for?"

"I know this may seem like a rather strange request, but could you marry us?" Destan asked, feeling uncomfortable — which was an enormous understatement. "I'm not familiar with the laws of this country; if you are allowed to or if something special is required."

"Does the young lady know about this?"

"Yes sir."

"Why the rush?" Justice Wan asked as he got a book from a shelf.

"I… it's complicated."

"I see." He nodded as he took a deep breath. "Well… if she is in agreement then I see no reason why not."

After a few more minutes, Callimay returned and noticed Justice Wan was teary-eyed, "This belonged to someone dear to you?"

He sighed as he set the book he had down on the table in front of him and picked up a photograph, "You remind me very much of her."

"I'm sorry." She bowed her head; and then after a minute — and hearing him groan — asked, "Are you well enough to get up, Destan? I'm sure he'll let us stay so we can wait for you to—"

"I'm fine. I need to get out of this as soon as I can." He grimaced as she helped him up. "I won't be long."

Justice Wan asked as soon as Destan shut the door, "The young man tells me you two want to get married. Is this true?"

Callimay answered, a warm smile covering her face as she looked down at the ring on her hand. "Yes. It's still hard for me to believe. It's only been two days since he asked me."

"He asked if I could perform the ceremony right now." He inquired; a curious look on his face. "Do you agree with how soon this is?"

"It's not what I dreamed about, but it doesn't matter what type of ceremony it is, the result's the same. That is what's most important."

Everything felt fuzzy for a moment, but then the fatal question was asked, "You are from the Creigam Freigh Society, aren't you?"

"I—" she hung her head. "I guess we didn't make it very far."

"I am not in any way on their side. Quite the opposite. … That is how I lost her. She was so eager to use this chance to turn things around for us as a family; she was one of the first to apply when it was released what was being built up there. She had only been gone five months when we received word there was an accident and she did not survive. The grief was too much for my beloved wife to bear. … She passed not but a month later. — I see the eager students arrive every year; and sure enough, not all of them leave. Something else is going on up there that they're hiding. I don't know what it is, but I have a feeling by the shape you two were in when I found you that you do. I do not wish to pry. Just answer me this: is there some other vendetta being accomplished under this façade the Society holds?"

"Yes." Callimay glanced back to the room Destan was in.

The fireplace crackled a few more times before he asked as he pushed a photograph to where Callimay could see it, "Maybe I am desperate to think she is not dead, but— do you recognize this girl? I know it is an older photograph, but she surely has not changed much."

The girl looked familiar. … After a bit, she gasped, "Hyra!"

"You 'have' seen her!"

"Yes. She's one of the students. But you— when did she attend?"

"Ten years ago." He answered in a bewildered tone as he took the picture back; him beginning to reminisce, his eyes glazed over. "She was just sixteen. Even with my status as Justice, the pay was not enough to afford higher education for her. With the tuition being free, my wife and I saw it as an opportunity for her. We did not agree with the other education, but thought it would be beneficial for her academically. I still remember sending her off that day — and regret it. … When you saw her, was she… happy?"

"Yes. I… I don't know what to say."

"She is alive." Justice Wan sighed in relief. "I know she will come home. There is still hope. Thank you."

Destan walked in with both of their uniforms, seeming to be confused about what to do with them. Justice Wan motioned to the floor, "Do not concern yourself with those. I will see to it they are destroyed so no one knows. — Where are you planning on going?"

He hesitated to say anything, unsure who to trust at this point. Callimay understood that, but at the same time she didn't see why she couldn't tell him. It's not like he was some horrible person. He was helping them, "I'm not really sure. I would like to go home for a little bit to gather a few things."

"By what I can gather, the two of you weren't planning on leaving so soon… let alone decided what to do after. Am I correct?" Justice Wan asked, starting to piece some things together.

Callimay could tell Destan wasn't pleased with being stationary and someone asking so many questions, so she looked at him and waited. He nodded rather reluctant as he looked to Justice Wan, motioning for her to come to him.

"Are you two from this country?"

"No," he answered in a mumble.

"Do you have your border passes?" Justice Wan inquired, revealing why he was asking all these questions.

"Destan!" Callimay gasped, a fearful look in her eye.

He didn't respond, but his actions answered the question.

"It is a good thing I found you two." Justice Wan took a deep breath and went over to his desk; pulling some paperwork out. "Being the Justice, I have the authority to grant temporary passes for any situation I deem reasonable. The only problem is… I usually have to make a few phone calls to check on the information you give me; which, depending on the country and time of day, can take a few days."

Destan sat up when he heard Justice Wan's offer to help, Callimay sitting down next to him and looking more optimistic. But then he hung his head and squeezed her hand while sighing in frustration, rubbing his face when he heard how long it would take.

"I said: 'usually'." Justice Wan was quick to clarify; filling out papers as he continued to talk, "I know enough to understand this is an emergency. Now I can't guarantee how far you will make it with what I can give you without verification. But seeing as how it is so late in the evening and knowing the type of people who work with the rails, you should be able to at least get out of the perish just fine. No matter how far you need to go, do 'not' fly. Yes, it would get you out faster, but they will catch the gaps much sooner. The consequences for that are—"

"Thank you sir," Destan said relieved as he sighed, looking up to him and then Callimay.

❦

Within the hour, Destan and Callimay were on their way: new though mismatched clothes, his wound tended to, Callimay's migraine gone, a free meal in their bellies, and their border passes and marriage license in tow. They weren't in the clear by any means, but they had a fighting chance to get to safety now. He even gave them directions and enough money to cover their train tickets, but reminded them in very plain and bold terms to take nothing but the rails.

If they had to cross paths with anyone after what they endured, Callimay was grateful it was Justice Wan.

This peace gave Callimay a completely different outlook on things. And part of it had nothing to do with the generosity of Justice Wan… she was married. But, when she looked over, it didn't appear Destan felt this way. Though think about it: he was injured and still shaken up from everything — he even used his ability for quite a long time — that was more than enough to have an effect on his emotional state. Who wouldn't be affected by it?

The sun had since vanished, leaving everything outside to fend for itself against the cold. Destan began to tense up a bit: two of them were unfamiliar with the area they were walking through, it was cold and dark, and on top of everything else, it Justice Wan's handwriting was difficult to read.

After a while of relying on listening to the train whistles, they finally found the rail station. She asked for his permission and called Fairove to see if there had been any unwanted visitors to the house.

He said there hadn't, so she told him she would be back to gather some things and that she would be gone for a while again.

Destan purchased the train tickets and they began their journey back to Callimay's home in the Northern Hills of Faberton.

She was nervous about their passes — as she could tell Destan was — but as Justice Wan predicted, they didn't pay attention and motioned them on when they saw they had signed papers.

They got on the train and found a wonderful blessing: they had the entire car to themselves. Callimay followed Destan and sat across from him, watching him as he stared off into the distance. He seemed tired and his eyes were glazed over. She couldn't blame him; he had gone through so much in only a few hours.

~ 19 ~

The train stopping woke Callimay from her deep sleep. At first she was confused, but then things began to come back to her. She then noticed she was alone; causing her to panic and jump out of her seat, "Destan! Where are y—"

"It's alright." He calmed as he put his hand on hers. "The way you were sleeping looked uncomfortable so I moved over here to see if I could help. It's alright. Just calm down."

"Oh."

"I didn't mean to scare you, Calli." Destan apologized, hearing her voice tremble.

"Really, anything even 'slightly' off is going to scare me to some degree right now. Where are we?"

"We're only about halfway. Brigon. The attendant went by a few minutes ago and said they'd be serving breakfast in an hour."

Callimay asked concerned as she wrung her hands, "Do we have any money?"

Destan nodded as he smiled; looking like he was fighting off a yawn, "Enough. Don't worry about it."

"Did you get any sleep?"

"I'm alright."

"Derelicts," they overheard someone scoff.

They turned and saw a scuffle out on the platform. A younger woman was screaming and trying to free herself from someone's grasp. The person holding her wore a white uniform of some kind; people with children rushing by while others gathered around.

Why wasn't anyone trying to help her!

A chant — as well as several other coarse words — began to rise amongst those who were on the platform, "Der-e-lict. Der-e-lict."

Seeing the sight reminded Callimay there was another danger lurking. The young lady looked to be about her age, and she was obviously left-handed as well.

Destan reached over and put his hand on hers. She looked up teary-eyed to his determined gaze.

I won't let anyone — 'any'one — take you away from me, he emphasized as he wiped the tears from her face.

Seeing his face helped calm her.

Out of nowhere it dawned on her: what Dakoe told her right before they left. Who did Destan lose? How did he lose them? What did the Society do to them? She knew it had to be what he mentioned on his application; but what happened? Were they left-handed too?

❦

About an hour after sunset the train stopped again.

"First call for Whipple Grove, folks." The attendant called out as he walked down the aisle. "We'll be here ten minutes. Whipple Grove."

"Closer," Callimay sighed as she tried to fight off a yawn.

The other couple in the car got up and retrieved their luggage from the overhead area. As they strolled to the door, Destan and Callimay could hear their conversation, "I wish they would have been one of our Falconers. Every cleat counts."

"Can't get them all, my dear." The man replied as he opened the door for her; having to set his briefcase down right next to Destan's foot so he could.

"I don't know why there are still Lone Wolves left. It makes no sense." She continued to criticize as she walked on.

"It's strange, dear. I know."

Callimay glanced down at the briefcase and saw something familiar. The family crest stamped on it… she couldn't help but think it looked like something she'd seen before; but not from a magazine.

As he picked up his briefcase, the man sighed, "I apologize for my wife's attitude. She 'is' the driving force of our business, but is usually more reserved in public. Our son is at Creigam Freigh Society, so with him being gone during Jubilee, she's venting her frustration about everything. … I hope you understand."

"Missing those you love can take a toll on your emotions." Callimay offered as it dawned on her who it was she was talking to. "Especially during the festivals."

"You both have a safe trip." The man smiled as he tipped his hat.

Syndicate scum, Destan almost spat at him.

W… we both know who they are, Callimay said frightened.

Who?

Toreon's parents.

How do you know that!

His briefcase. The crest. I knew I remembered it. Toreon's blazer had the same crest on its lapel. It clicked when he said their son was at the Society. Callimay explained as the train took off. *But why did he talk about their family business in reference to his wife's comment about Falconers? I thought they were like the bounty hunters of old from the Homeworld: loners who didn't want to work for anyone?*

You've heard of the Syndicate haven't you? Destan asked after he looked around in the car which was empty again.

A couple times. Toreon was the one who mentioned it. He said his family owns it.

So 'they're' the Monar— I'm sure they will be thrilled to find out he's been blabbing that everywhere. Destan rolled his eyes. *But, then again, they probably don't care what he does. … And that would explain Gallia calling him Prince.*

What?

There are a select few Falconers who work alone… like the one we saw earlier. He acknowledged as he sat back and put his arm around her. *But about the same time resistance groups started forming, the Syndicate did as well. Falconers were tired of building networks on their own and didn't want to be bogged down by all the minor details; and yet didn't have someone they could trust. So, the Syndicate came into being as a one-stop place for all of the above. And now they are the largest entity with full legal authority to uphold the International Law; 'serving' countless Falconers through finding reliable contacts called Informants who work on the front lines to find Derelicts. They set up meetings between Falconers and Informants and route the bounty rewards and such that these individuals would receive — taking their share, of course.*

So it's a way for the leadership to get rich quickly and 'legally'? Just like the whole reasoning behind the Eradication itself.

Pretty much.

"How do you know so much about this all? I've never gotten all of these details from my schooling and—"

"I think you've just been sheltered, Callimay," Destan responded as he stretched his legs and arms.

"You're probably right." She sighed as she looked down.

"It's not bad. Really, Callimay. Knowing all this doesn't make you any better or worse of a person. … Really? Knowing more about this can easily make life more dangerous." *'Much' more dangerous.*

☙

A few hours, train changes, and stops later, Callimay pressed her face against the cold glass of the window and almost squealed, "I told you it wouldn't be much longer. Look! This is our stop, Destan. We're home! … At least for right now."

They got off the train and she stood there for a moment. It was dark enough that almost everything was still drenched in shadows, but she knew where everything was… though it felt different, "It's strange. Even though I know this area better than any other place on this planet, it looks like it's changed since I've been away."

There was a new life in Callimay. Destan escorted her out of the station and then took her hand as she led him toward town. For as much as he wanted to keep his guard up, he couldn't help but relax and observe how happy and joyful she was.

As they walked along, it hit her: she didn't even know where Destan was from or if he even had a place to call home! Fear started to creep in: *What are we going to do if something happens?*

But the fear couldn't hold her when she saw a sight she'd loved so much: the first of the sun's rays spraying over Furlough Hill which was the hill — as it is classified — just north of Berchshire. The coastal terrain had more rugged hills than where they were, and Berchshire was positioned so it was one of the first areas around to see direct sunlight each day.

Callimay took a deep breath and then looked up, seeing a short-statured person standing in the distance. With it not being quite light enough for him to see, Destan wasn't quite sure what the person was wearing… it looked to be completely black. He tensed up a bit when he noticed they were keeping watch by the way they scanned the area and then locked on them.

"It's okay, Destan. It's Fairove." She smiled as she squeezed his hand and started running, leaving him behind.

"I'm so glad I was able to catch you before you headed up." He sighed, sounding thankful as he took a step back. "I hate to be the bearer of bad news, but you need to leave, Callimay. Now."

"What?" She asked as Destan caught up. "Why? We just got he—"

"When you called, you asked if there were any unwanted visitors at your house. … Well, about an hour later, some showed up. They're still there. I knew there'd be no way to reach you, so I've been waiting." Fairove spoke in a quiet voice as he looked around, checking for anyone within earshot.

"Who is it?" Callimay asked.

"The local authorities," he ushered the two of them to the side of the building close by. "What happened?"

"We need to go," Destan said firm as he took her hand.

"Why did they involve the local authorities? We're not criminals. Dakoe said it took them a few weeks to—"

"They weren't as desperate to keep him like they are to keep us under their thumb. Come on Callimay. We need to go."

"A… alright." She sighed as she looked around rather sad. "It was… good to see you, Fairove."

"It was good to see you too, Callimay. I will tell everyone I saw you and you're doing well. Take care." He waved, baffled as to what was going on and who this young man was.

"I promise I will come back," she swore as she turned back, trying not to sound choked up. "I'll come home, Fairove."

~ 20 ~

As they traveled back down the hill to the rail station, Callimay looked back to where the graveyard was. She paused and tried to rationalize staying just a little longer when she heard the faint sound of wind chimes: *Maybe if I ran—*

"We need to go, Callimay. I'm sorry."

She turned back and followed, trying her best to not cry. It was hard for her to remember what she said just a few months earlier about coming home and spending time at her mother's graveside to tell her about what she learned and the fun time she had. In the cruelest and vilest of ways, everything ended up being the complete opposite. Her spirit was crushed and weary. Deep inside she knew it wouldn't change anything, but all she wanted at that moment was to lie over her mother's grave and cry. She wanted to get the pain out; and with someone she trusted.

But what about Destan? He was the reason she was where she was. He was the one who put his life on the line to save her. He was the one who was alive… her mother was gone.

He looked tired and in pain, but she was willing to beg him to hold her. Yes, she knew they needed to get out of there, but surely five minutes wouldn't make that much of a difference… would it?

"Just wait until we get to the train, Callimay. Alright?"

"I…" she sniffled as he took her hand and rubbed it. "I just want to rest, Destan."

"I know. I'll get you somewhere safe just as fast as I can so you are able to. But until then we can't stop."

"Alright. … So now where do we go?"

"Where I live."

"But if they are already here, then they—"

"There's a lot about me you don't know yet, Callimay. Trust me when I say that in order for them to find where we're going, only someone with expert tracking abilities could even come close."

"I trust you. … How are we going to get there?"

"By train."

Callimay shook her head, sounding frightened, "But we d—"

"Remember what I just said?" He asked in an irritated and raised voice as he grabbed her arm.

Unfortunately, he grabbed her arm where it was injured, causing her to cry out in pain and push him away, "Destan!"

"I'm sorry Calli! … I forgot." He apologized, seeing her crumble to the ground. "I didn't me— Calli?"

A horrified look overtook her face as she dared to look up at him. He knew she was upset about not being able to go home. Him not being patient with her questions wasn't helping. He opened his mouth to say something, but didn't know what to say.

She knew someone would be by before long, so she got up and kept walking down the hill. He followed but still was at a loss as to how he could explain things were going to be alright.

❦

They stopped and Destan made a quick phone call before he got their tickets. Adding to the frustrations of everything, it turned out that the morning train was full. It was going to be a long wait for the next one. He asked if they could be on the waitlist in case someone canceled, but the booker didn't sound optimistic even though he agreed. It wasn't the best of circumstances, but what could they do?

Destan was trying to be hopeful and help Callimay keep her mind off the stress of everything, hoping she wouldn't worry, so he suggested they get some breakfast; asking her where a good place to go would be. She opened her mouth to say something without really thinking much about the question, but he knew what she was going to ask and answered in a calm tone, "Don't worry about money, Calli. The phone call I made was to get some. It's what I used to pay for the tickets."

"Oh. Okay then. … There's a small bakery on the corner of Main and Esteem just east of here. They just opened and it's early, so I guess it'd be the safest as far as people recognizing me and saying something about it. It's expensive though."

"Calli. It's alright. We can't look nervous. People are bound to pick up on that." Destan calmed as he saw her fiddling with her coat sash; putting his hand on hers. "I don't like the thought of staying, but maybe — just maybe — there'll be a cancelation on that morning train so we can get out sooner."

Of course she knew the way, but it wasn't hard for Destan to guess where they were going. Delicious smells of breads and spices seemed to ooze out of the building and flood the surrounding air.

Thankfully, they were the first customers. As he pulled out her chair, Callimay couldn't help but wonder about Destan and who he was. Who did he call that would be up at this hour? Could you transfer money this early in the day? Come to think of it, she didn't know where they were going.

With all this going on, her appetite wasn't much of anything so she didn't eat… according to Destan. He tried to get her to eat more, but she kept refusing, saying she was fine.

When he finished and paid the waiter, they left and headed back to the station. She sat where he could see her and waited while he got in line to ask about the tickets. Not but a couple seconds after he got to the window, he ran over with some papers, "Come on. Someone canceled."

"Really!"

"We've got to go now; the booker said they can't hold the train." He started making a beeline for the platform, his firm grip not wavering as he weaved in and out of people.

Destan had to steady Callimay as they got on; the train taking off the second their feet touched the car steps.

They came in and looked around the packed and bustling train car, thankfully finding the half-sized booth that was now theirs. A couple people nodded in acknowledgement of them, but most of them were preoccupied with their own lives.

The train jerking a second time caught her off guard; Callimay jumping up and yelping. When she realized what was going on, she sat back down and stared at the floor. A few moments later she could feel Destan putting his arm around her. She flinched and started to pull away, but he comforted, "It's alright, Calli. You're exhausted. Try to get some rest."

"But you are too."

"I'll be fine," his slight smile came across his face. "I'll sleep when we get home. It won't be much longer."

"Home…" Callimay sighed, sounding groggy as she leaned over.

He winced and pushed her away, "Ah! I'm sorry, I forgot—"

"Oh dear!" She gasped as she jumped back. "I'm sorry Destan."

"We both forgot. Don't worry about it, Callimay. I know you didn't mean it. Here…" he offered as he took his coat off; trying to keep her calm so she wouldn't draw attention to them. "Lie down here. It's going to be several hours before we get there."

"Alright. … I love you." She yawned as she curled up beside him and drifted off within what felt like seconds.

It felt like she just fell asleep when Destan gently shook her wrist, "We're here. Callimay? Wake up. The train won't be here long."

She opened her eyes and immediately looked out the window to see where they were. It was pitch-black so she couldn't distinguish much, but what she could see she didn't recognize at all, "And where is here?"

"Kerogen," he grunted as he stood and put his coat on.

"If it's just after ten, then we must be on the very edge," Callimay observed as she noticed the clock on the platform.

"See, you know where we are." He nodded as he took her hand.

"You mean you're from Kerogen?"

"Not actually." Destan shook his head; and then revealed in a casual manner: *I was born in the Northern Hills of Faberton.*

"What!"

"I'll explain while we ride back. Okay?"

⚶

When they got off the train, a tall and slender older man in full formal attire greeted them, "It is quite good to see you, Sir."

"It's good to see you, Rocher." Destan nodded as he offered his hand to Callimay and helped her off the train. "This is Callimay."

"I'm honored to see your integrity is intact, Sir. — It is simply a pleasure to make your fair acquaintance, Milady." He commented as he bowed in a respectful and formal manner.

"It's nice to meet you… Rocher." She nodded slow and unsure.

"No baggage to procure?"

"Nothing Rocher. We… we didn't have time to bring anything with us." Destan said frustrated as he looked down and shuffled his feet.

"I see. — Please. This way."

Destan let her go ahead of him as the two of them followed Rocher through the station. His speech as a whole was the most formal kind Callimay had ever heard; and his appearance led her to believe he had money… so it would seem. What else could explain the symmetrical and detailed nature of his suit? Not even his white gloves looked like they had a piece of lint on them! And then his sterling silver chevron mustache and matching hair were combed and kept in such a way that could only suggest this was his usual appearance.

"Destan? Is Rocher a friend of yours?" Callimay whispered.

"You could say that," he spoke in a normal tone; chuckling a bit. "Though I doubt he'd call himself a friend of mine… exactly."

The empty train station meant the only vehicle there was the one they would be riding in. Callimay jerked back and looked at Destan when Rocher opened the door; but he ushered for her to get in and then did so himself. After closing the door, Rocher made his way around the car to his seat; doing everything as if he were on autopilot.

Callimay sat on the middle of the bench seat, eyeing Destan as he stepped over her and flopped down beside her. He let out a groan which mimicked the leather creaking, and then stretched his neck.

Not but a moment later, Rocher rolled down the window which was between the front and back portions of the car; adjusting the mirror, "Might I ask if we need to attend to anything as we return, Sir?"

"No, Rocher. Just home." Destan shook his head as he sighed and sat back, closing his eyes as he mumbled, "Just home."

"Very well." He nodded; and then offered when he saw Callimay who was wide-eyed and curious, "It is quite late and our journey will be nothing short of pitch-black scenery, Milady. Please feel free to rest yourself. You both are in dire need of it I dare say."

"Oh," she yelped as she shifted her focus to him. "I— thank you."

"You're quite welcome, Milady." Rocher nodded in respect as he rolled the window up and started the car.

"And so now I'm sure you've got a million and a half questions," Destan sighed; not opening his eyes.

"I don't know where to start…" Callimay fumbled, bewildered by what she saw in the dimly lit, all leather interior with platinum-like embellishments — real platinum maybe? — and then looked back to him. "I mean: I 'really' don't know where to start."

"Well let me start by answering your question from earlier." He continued; his eyes still closed as he opened his hand to offer it to her. "It's true: I am from the same area as you. I lived about an hour further north in Heirway. The fighting in that area was — by far — the worst during the civil war. … My father was a biochemist at the University of Kerogen; their lead research scientist. When asked, to help he returned to Faberton during the civil war; continuing his work on formulating serums which would enhance the abilities of soldiers. The only thing was: they weren't ready. But with the dire situation being faced, the government forged ahead. The first few months were dismal at best; my father pleading to stop everything and work on the serums one-by-one to identify what was causing this lethal reaction… but he was blatantly ignored and his serums were twisted and tested on anyone who was willing to be injected with the poison. Without any power to stop what was happening, my father turned in his immediate letter of refusal and made plans to get my mother and myself back to Kerogen where things were safe. … The night we were supposed to leave, one of the men who was working with my father came and tried to 'talk some sense' into him. He refused to even let him in, so the man broke in and murdered my parents, setting the house ablaze to cover everything up."

Destan paused for a moment and opened his eyes; sitting up before continuing, "I was really young when it happened; Rocher is the one who told me many of the details. I have several memories of my father talking about people having abilities, both good and bad ones, but I thought those were just 'stories' he would tell me at night. — When Rocher told me what was going on, I didn't know what was real for a while. … The only thing that stuck with me that was real was seeing my mother and father that night. She was already gone and he was gasping for air. He must've been in shock because he kept repeating this phrase over and over again, not knowing I was there: 'I couldn't protect her. I couldn't keep her safe.' … Rocher grabbed me and pulled me out of the house right before it collapsed. He brought me here, and Kerogen is pretty much where I've been since."

Callimay was so shocked and stunned by what she was hearing. She couldn't imagine remembering every tiny detail like he had.

Now she began to better understand why it meant so much to him to keep her safe. The tears welled in her eyes so much it stung to keep them from falling. She refused to let them, though, because she wanted to be strong for Destan and support him.

"Why did he work for the government to help them?" She asked, remembering what he told her about the Eradication. "They—"

"He was trying to do what he could to minimize the damage being done." He shook his head; and then looked at her with sympathy as she began to cry, "Don't blame yourself Calli."

"I'm… I'm sorry." She tried to stifle her sobs and keep her emotions in check.

He asked somewhat hesitant; knowing a bit from what he read on her application but wanting to hear it from her. "I know you had a rough past because of the war. … Do you remember anything? I guess I should ask if you even want to talk about it."

All the tears rushed down her face as she bowed her head and explained, "I remembered some details when I was young; waking up in the middle of the night; screaming and going on about a 'demon ghost' in the house or talking about a lot of bodies and blood. … I still don't know what in the world 'demon ghost' meant to me. Where I am actually from I don't know. I don't know who my parents were or if I had or still have any siblings. Someone found me wandering the streets in late February of sixty-nine; covered in blood and rubble dust after a late-night battle in Quaverly. It was during one of the last major battles of the civil war. — But you probably already know that. — It was 'assumed' I was from there, but I didn't know how long I'd be walking or which direction I came from. They thought I had a concussion since I complained about my head hurting; them attributing my loss of memory to that… but who knows. … Things or words would seem familiar to me at first, but even those foggy memories are lost to me now. When I was told that a lady offered to take me in, I was so young that I didn't really know what else to say but 'yes'. The people that went with me said I acted like I knew about trains and wasn't scared about the trip, but again, I don't know why. … The first 'real' memory I have is seeing my mother's smiling face as she opened the door; the smell of cinnamon and tea rushing out with the warm air to greet me. … I found out later that she lost her husband in the war — albeit it was about six months before I came — and was left alone: like me."

"I'm sorry Calli." He wrapped his arms around her and rocked her.

"You had it worse, Destan. So much worse." She pointed out in anguish as she buried her face in his chest. "Y… you still remem—"

He consoled as he stroked her soft hair; resting his chin on her head, "But you're not emotionally scarred like I am. You don't have anger burned into you from seeing what someone's hunger for power does. You were spared; and I am so, 'so' thankful for that. I would never wish what I went through on anyone. Not even my worst enemy."

Destan and Callimay held each other for a while and cried.

Neither of them knew someone who could empathize with them and what they went through. There were still differences, but their freedom to speak to someone who knew what they were talking about helped form a stronger bond between them; let alone the fact they were both dealing with the same, real-life dangers of being who they were and how it played into everything.

After a few minutes, she realized one of the points he made, "Your father was the one who started this: giving people abilities!"

"Yes," he sniffled; taking a deep breath. "He was doing it to help, but realized the head of military research and others in Faberton weren't looking at it that way; so he started cutting off access to his work or destroying it. I don't know who the head of military research was or who was responsible for the manipulation of father's work that caused him to drop everything and try to run. If I had to guess, they're the ones who started sending out these Rogues. Why? There's another missing piece that's annoying me."

"That's… I…"

"Like I said, I don't know how this all fits together. And really, I don't know if these pieces belong to the same puzzle." Destan sat back and closed his eyes; then after a few moments of silence asked, "So I guess the next big question you have is why we're in this fancy car and I have a chauffeur, butler, conservator— or whatever you would like to refer to Rocher as?"

She was quiet for a few moments, but eventually nodded, "Yes."

"With the extensive reach and success of my father's work as the lead research biochemist at the U of K, he was paid quite handsome. He willed me the rights to everything he had, and so that income alone allows me the liberty of living this way." Destan explained as he began to talk slower and slower. "I don't know where all the money comes from, but it comes… every month."

Callimay sat there, struggling. Yes, she heard the Nevrille name held a high standing as far as money and prestige went; but this was just what others at the Society said. She was never the first one to jump aboard the bandwagon about such things which were mere gossip. But apparently they were right: Destan was a wealthy person.

"What?" He sensed she was staring at him.

"Why aren't you a snob?"

"There were plenty at the Society who thought I was."

"That's not what I mean. W… why didn't you use your money to stake your claim at the Society? You weren't dressed in rags when you came, but then again you weren't decked out like Toreon and so many of the others." Callimay observed as she tilted her head; confused with how he acted. "I know you were a bit… well, direct when you talked with people; but you weren't a snob about it."

"Money isn't everything. And a lot of times it makes things worse if you start using it to gain the upper hand. All it takes is one person with just 'that' much more than you have to send you to the gutter. It's not a horrible thing to have, but it can be dangerous if it isn't watched. Just like anything can be."

"I knew there was something different about you when we met."

"Me too," Destan responded as he yawned. "Let's get some rest, huh? We're safe now and Rocher will let us know when we're close to home. I'm sure you're still tired. It's been a rough couple days."

Callimay all of a sudden realized how exhausted he must be. He'd never answered her questions each time she asked, so she wondered if he slept at all since they left the Society. He would have been up over sixty hours to this point if so! Why in the world would he keep watch?

He was doing what his father couldn't.

And yet, the moment he was able to relax and recover, what did she do? Monopolize the time to find out details she could have waited for. She felt horrible. Destan was the one who needed rest and sleep; it didn't matter what she wanted to know. He was shot for goodness sake! — It's a wonder he was still able to hold a conversation.

All the evidence was laid forth and the jury came back with a unanimous verdict: it was her turn to keep watch. Sleep sounded so wonderful, but she felt the obligation to give him the protection he was giving her. Callimay wanted to show him how much she loved him and what she was willing to do without to keep him safe.

Destan was exhausted — there's not a person alive who wouldn't be — but even so, he could tell Callimay wasn't trying to rest. He opened his eyes and rolled his head over, seeing her looking out at the black night. In a way, it touched him to know she was willing to do this, but at the same time it saddened him she wouldn't listen to him. What she was protecting him from he couldn't begin to comprehend; he knew nothing could get to them where they were.

A second look revealed to Destan she was wringing her hands; probably to keep herself awake. He let out what sounded more like a grunt than a sigh as he shifted in his seat, "Callimay. Rest."

"I'm alright." She jumped.

"You're tired. Get some sleep."

"It's alright; you get some, Destan. I'll be fine."

"What in the world do you think you're accomplishing by staying awake? Just go to sleep. Rocher's got everything under control."

She wrung her hands and then looked back at him, "I… I can't."

"Why not?" He asked rather irritated.

"Because you've been the one to keep watch this whole time—"

"Calli," he cut off as he put his hands on the side of her face and turned her toward him. "It's my job to keep you safe. And believe me when I say: I do it gladly. But I need you to understand we're safe now.

There's no need to stay awake or keep watch. If anything happens, Rocher will let us know. Alright?"

After a few moments, she surrendered and nodded.

"Good," Destan sat back yet again and closed his eyes.

She glanced around a couple more times and then looked at Rocher. He didn't appear to be paying any attention; his focus on the road in front of him.

The scenery was picturesque even without any light to aid her eyes: they were coming down a grade toward the coastline of the Bulge Sea. With the moon in its first day of being new, the world outside looked black, cold, and sharp; no light to soften the rare shadow that was around or give even the illusion of warmth. The salty water looked so strange with distorted reflections from nearby lights: them surrounded by webs of darkened outlines.

Looking around at the surrounding area, which was cleared of trees, it felt like it was eaten away by this overwhelming view. All she could see was water to the east. It didn't look like there wasn't any end to it!

Now she wanted to stay away to look at what she could see of the outside world.

But, Callimay looked back at Destan. Seeing him asleep made her even more tired. For a moment, she hesitated before slipping her arms around him. He didn't flinch or push her away; not even letting out a sigh. She curled up on his lap and laid her head on his chest, being careful to stay away from his wounded side.

Everything wasn't meshing in her mind, but then again, she was exhausted. She mumbled a few words while she had her eyes closed and then looked up at him and smiled as she settled down, snuggling her head close to his heart that thumped at a slow and steady rate.

Destan sighed and shifted a bit, putting his arms around her and pulling her close to him as he whispered, "Just rest, Calli."

~ 21 ~

A few hours elapsed before Rocher woke them, telling them they were back. The tone of his voice hinted that he really didn't want to disturb them since they looked so peaceful, but Destan thanked him for letting him know.

Callimay turned and looked outside which was starting to become visible with the first sunrays. The road was flanked with dense woods and looked like a rural road even though it was well-kept. Rocher slowed to turn, but she saw no driveway or road in either direction.

"Don't worry," Destan forewarned as he took her hand. "This is what I meant by no one will be able to find us."

Rocher turned off the road toward the right and appeared to be headed directly for a tree; the car not jostling like she thought it would from going off the road. She held her breath, trying to trust everything was going to be alright while understanding why Destan said this had to do with why they couldn't be found.

Right as they should have hit the tree, everything around them changed. And what a change is wat! The area was cleared of trees and there was a stately mansion — that's right, a mansion — atop the gentle slope they were going up; extravagant gardens all around as well as various sized water fountains sprinkled here and there.

As they came to the front of the massive house, Callimay could see the ocean. It was a magnificent sight to behold: white-capped waves rolling endlessly into the horizon. What an amazing sight to wake up to each and every morning!

The potent smell of salt rushed into the car as Rocher opened the door. It was surprisingly warm compared to how it felt outside when

272

they got into the car. Callimay looked around in shock as she heard the roar of the ocean waves crashing against the base of the oceanside nearby as well as seagulls announcing the morning had come, "You can't see any of this from where we were!"

"You can't see this no matter where you're at." Destan grimaced as he struggled to get out of the car. "There's only one way in, and only someone who knew about this place would know where to look for it. You're safe here, Calli. Toreon can't find us."

"But how?"

"I'm not exactly sure," he admitted as he winced. "As close as I can tell, my father had this barrier built by some of his closest friends from different divisions in the science department at the U of K. I've never found its 'source' or the name of someone who worked on it to ask how it works. — Rain and sunshine get in, we can see out, animals and insects come and go as they please, the breeze blows, but people or machines can only get through that one entrance."

"Are you well?" Rocher asked; noting his slow, labored movements and the unmistakable sight of him favoring his right side.

"Not in the best shape, but it could've been worse," he looked down at his side which started bleeding again.

"Oh Destan!" Callimay rushed over.

"Let me support him, Milady. — I will make it my utmost priority to contact his physician so he will come hence forth to tend to him. … Sir's quarters are at the head of the stairs."

Callimay didn't bother to take in the grandeur of the mansion as she made her way up to the second floor; she was worried about Destan. Once Destan was in bed, she asked with desperation in her voice, "Please get someone right now. I can't rest until I know he's alright."

"Very well, Milady. I will see to it at once."

The room was as dark as night since the over-sized velvet curtains were still pulled across the full-length windows; only a single streak of soft light coming into the room where a gap was.

Callimay gently brushed Destan's jet-black hair out of his face and took his hand in hers. Pure adrenaline was the only thing keeping her awake at this point. She wanted to collapse and sleep, but seeing the pained look on his face kept her from succumbing to it. He needed her.

So, she curled up next to him and refused to let go of his hand; trying to stay as calm as possible, "Just hang in there, Destan. Please. Someone's coming to help."

Within the hour, Rocher returned, being quiet as he knocked. He heard hurried footsteps become louder, and then saw her face as she opened the door.

"Let me be brief in introducing Sir's personal physician, Milady."

This gentleman was about the same height and build as Destan, something which immediately stood out to her; his hair even looking similar in its cut and style. Of course the biggest difference was that he had a box beard which was beginning to show signs of age, hinting he'd been practicing medicine for a while.

Seeing that she looked exhausted and frightened, he tried to calm while not brushing her off; smiling as his deep voice said chipper, "You are Destan's bride I hear. Callimay, correct?"

"Yes. Yes I am. Thank you for coming so quick." She shook his hand and then opened the door, stepping back to allow them in. "Destan's still passed out. Please help him."

"His body's self-preservation instinct kicked in most likely. He's probably been in some degree of shock ever since the injury, and now since he knows he's safe, his body put him to sleep so it could begin to heal." The physician stated as he came up to Destan. "When did it happen? The injury I mean."

"Around five, day before yesterday. I don't think he's slept since."

He sounded hopeful as he removed the bandage Justice Wan placed, "Not too long then. Good. And I'm sure he didn't sleep. — Was there a bullet or any shrapnel removed when it was first cleaned and dressed?"

She gripped the bedpost, "No. ... Is he going to be okay? Please tell me he is."

"He will, Callimay. And whoever did this first dressing did him a great service. — Destan? Destan I need you to wake up for me."

It took a few minutes, but he pulled his eyes open as the doctor gently shook his shoulder; asking in a daze when he saw who was talking to him, "Lance?"

"Looks like you've given your bride a fright by passing out." He smiled as he patted his arm. "Now I've got to clean and sew this wound together, so you're going to feel some pain. I need you awake so you know what to expect. Do you understand?"

He nodded and then looked over to Callimay who was now sitting next to him. Destan took her hand and let out his little smile she had come to know as his way of showing he was happy. She sighed in relief as she laid her free hand on his and bowed her head to pray.

When Lance began, Destan winced and gripped her hand. She rubbed it as well as his arm with the softest touch to try to help keep his mind occupied. — To a certain extent, she could feel the pain he was feeling; but as strange as it may seem, it was more of the emotional side of what he was experiencing that she felt.

Destan glanced over, and saw she was in pain: *I'm sorry Calli.*

It… it's alright. I know you're not doing it on purpose.

Can't you stop that part of it?

I don't know. It seems like I can't break that connection.

I wish I could do something… anything to help you. Destan said sorrowful as he continued to look at her, seeing she was in so much pain. *Do you think Lance could help?*

She answered rather weak as she looked at him, still sounding worried: *Just get better. … Please.*

Doctor Gerould was soon done and put a fresh dressing on the wound. He gave Destan some medicine to help him sleep and then turned his attention to Callimay, "I will be back tomorrow to see how he is doing. If he is in much pain or the area starts to bleed again, do not hesitate to tell Rocher to contact me."

"I understand." She escorted them to the door. "Thank you so much for coming. I… I don't know about how to pay you."

"No need to bother, Callimay. Destan has everything already taken care of in that aspect." He smiled as he turned back; taking a moment before asking, "Would you be opposed to me giving you a hug? You look like you need one."

Without a word, she accepted his offer. Her emotions let loose for a minute or so, and then she stepped back and took a deep breath as she wiped her face, "Thank you."

"He'll be alright. … Just get some rest."

"I will."

"Sir is asleep now, Milady. If the necessity of assistance for either of you comes to light, the buzzer located on the underside of either nightstand beside the bed will notify me," Rocher informed as he came out. "Please do make an effort to acquire some rest for yourself. I believe Sir would rest much more secure if he knew you had."

She yawned as she shut the door, "I think I will. Thank you."

All the strength drained out of her as she dragged herself back to bed; her body exhausted on every front. You would have assumed the few hours of sleep she got in the car would have helped, but it was as if her body was addicted to it and wasn't satisfied with what "little" it was given. And then on top of everything her emotions were at rock bottom. What comfort Doctor Gerould offered did help, but again, her hunger for this assurance was almost insatiable.

Callimay slid her feet over the floor as if she were skating across it, but in reality, she looked more or less like she was stumbling over nothing and wandering around the room with no goal in mind. When she reached for the lower bedpost, her body told her it couldn't take another step or support her.

❦

Several hours later, Destan fought his eyelids to open them. At first he thought he was dreaming, but as he sat up and felt the throbbing pain from his wound, he was reminded: this was real. He then felt next to him and looked over, remembering Callimay was supposed to be with him, "Calli? Where are you?"

No response.

He struggled, grimacing the entire time, but got himself up. Destan stumbled to the end of the bed and saw her on the floor, face down.

"Calli? Calli wake up!" He exclaimed in a hushed tone as he rushed over and gathered her into his arms, brushing her tousled hair out of her face. "Calli, please. You've got to be alright. Calli! Talk to me."

It took her a few moments to understand what it was he was saying, but she eventually woke up from hearing his desperate voice and responded, "I'm alright. I guess I was just so tired that I collapsed."

"Oh Callimay," Destan sighed in relief as he pulled her close again. "You scared me so bad."

"I'm sorry. I wanted to get into bed, but my legs couldn't go another step. … I mean, I know why, but 'why' are you out of bed?"

"Making sure you're safe is more important to me," he groaned as she helped him to his feet. "Do you feel better now?"

"Much bet— ouch!"

"Oh Calli," he hesitated to reach out and touch her face.

"I guess I injured it when I passed out." She sighed as she looked at her bloodied fingers. "I'll have the doctor check it tomorrow."

"I'm sorry."

"A scar is nothing compared to— I'll be fine."

He stared at her, his eyes so soft in how they looked at her.

"I feel rested now."

"Good. I do too now since I know you're safe." Destan echoed as he walked over and opened a door, noticing she was looking around and holding her hand away from her. "You can clean up in here. There are bandages in the far-right cabinet. If you need my help—"

"Thank you. I'm sure I can manage. It's not that bad."

"Not to change the subject and ignore you… but: I would appreciate some food. How about you?"

"Sounds wonderful."

Rocher showed up within the minute, just as formal and pomp as before. Destan instructed him to have dinner prepared and set up for them on the veranda of the mansion as soon as possible, "Is there something in particular you would fancy, Sir?"

"Just something simple. Callimay's not used to 'our' normal."

"A commendable choice. As you wish." Rocher bowed and then left.

"It's the best I could do." Callimay came out and took her hand away from her face. "Not your caliber, but I don't think it's bad."

"Did you get a chance to look around yet?"

That was random. "No. I stayed with you."

"Would you like to?"

"Are you sure you should be walking around so much?"

"Did Lance say I was on bed rest?" Destan tilted his head and made a face. "I can't remember much of what happened."

"Well… no."

"Good. Would you like to?"

"Only if you feel up to it," she walked over and took his hand. "Then after you… Milady."

♭

It was now early evening, so the sun was beginning to pour through the grand windows in the upstairs hall as it made its nosedive for the horizon. Destan looked… well, he looked happy as he watched her stare with wonder at the majestic scene of the over-sized crystal chandelier in the two-story vaulted-ceiling vestibule that was framed with marble flooring, chestnut wood walls, and golden molding.

When they got to the first floor, Callimay was able to appreciate what she glossed over earlier. The size and lavishness of everything blew her away, but there was one piece of furniture that couldn't escape her notice. Just beyond the dining area was a beautiful concert grand piano that was positioned in such a way to offer a beautiful view of what lay outside the front of French doors — which led to the veranda where they would be eating dinner. Callimay was drawn to it and sat on the velvet-covered bench in awe for a moment; the glass-like wood felt unreal to her as she opened the fallboard.. She hadn't played in so long she didn't know if she could remember.

As her fingers graced the run of notes to one of the most famous pieces by the world-renowned composer from the Homeworld — Beethoven — her memory of playing it came back… pretty well.

The full and resonating tone of the piano filled the first-floor of the mansion, giving Callimay chills from its beautiful tone. And this was with the lid closed! She became lost in the song and didn't notice Destan, who marched up behind her.

"Stop it!" He demanded as he grabbed her hands off the ivory keys and put the fallboard down. "Don't 'ever' do that again."

Callimay wanted to ask why, but he stormed out, slamming the French door behind him. It was a wonder the glass — now quivering in its panes — didn't shatter from the impact. She sat there in shock, wondering what she did wrong. He never told her to stay away from it.

She heard the sound of a door opening and quickly looked back to see Rocher by a door near the dining table, "Oh Rocher!"

"Milady?" He responded a bit concerned.

"Do you know what in the world I did wrong?"

Rocher took a deep breath before answering in a somber tone, "No one has graced those ivory keys to call forth their melodious voices since Ma'am — that is, Sir's mother — did. I would recall it be twenty and two years now. … As it happens, your choice in classical music was a piece she frequented. Sir would oftentimes sit with her while she played. I dare say it is a fond and strong memory he still has of her."

Oh dear! Callimay gasped as she took off after him.

The sound of her footsteps clacking off the hardwood floor filled the emptiness left in the mansion. She raced outside and began desperately looking around. The veranda was rather large that she couldn't see to her left until she walked off it. Only then could she see him standing off in the distance. She ran as fast as she could, noticing where he was standing, "Destan! Don't!"

He stood there, staring off the cliffside at the foaming waves below, not reacting to her pleas in any way.

"Destan, please don't!" Callimay begged as she fell at his feet and grabbed his hand. "Destan I didn't know what I was doing. I'm sorry. I won't ever play it again."

She could sense his emotions were reaching the point where she would need to intervene, but she was so scared she didn't know what to do. His face was pale and his lips firmly pursed together, his green eyes piercing in their gaze and unmoving: *Please look at me. Destan! I… don't let these emotions take you over. Not again. … Fight it! If not for yourself, for me. Please Destan! — Please, God. Don't let this take him away from me. Please.*

It appeared he heard her because he looked down to her and then dropped to his knees.

"Oh Destan," Callimay wiped away the lonely tear from his face. "I'm so sorry. I never meant to cause you any pain. I just had only seen that type of piano from afar and wanted to— I should've asked first, I'm sorry. Please forgive me."

"You didn't know, Calli." He said under his breath as he bowed his head. "I'm the one who should be sorry."

"No." She shook her head, her hands and voice shaking still from her being panicked. "No, I should have—"

"Calli!" Destan gritted his teeth as he grabbed her by the shoulders. "Please! I… I just don't…"

"I understand. You need to be alone. Just… come back. Please?"

She waited, hoping he would say something to let her know he was alright, but he never responded. So, with nothing else possible she could do to help, she left; feeling alone and like she was failing Destan.

As she turned the corner, she looked back and saw he was gone. Now she felt grieved as she sighed and went inside.

❦

Callimay wasn't nearly as interested in touring her new home anymore; not since she was in this push-pull phase again with Destan. But in an effort to keep herself occupied, she made herself look around, trying to shove the feelings of this tug-of-war between them out.

Beside the piano was a lone door. The door handle on it was a bit different from anything she'd seen: it was sunken into the door itself. As she pulled on it, she could tell it wasn't the way the door moved, so she pushed on it… meeting the same resistance: *Even if a door 'is' locked, it has a tiny bit of give in the direction it opens. … That's strange. I wonder what in the world could be in there.*

After a couple more failed attempts, Callimay gave up and dragged herself over to where Rocher had been. There was a swinging door, so it had to be safe for her to go in… right? As she peaked inside, she let out a gasp; and it wasn't because there were two men in there working. Rocher, who just came in from another door in the back of the kitchen, looked a bit shocked as well. This pristine kitchen was something out of a high-end magazine. She'd only dreamed of having a place to cook and bake in like this. The island in the middle of the room looked about the size of the kitchen she'd worked in her entire life! There was so much to take in, but Callimay froze when the men stopped working and stared at her.

"I'm sorry." She apologized as she backed up, bumping against the corner of the countertop. "I was looking around and was wondering—I won't bother you."

The door swung back and forth as she stared at the grand dining table; it bumping into her a couple times to remind her she was still too close to it. She felt so strange. Callimay tried to shake it, but couldn't help but feel like she didn't belong there. Then it occurred to her: she never saw any other woman there. But, she had only been there for a little bit, so maybe she hadn't met them. Still, something felt off. The way the men looked at her; it was as if they were seeing an intruder.

She looked like something spooked her by the way she bolted to the other side of the room where yet another door was. This put her in a long and narrow hallway where several doors could be seen to her left; but didn't feel like adventuring down it. On the other hand, there was one right in front of her.

Behind this door, Callimay found a sunroom with a catwalk-type balcony around the perimeter and a crisscrossing interior. Her curious eye found a few tropical plants, a small pond with a water fountain, and a couple patio furniture pieces. It was nothing she would have imagined a sunroom to look like if any woman had been around.

Wandering around was the only "comfort" she had, but staying in one place too long reminded her she was alone. Callimay walked up the hall and looked around the parlor. The fireplace was lit and shed its ebbing and flowing glow over the pieces of furniture close by as well as its warmth. She scanned the walls for any photographs or portraits, but there was nothing. And no amount of investigation would reveal one little trinket: or what some called knick-knack. The coffee and end tables were bare of any lace doilies or cloth runners. There wasn't even a single fresh-cut flower or plant to be seen. Even if it had been a while since his mother passed, she thought he would have left everything as it was… and surely she had things like that around the mansion then.

The only thing that might have lent itself to the feminine style was what hung in the vestibule. She stared up through the crystals which gleamed and sparkled. She started up the stairs when she heard Rocher call out, "Milady? … I beg your pardon concerning our conduct earlier. Having guests in the kitchen isn't customary."

Guest?… "I'm sorry. I didn't mean to interrupt. I was just curious."

"Oh please do not feel you were at fault, Milady. You appeared to be out-of-sorts when you left so I wanted to take it upon myself to ensure you were alright." He asked in his formal tone and somewhat similar, yet different, accent to Destan.

"Rocher?" Callimay sighed as she sat down and leaned against the banister. "I… I 'do' feel very much 'out-of-sorts'. I know I just got here, but… I don't feel like I belong here. I just— I feel I'm intruding… a guest like you said."

"Pardon my ill-chosen words, Milady; I regret my lapse in allowing such language to slip past my lips. They do not properly represent my intentions. — We have been starved of the pleasure of a lady's presence around the residence for over ten years. Losing his mother was a hard truth for Sir to comprehend. When he became of age to legally be given those responsibilities, he requested in a very strong manner that all the female aides leave. I found out only after they were excused he could not, in his words, 'take any woman being around' and 'it was too much to bear'. — I must confess that Sir holds a rather nasty habit close to his person: suppressing emotions within himself and not seeking counsel to forge through those times. I believe this is described in the phrase: 'letting it fester'. I have made what attempts I could to show him the danger of this, but as you can attest to, it for the most part has been to no avail. — Though I would give a waiver for the past few years since he found religion. — With his absolute decision on the matter, the staff has yet to lay eyes upon a woman in such an extended period of time that you 'do' appear to them as somewhat of an intruder."

I was wondering what was wrong. She sighed as she closed her eyes. "Maybe I should go, Rocher. I wasn't raised like this. I'm not used to all this formality. — I'm not saying it's wrong. I… I just don't want to constantly be walking on eggshells, trying to make sure I'm doing the right thing. I don't want to hurt Destan any more than I have."

"If I could beg your indulgence, Milady. Do not ever purpose the thought you are at fault in any way. We — including Sir — are merely adjusting to these new circumstances and seek only to request your patience. You only just arrived! Please give this transition some time." He tried his best to encourage as he handed her a handkerchief. "I must say, when I heard him relay to me you would be accompanying him; I was fully expecting it to be one of Sir's fun-spirited jests he has quite the reputation for. I was a bit bewildered when I beheld you, but was of the utmost thankfulness and peaceful calm that Sir has been able to allow the fairer sex back into his life. I thank you eternally and beg on his behalf for your patience with him. … It is not lost to me how he continues to carry these nasty habits; I would contribute it largely to the fact he has been orphaned for so long since there is no substitute for a mother's love or father's instruction. I know I have failed him in this way and hope it was not a failure which will cause him — or you even — extreme heartache. … As far as you belonging, may I offer my words: change wouldn't in the least be an inconvenience for us. Sir has his moments of breaking off and being quite informal. I am sure those times will be of great importance and comfort to you when they arise. — Rest assured, those times will come. — And do not concern yourself with pleasing us. We are here to help you and do as you wish."

"Thank you for letting me know. It does help, me understanding what is going on here a bit more. … As far as his 'nasty habits', it's not the easiest thing getting information from Destan about things which bother him, or what I can do to help."

"If there are any inquiries Milady has, please do not hesitate to request my ear. I lay no claim to holding the answers to all the world's quandaries; but what I know which will aid you and Sir I offer freely."

Callimay reached up to her cut cheek with her hand, "I will."

He asked concerned as he stepped toward her, trying to help but unsure what to do, "Are you well, Milady?"

"I'm alright, Rocher. Destan didn't do this. — Do you think Doctor Gerould could look at it when he is here tomorrow?"

"I would think him to be delighted to have an opportunity to assist you." He nodded as he began to smile. "I will make it my priority to inform him about it."

"Thank you. … Oh! What time will dinner be?"

"At the top of the hour, Milady," Rocher said after he consulted his watch. "And I will take the duty of informing Sir upon myself. The grounds are quite new to you, so you need not worry seeking him out. He tends to wander when he's like this."

The landing for the stairs extended to the end of the mansion on the north side while it took a wide curve around the vestibule area toward the south; one wing extending off of it to the east.

Noting her outfit in one of the mirrors as she walked from bedroom to bedroom, she was curious if there were any clothes she could change into; so, she began to look through all the closets. As suspected: empty. Callimay went back into Destan's room and pulled back the curtains to reveal French-door windows which opened to a small balcony.

Just as she reached for the handle, she saw him outside talking with Rocher. Curiosity was trying harder, telling her to open the door and listen; but she reminded herself she couldn't constantly be the one trying to make sure the ground she was walking on was or wasn't eggshells. She needed him to tell her when something was bothering him — preferably before it was an issue.

Rocher handed him what looked to be some type of black leather jacket as he continued to speak. He stood and threw it over his back as he slipped his arms in it; nodding as he excused Rocher.

Seeing Destan in something other than what he wore at the Society was so foreign. Callimay stared at him for a while as he stood there, the jacket falling just above his ankles. It had to be of a thick, heavy-weight leather since it wasn't disturbed by the wind much at all.

Even though this was a bit troubling to her, the grief and sorry weighed on her more; her hand slipping down the windowpane. He looked so alone. And this wasn't what she was used to seeing from him: he liked being alone. No. No, this was more like the type of loneliness she recognized all too well. Callimay knew what it was like to not have anyone show unconditional love which could constantly be felt, even when the person giving it wasn't near.

She felt even more like she was failing to be a good wife to Destan; as if she weren't showing him love like she thought she was. She knew she wasn't receiving it from him, but if he didn't feel she was showing him any it would explain why he was acting this way.

Callimay hung her head and sobbed, falling to her knees: *What am I doing wrong, Destan? What is it? I will change, I just — I need to know what it is! And I refuse to read your mind. I want you to trust and tell me… but I don't know how to gain your trust so you will.*

After a few minutes, she gathered herself and used the door handle for support before turning back.

When she found the strength to look up, she saw a rain of dust in the air which sparkled in the sunlight. Callimay groaned to herself; not wanting to be light-hearted and cheerful like it was. If she was indeed going to be alone like this on a regular basis, how could she keep such an outlook and attitude about everything? … What had she done?

But part of her couldn't take this bleak and hopeless personality that she was allowing to infect herself. So, she shook her head, took a deep breath, made herself smile, and then went about finding what she was looking for in the first place.

As she went to open the door to what she assumed would be the closet, there came a knock. Unprepared, she jumped back and yelped. Another knock came and she realized it was the main door: *Get a grip, Rose Petal.* "Who is it?"

"It is Rocher, Milady."

"Oh. Come in, Rocher."

He opened the door and then vanished for a few moments; coming back with a towering stack of boxes which he then placed on the table closest to the door, "Sir had arrangements made to have these procured for you. I hope they are to your liking."

Whatever could they be? She pulled the top box down and looked at the embossed company name before opening it. *Array Customs? Why does that sound so familiar? … It was— Della got a job there last year, that's right. Then this must be…*

Inside was an assortment of outfits in the most beautiful rainbow of pastels and brights. And the types of fabric were only ones she had swatches of… and that was only for work!

"Alas, I fear we all lack the sure ability to decipher the sizing for woman's clothing with any kind of accuracy. Thank the stars above Sir relayed detailed instructions with such regards and necessary details which would have been overlooked if he had remained silent. If you find that any adjustments need to be made so they are to your liking, do not feel you are inconveniencing me. I hope you will find something suitable for the time being."

She ran her fingers over the cashmere and silk fabrics; sounding stunned, "I appreciate you all are doing so much to help me. … I will be sure to let you know if I need something, thank you."

"As you wish, Milady." Rocher bowed, closing the door.

Callimay took each outfit out and laid them on the bed to look at the styling and color choices; the luxurious fabrics seeming to slip through her hands like water. The pristine craftsmanship was amazing and the detailing beautiful.

One box in particular was a bit heavier than she was expecting; it containing about a dozen boxes that each held a pair of heels. — He even got her shoes! — Another was almost overlooked since it was so small; it holding a treasure chest of the most expensive kind: various jewels for her to wear.

Looking around at everything she now had, she couldn't think of one thing she was missing… and yet there was one last box: the biggest one. She gasped as she lifted the single article of clothing out. Her mind was running wild; describing it to herself in a language only she and others of that art would understand: an empire-waist A-line evening dress with leg-of-mutton sleeves, a mini train flowing from the floor-length hem, and lace-edging for the cuffs and bateau neckline.

The fact it was made from the softest silk or the lace was the finest, most delicate handmade lace wasn't what caused her so much joy… it was the color of the fabric: *It's just like my bedroom… orange.*

Nothing was going to keep her from trying it on first.

It was a perfect fit. Callimay was put off by the bandage on her cheek — it ruined the overall look: *It needs to be changed anyway.*

She swished the skirt back and forth as she looked at herself in the mirror, and then ran over to fix her hair and find some jewelry to complement it.

As she was looking through them, Callimay heard footsteps behind her. She whipped around, "You're back! Thank you so much, Destan!"

He had his arms opened toward her and stared at her in utter bewilderment as she ran over and threw her arms around his neck, "Everything is so beautiful. It's more than I could have ever asked for. I… I almost don't know what to say. You didn't have to go to all this trouble. I hope this didn't cost you too much. The jewelry looks real!"

"It wasn't any trouble, Calli. I'm glad it fits and that you like it. — I remembered you wore an orange blouse on orientation day when we met," Destan admitted as he held her close to hide his flushed face. "You looked so beautiful in it… I wanted you to have something special in the same color."

"It's my favorite color."

A moment later he let her down and cleared his throat, "And as far as the jewelry goes, some are real. I'll be the first to admit some are too rare for me to afford since they can't be found here and there's none coming from the Homeworld; so there are some costume—"

The clock didn't care it was interrupting; it had a job which it never failed to do: chime to announce the new hour.

"I'll change and meet you downstairs f—"

"You're not wearing that?" Destan gestured to her.

"You want me to?"

"Yes."

"Oh. Well. Alright then. Though I feel over-dressed now."

"That can be easily fixed," he all but ripped off his coat and tossed it to a chair on the other side of the room. "I won't be long. I'll meet you downstairs in a bit."

⅏

She went downstairs, feeling excited as she sat on one of the last steps to slip her shoes on. Having Destan with her made her forget the agony she went through not but an hour or so ago.

Callimay couldn't see herself but she felt like a princess… a five-years-old princess with hair dripping wet and frightened with her new surroundings; but given a new dress in her favorite color. She closed her eyes and replayed what she could remember of that memory.

Destan had since walked out and paused when he saw her waltzing around; the rainbows from the crystals in the chandelier paling in comparison to the diamonds she had on which couldn't even begin to rival her natural beauty. He leaned against the railing and gazed at her. She was so graceful and beautiful… and she was his.

He started down, trying to stay quiet, but caught her eye when he was about halfway down. She stumbled a bit as she stopped; looking embarrassed and hanging her head. Destan rushed down and put his hand under her chin to raise her face, "Why did you stop?"

"I… I looked like a fool," she mumbled, sounding ashamed as she looked away and closed her eyes.

"No, you didn't." he smiled as he laid his hand on the side of her neck. *Calli? Calli, look at me.*

Yes?

"You're just fine. And everything that happened earlier was my fault. Alright? It was 'my' fault. I should have said something before we came down." Destan apologized as he brushed her bangs behind her ear. "I shouldn't make you keep guessing what upsets me. You had no idea about the piano. I'm sorry, Calli."

Callimay leaned into his chest and gripped the lapel of his jacket. She knew this was a learning curve for them. In that moment she remembered: *Lord? I thank You for getting us to safety. I... I just ask for You to watch over us emotionally... as a couple. Help us to seek out how to help each other. Help us remember we're both learning how this is all supposed to look. And I pray we will look to You for answers neither of us have. In Your Son's Name I pray, amen.*

Destan heard what she was saying, but let her have the time she needed; even saying one himself for strength. They stayed there for a minute, enjoying the time of silence and peace. Callimay finally had what she'd wanted: a break.

"Tell you what," he said chipper as he took a step back. "I'm going back up so we can do this again."

"Whatever for?"

"You'll understand. Start dancing like you were."

"What?"

"Just do it."

"I... but... but, Destan." Callimay objected, him looking back at her somehow serious and soft at the same time. "Oh alright."

He went back into his room, and then after a minute or so walked out. She was dancing around as he told her to, but stopped again, just then realizing he was wearing a dashing five-piece Tuxedo.

It was easy to tell by the way he limped and took a labored breath with each step that he wasn't "himself", but he still looked like he felt so much better.

The second they embraced each other, she felt as if everything had turned a corner for the better. So much frustration and pain were behind them and they could work on healing... together.

"Better?" Destan whispered as he continued to gaze at her.

"Yes."

"Are you ready for dinner, Milady?" He exaggerated.

"Whenever you are, Milord." Callimay tried not to laugh.

"Oh!" He snapped his fingers and then reached into his pocket. *You're losing your mind, Boon. What's wrong?* "This was the main thing I had them go after. If this doesn't fit you, I would understand it more than everything else."

He handed her a small, black, velveteen box. She was fairly sure she knew what it was, but even so, when she opened it and found a set of rings in it for her and a band for Destan, Callimay almost dropped the box. The exquisite setting of diamonds in platinum — and if it weren't platinum it would be a disappointing downgrade from the rest of the jewelry he got her — was almost overwhelming.

The set for Callimay consisted of three bands that were decked out to the nines as it were: two thin outer one guarding the wide, euro-styled center band with a stone so imposing that it almost dwarfed her hand. Of course, Destan's was nothing but a plain, oversized band; but on a closer inspection there was a row of diamonds around each side edge. Seeing it stunned Callimay; she didn't think he would wear one. And even though they were small, there were diamonds on it!

"Do you like them?"

"I… I— they're beautiful, Destan. But these must have cost a fortune! Why would you spend so much on these?"

"And what of it?" He almost scoffed as he took her small, delicate hand in his. "Remember what I said about money?"

"I do."

"I'm only going to do this once, so I'm going to make sure it's done right — by my standards anyway." He smiled as he kneeled and slipped the trio of rings on her finger. "And I think you know when I say 'my standards' I mean in regards to frivolous things like the rings: I want there to be no doubt in anyone's mind we're married."

Callimay smiled as he stood and she took his hand to put his on, "You thought of everything didn't you?"

"Well, I had Rocher help me out with some things," he admitted; and then kissed her on the forehead.

She sighed as she kissed him on the cheek, "Thank you, Destan. Thank you for everything."

~ 22 ~

They spent the next week recuperating from their escape from the Society; during which time Doctor Gerould closed Callimay's cut without the worry of an overly-pronounced scar. He understood why the original type was used, but commented any normal, active person would have broken it just like she had. In one way, she was glad it wouldn't be so pronounced, but then it made her — and even Destan — suspicious of the medical staff at the Society. Did they do something else to her which wasn't the best and might put her at risk for being hurt later on?

Their first Sunday was strange. It was a very small group of men. Rocher was nowhere around and Destan wasn't willing to discuss why. Callimay was sad that in the chaos of everything when they left the Society, she didn't get to at least grab her Bible. Even Destan didn't seem pleased his was now gone. But what could they do? The Society most likely had them destroyed.

She was grateful his wound was healing quickly, but wasn't thrilled with what he decided because of this He started training since there wasn't that hindrance, but he had to pace himself — also known as: listen to Callimay's instructions. As much as he didn't want to admit it, he wasn't at one-hundred percent… and would spike easy.

In light of him training, Destan called a meeting to tell everyone what happened while he was gone and what they were preparing for… going so far as to put outgoing and incoming traffic to a minimum for two weeks. He did this in an effort to cut the ability someone could have to follow staff back without being noticed; yet without raising suspicions around the area concerning the absence of these individuals.

It was a surprise to Callimay that everyone was so calm after the meeting. But, she was so engrained with the usual reaction of small-talk and gossip starting after a meeting or when something was found out about a classmate at the Society. She forgot how real adults would normally react. Then she remembered when Destan found out about her ability, how he didn't have much of a response either. Of course, with her knowing about his father's work in this all it would make sense to not cause an uproar; but still.

⅁

Through all this, she was doing her best to be patient with him in general. She enjoyed the time after Assembly when they would discuss and talk about different things. Frankly, it was the most time they'd spend together during the week — and outside the realm of training — since he would oftentimes disappear for hours on end without saying anything. She would ask Rocher, who would in turn come back about an hour later and tell her where he was, or Destan — on rare occasions — would come himself to find her.

Getting used to someone else around all the time was new for her as well, but she was hoping he would be more open to listening when she felt she was being pushed aside or left out.

She found ways to entertain herself, but more and more she found herself wanting to be with him. One day she was in the sunroom looking out at the snow-covered landscape. It was only a small amount, and patchy at that. It looked more like heavy frost, really. Snow wasn't a common thing in this area at all. While she wrote with her finger in the frost on the window, Callimay sighed: *I spent more time with him at the Society where we 'weren't' safe and while we 'weren't' married. Now I… I don't—just because I'm safe physically doesn't mean that's all I need. At least I thought that's how it worked. — You promised you wouldn't leave me. You told me you understood what you were doing by marrying me. Is your understanding 'that' much different?*

Something else changed which struck her as odd. Well, borderline disturbing. But then again, she was seeing Destan in "his" environment for the first time. She knew what he normally wore was going to be a change from what she saw, but what was his everyday attire threw her

292

for a loop. He wore all black and favored that black leather, full-length, duster coat with no sleeves which Rocher gave him when she saw them in the garden that one time. Everything he wore was nice, but "all" black? He looked like a shadow walking around the mansion; especially after it got dark. It was nonintentional, but he scared her a couple times because of this.

She began to have more and more doubts about whether or not he married her only to keep her safe and not because he truly cared about her. The longer she spent time with him the more it became evident. He would oftentimes sleep in a guest room or stay up extremely late; and it was very obvious to Callimay that the only time Destan kissed her was their first day there… and it was on the forehead. She even tried to think of a time he did, but couldn't even recall him telling her he loved her. Not that this was a death sentence for their relationship, but it was hinting at something she was trying not to think of.

This grieved her more than maybe she ever wanted to admit, but she wasn't going to let his lack of affection and sometimes commitment deter her from making sure she upheld her duties in the relationship: she made a commitment to him and she was going to keep it.

Callimay kept praying Destan would be more willing to make sure he kept his commitment on a consistent basis instead of this "when it's convenient for me" timing.

∾

All this time, Toreon was finishing his training to get him in optimal condition. This whole development came as a blow to Mr. Freigh since he believed Destan would be the one to restore everything to the way it was prior to abilities being given to. He did agree though, that having the two of them left to their own devices was a dangerous liability and the situation needed to be dealt with sooner rather than later.

Various groups were sent out to scout for Toreon but they always returned with dead ends from wild rooster chases. They had a general idea of where Destan and Callimay were, but there weren't any solid leads to follow which would help narrow the search.

Even a surprise to him, Dakoe was able to avoid suspicion even after warning them. He was routinely sent out in these "recon" groups and would try everything he could if he thought they were getting close… somehow causing the trail to go cold. The most promising leads which came in were always assigned to him, so he was able to keep Toreon at bay that much longer. But even with every effort, Dakoe wasn't sure if this would last. He was hoping the time he was buying was going to be enough for them.

In light of the slip up with the paper files, Mr. Freigh eliminated paper trails altogether. Baleck warned him of this a few years prior when a student almost came into possession of another's file, but it was only one incident and Mr. Freigh deemed his own fault by carrying it around on his person.

Break was now almost over, so Toreon had a choice to make: find and eliminate Destan and Callimay or continue his "studies". Had this proposition been tabled two months earlier there would have been no way he would have left.

But now? Now he had a personal stake in this.

ॐ

Destan soon was getting report after report about people inquiring about him and a young lady who had been seen with him. He knew they were in the safest place on Quidoria, but he couldn't deny he was beginning to wait for the inevitable ending of Toreon showing up. But how could he find them? It was impossible: *Never assume something is impossible. The second you do is the second it happens.*

Callimay picked up on this unsettling in his emotions and tried to help ease it… but it never went away and he wouldn't tell her what was going on. With the amount and type of training he was doing, she put two and two together and kept getting: *Toreon is coming.*

She did her best to keep with his pace, but she could only last for so long. His emotions were spiking more frequently.

One day this all came to a traumatic head. Destan thought he was doing well and staying stable but then realized Callimay was no longer with him. He began to spiral out of control and became angry at her for stopping. It didn't take him long to find her even though she was evading him once she realized what was going on. He jerked her toward him, running over and throwing her off the cliff.

"Destan!" She screamed; frantically trying to reach out for him.

That shrill sound brought him to his senses. He jumped off the edge, knowing he wouldn't fall far; reaching out and hoping with everything that he could catch her before she hit the barrier.

Their fingers touched for a moment as he tried to grab her hand, but he didn't make it in time.

It sounded like he heard a "crack" when she made impact!

Dead silence as time seemed to stop; Destan staring in disbelief. He couldn't believe what he did.

She wasn't moving!

Destan gathered her in his arms, panic setting in. How injured was she? She wasn't bleeding, but she was breathing. Would she be alright? He couldn't get back up and carry her at the same time so he yelled again and again, his voice becoming more strained and broken with each plea for help. It felt like an eternity before someone answered him.

ℬ

As fast as humanly possible, Doctor Gerould drove out when he was told what happened. And as it turned out, she suffered a severe concussion, dislocated shoulder, two broken ribs, and a bruised spleen.

When she first woke up and saw Destan, she screamed and ordered him to get away from her; not allowing him to even be in the room.

He started to get angry and then realized: it wasn't her fault. He was the one demanding her to do this; pushing her farther than she could go. He was the one who lost control. He was the one who wouldn't listen. He was the one who tried to kill her! He was the reason she was terrified of him. No blame lay anywhere but on him.

Doctor Gerould came out not long after, "She calmed down just now and was going on and on about how frightened of you she was. That she had never seen you act like this toward her and she couldn't understand why. … With her concussion and whatever was done to her to give her the abilities she now has, her memory of what happened is overly amplified. I'm going to warn you now since I've never had someone with abilities in my care: this 'may' last for a week or so. My best guess is that it'll depend on how fast her body is able to recover. Just… don't be surprised if you hear her scream out every once in a while. And by that, I mean she could wake up from what she thinks to be a nightmare when in reality she is reliving what happened — like what she did just a little while ago. I've given her a strong sedative to try to help, but as you saw, she was able to break through it. — I wish I had both of your records. The way Callimay is overpowering those sedatives is completely unheard of!"

Destan, who was slumped over the railing next to him, asked, "Is she going to be alright? I mean is—"

"As long as she is allowed time to recover and come to terms with what happened, I assure you: there'll be no issues with her making a full recovery. There's nothing I've seen to make me feel otherwise. I would though, leave her alone for a few days after what she said just now. But you need to help her finish recovering, Destan. … You look at me like I'm some maniac telling you to fix what you broke when in reality you know only she can allow it to be fixed; but you've got to understand for her to make this choice she needs to see who you truly are. She needs to know what she saw earlier was the creation of the Society — not the hidden, true you which I think you've suppressed and hidden from her. I know you've never been keen to showing much emotion, let alone the type and amount needed for marriage; but you've 'got' to, Destan. You've 'got' to make yourself uncomfortable and prove to her you are not what she saw; that you do care about her. Don't just try, do! … I am speaking outside my medical expertise, I know. But I'm giving you advice as husband to husband. Don't let happen to you and Callimay be what ended up happening between me and Orpha. Don't find yourself at that point of no return. Don't allow her to become 'something' to you. Remind her quite often she is 'every'thing some'one' to you. Especially now."

"But how does that work? What does it look like?" Destan shook his interlocked hands. "I don't know how to. I spaz out!"

"Have you ever given her a compliment — of any kind — for no special reason? Just because?"

"I— not really."

"Knowing my track record, take my advice with a grain of salt… or a bucket," Doctor Gerould chuckled; and then became serious again, "A woman feeds off of verbal and physical feedback. It's how she's wired instinctively. It's how she's able to gauge where she stands with her husband. And by the look on your face I can tell you already know this isn't going to be easy. … It doesn't always have to be elaborate or fancy. Just tell her she's beautiful, remind her you love her, don't be afraid to give her a kiss in front of others, hold her hand… or smile when you catch her eye. I think you'll be surprised how the little things you do and say will do more than the big."

"But even those little things… I'm not even sure I can do those."

"Do you love her? … Destan, look at me."

"I…" he hesitated as he turned and stood to face him. "I want to protect her. I want to keep Callimay safe."

Doctor Gerould cringed as he bowed his head and shook it, "If you really wanted to protect her, you wouldn't put her through this emotional torment of being married to someone who doesn't love her. Physically protecting someone is just a fraction of the battle. You've got to be willing to protect her emotionally — protect her heart. Love her."

"But my father—"

"Do 'not' use Destry as an excuse, Destan Quinton Nevrille!" Doctor Gerould cut off; sounding and looking infuriated. "He did 'everything' in his power to protect Lylah in every — every — way. It just… it wasn't enough that one time."

"But that was all it took!" He slammed his fist on the railing.

"Do you know 'why' your father even had a place build here in Kerogen? Do you? Your father and mother had close to nothing when they got married. Lylah worked for me in my office in Heirway to help make ends meet while Destry finished his schooling down here. She was sick for him the whole time no matter how hard she tried to hide it. It tore her apart to only see her husband for a day and be away from him for almost a week with little or no contact. I offered to help so she could move, but she said she would only be a distraction and finishing his studies meant so much to him. Lylah said she was 'willing to endure that torture' — her exact words — because it would give them the stability they needed in the long run. Granted, he wasn't around her so he didn't know what she was going through. And since Lylah was more concerned about Destry she never told him how she felt. But I tell you what? The second he found out he dropped everything — skipped his next class — ran to the bank and spent every dime he had and could borrow to buy the small plot of land where the house stands that you still call home. He did most of the work by himself, but some classmates helped when they had spare time. I would even come with Lylah when I could. Your mother was a worker, Destan. She pushed through so much. I think your father took a lesson from her in that: Destry told me that he missed an important exam because he was so close to getting the house done; he refused to stop until it was and Lylah was with him. He worked all night and passed out just about the moment he finished. That exam was a pass/fail with no retake and what he needed to get to the next class. He gave that up just so your mother could be with him. … Do you understand what I am getting at, Destan? … Destan? Destan I know the Society is getting close to finding you both here. Fid—"

"How did—"

"Remember: you're not the only one who pays attention to what people say. Yes, the risk of you two being found is very concerning, but the risk of losing the love and devotion of the young woman in there is something you should be utterly terrified of, Destan Quinton." Doctor Gerould fumed as he shook his finger toward the bedroom Callimay was in. "I think deep down you do love her; I truly do. But I also think you don't understand what it all means. You're learning to put her safety above yours; though that's not saying much since you've always been reckless. You're not putting her wants and desires above yours."

"But I'm trying!"

"Are you?" He grabbed Destan's coat and shook him a bit. "Because it sure seems like you're trying to hang onto the lone-wolf mentality you've had for so long while fooling yourself into thinking you can hold onto her at the same time. — Let it go! You know she's the only one capable of keeping you alive when you lose control."

"I know!"

"She's stayed beside you even though you've locked her out. — Do you know what pain she goes through each and every time you train? She told me the amount of stress on her that comes from focusing while you're moving at such high speeds exhausts her so she can't even stand upright. Callimay also told me she feels the emotional pain you do, and it translates into physical pain for her."

"I know it does." He admitted in anguish as he ran his fingers through his hair. "She told me it does."

"Did she tell you how it feels?"

"No."

"Every single time your emotions spike it's like someone is taking a steaming-hot branding knife and running it through her skull and then twisting it while they — you — push it in farther. Having that on top of the migraine she develops from keeping in contact with you while you are moving at such high speeds— have you ever had a migraine, Destan? A 'true' migraine? Can you comprehend what type of pain she is experiencing? Do you realize what she goes through on a daily basis on that front alone for you?" Doctor Gerould graphically described.

"I didn't know." He groaned, now doubled over the railing. *Calli. I… I didn't know. … Why didn't you tell me? … I'm sorry!*

"She's sheltering you because she loves you. Do you see that?"

"Yes."

"Someone might think this is enough, but I'm not done. I know you're stubborn and hard-headed. I'm going to be the voice Callimay can't be… and won't because she loves you so much that she can't bear to voice her concerns. All that pain is horrible, but there's another pain she feels, Destan. Those countless hours after you're done training; while you're gone or mentally absent. What do you think she feels then? Compiling emotional pain atop horrendous physical pain never bodes well. Never. … What happened earlier? If nothing changes, this may be the last straw for her. You need to think about what pain and discomfort 'you' are willing to go through to keep her. Period!"

~ 23 ~

Just as Doctor Gerould said, Callimay had nightmares throughout the day; but they mainly occurred in the middle of the night. She always woke up screaming. Destan would wake up from these shrill bursts of noise but not move. He was in the bedroom next to her and could hear her start wailing, eventually calming as she fell asleep.

This went on for the next two weeks. Destan tried to see her, but each time she would shriek and yell at him to get away from her. At first, he would be frustrated she was still scared, but then seeing her wince from his emotional spike and remembering what Doctor Gerould alluded to: Callimay hadn't severed her connection to him. She hadn't given up on him even though she was terrified of him. Deep down she loved and kept watch over him.

The shoe was now on the other foot. It was his turn to work and not give up on Callimay. Each rejection hurt, but Destan began to see it somewhat as payback for all the times he rejected her. He knew she wasn't doing it for that purpose but he was seeing this coming from it. And, in a way, he needed it.

❦

At the end of two weeks, he woke in the middle of the night to the sound of her screaming. He lay there, trying to hold the tears back and stay strong, but couldn't stand it and got up, rushing over and leaning his forehead against the wall between their bedrooms.

Destan stayed there and listened as she calmed and was now softly crying. He wanted to comfort her; he wanted her back. Now that he knew what it was to lose her in this way, he knew he needed to change.

301

Things needed to be better like he admitted months before. Marriage didn't change any of those words. If anything, it made them even more cemented. But what could he do?

I know I've pushed you out. I know the pain you feel each time I do. I'm starting to understand I'm good at saying things when I'm able to get them out but completely miserable at following through. I know I hurt you, Calli. I know you're scared of me. I… I'm scared of myself right now. Toreon was right. It seems I have become the very person I was scared I was after I read through what happened back at the Society. … Lance said you need to see the true me, to see I'm not who I was that day. But the more I think about it, the more I wonder if who you saw that day is who I truly am on the inside: someone who has held in vengeance and anger for so long that they can't comprehend how to care and love for someone. Someone who is totally blind. — I can't lose you but I don't know anything but how to lose people. I really don't know what to do, Calli! I just… Destan confessed as the tears became too much for him to fight back. *God, help me! Heal her…*

A few minutes later Destan noticed there weren't any noises coming from next door. He ran to check on her, then went back to bed and lay there thinking more about what Doctor Gerould challenged him with; remembering what Callimay told him the day when he went searching for her after he'd thrown her out emotionally.

℘

The next day, Doctor Gerould showed up to see how she was doing. When he heard she was still having nightmares and sleeping most of the day, his expression changed to fear. Destan was right on his heels as they ran up to her room.

She was still asleep when they came in. Seeing the look on Doctor Gerould's face made Destan too frightened to ask what was wrong.

"Callimay?" Doctor Gerould asked in a booming tone as he rubbed her hand. "I need you to wake up. Come on. Wake up for me."

Calli? Calli it's Lance. The doctor. Wake up. Destan tried.

After a couple minutes and no reaction, Doctor Gerould took his Halo out and put it on her head. Destan sat beside her, taking her hand in his. It felt ice-cold and frail. His heart sank as he saw the doctor's expression change from fear to despair. Doctor Gerould looked right at him and opened his mouth but couldn't get anything to come out.

"No!" Destan gathered Callimay into his arms; refusing to accept what he knew was the truth. "No, you 'told' me she would be fine if there was enough time. You promised me she would come back!"

Doctor Gerould hung his head as he took the Halo off, "It must be due to whatever changed on a molecular level when they alter—"

"Get out of here, Lance!" He demanded as he flashed his green eyes at him. "Leave! Now!"

"Alright, Destan. I'm going."

He wept bitterly as he rocked her, staying with her all day and refusing to eat. All he wanted was to see her rich brown eyes that were so soft when they looked at him and to hear her sweet-sounding voice say his name. But all he could remember now was her screaming and looking at him with terror and fear.

He'd finally found someone to open his heart to. It was keeping the door open and allowing everything inside to be seen that was the issue.

As he sat there, Destan caught himself saying in the same tone as his father did, "I couldn't protect you."

Hearing those words come from "his" mouth in the exact way his memory held; it rocked him to his core.

Destan now understood that protecting someone wasn't only the physical side. The cascade of events which led to this was all due to his lack of valuing and loving Callimay. If he would've had the strength of character to exercise self-control and stop to notice she was maxing out that day, he would've stopped so she wouldn't have burned out. If he would've had the strength to talk to and understand her, Destan would've been able to fix so many things long ago. If he would've asked her why she was always so tired and pain-ridden after training, he would've spared her so much pain.

If.

If… the most powerful two-letter word known to man. One which holds the key to an infinite number of alternate realities, but those which can never be reached or explored. One which is all-knowing but only after the fact. One which holds the regrets of every single man and woman who ever lived — if.

"All I want to do is fix this, Calli." Destan cried as he cradled her seemingly lifeless body in his arms; his voice breaking more and more with each word. "I don't want to fix everything. I… I know I can't. The past is set in stone. My parents are gone and the others I cared about are too. But I just can't bring myself to accept that you're gone. This has to be something I can fix because it's happening now. … You mean so much to me. — I want another chance. Just one more. I 'want' to do everything differently. I… I want to do it 'with' you… 'for' you. I want to do it because I do care about you. I want to do it because… I love you, Callimay! I do! With every ounce of my life, I love you! I know I've never said it out loud until now. I know I never let you know. I guess it was because I didn't know. I didn't understand what it really meant until now. I didn't want to lie so I just didn't say anything. … But now I do. — Oh why take her from me, God! Why! I know You give and take as You see fit. I just— why allow me to see my errors and not be able to fix them like I should? Please don't do this! Please. Please give me back my Calli. Please, God. I'm struggling to see what You're wanting me to learn. Help me understand. Give her Your strength right now. Heal her. Let me have the wife of my youth back. I've learned I need to cherish her more than I am. Please, God. Please…"

ℬ

The next couple days, Destan spent most of his time by the cliff even though they were going through another bitter snap. His black attire proclaimed his overwhelming grief, his green eyes glassy and bloodshot from their overflow of emotions and lack of sleep, his drawn and pale face suggesting the time which had elapsed was a lifetime and a half rather than a couple days, and his quivering hands showed the longing for his love to hold them. The wind whipping around, his duster coat flapping and snapping, made his eyes dart in surprise and fear.

With the exception of Destan, the ocean spray froze anything it touched; it feared and parted around him so as not to be killed by the fire burning inside him… a fire which was a bed of glowing coals only needing the right conditions to roar back to a blaze.

From what Destan heard, Toreon just arrived in Kerogen. It was now only a matter of time. The impossible now became reality. He still had no idea what his abilities were but it didn't matter. Nothing mattered except making sure what the Society was planning didn't succeed. He knew once things began there would be no turning back and he would die — one way or another — but he had to try.

Destan recalled what he told Toreon: "When you're hanging off a cliff, you know you have to fight." Now he was fighting for someone other than himself… which made the fight worth so much more.

Callimay hadn't gained consciousness since her last nightmare. She was showing clear, strong vitals; even being able to breath on her own. But they all were fainting day-by-day.

Doctor Gerould had taken residence in the mansion so he could monitor her closely; and then after some discussion, he gained Destan's approval to bring in a nurse to help with Callimay when needed.

ЂD

One morning he caught a glimpse of Destan going in to see Callimay. Doctor Gerould stayed far enough away to respect his privacy, but still close enough so he could see and hear. He could barely contain himself when he saw him sitting there, talking with her as if she were there, and kissing her on the forehead: *I hope you didn't figure this out too late, Destan.*

He tried to stay with her, but couldn't bear seeing her in that state and hearing the constant ticks, beeps, and dings from the machines she was connected to. Hearing them becoming slower and weaker with each passing hour tortured him in an altogether different way. And yet, somehow he'd been able to form a normal life with Callimay; even though she wasn't "there". He'd heard how those in a coma could still hear, and so he wanted her to know: he cared for her, he was going to fight for her, and he was changing.

The only thing was, he didn't know if this was helping. Nothing ever seemed to change with her vitals in a good way. And Doctor Gerould never gave any inkling there was an end to this. How much longer could Callimay last in such a state? Could she stay like this forever? Would she ever regain consciousness? How much longer could Destan withstand this emotional devastation? Was he running from reality by keeping her like this?

~ 24 ~

It had been three months since they escaped from the Society and just over a month since Destan's episode with Callimay. Outside, the weather was similar to the landfall of a tropical storm. He woke to the sound of muffled the rain pounding against the window while the wind howled across the waters and through the trees. Lightning invaded the darkness for brief moments; leaving its voice of torturous and almost heinous laughter echoing in the darkened world.

As he opened the door, he saw Rocher carrying a breakfast tray down. Destan knew he was taking the one Doctor Gerould or the nurse had; but he clung to the hope it might — might — be Callimay's.

Rocher paused when he noticed him and turned to bid him good morning… but stopped short when he saw the look on his face. It tore at him even; seeing how much pain Destan was in.

"Quite the pinwheel for this late in the season," Rocher tried to evade the question he knew was coming. "The reports stated it should be at its eye come midday."

"Have you seen Callimay this morning?" He asked; that tiny bit of him hoping with everything that today was the day.

"I did. But only for a moment to check on Milady."

His heart sank. It was going to be yet another "normal" day. He motioned for Rocher to continue and wandered to Callimay's room. Destan took a deep breath as he reached for the door handle.

"Good morning Calli," he tried to sound chipper.

The same drowning sound filled the darkened room, lessening the grief he had of not hearing her voice answer him. It also hid the noises of the machines and monitors; so there was some good from this.

He dragged himself to the window and pulled a curtain back to let what light there was outside into the room, "It's not much, but it is 'some' light. Right Calli?"

After plodding over and climbing into bed, he took Callimay into his arms. She'd lost so much weight since she was being fed through a tube. Her hair which was always so silky and soft felt so frail and thin as he brushed it out like he did every morning. And her skin? It was pale, cold, and clammy to the touch; as if he were touching a porcelain doll, "Oh Calli. I'll ask Lance what I can do to keep you warm. ... I know you'd probably like to hear this. ... Today is my... my..."

Destan was overcome with grief. He put his cheek against hers and wept so much he felt as if his heart were being ripped out: *Why did it take this much for me to wake up and be willing to change? Why did I have to lose you? I finally have someone to love and you're gone.*

He closed his eyes, gripping her hair in his fists as he held her close. The desires of wanting the little things of what she would say or do made him further realize they meant so much more than any 'big' thing. Her smile, touch, eyes focused on him, sweet and calming voice saying his name or "I love you"; those were the things he was willing to beg for. He just wanted her back. Especially today. Today of all days. All he wanted was what he'd taken for granted.

Destan tenderly cradled Callimay's head against his chest and slowly rocked her back and forth for a long while.

As he opened his eyes, something on the vanity caught his attention. It was in the shadows but reflected and refracted the flickers from the lightning. He focused and saw a sight he hadn't seen in what felt closer to four months.

Once he laid Callimay down, Destan crept over to see if what he saw was real. As big as life, there, next to the jewelry she had laid out just over a month prior sat a glass vase full of red roses. As he got closer and closer, he could smell the ever-familiar scent he loved so much as it reached out and embraced him. There was an envelope next to them with his name written on it in Callimay's beautiful handwriting.

Unsure of what was going on and where they came from — let alone how in the world she wrote the note — Destan looked around as he walked back: *Rocher? ~ It had to be. He said he came in.*

As if scared of breaking it, he only used the tips of his fingers to open the envelope. Destan took a shaky deep breath, slipping his hand under hers and imagining he was hearing her say each word.

To my Destan,

I wanted to ask you, but you've been so busy and I didn't want to bother you, so I asked Rocher. He was so kind to keep this letter safe until today to be delivered with the roses. I know how much you love the smell of them and didn't notice any outside anywhere; so I had Rocher order a few dozen bushes. Please don't be upset with me; you seem to enjoy spending time outside so I thought the two would work well together.

In fact, while I'm writing this, I can see you standing out by the cliff. I admittedly wish I were with you, but I know you're working through things. I know things have been challenging — adjusting to me being here and all — but please don't forget I'm here. I don't say it to ask for attention alone, but rather to remind you no matter what you may be going through I want to help. I know that I only know a little about your past, but I can tell there is so much there which is weighing on you still. Please don't keep it locked up. Maybe if you could release at least some of it you could be more stable emotionally while you train; and I know how important that is to you right now.

Aside from all that, I wanted to tell you how much I love you and how thankful I am to have you in my life. I sometimes think of all the different decisions which would've put me in different situations right now; and even though this may not be the most preferable in some ways, I can't see myself in any better place than with you. I love you, Destan. I will until I die.

I hope your birthday is full of joy and gladness. Rocher told me you would be twenty-seven this year: which is how old I'll be this fall. It's so funny to me how all these little things seem to fall into place between the two of us — like God meant us for each other all along. I know the flowers aren't much, but I really didn't know what you would like. Please don't work too

*hard. Everyone deserves a break on their birthday. I will see
you at dinner if not sooner. Happy Birthday, Destan.*

> *Love,
> Your Calli*

After he finished reading it through a second time, Destan dropped
it and buried his face in his hands. His heart was pounding so hard he
could barely breathe.

Even though he couldn't smell much, the fragrant roses reached
through to him — like Callimay did no matter how angry he was.

As he looked at them, the memories of: first meeting her, when she
ran into him the first day of class, the first time he tutored her, being
out at the lake the first time, saving her, taking her out to the lake and
proposing to her, and so many other memories in between flooded
through his mind.

"I love you too." He sobbed under his breath as he sat there.

In most ways it was the worst birthday he ever had, but even so, he
was somehow able to see how this was the best one… as if looking for
the silver-lining Callimay always did: *Even when I don't think you're
able to give any more of yourself to me, you prove me wrong. You
show me again and again what it is to be selfless; reminding me what
true love is; reminding me how it looks to have the same love Christ has
for all of us. I know I've grown so much the past three weeks. I pray
you can see what a difference you've made in my life. To open my eyes
so I could finally see where I needed to grow. — I think I understand
now, God. At least part of what You want me to see. I've been such a
fool; a toxic combination of the rich young ruler, prodigal son, and the
priest who left the wounded man. How much more of a mess could I
have made everything? … But it doesn't have to stay that way. I can
stop the hurt, stop the pain. God please let Callimay be able to see the
change in me. I'm begging You: please, Heavenly Father. Please give
her the gift of seeing Your work in my life. Let her stay and be the
helper You've made for me so I wouldn't be alone. … Help me have
comfort in knowing Your will is wiser and far superior to what my
wishes are. I want Your will done. I ask all these things be in Your will*

and surrender myself and what I want into Your perfect and all-knowing hands. In Your Son's Name I pray, amen.

Destan sat there hunched over for a while and then sat up, picking up the letter and laying it beside the vase. He leaned over and kissed her lips, giving her hand one last squeeze while whispering, "I'm going to check on a few things since the eye of the storm is here. I promise I'll be back. I love you Calli."

As he stood, he stopped when he felt her squeeze his hand.

"Calli?" He rushed back to his seat and gently brushed the side of her face; his eyes wild with fear. "Calli, can you hear me?"

After a few moments and no response, Destan begged: *Callimay? Callimay, can you hear me?*

He sat there for a few minutes and begrudgingly let reality sink in: he "thought" he felt her squeeze his hand. Destan gave her one last kiss and then left.

ℬ

While outside, Destan kept glancing back at the window to Callimay's bedroom. Even though she wasn't "there", that was where he wanted to be. And he had this overwhelming feeling of someone keeping tabs on him. That alone made him want to be with her. He tried to stay on-task but his focus drifted so often because of these things.

The rain and wind began to pick up before long, so everyone headed in. Destan, on the other hand, wandered over to the cliff and stood there, trying to calm himself. He'd done this exact thing for years, but with things being "different" he didn't know if it would help.

He was furious to a certain degree, but he felt more sorrow than anything — regardless of whether or not he understood it. His duster was now snapping in the wind while the rain stung him as it peppered his face.

As time went by, he began to "feel" his emotions relaxing and subsiding… something he'd never been able to do without Callimay's help since gaining his abilities: *Maybe I 'can' control it.*

Not much later, he let out a large sigh. He was right. Someone was watching him… and they were now behind him. Destan acknowledged without turning to them, "I've known you were in the area for a while.

What took you so long? Did you stop and ask for directions? Though you asking for help sounds a bit… beneath you. Am I right, Falconer?”

“Pfft. Not so much as a hello to start things off? — Why would I expect any decorum? — Fine. We’ll do it your way: seeing this place was easy. Getting in wasn’t,” the person answered rather arrogant. “Gotta hand it to you, Nevrille. You ‘do’ have a way of tricking people into thinking they have you all figured out.”

“I just hold my cards close,” he replied as he turned around.

The sight of Toreon was something he could have done without for the rest of his life. He gritted his teeth when he saw him standing there. Toreon’s hair was slicked against his face, hinting he had been outside for a while, but his white trench coat and attire were spotless — not so much as a splatter of mud on his boots.

“Usually the villain is who wears black… like a ‘veiled’ Shadow.”

“Heroes don’t torture and murder others.” Destan sneered.

“It’s been a little bit since we’ve seen each other. How’ve you been?” Toreon smiled as he offered his left hand in friendship. “What? Not even going to give me that courtesy? Did I come all this way only to be slighted by a person I couldn’t care less about?”

Destan clenched his fists as he muttered, “Prince.”

“You’re smarter than I thought.” Toreon praised as he smirked and pulled his hand back. “So I was right… Doyen.”

“If you’re so sure ‘the myth’ is true, turn me in then.”

“Oh believe me, as tempting as it would be to get the reward the Syndicate would gladly fork over for you; I’d rather kill you myself. … I see you’re sporting a ring on that left hand. Which, if memory serves me correct, is only reserved for a wedding band. How is sweet Callimay doing these days? I trust you’re taking good care of her?”

“Quit with the banter, Toreon,” he growled as he gritted his teeth, his emotions spiking. “You never won when you tried.”

“True.” He continued to laugh as he began to walk to Destan’s left. “But what is a good fight without a little bit of dialogue between the two combatants prior to the ‘epic’ battle? Especially when both of them know who is going to win in the end.”

“Did you ever entertain the thought neither of us would?” He asked as he continued to stare down Toreon, finishing: *Calli? If you can hear me: I love you. I will do all I can to keep you safe. I don't know if I will win and come back to you, but I will do everything I can until my last breath. This I know I can promise you.*

The next second, he lunged at Toreon. As he reached out to grab him, he stumbled before catching himself. Destan looked around to see where in the world Toreon went, but he was nowhere to be found. Losing control of the situation started sending Destan over the edge: *Come on, keep it together Boon. Fight it!*

"Over here, punk."

He took off after him but Toreon disappeared the second before he was within arm's reach. After a moment of orienting himself, Destan looked around yet again and saw Toreon by the sunroom. He took off but was all of a sudden blindsided: Toreon was right next to him and laid a clean hit to his previously injured side.

Since Destan was moving so fast, he was launched into the air and hit the ground a few times as he tumbled to a long and painful stop. He shook his head a few times and struggled to get up, looking around again, "So what, you can run faster than me?"

"Sure, yeah."

That can't be it. … Which one is it? What does he have!

Destan tried to figure out where his voice was coming from but couldn't see Toreon at all. He took off running, but once again was blindsided, "Quit running into me, punk."

"Well… maybe if you'd stay in one place long enough I would be able to punch you. Then you wouldn't have to worry about me running into you."

Destan, behind you!

In a knee-jerk reaction to this warning, he dodged to the side; and then asked wide-eyed when he realized who it was: *Calli? Is it you! … Calli? Answer me… please!*

She calmed in her soft voice, *I'm here, it's me. — What's going on? Why are you— wait! Destan!*

Her advice was too late. Toreon repeated exactly what he had done the two times before: strike and vanish.

As Destan got up, he asked stunned, *Are you doing alright?*

I'm fine. You seem to be doing alright… emotionally, I mean.

Physical pain I can handle. He said more confident; but sighed as he looked around, *But you can feel it too. Are… are you sure you can't shut that part off Calli?*

Even if I knew how to I wouldn't. You couldn't make me. If I do that I can't watch over you. And I'm not about to abandon you. … It's a lose-lose situation, Destan. I'm sorry.

"There's got to be a way." *Can you see him?*

No. Oh wait, he's— now he's gone! It's like he's able to appear and then vanish at will.

Calli? He asked in a serious tone as he took off, making sure to stay where she could see him. *Calli I need you to break off of me and find Toreon. I will try my best to keep things stable while you're gone.*

Destan… are you sure?

I can take hits like this for a while like I said, but I need to be able to get to him. I can't win this fight by only playing defense. And then if you disconnect from me you won't feel the pain.

I won't d— wait.

What!

Destan, I can hear him 'and' you at the same time.

How!

I don't know.

Well, don't let him slip a— wait. Won't he hear you?

Not unless he has my ability, she said a bit more serious.

Isn't this going to wear on you faster though?

I'll last as long as I can, Callimay responded cheerfully; it sounding like she was smiling. *From what I'm hearing, he teleports because he can see you.*

Got it. Put something solid between the two of us.

Wait, Destan. No! He… he can see through things?

Teleportation 'and' x-ray vision? Well isn't that just great. Why am I surprised? He huffed as he stopped and glanced around. *So, there's nowhere for me to get away from him.*

No.

"That's how he found us. It's got to be." *But that means he can see you too.* Destan said concerned when he realized. *I need you to get out to me if you can. I know you're weak, Calli. But please… try.*

I'll meet you at the veranda. She nodded and turned away from the window. *Oh no. He's switched his focus to me.*

Where is he right now?

No response.

Calli, where is he! He repeated in a louder tone, turning to head for the closest door to get inside.

Right in front of me, she said terrified. *Destan, I—*

"Calli? Calli!" He shouted while throwing the door open.

"Inside voice." Toreon reprimanded in an uppity and snobbish tone. "Where are your manners? Goodness. Not so much as a knock on the door. And look at what you've done to the rug! Tsk, tsk."

"Let her go." Destan negotiated, trying to remain calm when he saw the Sai knife Toreon had at Callimay's throat. "This fight is between you and me. She's done nothing to deserve this. Let her go."

"Far from it. She started it all. Had it not been for her I wouldn't have paid much, if any, attention to you. … Well. … No, wait. Well, maybe you did— no. No, I was right. She started it all." Toreon thought out loud, his expression changing to the Cheshire-cat like smile. "She's the reason for everything."

Callimay didn't say a word this whole time. She looked terrified and too scared to move from being trapped by Toreon's free arm and the knife he had at her throat. Destan had gone over and over in his mind what the first time he'd get to see her awake was going to be like. And it was nothing like this. He was angry Toreon stole this one little thing he wanted so bad. — Let alone he was threatening his wife.

He started to reach out, part of him fighting not to cry, part of him mad beyond belief, and the other part frantically thinking of a way to talk Toreon down so he would let her go. But in this storm he saw her eyes and asked so tender: *Calli?*

Destan? She whimpered. *Destan what's going on? H—*

The next second, the two of them disappeared, "Calli!"

We're out by the cliff, she began to cry. *Hurry, Destan.*

I'm coming, Calli. Hang on. He did his best to sound calm, trying everything he knew to keep his emotions under control.

Destan leaped over the balcony railing and dropped two stories, rolling out when he hit the ground.

When he got there, they vanished again. Callimay would let him know where they were, but when he'd get within about twenty-five feet, they'd vanish again.

Toreon laughed the whole time, enjoying toying with Destan.

After going through the same routine for several gut-wrenching minutes, she realized: *Destan, listen to me. There's a small window where Toreon can't do anything. It's an extremely small window, but it may be enough if you can get to us fast enough. He has to focus on where he wants to go before he can actually 'make' the jump. It's a split second, but it's a moment he's not focusing on you 'or' me. Maybe I can see about knocking the knife out of his hand while you grab me?*

Alright. Split second. I can make it work. Don't worry about the knife. I'll get it. … I just hope he doesn't try to get out in the next couple jumps. — Where are you going next? He tried to calm himself.

The cliff, Toreon answered.

What in the—

The cliff, Callimay repeated.

I heard him say it, Destan said in disbelief.

You what?

I heard Toreon say it in my head before you did, he explained as he turned to follow them. *Are you functioning like a conduit between the two of us but it's only one-way? … I hope.*

Well whatever it is it really hurts.

I'm hurrying, Calli. I promise, not much longer.

Destan was able to follow them much quicker now and soon found where the split-second would work: *It's now or never, Calli. I won't let you go… I promise. Just don't let go of me. I've got you.*

In less time than it would take to bat an eye, Destan ripped Callimay away from Toreon… him unable to stop himself from making the jump he planned. She didn't pay attention to him saying he would get the knife, so as Destan and her fell, it slipped out of both their grasps and stabbed her. She tried to scream but she wasn't strong enough to even do that, "Calli!"

No! No, leave it, Destan. She wheezed as she put her hand over his which he had on the knife. *Please don't touch it. It'll hurt more if you touch it or do anything to it.*

He looked back and saw Rocher and Doctor Gerould standing near the front door of the mansion. Toreon was nowhere to be found, so he hoped he could get her back before he was able to regroup. And then on top of everything, the knife might be poisoned. He needed to focus and do whatever he was going to as fast as possible.

Destan gathered Callimay — who moaned and winced with every movement made — into his arms. As much as he could, he was trying to be careful; but all the painful noises she let out made him feel he was miserably failing, "I'm sorry Calli. I am."

After he got Rocher and Doctor Gerould's attention, Destan took off toward them. He kept a keen eye for Toreon's surprise attack and was so relieved when he was able to get her to safety — or somewhere which seemed safer.

"She'll be alright, Destan." Doctor Gerould assured him as he lay Callimay down; observing where the Sai was lodged. "It's not near any major structures."

"I don't know if it was laced or not." He shook his head, sounding extremely nervous. "Knowing his status in the Syndicate and the type of knives those are he might—"

"I'll take care of it."

"Calli?" Destan kneeled beside her, sheltering her from the cold rain pouring down on them.

"Yes?" She answered weakly as she worked to open her eyes.

"D— it's so good to see you." He paused when he saw her eyes. "Did he do anything?"

"No." She moaned.

"I'm so sorry, Calli. I… I lo— do you have anything left? How are you feeling?"

"Not much at all, I'm afraid. I'm sorry. Whatever I was doing— I'm so sore and weak, De—"

"Don't be sorry." He calmed as he rubbed the side of her face. "Just one more time, Calli. Please. I need you. Last as long as you can. It's all I can ask for… and I pray all I need. Stay here. I promise I'll stay close."

She pushed his soaking wet hair away from his eyes and answered in a whisper as she kept her eyes closed, Destan leaning his forehead against hers when he realized what she was doing, "God? Please keep

Destan safe. Give him Your strength and wisdom in this fight to know what You would want him to do. Help him fight off what the Society put in him to cause him to lose his sense of what is important. Help me to push the pain aside and do what I know I can to help. Please let it be in Your will that we make it through this alive. In Your Son's Name I pray, amen."

"Amen."

"Go."

She put forth all her energy and kept the conduit open. Toreon was frustrated Destan knew exactly when he did where he was planning to be, or if he changed his mind. His insults, though, fueled Destan's rage which began to break Callimay's ability to function as she needed to.

They skipped from place to place, Rocher and Doctor Gerould witnessing bits and pieces of the death-battle unfolding. The two young men quickly discovered the other was able to take a bit of a beating and not suffer much… though Destan knew Callimay could feel every ounce of pain he was enduring.

He'd been protecting it, but Toreon was somehow able to land a strike on Destan's side he had used as his punching bag earlier.

Things weren't looking good now. It was getting to the point that each time he got up, Toreon would immediately land another hit on Destan; knocking him back down. His emotions began to spike because of his inability to gain any footing to fight back.

"So. Callimay can feel your pain too, huh?" Toreon commented as he looked where Destan fearfully did. "Well isn't that a lovely little tidbit of information. Seems like you're 'constantly' causing her pain."

That made him finally snap; sending a shock wave to Callimay.

"Destan!" She screamed as she struggled to get up and away from Doctor Gerould and Rocher, stumbling rather than running after him; trying desperately to get a connection with him again. *Please. Stop! Destan! I can't lose you!*

All the rage and anger he had for the persons who murdered his parents, his friends, and almost his wife overtook him as he kept after Toreon. This influx enabled him to break through the memory gap he had; him recalling everything from the day he and Callimay were processed. He remembered the cruel way Toreon treated her and what he did and was planning to do. He remembered everything Mr. Freigh and Baleck said before processing. He remembered Callimay screaming and him trying to get to her before he fell unconscious; how terrified she was and begging him to keep her safe.

All these bottled emotions broke wide open. Nothing nor no one could hold them back. They were focused on Toreon with no restraint.

Rocher and Doctor Gerould went after Callimay, trying to keep her away from Destan and Toreon. She pushed away and worked her way back into his mind and pleaded with him to stop; but he spiked again, causing her to lose consciousness and collapse.

That's it. Come after me. Toreon smiled when he saw her drop to the ground; skillfully handling the last Sai he had as he licked his bloody lip. *You've got no safety net now, Cliffhanger. No failsafe to bring you back. It's just a matter of time. One way or another you're meeting your end today. And then it'll be her turn to pay. And believe me, I'll enjoy that part.*

As they continued to fight, Destan zoned out and couldn't see or hear anything. His focus was only on Toreon and making sure he didn't leave there alive. The plan Toreon had was working just as he wanted it to: Callimay couldn't help, so Destan had nothing to keep the monster inside him contained. He was expecting Destan to know how to fight and wasn't surprised of his skill level… though it appeared something was different. Destan was keeping up with him at first. What changed? It took him a moment, but Toreon realized Callimay was cluing Destan in on his thoughts and plans.

On the other side of things, Toreon only had the one Sai; so his strikes were limited and awkward at times. Destan used those moments to his advantage and got one good hit which turned the tide, Toreon taking the brunt of the beating now and losing the second knife he had.

Before long, he wasn't able to jump and Destan was able to get him on the ground. This wasn't at all what he saw happening! But he couldn't deny what was. He had no strength to do anything, so he put his hands up to surrender.

Destan didn't notice or care about this signal of surrender; about to do him in when he stopped and opened his eyes wide, saying horrified and out of breath, "Callimay!"

He scrambled to his feet and away from Toreon, trying to let the Sai go; shaking his hand like the knife was on fire. Destan searched the area, his heart pounding and him heaving and shaking as he gripped his chest, "Calli!"

Once he saw her lying on the ground, he ran over and dropped to his knees, accidentally splashing some mud on her face. She didn't react. He started rubbing her face, trying to get her to wake up when he flashed his eyes at Toreon and ordered, "Don't even think about it, Prince. You're not off the hook."

Toreon withdrew his hand and fell back on the ground, trying to recover: *How did it all go wrong? I had him!*

"Calli?" Destan asked almost frantic as he turned his attention back to her. "Calli come back to me. Calli please. I know I asked for you to do it one more time, but I— oh please don't let me have killed you. Calli! Calli wake up! Let me know you're alright. Please! Yell at me, tell me you don't want to see me ever again— just… just say something! Anything. … Yes, I'm begging. I'll beg for all eternity if I have to. — God please. Give me my wife back. Please don't take her away from me. Please, God. Please don't do this to me… not again. I know I need her. I don't think I can make it through an— please, God. — Calli!"

With nothing left to say or do, Destan yelled out in agony.

ℬ

Right before it started raining again, he carried her inside. He got cushions off the sofa and laid them close to the fire so she had something softer to lie on and somewhere warm to rest. The notable pain he had he did his best to ignore since what Callimay was going through was much worse. He was used to this. She wasn't.

The stab wound she had was not as dire as he thought; and thankfully the blade wasn't poisoned. It was just through the top part of her shoulder.

"She shouldn't have had to go through it at all. It's all my fault."

After making sure she was as comfortable as he knew to make her, he leaned over her and wrapped his arms around her. Destan jumped the first few times the logs in the fireplace snapped and popped, but soon grew accustomed to their noises; being able to somehow calm his thoughts and work through the consequences of his actions: *If I would have been thinking, this would've never happened. I know Callimay would say: 'compared to what could have happened it wasn't bad at all,' but… oh my Calli.*

❦

In the meantime, Rocher and Doctor Gerould restrained Toreon so he couldn't go anywhere. Callimay let them know how he was able to transport which jogged Rocher's memory. He left for a while, returning with what he was looking for just after Destan came back to his senses.

Toreon was now left without any way of freeing himself from his unique but foolproof imprisonment. It puzzled him how in the world they were so well equipped, demanding an answer as he struggled against them, "Who told you what ability I had?"

"Callimay." Rocher said curt and as stern as ever.

"How did she know?" Toreon muttered as he quit trying to free himself. "Baleck swore to me he—"

"You'll hold your tongue if you know what's best, scum."

❦

Destan sat by her side all evening. He was back to square one, again. Doctor Gerould promised she was only passed out, but he didn't trust him this time. She looked exactly as she did for the past three weeks.

Both Doctor Gerould and Rocher could see him with his head bowed, hands clasping Callimay's as they shook; his lips moving but not a sound being uttered as tears streamed down his face. Rocher started over but Doctor Gerould held him back, "Let them be."

"Perish the thought of me allowing an opportunity to support Sir run past my grasp!"

"He's getting all the support he needs, Rocher." Doctor Gerould gestured, knowing all along what Destan was doing. "Let's check and make sure our 'guest' hasn't tried anything stupid."

❦

He fought to stay awake — still terrified with what all happened and the uncertainty of if she was alright — but his over-worked, battered,

321

abused, exhausted, and emotionally drained body dealt with enough. Unable to resist it any longer, Destan passed out for a few hours and woke up just a little before midnight.

As he opened his eyes, he saw Callimay smiling at him, her face having a glow about it — and not from the hue of the fireplace. This was what he imagined seeing. This was what he wanted for a month.

And yet he hesitated for a moment. Yes, God gave him what he wanted, but now he had to do something with what he'd been given. He'd said this to her before, but she wasn't awake, looking at him, listening… aware.

But that thought soon faded as he remembered he wasn't promised his next breath. If he had something to say he needed to say it.

"I… I love you." He reached over and brushed the hair out of her face. "I love you so much, Calli."

It took a few moments to register, but then she asked, "What?"

"You're beautiful. You know that?" Destan smiled as he rested his hand on her neck and then leaned over to kiss her.

"I knew it— we're both dead." She screeched as she closed her eyes and rolled over, not giving him a chance to kiss her. "I di—"

"No, Calli." He defended as he sat up and turned her back to him. "We're still alive. Everything's alright now."

"Then why did you say— your forehead, Destan! You have a huge gash!" She gasped as she brushed his hair aside; grimacing when she reached up with her now injured arm.

"Don't worry about me." He calmed as he smiled; being gentle as he soothed her. "I'm just glad you're awake and alright. It's been a long month without you."

"It's been a month!"

"Yes," Destan laid his cheek on hers. "Thank you for the birthday present. I haven't gotten one like it in years. It was perfect."

"When was it? Did I miss it?"

"It's today." He looked at the clock and mumbled a bit before nodding, "Yep, still today."

"Happy Birthday, Destan. I love you so much."

"I love you too, Calli," he sighed after he kissed her. "I love you more than you'll ever know."

She was stunned, needless to say, while Destan was enjoying the true gift he was given for his birthday. Nothing was said for quite some time; but as usual, Callimay was the one to break the silence. And yet it didn't bother Destan one bit, "What happened?"

"If I had to guess, when you passed out is when all my memories from the past flooded back. Even my memories of the day Toreon started tormenting you and we were given our abilities. — I told you I'd get them back, though I don't have the foggiest idea how it happened. I was focused on wanting to kill him— then out of the blue, all I could think about was you and if you were alright."

"What about Toreon?" Callimay jumped up and looked around; gripping her arm to keep it steady so it wouldn't hurt so much. "Where is he? Is he al—"

"Rocher and Lance took care of him. He's alive. … For now. — Sit and rest, Calli. Please. I… I need to hold you. Please."

"I'm sorry." She sighed as she curled up on his lap.

"You're fine. I'm just tired."

"Well at least this is done with. Thank The Lord above for that."

"I wouldn't be so sure, Calli." Destan cautioned as he looked out the window. "Something tells me this storm isn't over yet."

The End

Or Is It?